BUG MAN

by

Peter Karl

TELEMACHUS PRESS

BUG MAN

Cover designed by DiDonato and Associates, Chicago, Illinois

Publishing Services by:
Telemachus Press, LLC
7652 Sawmill Road
Suite 304
Dublin, Ohio 43016
http://www.telemachuspress.com

Visit the author website:
http://www.AuthorPeterKarl.com

ISBN 978-1-951744-94-6 (eBook)
ISBN: 978-1-951744-95-3 (paperback)
ISBN: 978-1-956867-11-4 (hard cover)

Category: FIC050000 FICTION / Crime

Version 2021.11.11

ACKNOWLEDGEMENTS

My daughters and family have been a source of pride for me and I want to thank them for their encouragement and support throughout this writing process.

Special thanks to: Thomas Britten, a microbiologist and immunologist, who gave me encouragement to write this novel and the insight into how these microbiological agents work.

Gary Allmaier for his review and critique of the medical and pharmacological processes depicted in this book.

Retired Cook County Circuit Court Judge Frank De Boni and Cook County State's Attorney Kevin De Boni for their support and guidance through the judicial proceedings.

Deborah Shaw for her intellectual input in keeping the chapters focused and consistent.

Attorney Samuel Fifer for his constant input and discourse, support and encouragement through the months of writing this manuscript.

Forensic Psychologist Doctor Bruce Chambers for providing insight into the criminal mind and why serial killers act the way they do.

Peter DiDonato and DiDonato Associates Incorporated for their design of the cover for "Bug Man."

BUG MAN

CHAPTER 1

Balamuthia Mandrillaris is very rare. It is almost impossible to detect this amoebic encephalitis unless one knew exactly what to look for and that made him smile. No one has ever survived this brain-eating organism once infected. The hairless man was getting sexually aroused as he studied the specimen floating on the glass slide under his Zeiss Inverted Phase Microscope at 40-X power of magnification. Bugs were his passion, he could manipulate them to kill, infect or cause great bodily harm. It all depended on how he dispersed them. He was saving the Balamuthia Mandrillaris for Dr. Louis Yako, the psychiatrist who had *the nerve to proclaim me mentally fit and that I deserved prison not psychiatric treatment.*

He appeared to have alopecia areata, the autoimmune disorder that causes hair loss, but he didn't. Shaving his body of its natural thick, course black hair took too much time and it left his skin with irritating rashes so he removed all of his hair with laser treatments. The esthetician got an unnerving feeling during his 25th and last treatment when he smiled as she erased his eyebrows.

He knew she thought he was *weird* but it didn't faze him. He could kill or maim her anytime he wanted, and nobody would know. His devilish smile widened.

~~~~

The two-flat brownstone on Chestnut Street was set back 20 feet from its black wrought iron fence. The immaculate, thick Kentucky bluegrass was perfectly manicured and edged by hand with a knife. The brown paver walkway glistened from the afternoon's pure sunrays highlighting its clear protective sealer.

The hairless man paid 3.3 million dollars in cash under the name of Brandon Martin and then immediately invested another 1.2 million dollars to remodel it. Two and three flats comprise 30 percent of Chicago's housing stock. The only thing that draws attention to them is the neighborhoods in which they were built, and whether or not they were pristinely maintained or the degree of their neglect.

Billy Bob Winkler's Construction Company accepted the remodel contract without hesitation and the first $250,000 installment was paid at signing. No questions asked. Winkler was about to inquire, why Mr. Martin wanted the construction area vacuumed every night before his workmen left the site at the end of the day, but he had second thoughts. *What the hell—time was money!*

The stainless-steel spiral staircase leading from the first floor to the second was not illegal under Chicago's strict building codes but it was unusual. The second floor was sterile. The white marble tiled floors and white marble tabletops ran faultlessly symmetrical. The stainless-steel counters, shelves and cabinets that lined the walls were smudge less. It looked antiseptic. Hundreds of recessed LED bulbs were prolifically positioned in the twelve-foot ceiling to produce bright but shadow less light. Eerie!

The walls were insulated and soundproof with an abundance of electrical outlets every three feet, exactly two feet above the counter tops. Precise.

The kitchen sinks were also stainless steel, all with different sizes and depths along with high tech devices that produced instant hot water. Bland.

The quiet, energy efficient H-VAC system produced a temperature of 72 degrees Fahrenheit year-round and the perfect balance of humidity.

Brandon Martin worked in his lab naked most of the time. Everything had to be flawless and managed to perfection. After all it was a matter of life and death. Controlling.

The first floor had no personality. Monochromatic. The same white marble floors. White walls. White kitchen counter tops and cabinets. Stainless steel sinks. The glass hand soap dispensers had stainless steel plungers. White appliances. White porcelain dishware. Anemic.

The living room had a $40,000 white leather Minotti sectional couch facing the front picture window that was so spotless; it gave the impression of being glassless. The glass coffee table sitting on a chrome frame accepted the sun's refracted rays that inched into the antiseptic room. No family pictures. No smiling faces. Nothing personal. Ominously deceptive. Spiritless.

The master bedroom was outfitted in white furniture. White lamps. The California king bed sitting in a pure white frame and headboard was adorned with a triple layered white duvet. No color. Pure but sinful.

The wall adjacent to the exit door was mirrored from ceiling to floor. Soulless.

The second bedroom and dining area were gutted and made into one big dressing room that offered the only real color in the house. Rachel Welch and Jon Renua wigs of every color and length imaginable were displayed on white mannequin heads—male on one side, female on the other. The walk-in closets contained male outfits in one and female outfits in the other. Disguises.

The man known as Brandon Martin never looked the same two days in a row when he left the house. He blended into every environment he entered virtually unnoticed. He was a chameleon. A killer.

CHAPTER 2

"**N**ews ... Michaels."

"Hey Peter, its Patricia."

It was a voice he would never forget. Sexy. Raspy. Suggestive.

Patricia Dickerson worked for the Center for Disease Control in Atlanta. Michaels met her when he was doing a series of stories on the West Nile mosquito outbreak during the summer of 2014. Chicago was the largest city at that time affected by the virus with more than 70 people infected and five young adults suffered the severe effects of meningitis and/or encephalitis.

The entire nation was put on alert in 2012 when North Texas reported 663 human cases and 18 deaths in August of that year. During that period of time, the CDC reported 1,118 human cases and 41 deaths from the virus nationwide.

Michaels smiled as he recalled the short tryst; they shared for about six weeks. "Hey Pat, what's happening?" He felt warmness in his groin, and a hint of a smile of sexual satisfaction slowly creased his lips. He looked around the room to see if anyone was looking in his direction.

"I'm giving you a heads up. Something strange is going on up there."

His coquettish grin disappeared. "What are you talking about? What do you mean, strange?"

"Seven area hospitals are reporting some very alarming symptoms, affecting maybe dozens of people. We don't know what it is right now. We're sending a team to Chicago later today. So, I guess, I'll see you soon."

Michaels' romantic mood now shifted into reporter mode, his senses on high alert, "What are the symptoms?" He asked reaching for his notebook.

"Coughing, fever, chills, shortness of breath, bleeding from the nose and mouth, ultimately suffocation and death. Some people reported 'they thought they were having a heart attack.' Rare shit. Scary." She gave him a list of the hospitals and hung up.

Michaels was on his feet and moving quickly. "Hey Dave, come on let's go. We have to stop everything we're doing. The shit has hit the fan at Northwestern Hospital, we've gotta see Rivers now!"

David Beedy, Michaels' producer and dear friend, was sitting back in his chair with his feet up on his desk, reading a report from the city's health department on the spiking increase of AIDS cases in the LGBTQ community. He shot to his feet, grabbed his reporter's notepad and was immediately out the door, "What's going on?" Beedy never hesitated when he saw that look in his partner's eyes.

"Maybe terrorism!"

"You shittin' me!"

Phil Rivers was the WMAC-TV News Director. He always gave Michaels a lot of leeway when it came to his investigative reporting. Rivers liked order and organization. Michaels often flew by the seat of his pants and broke a lot of big stories. He always followed his gut and was sued for millions of dollars over the years, but he never lost a lawsuit.

~~~~

Northwestern Hospital's Emergency Room was busier than usual for a late Friday afternoon in July. With rare excitement in their voices, Chicago Fire Department EMTs shuffled in and out, yelling orders and descriptions of how they found their patients, what meds were given, what their vitals were, and the unexplained blood coming from their mouths and noses.

The ER looked tired and worn, 33% of the fluorescent ceiling lights were burned out adding to the dreary ambience. The cream-colored walls were scarred and bruised from crashes of hurried gurneys being quickly maneuvered down the hallways. The beige colored floors, though mopped on every shift, were scuffed and streaked from the dirty rubber heels of first responders' boots and the sudden stops of gurney wheels to prevent a collision in the fast-moving patient traffic.

"This is the fourth patient I have had today with these symptoms. I've never seen anything like this." Dr. Melanie Karlton said with eyes wide-open taking in the chaotic scene unfolding all around her. "We need someone down here from pathology, STAT!"

~~~~

"I just got off the phone with a friend of mine from the CDC. Something huge is going on here. Some sort of bio-terrorism?" Michaels proclaimed excitedly.

"Settle down, Peter." Phil Rivers never saw Michaels this anxious; it actually alarmed him. "What are you talking about? Bio-terrorism? You gotta be careful not to scare the shit out of everyone."

"Look, I just got off the phone with another source at Northwestern. They have several cases over there of people suffering from all sorts of weird and complicated symptoms. Shit, people are bleeding from their mouths and noses." Michaels explained with a look of disbelief because of the enormity of this outbreak. "They've never seen anything like it."

"We can't just be calling this bio-terrorism until we are certain what this is." Rivers said expressively, his eyes now showing grave concern.

"That's just it. They don't know what it is! They've never seen anything like it." Michaels' expression had everyone in the room growing more disturbed.

Beedy's cellphone chirped. He looked at the screen, stood up and walked away from Rivers' desk as a serious look crossed his face, nodding. "No shit! When?" One beat. Two beats. "Yeah, thanks." Beedy had a blank stare, his skin colorless, a ghostly pallor.

"What is it?" asked Michaels with a premonition of pending doom.

Almost whispering, putting his cell phone in his back pocket, Beedy said, "Make that eight hospitals. Elmhurst Memorial just admitted two more patients with the same symptoms. They're putting them in isolation."

Phil Rivers, who was standing, fell stiffly back into his chair. He started flipping his tie with his fingers. A nervous habit he picked up years ago, whenever, he knew he had crisis on his hands and he wasn't quite sure how to handle it.

"Peter be careful. Keep me updated."

CHAPTER 3

It took nearly eight months to harvest the Anglostrongylus Cantonensis, an invasive deadly parasite known as rat lungworm. The man known as Brandon Martin methodically and patiently placed his worm embryos in petri dishes, some with lettuce, others in dry, plain bottom dishes, and yet others in moist environments. He positioned them in three, high-powered HQ-9, 2.75 cubic foot incubators feeding them a daily diet of rat feces at varying degrees of heat. The worms on the lettuce grew faster and stronger. The main nutrients included beef broth as the main staple along with rat feces, protein media and amino acids. The vermillion microscopic parasite matured slowly and steadily, once the proper regime and temperature was established. He patiently waited five and a half months to cultivate this weapon and now he was confident it would work.

Its prodigious, deadly physiognomies would last approximately two hours after it was exposed to air. The worms passed their final test of survival in the host creamy blue cheese dressing because they had built up a tolerance against an acidic environment that surrounded them. They would infect and kill as planned. Once ingested, there is no known antidote to stop it from eating away at the pleura lining of the human lung.

The hairless scientist was excited as he examined his creations that were squirming and twisting under his powerful Vogue 333 clinical microscope. *Maybe I'll get more than one tomorrow,* He mused as he stood up and walked to the stainless-steel spiral staircase thinking about how he was going to put his deadly plan into motion.

~~~~

He decided on the Rachel Welch brunette medium length wig, red lipstick and red fingernails. The plain black linen pantsuit and off-white cotton blouse with a high neckline fit comfortably on his toned, lithe body. The gray, lightweight p-coat looked almost elegant. Not expensive. Not extravagant. The one-inch black pumps made him five feet; six inches tall. The brown tinted contact lenses camouflaged his striking green eyes. The black floppy hat covered his forehead and shadowed his face. The oversized sunglasses were there to protect his identity not his eyes.

He checked himself in the full-length mirror. Perfect. Ordinary. Hiding in plain sight.

When the woman dressed in the gray p-coat left the brownstone and walked to the Blue Line El train station on State Street to go downtown, no one noticed her. She was just one of the 1.7 million passengers a day that used the CTA, the Chicago Transit Authority system. She sat near the rear door, head down, eyes alert. The train stopped at the underground station at 60 West Washington Street. Passengers exited into a maze of tunnels and walkways that led to shops and restaurants, she blended in with the rush hour traffic ... unnoticed.

In the heart of Chicago's Loop, there is an underground city that not many people know about unless they work or live in the area. This pedestrian walkway system of tunnels, links 40 city blocks in the

Central Business District, known as Chicago's Loop. Tens of thousands of people use it daily because it is normally safe, convenient and a quick way to move around the city particularly during the winter months or on rainy days. The ped-way connects more than 50 buildings both public and private including public transportation stations like Chicago's Red Line and Blue Line subway trains directly under the Richard J. Daley Center.

It was 11:30 am when the El train's doors swished open. He/she turned right and immediately zeroed in on the Kale Town Café, a very popular eatery for the employees at City Hall, the County Building and the Daley Center Courthouse. If the clerk with the pitifully dyed orange hair followed her weekly routine, she would approach the KTC salad bar shortly after noon.

He/she picked KTC because every Wednesday, the clerk with the orange hair took full advantage of the fresh, generously supplied salad bar. It was cheap, healthy and fulfilling. The homemade chunky blue cheese dressing was to die for and the clerk never varied her choice of ingredients or dressing. He/she decided that is where he would dump the two ounces of rat lungworms. The worms would go unnoticed for at least an hour before they turned a ghastly yellow/green color, but by then the clerk with the orange hair would be already walking back to the courtroom of Judge Harold Wolfe.

Antoinette Barettelli was one of those women that everyone liked. Her bright orange hair only added to her outgoing spunky personality. At fifty, she had a finely tuned athletic body from Pilates three times a week after work and a healthy diet that didn't allow red meat. Her skin appeared wrinkle free. A voluptuous smile on her full red lips that often filled her face made men fantasize about her sexual appetite.

She lunched with the same two women almost every day. Very little ever troubled her so when the three of them were talking expressively and laughing while standing in line at the salad bar, she uncharacteristically became unnerved when the woman in the gray p-coat nonchalantly stepped in front of them. She felt a strange vibe and became irritated. She struggled to keep her composure, she found herself pissed off, and she didn't know why because it was so uncharacteristic of her personality.

The rude woman slowly and methodically filled her plate with lettuce, tomatoes, yellow peppers and pine nuts. When she got to the salad dressings, she hesitated and pretended to act indecisively, that's when she inconspicuously slid the plastic tube with the retractable lid into her palm and dumped the rat lungworms into the salad dressing container. She played with the ladle, mixing the deadly worms into the chunky blue cheese dressing and said aloud as if frustrated, "Oh my God, I just can't decide." She shuffled to the French dressing and generously applied it on her salad. She then walked to the cashier, paid cash for her takeout lunch and left the Kale Town Café, her floppy hat hiding her face from the security camera.

Antoinette Barettelli riddled her friends with questions as a suspicious expression crossed her face, "I don't know why that woman bothered me. Didn't you think she was a little pushy? Did you see her? She cut in front of us and then acted odd."

"Who are talking about, Toni? I didn't pay any attention to her. Fuck her, anyways." Her friend said with a flick of the hand dismissively then added, "Forget about it," and then they all laughed.

"I never saw her before, but she dresses nice. Must be a lawyer or something." As if scripted, when Toni got to the dressings, she scooped out a generous portion of the chunky blue cheese and gently spread it over her salad with a big inviting smile. Her two friends moved forward and smothered their salads: one with Italian, and the other Ranch.

In 24 hours, the spirited lady with the orange hair and funny personality, known as Toni to her friends, would start coughing and wheezing. In 36 hours, she would start gasping for air. In 48 hours, blood would start trickling from her nose, finally she would collapse, have a seizure and be rushed to Northwestern's Emergency Room, clinging to life.

CHAPTER 4

D r. Melanie Karlton was five-feet-ten-inches tall and very attractive in an exotic way. Her long, thick brown hair that normally fell over her shoulders was in a tight ponytail accentuating a flawless face. Her big gray leopard like, circular glasses, commonly known around the hospital as "Peepers," hid the beauty mark on her left eye, but they highlighted her high, smooth, sensuous cheekbones.

Dr. Karlton looked up from the pathology report she was reading on her computer screen when she heard the excitement in an EMT's booming voice as he brought in his second patient of the day suffering from affixation and severe bleeding from her mouth and nose.

"Take that patient to room one." Dr. Karlton commanded. "Clear rooms three, four, five and six. We are going to isolate everyone with a bloody nose. Do it now!"

The charge nurse looked over at her, nodded and then yelled "Terri, Patrick and Philip, you guys are the only people I want touching these patients. Gear up and isolate them from everyone." Hosea Hernandez's green surgical scrubs were stained with sweat. He was on his feet, moving quickly to the emergency cabinet that held the sterile isolation drapes that he would immediately hang to quarantine the area.

"I am declaring this a HAZMAT crisis." Dr. Karlton ordered standing and searching the room, taking full command, establishing herself as the only "Go to person" in the ER. "We are initiating our emergency medical protocols until we know exactly what we are dealing with here," she proclaimed. Once again, she quickly re-examined the pathology report that she had ordered two hours earlier. She was clearly not happy to see the word, "Negative."

Dr. Melanie Karlton was in the eleventh hour of her shift and her adrenaline was flowing at full speed. She was well liked in the ER even though she was a stickler for training and a strict disciplinarian. Male patients often gawked at her because of her beauty. Her dark blue scrubs accentuated her stunning green eyes. Her white lab coat highlighted her lovely face, but it did little to hide her slim, shapely figure. Generally, her re-assuring smile brought calm, but now it morphed into a worried look. Silently forcing all the nurses and pa-tient care techs that normally moved in a calm, easy pace to take no-tice. They kicked into double time and high alert. A control freak, Dr. Karlton hated not knowing what she was dealing with. She had never felt this helpless.

~~~~

The hospital had a mock HAZMAT/disaster training session with the Chicago Fire Department just five months before. A similar scenario was utilized on that training day. Instinctively, she reached for the red desk phone at the nurse's station, immediately connecting her to the dean of the hospital's office. "I have declared a medical emergency! Unknown origin! We have a major, major crisis down here. I believe it could be an act of terrorism."

People in the ER momentarily seemed to freeze in time and focus their full attention towards her ... staring. At that moment, everyone seemed to realize the importance of the situation they were facing and all activity resumed instantaneously with purpose and more clarity.

"Calm down!" Dr. Chester Cunningham retorted. Dr. Cunningham had the moniker CC; he's been in charge of the hospital for as long as anyone could remember. He looked like and reminded everyone of **Dr. Marcus Welby M.D.**, the popular television show starring Robert Young from 1969 through 1976. Dr. Welby never appeared rattled but this was not some television drama.

"You can't go off the handle and talk terrorism. What do you know?"

Dr. Cunningham asked soothingly. Trying to bring calm to what he thought may have been chaos.

"That's just it, we DON'T know. We don't know anything … accept; I've never seen anything like this before. Pathology has no clue yet, but I am telling you, we have to isolate these patients." Dr. Karlton explained tranquilly and patiently. Raising her hand to her forehead, she winched as if she had a headache, and continued, "Something really dreadful is happening. We have eight people down here with undetermined life-threatening symptoms and I don't know if they are contagious."

"Are you telling me you want me to activate SORT?" Cunningham asked with restless eyes.

"Yes, CC that's exactly what we should do … and stat!"

~~~~

The Chicago Fire Department's Special Operations Response Team (SORT) took over the east parking lot, closest to the Emergency Room. They established a perimeter and began unloading and setting up their quarantine and sterilization tents. Most ERs do not have many segregated areas within the hospital to handle a large number of patients that need to be isolated in rooms with a negative airflow to contain any contaminated air.

People walking in and out of the hospital were astonished when they saw Chicago firefighters dressed in white and blue heavy isolation suits, and yellow respirators, assembling three huge tents with eight-feet tall fans. It looked like something from a sci-fi movie.

Visitors with cell phones were recording all of the activity as daylight was dissolving into dark gray storm clouds. They had no idea what they were encountering, but that didn't stop them from taking their pictures. It was something to tell their children and grandchildren or perhaps sell to a television station.

After the tents were set up within the isolation perimeter, a clear thick plastic tunnel was created that led straight to ER room number one, and the infected patients.

~~~~

Hosea Hernandez and three other nurses were now in white protective suits with oxygen masks, hand ventilating four patients. They were perspiring profusely, fogging up their protective eyepieces, which in turn hindered their vision.

The first four patients to arrive that afternoon were on ventilators but the hospital had no more available in the emergency room. Ventilators are very expensive and hospital bean counters carefully control how many are needed and where they're dispensed.

Northwester's hospital is an academic medical center that's ranked number one in the state of Illinois. Within the hospital complex, the campus has five other pavilions that provide all the medical care known to mankind. Most of the ventilators were in use in other critical care units throughout the hospital campus. Every piece of life saving equipment was being utilized.

The four nurses pumping air into the lungs of their patients felt as if their arms were going to fall off as their fingers began to cramp after two hours of the nonstop rhythmic squeezing of the football size air bags.

Hernandez's patient was struggling hard to breath. She was a very distinguished looking 50-year-old woman with orange hair. He finally relaxed and flexed his tired fingers when he got her into a sterilized quarantine room. A ventilator was set up waiting for the medical team to slide her off the gurney and onto a bed. Dr. Mel, as she was often called, immediately took control, barking orders to save her life. The doctor's eyes were sad and tired. She worked feverishly as they hooked the patient to a monitor that measured all her vital signs. Her blood pressure was sinking rapidly and her oxygen level seemed to evaporate as her pulse oximeter measured less than 60.

Very little ever surprised Hosea Hernandez, who had been an ER nurse for eleven years. He had dealt with multiple gunshot wounds from gangbanger turf wars, horrible trauma from head-on automobile accidents, even a suicide victim, who survived a five-story jump out of an apartment window but the look in his dark brown eyes this evening revealed anxiety, pain and uncertainty. He was taking deep breaths to relieve the stress that had built up, trying to save the lady with orange hair.

Hosea Hernandez drank beer with Peter Michaels on many social occasions, and he couldn't wait to get his sailing buddy on the phone to describe the most incredible experience of his life as a nurse. As he dialed the familiar number, he thought, *I hope that shit didn't contaminate me.*

CHAPTER 5

C yril Dobonovich, AKA Brandon Martin, a child phenome-
non, was absolutely brilliant. He was first in his 1993
graduation class from Chicago's revered St. Ignatius High
School at the age of twelve, excelling in every subject. Biology was
his most fervent love. The biggest problem he had in school was
boredom. The Jesuits recognized early on, that he was a prodigy, and
that he had a photographic memory.

The second time Dobonovich went to the mandatory student
mass, he memorized every prayer in the breviary. He hated religion
and God. Science is what he adored and worshipped. The thought of
going to church was a total waste of his time. He was an odd-looking
child without many friends, because primarily he preferred to dissect
a frog than to talk to any classmates. Puberty came early. At age
eleven, course black hair began to sprout all over his body.

Dobonovich was even bored at Loyola University, another Jesuit
school on Chicago's lakefront. He majored in Biology, Chemistry and
the Earth Sciences. His lowest grade was a B+ and his narcissistic
personality would not allow him to accept any form of failure. He
vehemently argued over his test score with his professor, Dr. James
McKenzie, PhD. that he was correct claiming that the professor was
not well informed about Creutzfeldt-Jakob disease, the subject of the

argument. Dobonovich claimed a cure was close but no scientific evidence backed that thesis.

"I know more about the effects of the Creutzfeldt-Jakob disease than anyone on the planet." The young student screamed, spittle spewing from his mouth as he approached Dr. McKenzie in his office, waving his test paper.

The startled professor jumped to his feet and instinctively pulled at his woolen sweater sleeve to cover his wristwatch. "Young man, you are barely a teenager. Don't come here arguing with me about an antidote. You don't know as much as you think you do. There is no treatment."

"I don't care. I know; I will find a treatment before anyone else." The inflamed, young Dobonovich declared as he threw his test paper at the professor and continued his rant. "You know nothing. I'm smarter than you'll ever be. Fuck You."

Commonly called Kuru, Creutzfeldt-Jakob is a very rare infectious protein found in contaminated brain tissue. Dobonovich was obsessed with the subject matter. After he lost his academic argument, he despised Professor McKenzie even more and vowed that one day he would make the old man pay for his humiliation.

It took only six semesters for Dobonovich to finish his triple major sciences degree. The B+ deprived him of the highest-grade point average ever achieved in Loyola's history and this incident planted the seeds of revenge that would one day make him one of the most despicable and diabolic killers in Chicago's history.

Dobonovich's warped mind absorbed everything about viruses, germs and diseases so when the Washington, D C, Technical School of Infectious Diseases offered him a full grant for a master's degree, he accepted their scholarship immediately. Summer school offered limited classes but he didn't care. He couldn't wait to get started and move out of Chicago and away from Professor James McKenzie, not to mention some other mortal sins that he committed.

He never brought a book to a classroom or lab session. Once he read the material, his memory took over. Every student at Washington Tech knew who this 15-year-old genius was. All the stares made him more self-conscious and drove him further into his shell of self-loathing and hatred.

As a young student, his five-foot five-inch frame was scrawny. He survived on junk food and grape soda. His teeth were starting to rot from lack of oral hygiene forcing anyone who had the opportunity to talk with him to social distance. His course black hair grew wildly and his bushy eyebrows drew attention to his thick eyeglasses. He shaved twice a day because his five o'clock shadow started well before noon. He averted eye contact with people who ogled at him. His beloved bugs didn't look back. So, he gladly embraced his dark world of atrociousness, plotting his revenge against anyone who dared to challenge him or his intellect.

While doing some routine research on sexually transmitted diseases, Dobonovich discovered Chancroid, a bacterium that settles in a man's genital area. The affects were extremely painful. Although the bacteria are mainly transferred through sexual activity, he made up his mind that this was how he would punish Professor McKenzie. He would develop a delivery system that could encapsulate the bacteria.

With a master's degree and a PhD by the time he was 17, he began publishing results of studies he conducted on a rare form of a complex micro-bacterium tuberculosis strain. He utilized a microscopic, automated acid platform that led to the detection of rare mutations for an antibiotic treatment. His scholarly reputation was growing as fast as the deadly microorganisms that he was secretly cultivating.

School became more and more tedious. All of his spare time was devoted to research. The arrogant Dobonovich cloaked himself as a research fellow in biology giving him the fraudulent credentials; he needed to apply for academic study grants. With a sociopathic ego, his feeling of superiority flourished. His associates were mere minions not his equals. Every final exam offered him no challenge and was a waste of his energy and talents. He begrudgingly took them only to advance his personal scholarly credentials.

Research and money became his only passions.

The Austrian Institute of Virology offered him a postdoctoral fellowship with teaching opportunities and tenure. He accepted the position without hesitation knowing that Vienna's population of nearly two million people offered him the opportunity to disappear into his dark environment and away from those who dared to question any of his intentions and motives.

The Institute of Virology gave him access to a number of extremely dangerous infectious agents and he took full advantage of every single opportunity made available to him. He hid behind the guise of grants from the World Health Organization as he created his own private processes to grow, purify and isolate various viruses and to develop vaccines to protect the human race for which he cared little. He reported to the W.H.O. that unfortunately his procedures were all failures although he knew how successful they really were.

After his first two years at the Institute, he clandestinely established his own private laboratories in Linz, Salzburg and Innsbruck, where he started to develop his unique methods to discover antidotes and vaccines for the deadly agents that he created and separated. With the special chemical compounds that he advanced; he was able to remove the most active components from potentially deadly principles. He then created peptide sequences for very specific infective agents that he could isolate and preserve.

He would patent his achievements when he returned to the United States.

One night after a very hectic day of travel to Innsbruck and many long hours of research, a tired, Dobonovich was working on his antibody for Kuru, the slow brain-eating virus. When he finished isolating a sample, he smiled a triumphant evil smile, and he prepared to freeze the sample by aerosolizing the virus into a self-sealing pressurized container. He took off his protective glasses and wiped his eyes and face with a wet washcloth. He cracked his knuckles and shook his fingers to relax. He moved back to his workspace with a metal overhead shield to continue the isolation procedure and that's when he accidently applied too much pressure to his air hose nozzle, which startled him causing him to take a deep breath. It was a critical mistake that dispensed microscopic fragments of the toxin into the air. As he tried to adjust his cloth-filtering N-95 mask, he realized he forgot to put it back on after he gloated about his success just moments earlier. It was the first and only time he could remember that he violated his strict safety protocols. Unhindered, however, he finished freezing the specimen and didn't give his mistake a second thought because for him it would be incomprehensible that it would have any personal consequence in any way.

CHAPTER 6

"News ... Michaels."

"Hey, Man, it's Hosea."

"What's up brother?" Michaels and Hosea Hernandez were friends for a long time. They drank beer and sailed together on many summer weekends. Hernandez even crewed on Michaels' beloved "Dr. Detroit," a 40.6 Beneteau on four Chicago to Mackinac races.

Hernandez was generally calm and composed, but excitement was overflowing, when exclaimed, "You better get your ass over here right away. We got some shit going on and nobody, and I mean nobody, knows what we're dealing with."

"Yeah, I heard about it earlier and I am waiting to hear from a friend who works at the CDC. She's on her way there." Michaels said as he pulled off his Harley Davidson tee shirt and reached for his dress shirt and tie.

"Well, she's already here." Hosea was drying his hair with a hospital towel. "I just got out of a sterilization shower. My arms are ready to fall off. I just finished two hours of ventilating a patient by hand. It's bad man!" Hernandez took several deep breaths to calm himself. "Dr. Karlton has declared a 'HAZMATt' emergency. We're under attack."

Michaels hung up the phone and charged into News Director Phil Rivers' office. He didn't know he was disrupting a private meeting, and he didn't care. "Sorry, boss. Northwestern Hospital has declared an all-out 'HAZMAT' emergency. They set up a quarantine area in the parking lot. I told you, it could be bioterrorism."

"You check that out Michaels." Rivers stood up at his desk as a concerned look transmuted across his face. His left hand instinctively reached for his tie hanging loosely around his neck and his right forefinger shot out at Michaels like an arrow off of a bowstring. "Damn it, Michaels, I don't want you to scare the shit out of this city."

"You know me better than that!" Michaels responded with a boyish grin that over the years became his unofficial trademark.

Rivers drop his finger, frowning, "Yeah, that's why I'm telling you. Be sure!"

~~~~

Michaels loved working with Paul Nagaro as his "shooter"—a common television term for a cameraman. Nagaro, an Emmy-winning photojournalist, was Japanese, five feet-eleven inches tall. His smooth jet-black hair cut slightly over his ears was starting to show speckles of gray at the temples, and it was gelled and combed straight back … stylish. Always a very sharp dresser, he never seemed to get dirty, his designer jeans were impeccable, every pair of tennis shoe he wore were never scuffed, and immaculately white, like he walked on water instead of the filthy streets of Chicago. More importantly, he had a keen eye; he sensed action developing before it actually happened. He never missed the "money" shot. He's good—very good.

Michaels knew as soon as he schmoozed his way close to the ER parking lot, Nagaro would instinctively start gathering every interesting video shot available. The live truck would be setting up within minutes.

Michaels wove his way through the chaotic activity in the make-shift HAZMAT area, trying to talk into his cellphone over all the background sound, "Hey Pat, when did you get into town?" Michaels asked.

Patricia Dickerson was second in command of the eight-person CDC team that was sent from Atlanta. "About an hour ago, I can't talk long. I am trying to put together the information for our M & M Report, but we don't know yet, what we're dealing with here. I just put more samples on our jet to see if the scientists in Atlanta can figure this out."

Morbidity and Mortality Reports are an analysis of the findings from a medical investigation. Once an organism or infectious disease is identified, the CDC tries to determine what it is and what type of injuries it can cause. If any injuries are intentional, a "code red" goes into effect and extreme safety measures are put in place. The CDC wants to know immediately, if there is any known effective vaccine for any suspicious finding. The M & M report gives a description of the symptoms and aggravating effects along with a prediction for mortality.

"What does the hospital say?" Michaels asked as he entered the ER door, nodding at the security guard, who recognized him with a slight grin.

Dickerson was in the middle of all the commotion at the ER nurse's station. Her blonde hair was pulled back in a ponytail and her blue eyes that accentuated her high cheekbones looked tired. Her pretty face was shadowed with anxiety, as she warily responded, "We have been unable to determine what we are dealing with, and that is why I rushed more samples out. It is ugly here. I gotta go. I'll call you when I can."

Michaels was startled by the quick response. "Wait! How many cases are we talking about here?"

A frustrated Dickerson let out a short but loud sigh and rolled her eyes. She was agitated, "More than 20 victims so far, and I think eight hospitals. Bye."

Michaels was stunned, looking at his cellphone he mumbled, "Did she just hang up on me?" and then shook his head.

Nagaro approached with a gleeful look. "I got a lot of good stuff. I'm heading to the truck to edit. How many seconds do you want?"

"Two minutes." Michaels responded without hesitation as his mind was writing his script. "You didn't breathe in any of this shit, did you?"

Nagaro's face turned from inquisitive to apprehensive, "What the fuck, Peter! What are we dealing with here?"

"I don't know Paul. I don't know."

~~~~

Dr. Karlton was on the phone speaking in hushed tones, almost whispering. She was startled to see Peter Michaels standing in front of her.

"How the hell did you get in here?"

Michaels shrugged his shoulders and put his palms out and gave her that innocent boyish look as if being scolded by Sister Mary Stevens in grade school. "I've been in and out of here a thousand times. What's going on?"

"You got to get out of here. Part of this ER is on quarantine." Dr. Karlton said looking over her shoulder worriedly.

"How many you got infected here?"

"How do you know about this? You gotta go. I swear, Peter, I don't want to call security."

"Just tell me how many and I'm out of here. I've got 15 minutes before I am going live outside."

"Eight! Now go!"

"What about other hospitals?"

Dr. Karlton stood up and pointed to the door. "Check with the police. Go!"

Michaels reached for his cellphone as he turned and rushed out the door. He hit the speed dial button for Sergeant Bob Kennedy, a source he's had for years, who was in charge of the Chicago Police Department's Office of News Affairs.

Kennedy responded on the first ring when he saw who was calling. "I'm with the boss right now. I can't say much." Kennedy said with a stern look camouflaging his face.

Jackie Jackson was the Superintendent of Police. He was getting ready to retire but this act of terrorism had his blood rushing and his adrenalin pumping giving him second thoughts.

"I'm on the air in a few. Give me something."

"Four dead. Fourteen critical. At least four more in isolation."

"Anything else?"

"Shit Michaels ... Ain't that enough? Oh ... By the way we're calling in the FBI."

Michaels was sweating as he positioned himself in front of his camera. Nagaro started to wire him up and gave him his IFB earpiece. He immediately heard Ron Magers, The WMAC anchorman ask, "What's the lede?"

Michaels said "bioterrorism, FBI and four dead." He knew Magers would adlib a perfect lede into his on-camera story. Michaels hated live shots because he was deathly afraid that he would drop an F-bomb when he got personally involved in a story. Tonight, was such a time. Michaels could hear the station's musical theme in the background and the announcer introducing the Ten O'clock News with Ron Magers.

"Tonight, the City of Chicago is on high alert after an incident that has already claimed at least four lives. There is concern that this could be an act of bioterrorism and Channel Six News has learned that the city is calling in the FBI's Terrorist Task Force for help. Peter Michaels is live with exclusive details. Peter."

Michaels looked into the camera. He didn't have to be dramatic. The look on his face said it all as the red tally light cued him to speak. By the time he finished his story, the City of Chicago was in shock. Terrorists hit home for the first time with a suspected biological attack in the city's history.

CHAPTER 7

T he hairless man known as Brandon Martin just finished fitting the final glass panel of his Bio Safety Lab (BSL) into place. He was testing the seal on the double doors when he heard Ron Magers announce that the city was under siege by a bioterrorist attack. He grabbed a sterile white terrycloth towel to wipe his forehead as he settled in front of his 80-inch Vizio television set. An opprobrium smirk slinked across his Botox filled face. *What fucking fools,* he thought as he listened to that reporter Peter Michaels blabber on. *Terrorism. If they only knew.*

His glass modular clean room was delivered in separate pieces, three days earlier by a private mover. Brandon Martin worked tirelessly and meticulously to erect the room where he created death in numerous microorganisms. He was recalcitrant and worriless about any of the BSL materials being traced back to him because they are not regulated, locally or federally.

The incubators and the lyophilization refrigerators fit precisely on the stainless-steel tables. He could flash burn and vaporize any material in his high temperature incinerator. The ventilation scheme perfectly aligned with his one-way exhaust fan systems that sucked out any contaminated air into Chicago's atmosphere. He could also reverse the airflow to produce positive pressure within his clean room. He already began to isolate his newest deadly viral sequences for his victims.

He knew exactly how he would terminate his next enemy. His attorney, the man, who failed him miserably years ago. It was time for sleep. Four hours was all he needed.

~~~~

It was late Friday afternoon when the death pattern began to reveal itself. Peter Michaels was on the phone with Sergeant Bob Kennedy, the Director of the News Affairs for the Chicago Police Department.

"What happens now that you determined that a massive crime has developed, what do you do?" Michaels asked.

"Well, all first responders contact the Crime Prevention Information Center. You know, it's here at headquarters on the fifth floor. You've seen it before, right? It is literally the city's crime fighting nerve center." Kennedy said.

"Yeah. Yeah. A bunch of different law enforcement agencies are there. Right? What's it called again?"

"C-PIC. It's our first line of defense once we determine if a devastating crime was committed. Remember, you gotta go through two security doors to get in."

"Oh, yeah. The room looks like you're in a 'Star Trek' movie. All kinds of TV screens and shit."

"Yep, it has every form of communication equipment you can imagine. Information is gathered, analyzed and distributed. Action strategies are developed and then implemented if necessary."

"What happens next?"

"Well, OEMC is contacted and all city services are put on full alert but listen I gotta go. I'll call Commander Shaw over there and set you up with an appointment. You should go see it. It's very impressive."

"Will they let us take some pictures? I'll send my producer over with a cameraman."

"No problem. Here's Shaw's number."

~~~~

Chicago's Office of Emergency Management and Communications is a state-of-the-art facility that coordinates every type of city service that is available for any type of emergency that occurs.

When producer David Beedy and cameraman, Paul Nagaro arrived, the guard announced they were expected and issued them credentials. OEMC's headquarters at 1411 West Madison Street is a five story, red brick fortress protected with cement pillars to deter any vehicle penetration.

"Man, I have to take my long shot from back here at this fence line." Nagaro said. "This place is fucking huge."

Commander Jerry Shaw greeted them as they exited the elevator on the second floor. Shaw had an eternal smile that made everyone who entered his stronghold feel at home. His handshake was firm.

"Let's start in the 911 center." He announced businesslike.

"How many people work here?" Beedy asked.

"We have a total of 2,500 employees. We coordinate and execute every service related to all of the city's events, including emergencies and disasters. We also operate a citywide communication system and offer technological support to law enforcement, emergency medical services, fire services, Streets and Sanitation services and traffic control within the 250 miles of Chicago's city limits."

"I've read that you guys have pretty sophisticated cameras all over the city." Beedy rhetorically asked.

"That's right, Dave. The OEMC controls over twenty thousand cameras strategically located throughout the city. These cameras can detect the sound of gunshots and produce video as they zoom into the precise areas where the shots were fired."

As Nagaro shot video, everyone sitting at their stations turned their heads to protect their identity. Some of them were undercover operatives when they weren't assigned to OEMC.

"Does the C-PIC have full access to all these cameras?" Beedy asked.

"Yep. They can call up any camera, anytime."

"And this place is what, again?"

"It's the Emergency Control and Command Center. It is one of the most advanced and sophisticated electronic and communication systems in the world. We have more than a hundred individual stations set up amphitheater style. Notice how everything is facing the main command post." Shaw explained.

"This is pretty impressive commander. I'm not kidding you. Looks like you got every law enforcement agency involved here."

"We do; Chicago Police and Fire, State Police, FBI, DEA, Homeland Security, even the CIA is present if it involves terrorism."

"Excuse me commander, this just came in for you," said a police officer handing Shaw a folded note.

Shaw read it and his smile converted to a frown.

"What is it?" Beedy asked.

"It looks like breaking news, Mr. Beedy. The superintendent just put us and the C-PIC on the highest 'code red' alert and he's calling in the FBI's Joint Terrorism Task Force."

~~~~

Special agents were already gathering on the 5th floor of Chicago's new ultramodern FBI field office at 2111 West Roosevelt Road. Members of the Joint Terrorism Task Force (JTTF) are literally hand-picked. The best of the best from the CPD and the FBI.

The tools available to them to respond to a terrorist attack are so refined that they defy the imagination. Helicopters, planes and drones equipped with electronic magnetic impulse lasers and sound wave technology to destroy enemy drones can be launch in an instant by Homeland Security. Electronic listening devices can be placed in a room by remote control. Communication channels that connect every law enforcement agency on the planet operate 24 hours a day.

There was no chatter from known terrorist organizations about this latest attack. Strangely no one was taking credit for these mass murders that had the city of Chicago in shock. The JTTF was on edge because of the lack of acknowledgement. Law enforcement and medical investigators were at ground zero with very little information with the exception, that they knew there were 24 victims.

The investigation was code named **Operation Firefox.**

CHAPTER 8

Saturday mornings in the summer were usually quiet in the WMAC newsroom. Weekend reporters and producers were generally the per diem hires. They were less experienced, young, hungry rookies trying to make a name for themselves as they vied for the best story of the day. This July morning, however, was different, the entire investigative unit, the main anchors and the top general assignment reporters were summoned to the station to meet with the new general manager, Larry Voss to discuss the next steps of how to handle this terrorist attack.

Peter Michaels was there long before anyone else. He just got off the phone and found out six more people died. All seemingly random. No known connections. He wanted to walk and think. An overnight rain caused a precipitous drop in temperature from the day before. The steam from Michaels' Dunkin Donuts coffee was lingering in the chilly morning air when he realized he was on Chicago's Magnificent Mile (Michigan Avenue) after a shopper inadvertently bumped his arm and broke his chain of thought as he headed for the river and a park bench.

The green, brown water of the Chicago River was sparkling like a million diamonds as the sun's rays breaking through the gray morning clouds created the illusion of tiny mirrors on its now glimmering surface. Michaels loved living in Chicago. It was vibrant and ten times cleaner than New York City. If only the crime rate would show some more respect. If only this terrorist attack didn't disrupt his city.

He found a bench, sat down, sipped his now cooled coffee, and abruptly found himself in a hypnotic state after absent mindedly staring at those tiny mirrors reflecting off of the polluted water that flowed westward, meandering toward the Mississippi River and ultimately discharging its waste into the Gulf of Mexico.

Michaels was transfixed in deep thought. He had sources all over the city in every department of public service: police, fire, public defenders, defense attorneys, prosecutors, judges, and even janitors, who cleaned buildings. He was also very close to a high-ranking member of the CDC's medical investigative team. No one knew anything new except at least 16 people were dead and eight others were clinging to life.

The blaring siren from Chicago Fire Department ambulance #68 shattered Michaels' tranquility bringing him back to reality and the present moment. Gray, gloomy clouds started to curtain the sun as the temperature struggled to warm the morning air. Michaels stretched, yawned, stood up and a sharp pain shot through his lower back. He was stiff and achy. He winched as he started to walk back towards the NBC Tower pulling out his cellphone.

"Hey, where the hell are you?" his producer David Beedy asked, nervously walking around the I-Team's office.

"I've been walking and thinking. Anything new?" Michaels responded trekking back to meet his colleagues.

"Yeah. We now have eight hospitals for sure treating victims and two more died. It's ugly."

"I'll be there shortly."

"You better get your ass here. They want to start early."

~~~~

The highly polished cherry wood table in the middle of Larry Voss's conference room was designed to make everyone feel that they were an important part of every conversation that took place around it. The room was generally used to discuss business deals and strategies for the upcoming rating season, but today it was being used to plan a stratagem for news coverage of something that had never occurred in Chicago before, massive deaths from an apparently terrorist attack.

The wall that everyone noticed as they entered the room was covered with journalism awards, many of which Michaels had won. They were all set in sterling silver frames except for the George Foster Peabody Award, which was the equivalent to the Pulitzer Prize for newspapers. It was the centerpiece of the display proudly exhibited in an exotic mahogany frame. It was Michaels' favorite.

~~~~

Peter Michaels was always an informal person who spoke his mind more often than he should, but this morning he was unusually quiet. He and his producer David Beedy were casually dressed in jeans and opened collared shirts. He wondered whether he should have worn his blue Armani suit and his red power tie for this particular meeting with the new GM Larry Voss and his news director, Phil Rivers. He felt relieved as the two of them walked into the room with their shirt-sleeves rolled up and no ties. Voss canceled his usual Saturday morning golf match. He was not smiling.

"What have we got so far?" Voss asked in anticipation of quick responses.

Everyone was silent and then all eyes shifted to Michaels, who was standing in the corner with Ron Magers on one side and Beedy on the other. Magers' black hair was perfectly combed back. His graying temples gave him an aristocratic appearance even though he was casually dressed in blue jeans and a light blue oxford shirt with no tie. He never took notes. His near photographic memory served him well in the anchor chair where he never suffered a second of dead air.

Beedy, on the other hand, was always taking notes. He had a yellow number two pencil tucked in his right ear and a ballpoint busily scribbling in his reporter's notebook. He was one of the most organized people in the newsroom. He cataloged everything and kept impeccable records of any project he ever worked on.

"What?" Michaels said with a sheepish grin, knowing everyone was staring at him. Silence. One beat. Two beats. He pulled his notebook out of his back pocket. "There were ten victims at Northwestern, two at Loyola, three at Christ, four at the University of Chicago, three at St. Joe's, two at Resurrection, two at Evanston and two at Elmhurst. Twenty-eight in all. I think at least 14 have died. The others are all critical and unlikely to make it through the night."

"Have they identified what killed these people yet?" Rivers asked looking around the room.

"The headline today is the autopsies that are scheduled to begin at noon. The feds are waiting for some of their forensic guys to get here. Dr. Crine has been brought into the loop. That's good for us. We go back a long way." Michaels responded knowing that he had a great connection with Dr. Crine.

Doctor Robert Crine was the Cook County Medical Examiner. He was hoping to retire within six months. This case may be his last after twenty-five years of service in Chicago.

Michaels developed a great rapport with him after the stories he did years ago on the heroine substitute T's and Blues as a new killer of drug abusers. As a result, Dr. Crine changed the causes of death for 17 victims from heroin overdoses to T's and Blues overdoses. They've respected one another ever since.

"What does your ... cough ... cough ... girlfriend say?" asked one of his colleagues with a giant sly grin.

"Which one?" Michaels retorted.

Everyone laughed because they knew Michaels had a relationship with the CDC investigator assigned to this case.

"I haven't had much of a chance to talk with her. She is up to her ass in alligators with all of this. She texted me last night. I hope to talk to her this afternoon." Michaels said as he closed his notebook and slipped it into his back pocket.

"Okay! Let's filter all information through Magers and Beedy." All eyes shifted to the new general manager, who had a reputation of letting his news people do their thing and not interfere. "Don't be afraid to share. This story is bigger than any ego. Let's get cracking." Voss ordered.

CHAPTER 9

S ome police officers would argue that Detective Jack Warren, who had the highest IQ on the Chicago Police Department, was not that smart. He gave up a brilliant career as a surgeon to become a cop. While working in the ER at Cook County Hospital during his second year of residency, he was attending to three gunshot victims. The detectives working the case had a calming effect on the victims' family members. This mesmerized Warren. After he extracted an AK-47 round from a gangbanger belonging to Black Disciples' chest, a half inch from his heart, Warren went over to Detective David Grauzer and started talking to him about working a homicide case. He made up his mind to change careers at that moment.

He graduated from the Police Academy number one in his class in academics, physical fitness and firearms. He was top shot, the highest honored that could be bestowed on a graduate. The Commander of the Training Academy contacted the superintendent to make him aware that recruit Jack Warren was a superior student and destined for great things.

Promotions came quickly to Warren. At age 30 with just five years on the job, he already made detective. It was unprecedented on the CPD. He was brilliant and as he worked a homicide case, he had the ability to absorb and analyze vast amounts of information. His brain moved facts around as they unfolded like they were chess pieces moving from one square to another until he arrived at checkmate.

The superintendent of police wanted his up-and-coming star on the FBI terrorist task force.

Warren didn't look like a computer nerd but computers didn't scare him. He knew more about technology than any "Geek Squad" that was often called in to fix unknown problems.

At six feet, his muscular 178 pound-frame, accepted his tailored made clothes to be part of his skin. He seemed to glide when he walked into FBI headquarters on the 5th floor. The secretary with short red hair and green eyes that greeted him was awe struck by his penetrating deep blue eyes when he said, "Hi. I'm Jack Warren. I am supposed to report to the Joint Terrorist Task Force. Where do I find Special Agent Tom Eiseman?"

"Yes, he's expecting you. Go through the double doors and turn right you can't miss it." She responded with blinking eyes and an opened mouth.

The room was humming with activity when he entered, but it was not what he expected. It was not high tech. It looked like any other office space with beige cloth cubicles dividing all of the work-stations. The walls were painted eggshell white. Desks were decorated with personal effects of the agents occupying them. Family pictures. White Sox and Blackhawks paraphilia. Even a Philadelphia Eagles flag. No one looked up as he sauntered in. Every agent in the room appeared to have a phone attached to his or her ear, and investigative files in front of them. Sixteen victims now dead, twelve more were barely alive, clinging to life. Comatose.

Warren assumed Special Agent Eiseman was the man in the front office. The one that had, the only windows in the room. They were tinted. You could see out but nobody could see in. Bullet proof. Secure.

Warren stretched out his hand to greet his new boss. "Excuse me, sir. Are you agent Tom Eiseman?"

"You must be the 'whiz kid.' Jackson speaks very highly of you," he said standing up revealing a once muscular body of an offensive tackle for the University of Illinois. His neck was thick and his smile friendly and engaging. His handshake was firm and strong, leaving the impression that his fist had broken a few noses during his long career.

"Thanks ... I guess," said Warren as his eyes systematically searched the room taking in nothing unusual, except two large TV monitors. Each screen had four different quadrants filled with black and white moving pictures. Plain. Simple. Safe.

"What do we have?" asked Warren trying to get immediately involved in his new assignment.

"We have identified all of the victims." Eiseman responded, shuffling a stack of folders on his desk.

"Do we know where they all worked?"

"That's your job. Once we figure that out, we should be able to find the origin of the attack."

"Do we know when it happened?"

"No! Not yet, but I assume in the middle of the week. It took a few days to unfold."

~~~~

Dr. Robert Crine's victim/patient had bright orange hair and black tattooed eyebrows. Antoinette Barettelli was once very pretty. Now she was contorted and gnarly. She suffered a severely painful death. Crine was a stickler for protocol but he wasted no time removing her heart, weighing it and going straight to her lungs. All the victims bled profusely from their noses and mouths. *It had to be from their lungs,* he reckoned. He took the right lung first and laid on a stainless-steel tray and weighed it. He flipped down his magnifying eyeglasses immediately discovering dozens of BB size nodules that were exposed. He plucked out several samples, put them under his microscope and maggot type worms were revealed. They turned a bright avocado color from the center outward once they were exposed to air. He then explored her stomach and found similar worms. He found nothing in her windpipe.

He was instructed to call the Joint Terrorism Task Force if he found anything suspicious. He dialed the number he was assigned, put the call on speaker and continued dissecting his samples.

"Detective Jack Warren." It was his first call at the JTTF. His nerves immediately settled when he heard the familiar voice.

"Hey Jack. It's Dr. Crine. I didn't know you were detailed to the task force," he said with a smile as he wiped his forehead with the back of his latex gloved hand.

"Yeah. I started this morning. You got something for us?"

"Yup ... they were poisoned from something they ate. I found maggots, teeny greenish worms in her stomach and lungs. They probably migrated once they were ingested. There was nothing in her throat. It came from the stomach. I'm positive!" Crine said as he returned to his microscope as if to double-check his information. "I think you should get the word out to everyone doing an autopsy—start in the lungs and stomach." He hung up abruptly not waiting for a response.

Warren immediately pressed a button on his secure phone that directly connected him to Special Agent Tom Eiseman, who picked it up instantly.

"Whatta yah got?" Eiseman asked as he rubbed his furled forehead, closing his eyes.

Warren told him what Dr. Crine reported and Eiseman pressed a link on his computer that sent a message to all the special agents who had a top-secret security clearance and summed them to the SCIF (pronounced skiff). The Sensitive Compartmented Information Facility is a secure room where all high priority and classified material is discussed. Any person entering the room must have a classified top-secret security clearance. All cell phones, laptops, recording machines, photographic and other electronic media devices were surrendered at the door and placed in a sealed and locked metal box.

To cut red tape and save time, Special Agent Tom Eiseman required everyone who entered his SCIF to leave everything other than a ballpoint pen at or in their desk drawers. All information, activity and conversations inside this secure room were highly confidential, sensitive and restricted from any disclosure to the public.

~~~~

Patricia Dickerson was on the CDC jet with more than 30 autopsy specimens in median transport vessels but she was diverted from Atlanta to Fort Detrick in Maryland to test the samples. Some specimens were placed in liquids, formaldehyde, warm and cold fresh or salty water. Others were left in the pleura of the lungs. Several were exposed to air.

Fort Detrick is the top United States Army Medical Command installation. It has the latest and most sophisticated research equipment, instruments and methodology to identify unknown pathogens, viruses, bugs, microorganisms and parasites. The government also conducts biomedical research and development on its 1200-acre campus located in Frederick, Maryland. There are different laboratories for Biodefense exploration, Biological research, infectious diseases evaluation and the assessment of foreign plant pathogens. The first major study on the scientific aspects of Anthrax was conducted here. Fort Detrick also had its share of failed test and contamination scares. It is often referred to as "Fort Doom."

~~~~

Dickerson was immediately on her computer searching for any known parasite, microorganism, bug or worm that would settle in the lungs. This was their first big lead and twelve victims were still clinging to life.

"News … Michaels."

"Hey! It's Pat. We got something." She said with excitement in her voice.

"What?" Michaels responded as he jolted up in his chair and looked for something to write on.

"Worms."

"Worms. What the fuck!" He responded with a questioning look unfolding across his face.

"Your buddy, Crine was the first to discover it. The FBI's guy was a few minutes behind him. It's confirmed. We are absolutely positive it came from something they ate."

"Do you know when or where?" He asked as he stopped writing, looking off into space.

"Nope, the pathology definitely indicates it started in the stomach."

"What's next?"

"We'll try to identify the worm or whatever it is and see if there is an antidote or vaccine. Eight people are still alive." She proclaimed with a glimmer of hope in her eyes.

"Stay in touch. I'll talk to you soon." Michaels hung up phone and then dial the news hotline to report. "The killing agent is some kind of parasite that grows into a worm that eats its way from the stomach into the lungs. There is no known cure."

CHAPTER 10

T he hairless man transferred $750,000 from the account of the man known as Brandon Martin into the new account of a 35-year-old man about to be born, named Charles Darrow. He killed off Brandon Martin with click of a keystroke and he created a death certificate inside the vital statistics information platform on the hard drives of the computers in the Cook County Clerk's office. He already shredded Martin's driver's license and passport. Charles Darrow would exist for two or three weeks depending on how long it would take his new experimental neurodegenerative virus cultures to mature.

The blonde woman, who dispensed the rat lungworm in the blue cheese dressing at the Kale Town Café, existed in his mind as Darlene Johnson. She would never be seen again, he created Ruth Hayward. Her driver's license and passport would be ready in a day or so. The forgeries were always flawless. Always perfect. Always fool proof.

Money was the least of Dobonovich's concerns. He had more than $250,000,000 in Swiss bank accounts and offshore accounts in the Bahamas. All hidden behind numbers and fictitious identities that he had fashioned over the years. He preferred numbers to names. Harder to trace and he didn't like people.

His headaches were getting much more severe. He grasped the edge of the stainless-steel table and lowered himself onto his lab chair, and he thought about when he first noticed them. It was more than ten years ago after he returned to Chicago in the fall of 2004 from Austria as Dr. Cyril Dobonovich with PhDs in Biology and Chemistry from The Austrian Institute of Virology where he specialized in infectious diseases.

His fortune amassed daily from a continuing stream of royalties from patents, he developed with the proprietary research he concealed and stole from the Austrian Institute and the World Health Organization.

His discoveries caught the attention of big pharmaceutical companies after he developed a unique process to grow, isolate and then purify viruses that led to vaccines and antidotes quickly. He did all this in his clandestine research laboratories in Lake Forest, and Frankfort, Illinois and Milwaukee, Wisconsin.

These strange new headaches started to affect him and his temperament. He would often have angry outbursts while working. The first one started after his visit to Professor James McKenzie at Loyola University right after he returned to the states. The unsuspecting, aging professor was surprised to see his gifted pupil after all these years. He had no idea how much Dobonovich hated and despised him. His student looked different. Older. Bearded. Wild hair. Thick eyeglasses. All of this was about to change, but his distinctive high-pitched voice would be hard to alter.

After a humble greeting, Dobonovich sat down in one of the chairs in front of the professor's desk, slid his hand into his coat pocket, grasped the capsule of Chancroid bacteria and went into a rage.

"You sorry pathetic old man don't you know I am the smartest person in the world? You should have recognized that years ago when you gave me that humiliating grade in Biology after my discourse of Kuru."

Shocked and scared, almost tongue-tied the old professor managed, "Young man how could you harbor this hatred for so long?"

The professor's hands trembled. His voice seemed to squeak. "You call me pathetic. You sorry bastard get out of my office before I call security," he said as he attempted to stand up.

At that moment, when the professor's head was down, Dobonovich dropped the capsule of Chancroid bacteria into his coffee cup. "Sit down you old fool. You will never see me again but you will always remember me. I guarantee it." He got up and walked out of the office with a malevolent grin thinking, *your body will rot and you will have unbearable pain* then he laughed a ghoulish laugh and never looked back. The following day medical procedures were scheduled and he knew he would never look the same again.

~~~~

Peter Michaels was on the phone with Pat Dickerson. He was exhausted, and sprawled out on his green leather living room couch, listening to the soothing sounds of water splashing on the hulls of sailboats gliding through the sea. He was sipping a cold bottle of IPA beer, momentarily out of reporter mode, falling into romance mode. "When are you back in Chicago?" He asked softly.

"Soon, I hope. I'd like to see you again. The scientists here are brilliant but boring." Dickerson was in a similar mood laying in her hotel room with her head propped up on two pillows and a glass of Dewar's scotch smothered in ice wrapped in her hands.

Michaels smiled, "I hope you don't find me ... boring?"

"You and I both know this is going to go nowhere. You in Chicago. Me in Atlanta."

"Yeah ... but let's not worry about it now. You never know. Call me when you're back."

"I'd like that. Sleep well."

They both hung up smiling.

~~~~

The doorbell rang and broke Dobonovich's train of thought. He got up, looked through the peephole to see the UPS driver walking down the steps and back to his truck. It was a rare and expensive late Sunday night special delivery. He smiled as he opened the door and picked up the package no bigger than a shoebox. The contents securely packed. The delivery from Southeast Asia by way of Oakland, California was artistically wrapped, every corner folded perfectly, it had to be protected. The address label was blocked printed, untraceable. The four vials inside looked like bottles of imported hemp oil thanks to the eyedropper caps. The disguise would fool any customs x-ray machine. The four eight ounce bottles of Anthrax would soon multiple and his last hurrah would place him in infamy. His smile turned venomous as he proudly picked up his package of revenge and headed to the sterile, airtight BSL, and the incubators that would grow the feared and deadly toxin.

CHAPTER 11

P eter Michaels loved Chicago style hotdogs particularly at Jimmy's Original Red Hots and Polish. They seemed to taste better there; maybe it was the greasy fries that came with the dog, all wrapped in a bag. The small rectangular red brick structure at Grand Avenue and Pulaski hasn't changed since 1954.

A Chicago hotdog is unique: it's an all-beef dog resting in a poppy seed bun with yellow mustard, white onion, sweet green relish, hot sport peppers, tomatoes, dill pickle wedges and celery salt. They're offered in many restaurants around the world but they're really not the same. Eating them in Chicago gives them that extra ambience and taste.

Michaels was sitting in his car listening to Jimmy Buffett, getting ready to bite into his hotdog when his cell phone rang.

"It's Peter."

"Hey, it's Jack."

The two of them met drinking beers at Buddy Guy's "House of Blues" last year. They were 20 years apart in age, but they both liked beer and blues, and they lived in the same building at 880 South Michigan Avenue. Warren on the fifth floor (501) and Michaels on the tenth (1002). Their views of Lake Michigan, the museum campus and Grant Park were fantastic. Michaels' was spectacular.

"What's up brother?"

"We have identified all 28 victims. I am sorry to tell you but you may know at least two of them."

Michaels took a deep breath and put his hotdog on the passenger seat. "Who are they?"

"Antoinette Barettelli and ..."

"Oh, shit man! She was like the best." Michaels interrupted as gloominess overtook him.

"... And Nina Kovak. She worked in city hall."

"Yeah! In the clerk's office. I know em' both. Whatta you got?"

"None of them lived close together but they all worked in the same general area around the Daley Center."

"Do you think this is political? City hall, the county building, courthouses, state offices ... that kind of thing?"

"We don't know. We'll be all over it first thing in the morning. We are contacting the next of kin now."

"Are there any survivors?"

"Three more died and nine are still hanging in there but it doesn't look good. There is no known antidote. Maybe I'll see you later."

"Yeah, maybe ..." Michaels voice drifted off. He opened his car door, leaned outside and threw up.

~~~~

Edmond Jenkins was one of Chicago's best-known and wealthiest defense attorneys. His reputation over the years was legend. His client list contained some of the most high profile criminals not only from Chicago but nationwide: mafia kingpins, drug lords, and gang-leaders, even a rich scientist. He was starting to show his age, chubbier, balder, and less ambulatory. He walked with a cane but never complained ... always smiled.

He was old school and still took his notes with a fountain pen filled with blue ink. He dressed flamboyantly, bright colored sport coats, contrasting shirts, gaudy ties. Everyone liked Eddie Jenkins. His personality was abundant.

The Ten O' Clock News with Ron Magers was on his 65-inch television in the master bedroom as Jenkins was getting ready for bed. It was very unusual for the main anchorman to do the weekend news. Jenkins listened intently as Magers introduced Peter Michaels, who seemed to be ahead of everyone else covering this terrorist attack on the city. All 28 victims have now been identified, but no names were released.

Funny, Jenkins thought, *it appears many of them work in the courthouses where I practice, Hum*. He was not in any hurry to get to bed he knew tomorrow was an unusually light day for a Monday. He looked at his digital calendar, no court until 1:30 but an interesting appointment at 10 a.m. Sister Mary Thomas—vs.—The Chicago Archdiocese.

~~~~

The nun's habit and headpiece were gray. The collar and bib were white and heavily starched. Her skin would be pushed slightly forward further distorting any facial features. The natural brown colored wig would be completely veiled. The wire rim glasses had a slight red tint. His contact lenses were light blue, not striking but enough to distort his green eyes. Nothing to draw attention to the face. Plain and simple. Undistinguishable.

He secured the short wig on the mannequin head and brushed it. His Machiavellian thoughts were sexually arousing him, as he walked to his bedroom. His television set tuned into The Ten O'clock News with Ron Magers and that investigative prick, Peter Michaels.

As he slithered his naked body between the pure white, sterile sheets, he thought, *tomorrow one more of them would die.*

CHAPTER 12

"**O**peration Firefox" was in full swing early Monday morning. Fourteen agents from the JTTF would visit the offices of all 28 victims of the terrorist attack asking questions as staff members barely had time to sit down for their coffee at 7:30. All of the victims worked within a mile radius of the Daley Center. Not all were government employees. Some worked for law firms. Another was a CPA at a small accounting firm on Madison Street. Another was a hair stylist, who made more in tips than she did from cutting and styling hair at a popular salon on LaSalle Street.

The agents wanted to know the victims work habits, friendships, social activities, and any extraordinary travel arrangements. Did they use public transportation or private vehicles, where did they park, where did they eat? They wanted to see if there were any patterns of behavior that ever intersected. Supervisors, secretaries, clerks, even the janitors were scheduled to be questioned. All were dumbfounded. All were scared. All were nervous. Most were crying.

Special Agent Jack Warren wanted to talk to the friends of Nina Kovak, one of Peter Michaels' sources. Her desk partner Sara Petro knew her the best. They worked together for 21 years. "Nina loved it when Peter Michaels came in here. She was always ready to help him. Do you know him?"

"Yeah! We met a couple of times." Pause. The detective gave one of his exasperated looks and shook his head trying not to grin. "So, you knew Ms. Kovak for more that 20 years?"

"Yes. We went to each other's family picnics. Our kids even met on several occasions." Ms. Petro was ringing a white linen hand-kerchief in her shaking hands. Her blue eyes were engulfed with red veins from crying.

"Was anything bothering her?"

"Oh no. She was happy most of the time, although we shared those stories of heartache and joy, you know what I'm saying, wed-dings and funerals."

"Did you guys eat together?"

"Oh yes, at least two or three times a week."

"Where did you eat?" asked Warren.

"It varied. One day we'd have pizza. The next day we'd have salad." She stopped suddenly and pensive look curtained her face. She took a deep breath and continued. "The next we might have sandwiches from Subway and sit outside. You know, we just liked to get out of the office. Some of these people who come in here can be pricks. Demanding. Hollering. You know, you're not helping them fast enough. That kinda shi … stuff."

"Ms. Petro this is very important. We believe Nina may have been poisoned. Can you be more specific?"

A troubled look now blemished Sara Petro's face. Her red eyes drifted upwards as if thinking harder and trying to recall anything, "No. Not really. Like I said, we ate at a lot of different places."

"Thank you. Here's my card. If you think of anything, no matter how small or insignificant. Call me, I answer that number 24 hours a day."

~~~~

The driver of the 156 bus didn't give the little nun in the gray habit a second thought as she boarded his bus on LaSalle Street and Chicago Avenue, after all Holy Name Cathedral was just a block away. However, he did notice that her fingers looked a little strange as she dropped her token in the glass collection tray. Retirement was just six months away and 27 years of the same mundane routines left the driver rather languid. Her long sleeves camouflaged her hands as she made her way to the rear of the bus. No one noticed the skin colored latex gloves that were protecting her fingerprints. She sat in the last seat on the right, turning her upper torso slightly and lowering her head so no one on the bus could get a good view of her face. She never took her eyes away from the buildings as they apathetically passed by. On the eighth stop, eleven minutes later, she joined the rest of the passengers and exited by the rear door.

The Daley Plaza's courtyard was smothered with blue and white squad cars and what appeared to be unmarked police cars were parked off the street and up on the curbs blocking walkways. The vehicles that parked in the makeshift police parking lot around the perimeter of the war memorial and its eternal burning flame seemed to extend a certain reverence to all the soldiers who died for our country.

The view of the massive 50-foot reddish landmark sculpture by Pablo Picasso was not hindered and tourists were not yet climbing onto it and sliding down its face. They were having their morning coffee in their hotel rooms. The visitors would start their activities around ten, after office worker traffic thinned out on the sidewalks.

Pedestrians stepped out of the way showing respect to the nun dressed in gray as she walked through the morning crowd heading to the courtrooms on the 12th floor of the Richard J. Daley Center.

When the Daley Center was completed in 1965, it was the tallest building in downtown Chicago. It is one of the city's biggest tourists attractions. Millions of people pass by it and through its halls every year. It is a national landmark and was made famous in part by the climatic scenes from the 1980 film "The Blues Brothers." Other famous films, "The Fugitive," "Batman Begins," and "Batman: The Dark Knight" also featured the 65 story glass structure.

The Richard J. Daley Center houses 120 courtrooms and hearing rooms as well as the Cook County Law Library. The Cook County Sheriff's Office also occupies a large portion of the building.

Antoinette Barettelli was a sheriff deputy, who worked in the courtroom of Judge Harold Wolfe. Courtroom 1204.

~~~~

Peter Michaels made it a habit to act like he belonged in any room that he ever entered. It was no different as he strolled into the chambers of Judge Harold Wolfe as two special agents from the JTTF were leaving. He nodded to them and they gave him that "fuck you" look as they walked past.

Judge Wolfe looked distinguished. He was 65-years old, five-eleven with white hair, combed meticulously straight back, stylishly touching the top of his white collared shirt. His eyes were blue and red and tired. He shed a lot of tears since he found out his beloved clerk of 17 years was murdered in a senseless act of terrorism that no one could explain. He regained his composure after spending the last 45 minutes with the two JTTF agents.

"Come on in," he said and motioned Michaels to sit in one of the maroon colored felt armchairs in front of his dark mahogany desk. Green bound law books of all the recent Appellate Court decisions lined his matching mahogany bookshelves. Judge Wolfe looked spent as he rubbed his eyes with both hands and said, "She really was a good shit. She kept me organized every day." He was shaking his head, fighting back another emotional explosion. "I can't imagine anyone doing something like this."

"She was always great with me."

"She loved you."

Michaels blushed. He was a charmer but he always treated his sources with a great deal of respect. "I remember when her son had phenomena, I made her my world famous Pasta Fagioli. She never forgot that."

"Peter, she wouldn't hurt a fly."

"I'll never forget how many times she told me the story about the time you had that drug lord on trial and two gang bangers stormed into your courtroom and took everyone hostage. That police standoff lasted, what … 12 hours? She never lost her cool."

"She knew how to handle herself under pressure."

"She told me the only time she was ever unnerved was when you had that crazy scientist on trial for beating one of his co-workers within an inch of her life."

"Yeah, that was about ten years ago now. He was one weird son of a bitch. Wild hair, thick course beard, coke bottle type eyeglasses. Scary looking bastard."

"You got anything I can look into? Any thoughts? Was there anything unusual last week?"

"No … everything seemed normal. I will tell you. You should talk to Sue Lopez and Lisa Middleton. Susan works in the clerk's office and Lisa works at the law offices of Carlin and Miller. Paralegal … I think." Judge Wolfe paused in thought … staring past Michaels. He suddenly blinked and continued, "They had lunch together all the time." The judge leaned forward, reached for his tattered Rolodex file, flipped through the worn pages, found what he was looking for, and wrote down two numbers and handed them to Michaels.

"Thanks, your honor."

"Let me walk you out. I have to stretch my legs."

Both stood up like creaky old men and Judge Wolfe put his arm around Michaels shoulders as they ambled into his courtroom that had not yet awakened. The morning's pedestrian traffic was starting to pick up. As they walked in hushed conversation, they both noticed the short nun in a gray habit sitting in the last row of the gallery.

"Thanks again judge. I'll keep you informed if I learn anything."

They shook hands and judge Wolfe returned to his chambers and Michaels walked toward the exit. He nodded to the nun.

She peeked a glance at him over the book she was apparently reading.

"Sister." He said and smiled as he studied her.

She turned her face away shyly as if to ignore his greeting. Expressionless.

He observed, the back cover of her book had a bold red symbol of Satin. *Odd,* he thought, *why would a nun be reading a book about the devil and cults?*

CHAPTER 13

L
ike clockwork, Eddie Jenkins arrived at his office at 7:30 am, even though he had no pressing morning appointments, he was a creature of habit. He didn't sleep well. He was a little agitated that's why he decided to dress more extravagantly. His bright orange sport coat, lime colored shirt and blue tie decorated with white seahorses made the janitor, who was dusting his big ornate desk, smile broadly revealing a mouthful of perfectly straight, brilliant white teeth.

"Mornin' Mr. J." Leroy Williams said with his Memphis accent that he never lost after living up north for more than 40 years. Williams was six-foot-three inches with a slim, wiry build. His shoulders were slightly slouched and he walked with a determined pace. His graying temples and mustache along with his gold horn-rimmed glasses gave this light skinned African-American the distinguished look of a college professor.

"Good morning to you, Leroy."

Leroy Williams had been a client 14 years ago, accused of assaulting his girlfriend. Jenkins convinced the judge that the charge was not an assault but was merely a lover's quarrel. He got Williams's five years probation and job. Leroy Williams has never missed a day of work since he started cleaning all the offices of Jenkins, Franklin and Revere.

The seven partners and 25 other associates of the firm occupied the entire 18th floor of the Sherman Oaks Office Building at 75 West Washington Boulevard.

Edmund Jenkins had the most extravagant office. He was the founder and biggest moneymaker in the firm. His office was kitschy. The walls were bright yellow. The ceiling was also yellow but less abrasive. His treasured oil paintings of Revolutionary War battles that hung on the walls were in garish frames. His impressive law credentials that decorated the area behind his desk were the only things conservative in the room. The focal point was his diploma from Harvard Law, Class of 1969. Valedictorian.

His office was walking distance to the Everett McKinley Dirksen federal courthouse on South Dearborn Street and the Daley Center just across the plaza. Years ago, he welcomed the strolls to the courthouses, but the passing of time made his arthritic knees ache more, thus dimming his desire to take those walks. He was a candidate for knee replacements ten years ago but as a skier, he hated the thought of giving up the only sport he had ever enjoyed. So, he put off any effort to have the surgery but now he had no choice.

Chicago's cold winters served as a constant reminder of the chronic pain he felt with every step. The realization of retirement started to fill his thoughts since the New Year began. Money was not a problem. It was his EGO, being out of the limelight, missing the calls from reporters looking for a scoop, being the center of attention when he was litigating a high profile, controversial case. In the past the idea of retirement was always pushed aside but a recent trip to Scottsdale, Arizona rekindled the feelings of less pain and warmer temperatures. He planned to announce his retirement around Thanksgiving, just a few months away.

Gertrude Van Hee was his only secretary for the last 25 years. Age did not deter from her natural beauty. Her gray hair was expertly coiffed. Her blue eyes were happy, and expertly trained. She was exceptionally observant. Her ever-present smile relaxed everyone she spoke too. Her perfectly manicured fingernails displayed clear polish that never seemed to be chipped. She brought him his one and only cup of coffee allowed for the day at precisely 8:15. Italian Lavazza with double cream, room temperature, easy to sip.

"Thank you, Gertrude. Slow day for once." He said with his sly grin.

"Yes sir. It's not every day though that we see a nun suing the church. I am anxious to hear what she has to say." Gertrude was very catholic. She never missed Sunday mass unless she was in the hospital and that happened only twice in the last three decades when she gave birth to her daughter and son.

"Hum." He mumbled as he accepted his coffee cup with **HARVARD** emblazed on it. He picked up his dark mahogany cane with his left hand and walked over to his heavily tinted window that blocked the intense rays of the rising morning sun. He somehow spotted and fixated on a little nun in a gray habit walking across the Daley Plaza straight for his building. He took a sip of his Lavazza, which produced a grin of great satisfaction, and he returned to his desk. He set his cup down and opened his very large and very old-fashioned leather briefcase that he always set on the left side of his desk. He pulled out his only court file for the day, Anderson vs. Anderson. One family member trying to get her brother committed to Madison Mental Health Center.

The firm of Jenkins, Franklin and Revere specialized in all aspects of mental health issues. In civil actions, they took either side of the issue; if their client wanted to commit a family member or relative to a mental institution, they would vigorously pursue their wishes or if their client wanted to fight institutionalization, they would aggressively defend that position.

In criminal cases, Edmund Jenkins was the master of the insanity plea. He was successful in every case that he employed the old traditional defense of "not guilty by reason of insanity" for his client.

The firm's most notorious case that occurred more than ten years ago involved a crazy doctor, who beat his assistant too within an inch of her life. It was the first time they had ever beaten the prosecution's secret weapon. Dr. Louis Yako, arguably the most noted forensic psychiatrist in the United States legal system. Dr. Yako's credentials were so numerous, attorneys on both sides of the cases he testified in, would stipulate to his expertise because it would take more than 15 minutes to read his extensive and impressive curriculum vita into the court's record.

Jenkins was convinced if the victim had died before trial they would have lost. The poor woman was in a coma for years and she died shortly after the mad scientist who beat her with a microscope was released from the insane asylum. It was the one case that Jenkins wished his firm had not accepted. He knew the guy was crazy as a shithouse rat and Jenkins also believed that his client knew exactly what he was doing when he attacked that poor research assistant. It haunted him for years because he felt like he sold his soul to devil for the huge contingency fee and hundreds of thousands of dollars in legal fees that were paid for in cash.

~~~~

Susan Lopez was gripping a damp Kleenex tightly in her hand. She almost called in sick because she hadn't stopped crying since she heard the news about Toni B.

Ms. Lopez had short brown hair and sad blue eyes. She was petite and normally had great posture but today she was hunched over and looked frail. She hadn't slept in 36 hours. Antoinette Barettelli was her best work friend.

"Toni was just a great person. You know that Peter. You dealt with her many times. I don't understand any of this shit."

"I know. Toni was always very good to me." Michaels said as he lowered his head, closed his eyes and waited a beat. "So, tell me about last week."

"It was like any other week. We work. We meet for lunch. We work. We go home. End of another fucking day."

Michaels was used to her "F-bombs." He had known her for years through her brother, Mark. They all sailed together particularly on Wednesday nights in the "Beer Can Races" sponsored by Chicago's competing yacht clubs, but this was not a social call. "Where do you eat lunch?"

"We go to a lotta different places in the area; Albert's across the street, that Thai place on Madison, Number One Son on State, KTC in the underground, Rockets on Washington, Stella's on LaSalle. I don't know, a few other places, I guess." Sue Lopes burst out crying again.

Michaels handed her another Kleenex. "Look here's my card. I'm sure you have my number but Sue if you think of anything else, please give me a call." He left it on her desk, patted her on the shoulder as he stood. "Why don't you go home. The judge will understand."

"I think I might," she said as she put her head in both hands and started to heave silently, her back arched as she started gasping for air. "I can't believe this is happening. Those bastards."

~~~~

Jack Warren and his partner, FBI agent Francine Valentino did not return to FBI headquarters with the other Joint Terrorism Task Force members. Warren still wanted to talk to more associates of Nina Kovak. For the most part, these victims came to work, put in their eight hours and went home. Lunch times varied and so did the places they all ate. Men and women, all different ages, all different backgrounds. No common thread. Warren tried to move the pieces of the puzzle around in his mind. He was stuck.

"We don't have enough information yet. I don't see a pattern here." His phone buzzed. "Shit."

"What?" asked agent Valentino.

"Two more people died. Mr. Cortez and Mr. Ventimealla."

"Do we even know what killed them yet."

"Yeah, worms."

~~~~

Patricia Dickerson was deep in thought when one of the Fort Detrick research scientists, Dr. James McBride, who just finished an antibody diagnosis of a parasitic infection control agent exclaimed "Anti-Physiognomies Peroxidious."

"What's that?"

Dr. McBride ignored the question. He was still focusing his high-powered microscope. His brown eyes strained as his wire-rimmed glasses touched the soft rubber lens protectors. His mind raced, searching for a solution. "A possible antidote that may stop or at least slow the poison in their systems."

"What kind of poison, James?"

"They were poisoned by Anglostrongylus Cantonensis, more commonly called rat lungworms." He looked at Dickerson then returned his attention to the photomicrograph of the stool specimen he had just produced. "I'm positive. No question about it. All the worms have got to be dead by now but their excrement is the actual poison from their systems. These guys were feed rat shit to survive in their contaminated mediums."

Dr. McBride leaned back in his chair, closed his eyes and thought for a moment. He moved over to a more powerful microscope, examined the slide again. He swiveled in his chair and with a slight push he gracefully glided like a figure skater over to his computer. He started to type rapidly, now totally engaged with his monitor and when he found what he was looking for he cried out, "Fuck!

These worms were home grown. I'll bet a million bucks. They are almost twice the size of any rat lungworm specimen ever recorded in all of the research that has been done on these creatures."

"Will that effect the antidote?" Dickerson asked.

"The Peroxidious may stop it or at least stall its effects on our victims but I don't ..." his train of thought stopped and he shook his head negatively.

"How soon before you can produce this Peroxidious antidote?"

"Maybe 18 hours. Not sure."

"Do it. We may be able to save the last seven."

Dr. James McBride brushed his fleshy fingers through his long, gray, curly hair and sighed, "That's very unlikely. Most people don't survive 96 hours." He turned towards Patricia Dickerson a forsaken look shadowed his face and his sad eyes portrayed his despair, "I sure hope it will work but to tell the truth, I don't think we'll be in time."

Dickerson grabbed her cell phone and hit the speed dial icon for Special Agent Tom Eiseman's private number and relayed the latest discovery.

"Most people don't survive 96 hours. At least this gives us a rough outline for a timeline." Dickerson said with a glimpse of hope in her voice.

"Hopefully, we can figure out when and where it happened" said the special agent but he was shaking his head and rubbing his mouth with his left hand, an old habit he had when he received bad news. "I just got word a few minutes before you called. They're all dead. All 28. We're too late."

CHAPTER 14

The last time Peter Michaels was at the prestigious law firm of Carlin and Miller was a few years ago after the city reached a high profile civil rights agreement with the three men accused of killing two detectives. It ended up being a wrongful conviction case that shook the core of the Cook County's legal system, and pissed off the entire Chicago Police Department.

Lisa Middleton's cubicle was on the eleventh floor in an open area that was not very private, so she and Michaels moved to a small-unoccupied conference room nearby and shut the door.

Lisa eyes were hazel and swollen. She was cried out and in a mild form of shock. Her short blonde hair was mussed from running her manicured fingers through it a million times since she heard the news of Antoinette Barettelli's death.

"You never ever think something like this could ever happen to someone you know. Drive by shooting, yes, but a terrorist attack in Chicago. No fucking way." She said shaking her head and biting her chapped lower lip. Lisa and Sue Lopez were sisters in law. The language was no surprise to Michaels.

"Listen, I know you talked with the Terrorist Task Force guys. I don't want you to keep reliving this horrible thing but ..."

"Listen, I'm telling you what I told them. Our daily life was just very routine. We work. We eat. We go home."

"Did you guys eat together every day?"

"Most of the time. My job may have me in court some days through the lunch hour and I don't get time to eat, but I eat with Toni and Sue, three or four times a week. If I can."

"Yeah, I know." Michaels started turning the pages of his reporter's notebook. "Sue told me about all the restaurants you go to. You guys go to a different place every day. Right?"

"Every day except Wednesdays."

"Whatta mean?"

"Every Wednesday, we go to KTC for salads. They're fresh. They're delicious and they're fucking cheap. You get a lot for your money."

"KTC?"

"Kale Town Café."

"Did you eat there last Wednesday?"

"Yes. We eat there every Wednesday. Without fail."

~~~~

The smell of fresh brewed coffee floated in the air ever morning in the reception area of Jenkins, Franklin and Revere. The firm's name, which could be seen from the elevator threshold was etched in on an oversize inch thick Lucite display and prominently hung behind the receptionist's desk. The steady cacophony of telephones ringing and client's chatter filled the room every morning. The Faux walnut walls once looked rich, but the clutter of case files, manila envelopes, coffee cups and yellow post-it notes visible on the receptionist's desk shattered that image. The marble floors were mopped and buffed every morning before the double glass doors were unlocked. A coffee table surrounded by a black leather couch and four matching chairs, offered copies of the Wall Street Journal, the Chicago Ledger and the

Daily Sun. A potted Ficus tree and an oversized Indian rubber plant both capable of survival with minimum care sat in each corner.

The receptionist behind the glass partition suddenly became aware of her cleavage when she looked up and saw the nun in a gray habit walk into the office. Pam Rakoczy was the product of a catholic education. She had a tattoo of the Chinese love sign on her neck under her left ear and another tat proclaiming MADE IN THE USA on her right elbow. She became very self-conscious because her low cut blouse had the top two buttons, unbuttoned, revealing her well-endowed cleavage. Her Hungarian father and mother always taught their children to respect the priests and the nuns at Saint Dominick's elementary school. Her cheeks turned as red as her blouse. "Can I help you, sister?" she asked with an embarrassed smile.

The man/nun had to concentrate on Pam Rakoczy's hazel eyes and not her breast. "Yes, thank you. I have an appointment with Mr. Jenkins at 10 o'clock." The nun responded with a coy grin. *He'll be dead by three,* the disguised killer thought.

"I'll check, please have a seat. Can I get you anything? Coffee? Water?"

"No. No thank you." *No DNA,* the man/nun thought.

The receptionist dialed a number and whispered, "There's a nun here to see, Mr. Jenkins. (Pause) Yes. Ok." She looked over towards the nun and smiled, "It will be just a few minutes sister" and unconsciously, she reached up and clasped her opened blouse.

~~~~

Eddie Jenkins was buttoning his flamboyant orange sport coat as his secretary Gertrude Van Hee escorted Sister Mary Thomas into his office. He greeted the small nun with a smile and an extended hand.

"Sister Mary Thomas. Nice to see you. Please ... have a seat."

You smarmy fuck, the man/nun thought as she slightly shook his hand with all the confidence in the world that the attorney would never recognize him/her after all these years, and all the plastic surgeries. *Fuck you, you idiot.* She smiled, sat down and placed her backpack on the floor.

"What can I do for you, sister?" he asked as he closed the open file on his desk and slid it to the side.

"I am thinking about suing Fr. Hector Ortiz over at St. Francis. He has been sexually harassing me for a long time and I can't take it anymore." She lied. "It's been just awful." She put her head down and feigned sadness … shaking her head ever so slightly to add to the subterfuge.

The man/nun proceeded to conjure up a story of the priest making sexual advances towards her over a period of three or four years when Jenkins's secretary peeked her head around the door.

"Sorry to interrupt Mr. Jenkins but Judge Wolfe's office just called. He's cancelled his docket for the day."

"Did he say why?"

"Yes. His clerk, that lovely lady Toni Barettelli was one of the victims of that terrorist attack last week. Everyone over there is very upset. It's just awful."

The man/nun had to contained his exuberance when he heard the news that he managed to interrupt the court system.

"Oh my God, Toni was such a great person." Jenkins said as he looked over at the nun, who appeared to be flaccid.

When she caught his gaze, she made the sign of the cross and said, "God protect all of them."

A flash of recognition instantly sparked in Jenkins's memory. It was the way she signed herself that cause the reminiscence jolt to his near photographic memory. The bizarre motion of how she raised her hand to her forehead triggered the reaction of something from his distant past. Jenkins mind was racing, trying to recall the movement. *What was it?* He didn't realize that the quizzical look on his face betrayed him.

Fuck, fuck, the man/nun thought as she looked down and pretended to mumble some prayers for the dead but her mind was also racing. Cyril Dobonovich had a strange way of reaching up and pushing his eyeglasses off his nose. It resembled the beginning of a Nazi salute. "Heil Hitler."

Jenkins stood "You'll have to forgive me sister. I need to talk to my secretary. Can I get you anything? Coffee? Water?"

"No thank you. Perhaps I should go."

"No. Just give me a minute."

That's all I'll need you dumb fuck. "Please take your time." The man/nun encouraged as she reached into her habit pocket and found the capsule of the deadly microorganism. DARMADODIMINE EXTRACT. He carefully packed more than he needed of the microorganism two days before. The man/nun's eyes darted back and forth. *Don't panic.* His first headache in a week started to build and his hand had a slight tremor as the man/nun broke the capsule and dumped most of its contents into the remainder of Jenkins's cherished Lavazza. *Three hours and you'll be dead, you bastard.*

The man/nun was already seated when Jenkins returned. He appeared to be calm but inside his blood pressure was rising.

"Now, where were we?" Jenkins asked.

"Listen Mr. Jenkins why don't I come back next week. This sexual harassment has been going on for a long time, a few more days isn't going to change anything."

"Are you sure? We have plenty of time now that my afternoon has been cleared."

"No. No. It seems everyone is upset. I have no problem coming back later. This last weekend has everyone on edge with that awful terrorist thing. I am going to go to the Cathedral and pray for those poor victims for the rest of the afternoon." She picked up her backpack, stood and said, "I'll check with your secretary and reschedule," and she was gone.

Jenkins sat back in his chair, looked up at the yellow ceiling seeking comfort but his mind was probing and pecking at his memory looking for answers and too what, he wasn't sure. A movement. A hand gesture. What was it? He reached over for his precious coffee and drained the last of it. He felt a bitter taste in his mouth.

CHAPTER 15

T

he lunch hour was winding down when Peter Michaels walked into the Kale Town Café, only five tables had patrons finishing their salads. It was the third restaurant on his list. The KTC salad bar was magnificent; three different types of lettuce, beets, avocados, onions, scallions, bacon bits, hard boiled eggs, several shaved cheeses, along with crumpled blue cheese, pine nuts, pumpkin seeds, walnuts, celery, carrots, tomatoes, cucumbers, garbanzo beans, cranberries, dried tart cherries, hearts of palm, artichokes and anchovies along with seven different dressings; Italian, French, Ranch, Caesar, chunky blue cheese, Thousand Island and olive oil and balsamic vinegar.

The KTC operation was efficient, disposable plastic plates, bowls, cups and clear thick plastic silverware. All recyclables. No dishes to wash. Manpower at a minimum. Its cost conscience owner Carter Hix looked up as he was gathering the remaining lettuce into a chilled container, he recognized Michaels from television. He set the stainless steel container down, wiped his hands on his apron, smiled and extended his hand. "Mr. Michaels, a pleasure to see you. What can I do for you?"

"Can we sit down and talk somewhere?"

Carter Hix's smile transformed to a look of trepidation as he led Michaels to an empty rear table. His stomach began to produce acid and pain. "Is dare somethin wrong?" He asked in his Southside accent.

"I'm not sure. Do you know Antoinette Barettelli? She's the lady with the bright orange hair?"

"Oh, yes. Toni, nice lady. Why?"

"She ate here last Wednesday and now she is dead."

"Dead! Whadda you mean? You think I had somethin to do with it?"

"No! No! She and her friends eat here every Wednesday. Don't they?" Michaels didn't wait for answer. "Did anything happen last week that you thought was strange? Anything at all?"

Hix was a tall man, six-five. His skinny tattooed forearms were leaning on his boney thighs, his hands were folded with his fingers interlaced. His stained white apron was untied and draped around his neck touching the floor. His face was thin, his deep-set brown eyes were closed as he thought. His right leg was nervously bouncing up and down and then it abruptly stopped, he jerked his head up and his eyes seemed to jump out of his head, "Yes, yes, last Wednesday somethin weird did happened."

"What do you mean?"

"Mr. Halstead, one of my customers calls me over right before closin time. The blue cheese dressin had these small green, yellow little globs of stuff floating on the surface. I never saw anythin like dat before."

"Green yellowish globs of stuff. What did you do?"

"I got it the fuck outta dare. That's what I did."

"What do you mean … out of there?"

"I dumped it in anudder container, took a spoon of it and smelled it."

"Did it smell?"

"No, not really. I swished it around a little, you know, then I washed dah shit down wit hot water. I put on the rubber gloves, you know what I mean, and washed it two or tree more times and then I put bleach in the container and cleaned all the udder stuff up."

"Do you know Nina Kovak?"

"Yeah, I know her. Why?" He was getting agitated. "Hey what's dis all about?"

"Did she eat here on Wednesday?"

Hix thought for a moment, "I am not sure if it was Wednesday or Thursday but I know she ate here last week. She eats here at least once a week. Very good customer."

"Thanks, you have been a great help Mr. Hix." Michaels said as he stood up and took his cell phone out of his pocket and dialed Sue Lopez.

~~~~

The man/nun was in a hurry but he walked slowly and cautiously down the hall to the elevators. He didn't press the lobby button. He knew there was a unisex bathroom on the 15th floor from his previous surveillance of the building the week before.

He entered the unoccupied restroom, took off the nun habit, cut it into pieces and dropped some of the cloth bits into the trash can and covered the contents with wet paper towels. He pulled out a Cubs hat, donned it and stuffed the rest of the habit into his backpack.

When he exited the building, he was dressed in khaki shorts, white sneakers and a Cubs tee shirt and hat. He acted nonchalant, not in a hurry, never looking up at the security cameras. His pulse rate had slowed down considerably and his blood pressure returned to 120/70. His headache was diminishing and his malignant smile was widening. He joined the rest of the cattle herd of workers mindlessly returning to their offices on this hot summer afternoon. He was just another Cub fan walking in plain sight down State Street attracting no attention. Sister Mary Thomas disappeared into thin air as pieces of gray cloth were deposited in the trashcans that line Chicago's downtown streets.

~~~~

Peter Michaels hung up with Sue Lopez and Lisa Middleton. He immediately dialed detective Jack Warren. "Hey Jack, I know where they were poisoned."

Warren had just returned to the JTTF office, dejected. The puzzle in his mind was still scrambled. He was on his way to join the task force meeting that was already in progress in the SCIF. Warren stopped in his tracks and put his index finger in his left ear so he could hear more clearly. "Whatta mean?"

"I bet you a hundred bucks all the victims ate lunch at the KTC in the underground ped-way last Wednesday, and I bet all of them put chunky blue cheese dressing on their salads."

"How do you know? Why blue cheese?"

"I don't know but I do know Toni and Nina both had lunch there on Wednesday. I guarantee you … all of the victims did the same thing and put blue cheese dressing on their salads. Her friends were lucky, I guess. They don't like blue cheese but Toni loved it, even bragged about how good it was at the KTC."

"I owe you." Warren didn't bother to dump his phone in the metal security box outside the SCIF room. He took everyone by surprise when he burst into the room and blurted out the information that Peter Michaels just relayed to him and ordered, "Send the nearest patrol officer to KTC and keep that place open until we can get there." Everyone looked astonished as this rookie CPD detective appeared to take command. "I think all of you should recheck with the people you just interviewed and ask them if their friends had lunch at the KTC and put chucky blue cheese on their salads last Wednesday. The blue cheese dressing is the key. I think they all put it on their salads and now they're all dead."

All the agents at the same time looked over at their SAC, Tom Eiseman, who's surprised looked turned into an admiring smile. He said, "You heard the man! Check it out." To Warren, he indicated with his index finger, follow me into my office.

Jack Warren thought *I just fucked up!*

CHAPTER 16

S ergeant Tyler Crane was on his way back to City Hall when he heard the call come over his portable Motorola radio attached to the epaulet of his starched short sleeve white uniform shirt. The tall, thin Crane did an about face and double timed back to the Kale Town Café. He was the last to leave and he saw Peter Michaels interviewing Carter Hix earlier. He now knew they were talking about the terrorist attack and he got an uneasy feeling in the pit of his stomach.

Hix was just about to pull down his security gate and lock up for the day as Sgt. Crane approached him breathing hard. "Not so fast there, Mr. Hix."

"Hey, Sarge! What's wrong? Is dare a problem?"

"Not sure, Mr. Hix but detectives are on the way to talk to you and we were ordered to catch you before you left."

"What do they want? Did I do somethin wrong?" Hix asked as his smile melted into a total look of panic and dejection.

Sgt. Crane reached for his microphone turning his head, "Dispatch. This is 186. I have the person of interest. What should I do?"

"186. Stay with him. Detectives are in route."

"Copy that!"

~~~~

Peter Michaels was talking to his producer David Beedy, as he exited the County Building at Clark Street. He saw three Chicago Fire Department trucks and two ambulances parked in front of the Sherman Oaks Office Building, totally blocking traffic on Washington Boulevard.

"You hear anything that's going on at Sherman Oaks?"

"No! Why?"

"I don't know but something is happening. Cop cars, CFD trucks and ambulances. Traffic is at a total standstill around the hall."

"I'll check," Beedy said and hung up.

Michaels had a great rapport with Chicago's fire fighters and first responders. He did a very favorable piece on their HAZMAT preparedness training exercise a few months prior. Michaels was searching for someone he knew when he recognized the name **SLOAN** stenciled on the back of his heavy protective coat. "Hey … Lt. Sloan, what's going on?"

Lt. Charles Sloan turned around and smiled when he saw Michaels approach. His coat was unbuttoned in an attempt to cool his body heat. The temperature was in the upper eighties and the sun was scorching hot, high in the blue cloudless sky. Sloan's helmet, with the insignia of Engine Company 99, was pushed back off his forehead. The once white towel he used to wipe his face was damp and splotchy with dirt and grim from his sweat. He put the bottle of water he was drinking into his right pocket and extended his hand to greet Michaels.

"Not sure but my EMTs just informed me that what they found may be a crime scene."

"Crime scene. What … murder?"

"Not sure."

"Who is it?"

"Some big time defense attorney … Eddie Jenkins."

Michaels jaw dropped. He had known Eddie Jenkins for more than 20 years. Jenkins was an incredible source when he investigated corruption in the Cook County court system. "I gotta get in there."

"I don't think they are going to let you up there just yet, Peter."

Michaels noticed four unmarked police cars pull onto the Daley Plaza near the war memorial and saw detective Jack Warren hurriedly exit his dented, dirty, ugly green vehicle and rush into the county building. Michaels knew exactly where he was going. "Thanks lieutenant but I gotta try."

~~~~

Gertrude Van Hee pressed the intercom button and asked "Are you hungry? It's almost one. Do you want me to order you a sandwich or something from the deli?"

"No! Just bring me some cold water." Jenkins replied.

After more than 25 years of service to Edmund Jenkins, Gertrude Van Hee knew her boss better than she knew her husband of 40 years. She had been by his side for many 18-hour days when he was involved in a major case. She would do anything for him. The bonuses he provided her over the years set her and her husband up financially for the rest of their lives. When Edmund Jenkins retired so would Gertrude Van Hee. She was very disturbed by the sound of his voice. She quickly got up from her desk, went to the office kitchen and retrieved a clear plastic glass, filled it with ice and grabbed a bottle of water.

Oh, my God.

"Are you alright, Mr. Jenkins?" she asked. Her hands trembled as she entered his office with the water looking at his crimson face.

"I'm fine. My stomach is a little off. That's all!"

He wasn't fine, but he didn't want to alarm anyone, especially one of the people, he held in the highest esteem. He had felt a little fluey the week earlier. "I'll be fine. I'll call you if I need anything. Don't worry."

Gertrude reluctantly backed out of his office, never taking her eyes off of him until she closed the door. She sat down at her desk and apprehension overwhelmed her. Gertrude Van Hee did something that she had never done in 25 years ... she spied on her boss by turning on their private intercom.

Jenkins was breathing deeply almost heaving. He slowly took a sip of the ice water and bent over with horrible cramps. The pain was sharp, excruciating. He imagined someone stabbed him in the stomach with a stiletto. *Was that sister what's her name smiling at me. Am I hallucinating?* He tried to stand but his legs felt strange. Weak. Shaky. Non-existent. His upper torso felt like it was on fire. His breath was suffocating him. He reached up to loosen his beloved tie. He attempted to scream but his larynx produced no sound. Paralyzed. *Fuck!* Both his hands were now flat on his desk. He tried to force himself upright. *The sign of the cross. The hand movement. Was it him? The nun was Cyril Dobonovich. That mad son of a bitch.* Life was flashing in front of his eyes. The trial. The threats. The screams. The hand movement. Every time Dobonovich reached up to push his glasses off the tip of his nose. The unique hand movement was no longer a memory; it was now a cloudy vision that kept repeating itself as he was losing consciousness. He became lightheaded and faint. Then the vomiting started. Reddish discharge was coming out of his mouth and nose, dripping onto his desk calendar. Leaning on his left hand, he reached up with his right and tried to further loosen his tie. He cried out "Geerrrtruuuuddee."

She thought she heard some moaning earlier but then nothing. However, when she heard her name, all the hair on her body perked up like an electric current just shot through her entire system. The pure agony in that cry jolted her. At 68 years of age, she sprang out of her chair like a runner out of the starting blocks. Her wrists stung as she hit the heavy door with both hands. She was aghast at what she witnessed.

Edmund Jenkins, one of the most powerful and respected defense attorneys in the history of the Chicago Bar, was wheezing for air. Gasping for life. His face was beet red and covered with perspiration and fear but mostly despair. His eyes were wide open, questioning! He collapsed behind his desk.

Gertrude Van Hee fell to her knees, put her head near his mouth, smelled his ugly breath and heard his last words. "It was that mad sea."

She had no idea what he was talking about. She was bewildered and shocked. One of the most important persons in her life other than her family sucked in his last breath and died in her arms.

~~~~

When the EMTs entered Jenkins's office on the 18th floor, his body was lying face down on an ornate Persian rug behind his big mahogany desk. The back of his ears and neck were vermillion. The way he had collapsed produced a surreal picture for the first responders. His left arm was awkwardly bent and his right arm was hidden under his torso. Joan Myers, the ranking EMT touched his carotid artery with two fingers that were covered with a blue latex glove, searching for a pulse. There was none.

Myers was a small sized woman with muscular arms from lifting weights at least three times a week. She had been a paramedic for 18 years and was the first on the scene of many emergency calls from heart attack victims to deadly gunshot wounds. A loud gasp echoed through the room when she rolled Jenkins onto his back and witnessed the horror on his face. The forefinger of his right hand was still hooked into the half Windsor knot of his bright blue tie adorned with white seahorses. His eyes were wide open and lifeless but filled with fear. His pupils were dilated. His thin ruffled blonde hair and his lime-collared shirt accentuated the dark red color of his skin. His lips were circular and the rose colored foam that bubbled from his mouth began to crust, giving off a malodorous hint of rotten meat.

"Everyone out of this room" Myers commanded as she reached for her portable two-way radio. "Lieutenant, you better get the police up here, right away. This ain't no heart attack. It looks like a murder to me."

"Whatta mean?" Lt. Sloan responded.

"I'm telling yah! He was killed … probably poisoned."

CHAPTER 17

T he tall skinny homeless man was silhouetted in the dark recess of the entrance to parking garage for the Channel 8
news trucks on Lake Street. He was flummoxed when the
Cubs fan drop something into the trashcan. His dirty face with alert
eyes and a wild unattended full beard peeked around the edge of the
building as he watched the little man cross the street and do the same
thing on the corner of Clark Street. The ex-Army ranger unwittingly
and instinctively kicked into combat mode because the hairless man
with sunburned skin appeared suspicious. He kept mendaciously
looking over his shoulder before he dumped the next handful of gray
material. The vet was diagnosed with PTSD when he was medically
discharged in 2015 after two tours in Afghanistan. The nametag on
his filthy dirty camouflage fatigue jacket identified him as Chalmers.
The combat patch on his right shoulder distinguished him as a member of the elite Second Battalion, 75th Army Ranger Regiment. He was
six-three with a 29 inch waist, weighing 141 pounds. The man
named Chalmers was starving to death; he didn't know it and he
didn't care. Everything he owned was in a grocery store shopping cart
that was overflowing with things of no value except for his distant
memories.

He reached into the trashcan and pulled out a few pieces of the discarded gray cloth. His eyes got larger when he put his black stained calloused hand into what appeared to be a pocket, and he found a small broken capsule with a substance that felt like sugar and looked like cocaine on his dirty finger. It didn't smell sweet, and it tasted very bitter. He spit and smacked his lips after he swallowed the remaining contents of the capsule. Despite the blistering heat and the suffocating humidity, he pulled his woolen Chicago Bears hat further down on his head and pushed his cart towards lower Wacker Drive and his cardboard home.

~~~~

Wayne Phillips was the first African American to make partner at the firm of Albanese, Copland, Byers and Brittan. He was a brilliant trial attorney, who honed his skills as a lead prosecutor for the Cook County State's Attorney for 20 years. The ex-marine was invited to join the prestigious firm five years ago in 2014 but he refused the offer unless he was made a full partner. The stunned solicitors were flabbergasted at Phillips's bold refusal because they offered him four times his annual salary as a prosecutor to start, along with quarterly bonuses. The following day the partners acquiesced to his demands and Phillips gave his 30 day notice to the Chief Judge and filed the retirement papers for his pension and back pay for the 22 weeks of vacation time that he accumulated.

Phillips was an impeccable dresser. He wore hand tailored suits and shirts. His ties matched perfectly with every suit he wore. He was five-eleven and lithe. At 55 years of age, he was remarkably fit from working out at least four times a week. His neatly trimmed hair was graying at the temples giving him an aristocratic appearance. He was deferential to his juries. He had a hypnotic effect on them. He only lost one case as a prosecutor that ever bothered him. The mad scientist that was committed to a mental institution instead of sentenced to death by lethal injection. Even with expert testimony of the world-re-nowned psychiatrist Dr. Louis Yako, the jury sided with the defense because of the victim was alive at the time of the trial, albeit she was in a coma, kept alive with a ventilator for years.

At one time the justice system called it, "Not guilty by reason of insanity" but now it's "guilty but mentally ill" with the defendant entrusted to an insane asylum with the possibility of freedom if he or she responded to treatment.

~~~~

Detective Jack Warren was making a fist, trying to calm himself down, "You found some unidentified shit in your salad dressing and you just washed it down the drain?"

"Detective, you know in da food business, creams curdle, and milk gets sour, food spoils. I didn't have no idea what dat stuff was." Carter Hix implored with his voice and his eyes.

Warren looked from Hix to his cell phone as a text message from another JTTF agent confirmed that the victim he was assigned to had chunky blue cheese dressing on his salad last Wednesday. The puzzle in his mind had some pieces coming together. He hit a speed dial number even though his gut told him it was a long shot.

Special Agent in Charge Tom Eiseman picked up on the second ring.

"What do ya got?"

"I think we have to shut this place down and get the FBI's best forensic guys here and see if our CSI people can recover anything in these drains and sewer pipes." Warren entreated.

"I'll get them over there in the next 24 hours, but right now lock down the scene," Eiseman ordered.

"If we need a court order to close this place, we better get it. This jag-off washed everything away." Warren said with a look of disbelief fanning across his face.

"I'll get the Department of Public Health to shut him down. See if he has any security footage," said Eiseman as he hung up.

Warren clicked off and looked around for any security cameras and said, "Mr. Hix, Is that the only camera you have watching this place?"

Carter Hix nodded. He was emotionally drained and physically shaking. His life savings were invested into the KTC. His dream was now a nightmare, he knew he would be out of business by the end of the week. Dejectedly and barely audible, he responded, "Yes. I only have the one, but it covers the entire restaurant wit a wide angle lens."

"Do you have footage from last Wednesday?"

"Yes. I can get you the disk."

As Carter Hix got up to fetch the videodisk, his shoulders were hunched over, his arms were hanging dolefully by his sides and his gait turned into a resigned shuffle of despair as if he had invisible shackles clasped around his ankles. Tears filled his eyes as a team from the Chicago Department of Public Health entered his restaurant with an order to place the Kale Town Café under quarantine. The KTC was now a crime scene.

~~~~

The JTTF agents returned to headquarters and prepared for hours of work viewing and scrutinizing their newest and only piece of evidence of the attack. The incident occurred six days earlier but they now knew where and when the terrorist attack that killed 28 people took place. What they didn't know was more disturbing. There was still not a single word of chatter from anyone or group claiming responsibility on any of the law enforcement channels of communication they were monitoring.

Jack Warren's puzzle was trying to take form but the pieces were becoming more blurred and disfigured like trying to fit a square peg into a round hole. It made no sense.

The JTTF video screening area was nothing extravagant. The 20 by 20 foot room had six, 55-inch monitors hanging on the beige walls. There were eight desks with viewing stations that could remotely switch into any one of the monitors.

FBI tech, Donna Blake, had already downloaded the videodisk from the KTC security camera. It was a black and white, wide shot of the entire restaurant that included the cashier's station. The picture appeared on all the monitors.

"Hey Donna, can you tighten it up a little and bring up the time code on the video?" Detective Jack Warren asked.

Agent Donna Blake had an animated round face with expressive, penetrating brown eyes that she could sarcastically roll, communicating that "fuck you" look when she was challenged to perform a simple task.

As the picture got larger, it also got grainier. Jack Warren, his partner and two other agents were glued to their screens, each playing with size and speed.

"There's the court clerk! What's her …"

"Antoinette Barettelli" said agent Francine Valentino, Warren's partner.

"Yep, there's Sue Lopez and Lisa Middleton with her" said agent Rene Champagne. "I interviewed her … Lopez."

The time code on the video was 12:10 pm.

"Freeze it … there," said Warren concentrating on his desk screen.

"What?" asked Valentino.

"Yep! there they are. The three of them. Roll it … half speed." Seven sets of eyes were now focused on the middle monitor. The video frames moved at a snail's pace. "There … freeze it."

Warren jumped out of his chair, went up to the monitor and pointed with his pen. "Her. Watch her." Everyone's attention zeroed in on the woman with the gray p-coat, floppy hat and oversized sunglasses.

"Normal speed."

The tech rolled the tape again.

"Stop. Did you see it?"

"See what?" They all exclaimed.

Donna Blake played it again and this time her gaze was like a laser, focusing on the woman's right hand.

On the fifth replay, "Yes. Yes. She looks like she is mixing something into the dressing."

Agent Valentino said. "The other patrons just dip the ladle, once maybe twice and pour it on their salads. 'Floppy hat' is actually mixing something into that dressing." An expressive look of alarm and disbelief filled her face as she shook her side to side. "Unbelievable!"

"Rewind it … slowly. (beat) Stop. Look at her hand. Is she pouring something from her sleeve?" Warren wondered out loud, combing his fingers through boyish curls.

Everybody, except Blake, was now out of their chairs and walking up to the monitor as if that would make the pictures clearer.

"We've got our terrorist." Agent Champagne declared.

Donna Blake was a computer genius working as an FBI consultant. Blake was six-one, large boned and looked like she could kick anybody's ass who stood in her way. She was a take-charge person.

"I'm taking this footage to Quantico, ASAP and I'll run an image analysis. We should be able to determine how tall our **Unsub** is." "Unsub" is a term FBI agents, use for suspect. Chicago Police simply called them "Bad Guys."

Blake continued, "We can determine how much she weighs. We can analyze her gait. You know, the way a person walks is like a fingerprint. No one really walks the same way," she said with a sagacious grin.

"How long before we get any results?" asked Warren.

With pursed lips and a quizzical look, tilting her head, Blake replied, "We should have something concrete in 24 or 36 hours."

CHAPTER 18

R on Magers, WMAC's main anchorman, looked up from the newspaper he was reading with his feet up on his desk and his glasses perched on the tip of nose when Peter Michaels walked into his office without knocking and unannounced but expected.

"Busy news day." It was a statement not a question from Magers.

"Man … Mage, I can't believe it. I find out three great sources of mine are dead in a single day. All apparently murdered?"

"Eddie was murdered? I thought it was a heart attack."

"I tried to get up in his office but the cops had it sealed off tighter than a drum. I saw Tony Quag there. He's the number one homicide detective from Central. So, it's not a stretch to think murder."

Tony Quagliaroli got the sobriquet "Quag" when he was in grade school because no one could pronounce his Italian surname. He is assigned most of the heater cases in Area Central. When Tony Quag walked into a room, everyone knew he was the police. He just had the look … "detective." There was a percipience about his demeanor. No detail, no matter how small, escaped his attention. He had the highest clearance rate of any homicide detective on the job.

The Chicago Police Department was formally divided into six different areas with four separate police districts in each of the areas, but the shortage of manpower, the increase in homicides and violent crimes along with the skyrocketing crime rate ultimately led to a redistribution of CPD resources. Three new geographical areas were created, Area North, Area South and Area Central.

Area Central Headquarters was located at 51st and Wentworth, overlooking the Dan Ryan Expressway for easy access to every major traffic artery in the city. Major Crimes occupied the entire second floor.

"Did you get a chance to talk with Quag?" Magers asked.

"Naw, he kinda hinted to call him later. I will."

"Well, at least they got some movement on this terrorist thing."

"I don't know, Mage. Something isn't right."

"What do you mean?" He responded with a quizzical look.

"I just have a gut feeling. Nothing I can report yet, but if it were a terrorist attack, wouldn't you want to kill as many people as possible?"

"Yeah. What are you saying?"

"Well … why just put the poison stuff in one salad dressing? Why not more?"

"I don't know but we can only report, what we know. Your script looks good. Let's go do this thing." Magers said as he stood and started walking to the studio.

~~~~

The hairless man with a new driver's license that now identified him as Clarence Tomas, stepped out of an ice cold shower. His sunburned neck and arms were not only uncomfortable, but it was also a source of aggravation to him because it was a detail, he had overlooked …

sunscreen for his delicate skin for the hour long walk back to his two flat. He was positive no one saw him enter through the backdoor and the lights in the basement apartment were off.

Clarence Tomas applied generous amounts of soothing Aloe Vesta on his blistering skin. After he dried his hands, he slipped on latex gloves and opened one of his refrigerators. The Paradomaxia Orthogenics was now fully matured in its silver medium.

He ground up some heavy gauge macro glass into a clear, razor sharp, microscope powder that could not be detected by the human eye. The slightest pressure from a single touch of it would cause penetration of the skin's outer dermis and carry the lethal agent into the victim's bloodstream. He engineered the lethal pathogen so death would occur in hours.

His malignant smile widen as he pedantically combined an adhesive agent with the Pardomaxia Orthogenics and the razor sharp substance into a talcum powder type mixture. It was created to re-lease over time and cause a horrific, painful death. Clarence Tomas sealed the container and placed it in a secure, temperature controlled cabinet and locked it.

He then went into the living room and turned on the TV. He was surprised when he heard anchorman Ron Magers say, "Tonight. The sudden death of highly respected attorney, Edmund Jenkins is being considered a homicide." After Magers finished that story he intro-duced Peter Michaels, who had breaking news of the terrorist attack that occurred last week.

Clarence Tomas's smile turned into a maligned frown when that investigative reporter Peter Michaels appeared on the screen and re-ported that "Authorities have discovered the terrorist attack that took 28 lives apparently started at the Kale Town Café last Wednesday. And police and the FBI, now have pictures of the killer."

~~~~

Patricia Dickerson was sitting in the far corner booth at Kitty O'Shea's Irish Pub in the Hilton Hotel on Michigan Avenue with a half empty stein of Goose Island IPO in front of her. She was tired, lonely and horny. She broke off an eight-month relationship before she left Atlanta for Chicago and Fort Detrick.

Although medical researchers identified the rat lungworm used in the terrorist attack, the fact that they couldn't develop an antidote in time to save any lives weighed heavily on her. She was fingering her glass when Peter Michaels came in and sat down in the chair opposite her. She smiled. "Hey."

"Nice work. I've read that, that rat shit stuff is very difficult to detect."

A waitress dressed in a leprechaun type outfit came over and Michaels mimed *I'll have the same.*

"Fucking terrorist." Dickerson said.

"What if it isn't terrorism?"

That immediately got her attention and shattered the gloomy funk she was in, "What are you talking about?" She asked now fully alert.

Michaels explained his theory of why poison just one salad dressing, when the total number of deaths could have been so much higher by contaminating more containers. "Besides, nobody has even claimed responsibility yet. Don't you think that's odd?" He asked as the palms of his hands turned upright in the gesture of a question.

"I don't know. This is the first time I have worked on something tied to terrorism." Dickerson responded. Her hand instinctively moving to her lips.

"Actually, me too. I bet I am the only person in Chicago that is thinking this could be something different." Michaels said as he noticed Dickerson's open blouse revealing a sexy laced bra.

"I don't want to be a killjoy but I'm exhausted." She looked at him flirtingly, reached out and touched his hand while producing a kittenish grin. "You want to go reenact 2016?"

"Sure." Michaels said with a responding "Let's Go" look.

~~~~

Cook County Medical Examiner, Dr. Robert Crine was due home for dinner an hour ago but his friend's corpse was laying in front of him on a cold stainless steel slab. Dr. Crine removed the sheet covering Edmund Jenkins's body and flipped down the protective magnifying shield on his headgear. The overhead fluorescent lights were humming as they made the drab green autopsy room bright. Before rinsing off the body, he closely examined Jenkins's mouth. The moist reddish foam secretions that the EMT discovered earlier were now crusty and dry and odorless. It looked like day old cotton candy. Dr. Crine gently scrapped the remnants into a sterile petri dish, sealed it and placed it into an evidence bag. He would over night the specimen along with blood samples to the State Police Crime Lab and request an expeditious diagnosis and toxicology report.

After the medical examiner removed Jenkins's major organs, he silently and almost prayerfully shook his head. The heart was grotesquely enlarged, probably from his younger years and two packs of non-filtered Camels a day. A healthy liver is the color of an Irish Setter. Jenkins's liver was soft, mushy and battleship gray. It was twice the size of a normal liver not only from the Vodka on the rocks that he splurged on nightly for more than 30 years but also because of the multiple tumors that were encased within it.

The pancreas was nine inches long. It looked like a tumid fish because a cancerous tumor the size of a Jubilee plum was about to exploded and infiltrate the healthy tissue around it. Dr. Crine softly placed the organ on his scale knowing that it would exceed the normal average weight of 80 grams. It weighed 133 grams. Edmund Jenkins had stage four-pancreatic cancer. He literally was a dead man walking.

After Dr. Crine finished the autopsy and turned off his dictation microphone, he covered his friend's body with a fresh sheet and rolled it into refrigeration chamber-18. After he secured the door, he closed his eyes and thought, *you would not have made it to Christmas, my dear friend. At least you were spared the agony and discomfort of chemotherapy and radiation. I hope they nail the bastards who did this to you.*

CHAPTER 19

The Chicago Board of Trade's parking garage was located at the corner of Clark and West Van Buren Streets. The retracting heavy metal entrance and exit doors were operated by a card fob or sensor implanted in the car's grill or license plate. The entry ramp was slanted at a 45-degree angle and once inside, a fob was required to lower a three-foot high iron security barrier that protects the property and privacy of every patron. The barrier was painted black and white and screams "DON'T EVEN THINK ABOUT IT." An armored tank couldn't go over it or around it. The interior walls and the structure's concrete columns were painted pure white. The floor was a glossy gray and the 85 parking spaces were demarcated with yellow lines. However, more than 110 vehicles could be parked on any given day. High beam florescent ceiling lights brightly illuminated the interior. Eighteen close circuit cameras that were strategically located throughout the garage provided a sense of ultimate security. Parking was a bargain at $450 a month for anyone who came to downtown Chicago on a daily basis, including weekends. Every patron left their keys in their cars just in case the attendants had to shuffle any vehicles to prevent getting blocked in. Also, the hand car washes that were offered for twenty dollars cash were considered the best bargain in downtown Chicago.

The glass enclosed security office was a 12 by 12 foot space that housed the monitors that received the signals from 18 HD security cameras. The office, however, was hardly ever manned after the opening bell sounded on the trading floors, six stories above.

Wayne Philips was more concerned about convenience and not security when he parked his navy blue, 2018, $185,000 Gran Turismo Maserati right next to the maintenance door. He wanted easy access in and out of the garage. The law firm of Albanese, Copland, Byers and Brittan was located less than 250 yards away just across the street from the Dirksen Federal Courthouse. Philips's corner office located on the 20th floor provided a beautiful view of Lake Michigan. Life was very good to the former prosecutor, who was now practicing almost exclusively in federal court, handling product liability lawsuits with multi-million dollar settlements.

~~~~

The FBI's crime scene investigators were finishing up vacuuming the black slick goo from the water drains of the KTC's kitchen sinks. The agents were dressed in white HAZMAT protective suits. One navigated the pipes with a quarter of an inch wide tube that had a light attached on the end. The tool looked like a snake that plumbers use to unclog sewers. His yellow rubber gloves glistened from the flow of water and the rays from the lights that were aimed directly at the sinks. He was tall and heavy-set. His brown hair was cut like a marines; shaved on the sides and flat on the top. When he took off his headpiece his face was covered in sweat but his smile left no doubt, he was used to the discomfort.

"I got most of it but I don't think we'll get much to work with." Agent Eddie Marino said, stretching out his shoulders trying to relieve the pain in his back from bending over for more than an hour.

The other agent who gathered the evidence in pint-size jars was smaller. When she took off her headpiece, she had a studious look on her face. Her thick natural blonde hair was cut short and was spiked. Her blue-green eyes were intense. She arranged the jars of evidence on a small stainless steel table and starting filling out the spaces on the evidence bags to maintain the line of custody. She did not look up when agent Jack Warren entered the room.

"What do you think?" Warren asked trying to project a glimmer of hope, showing the agents his credentials.

Agent Colleen Olton could not help expressing a coquetry grin when she looked over at Warren, who looked like he belonged on the cover GQ. His tan sport coat and dark brown Elton shirt were unbuttoned. He didn't look like a typical FBI agent.

"I'd be surprised if we find anything in this shit. It has been at least six days since this incident occurred. I am not very hopeful. Like I said, a lot of water has washed away any surface trace that's for sure." Agent Marino said.

"You never know though. We'll get this back to Quantico and run some analysis." Agent Olton said with her head tilted and her eyes gleaming. "Who do we call?"

Warren was used to flirtatious women. He quickly scrutinized her and wondered why a woman who was fairly attractive would have so much plastic surgery at such a young age. "You can call any one of the agents at the JTTF," he said handing her his card with the general office number on it.

"You got some weird shit going on here agent Warren." Marino said.

"Yeah ... I know and I think it is going to get weirder and weirder until we solve this thing."

~~~~

Dank and smelly car exhaust fumes hung heavy in the air and Peter Michaels's eyes that were protected by his motorcycle goggles stung, but it didn't affect his ear to ear smile as thoughts of his reunion with

Patricia Dickerson, the night before flashed through his mind. The loud roar of his Harley Davidson's Screaming Eagle mufflers alerted sleepy drivers of his presence on lower Wacker Drive.

His smile was transformed to a grimace as flashing red lights from the CFD's Engine Company 71 grabbed his attention. He quickly made an illegal right turn from the left lane, ignoring the screeching tires and the blaring horns along with every driver giving him the finger, as he focused his attention on the body lying on the ground, surrounded by several first responders. Instinctively, he lowered his side stand, killed the ignition, pocketed the key and slowly swung his right leg over his black leather seat. He was in familiar territory now, the underground homeless city that provided shelter for hundreds of men and women who roamed the streets of Chicago. It reminded him of a dark cave with four by four foot, soot covered concrete pillars, constructively placed in this subterranean world to support the weight of Michigan Avenue above them.

Michaels went undercover as a homeless person the year before to document how cuts in the county and federal government's mental health budget affected the lives of Chicago's homeless population. He spent three days and two nights living with these poor souls and secretly videotaped life in this cardboard and blue tarp encampment that many suffering from mental health issues, called home.

"What's going on?" Michaels asked the CFD officer, whom he didn't recognize, but who seemed to be in charge. Michaels was taking off his leather gloves and his alert eyes were moving back and forth, his mind photographing the scene.

"Another homeless vet ... dead." Responded the officer in a white shirt with two bugles on his collar.

Michaels extended his hand, introducing himself asking, "How do you know he's a vet?"

The captain didn't recognize Michaels at first dressed in his black leather motorcycle jacket. He grinned and nodded saying, "Surmising ... I guess from the fatigue jacket he has on."

"What's his name?"

"Chalmers."

"Chris Chalmers?" Michaels exclaimed in shocked disbelief.

"You know him?"

"Sorta. I interviewed him last year when I did a piece on the city's homeless."

"Oh yeah … I remember that story." A look of recognition flashed across the captain's face. "You know where he's from?"

"Addison or Villa Park, if my memory serves me correctly. He did two tours in Afghanistan." Michaels surprisingly had tears welling up in his eyes and the lump in his throat seemed to swell, as he looked down at the body. "He was awarded the Bronze Star and two Purple Hearts. He comes home and wham, PTSD." Michaels' face was shadowed in sadness. He shook his head from side to side, slowly. "It fucked him up."

"Well at least he's not one of the 20 vets who will commit suicide today."

"How do you know it wasn't suicide?"

"Because a witness said, 'He tasted some shit that he found earlier. A couple of hours later he went into convulsions, grabbed his stomach and his throat then just feel over dead,' so, I guess I'm just surmising again."

"Thanks" Michaels said as he got back on his 2016, black, Harley Street Bob and thought, *Shit, four people I know have died in the last eight days.*

~~~~

Detective Jack Warren was at his desk with his feet propped up, his cell phone's wireless ear buds were set at the highest volume possible to drown out the JTTF office noise as he listened intently to Donna Blake's initial findings from the KTC security video.

"What the fuck does that mean? Not a woman?" Warren responded, jumping to his feet when Blake dropped the verbal bomb.

"It's the gait. The way she ... he walks. It ain't a woman," said Blake with that expressive look she gets when she's excited. Her eyes widen and a smile expressed itself knowing it was a fantastic discovery.

"You positive?"

"Yep ... 98 percent. I'm sure when everything is said and done. It'll be 100 percent."

"What else?" Now Warren was pacing. Thinking. Trying to move some pieces of the puzzle around in his mind.

"We think, he's five-three or four, maybe five-six at the most."

"And ...?"

"And maybe 140 pounds."

"And ...?"

"I am not sure all of the other analysts will agree with me, but I see a couple of other things. They're ... minute."

"Talk to me" he said as his mind raced.

"There's ... this little gimpy thing with his gait. It's not there all the time. Kind of a hitch or something. I'll show you. You tell me."

"And ... what's the other thing?"

"It's minuscule as well, but the way he lifted the ladle. It was weird. I can't explain it. I'll show you and you tell me if I'm nuts." Blake said as if she was questioning her own unique observation.

"You know, I will." Warren said.

"Yeah. I'm expecting it."

"Son of a bitch, this is getting really weird." Warren surmised, shaking his head and frowning.

CHAPTER 20

T he oversized aviator sunglasses were a bargain at Wall Mart and they perfectly covered his striking green eyes. Dark contacts lens were out of the question. He needed to be precise when he dusted the door handle of his next victim's car. His blue uniform shirt had long sleeves and a white name patch over the left breast with "Chuck" stenciled on it in red block lettering. His black hair was covered with a nondescript blue, wide rimmed baseball cap. His red toolbox looked like any other except for the skin colored latex glove on the hand carrying it.

The late afternoon's blistering heat was shimmering up from the concrete sidewalks creating a mirage effect. The humidity seemed to smoother pedestrians who dared to challenge it. No one noticed Clarence Tomas pick the lock on the maintenance door to the underground parking garage. The navy blue, Gran Turismo Maserati was where it was always parked since Wayne Philips purchased the coveted spot years ago. Tomas knew the overhead security camera would not capture his face. On every one of his reconnaissance missions, he ever so slightly pushed the camera's lens up. The subtle changes were so delicate, they went unnoticed by any guard monitoring the camera's output. Tomas slithered against the wall and drop to his knee at the driver's side door. He opened his toolbox, took out the container of brain eating, Paradomaxia Orthogenics and generously applied the clear talc on the driver's door handle with a makeup type brush. The killing agent would remain potent for at least four hours. This batch of Paradomaxia Orthogenics was engineered so death would come approximately three hours after contact. Tomas took a microfiber rag and gently wiped the door clean of any telltale residue. He smiled malevolently as he stood up and made his way to the door. *That black, arrogant bastard will die tonight,* he thought.

~~~~

Peter Michaels had finally reached detective Tony Quag, "Hey Quagliaroli, can you tell me how Eddie Jenkins died?"

Tony Quag smiled. Peter Michaels was probably one of the only people on the plant who called him by his real name. "Yeah, he was poisoned, we think."

"Dah … I know that. Can you tell me what he went through?"

"Peter, right now I can't get that specific with you." Quag said, rolling his eyes.

"Okay, tell me if I'm wrong. He probably had a sharp pain in his stomach and bent over. He gasped for air, like his windpipe was strangling him. He then went into convulsions and drops dead. Am I right?"

Tony Quag was slouched into his chair in deep thought when the phone first rang, now he shot straight up with a look of utter amazement on his face. He instinctively reached to loosen his already loose tie; this material was not released to anyone. "You know anything else?" Quag inquired incredulously.

"Not sure but I think there was a foul odor coming from him. Am I right?" Michaels asked in an assertive tone, crossing his fingers hoping he was correct.

"How'd you find that shit out, Michaels?" Quag retorted in disbelief that someone leaked confidential information to a reporter, but he also knew that Michaels had sources in every government office in the city.

Michaels grinned; he knew he was right on with what he overheard the EMT say outside Jenkins's office. He felt better about the request he was about to make, "Look this homeless guy I knew from that story I did last year was found dead this morning at his encampment under Michigan Avenue. They will never do an autopsy on the guy unless there is a solid connection to an important case, and I gotta tell you, I'm 99 percent certain that Chalmers death is connected to this case somehow."

"Peter, What's the connection? There is none. Notta! Capeesh!"

"How do you know? This guy, his name was Chris Chalmers, he was a decorated war hero. Bronze Medal. Purple Hearts. First of all, he deserves more than a pauper's funeral."

"That's a stretch, Michaels."

"Tony, this guy was on streets all the time. What if he saw something or stumbled across something, he shouldn't have to die in vain?"

"Peter, the ME can't autopsy every Tom, Dick or Harry. They are backlogged as it is." Quag said, a tired look filtered across his face as he put his head into the fingers of right hand, slowly massaging his forehead.

"I know Quagliaroli. It is a long shot, I know, but what if it's not?" Michaels pleaded.

Tony Quag had a soft spot for Michaels, even if it was only because he used his baptismal name, "I'll see what I can do."

~~~~

Detective Jack Warren hung up the phone with his beer-drinking neighbor. He did not share any information about their investigation but Peter Michaels got him thinking outside the box.

The investigation was now eight days old. They knew where it started. They knew the terrorist/unsub was male by his gait and that he was not very big. They also had absolutely no idea what he looked like. He was a master of deception. There was no chatter on any law enforcement communication channels claiming responsibility.

SAC Tom Eiseman motioned detective Jack Warren into his office and simulated "sit down." When he finished his phone call, he engaged Warren, "You don't look happy."

"What if this isn't a terrorist attack?"

"Look Warren, you can say anything you want, but there is no question this is at least an urban terrorist attack. For Christ's sake, 28 people are dead." Eiseman implored with an expression of exasperation.

"I know. I know. There is no question, this was a well-planned attack but what I don't understand is … Why didn't he put this shit in more salad dressings? He could have killed twice as many people or more." Warren responded with an inquisitive look.

"I just got off the phone with the CDC. They have no doubt these rat worms were home grown. The fuckers are biggest rat worms ever recorded by far."

This was new information to Warren, who became more alive with the latest detail. "How do we know?"

"I'll have this Dr. McBride's report from Fort Detrick within the hour and I'll go over it with everyone when I have it in my hand."

"Yeah, I'm waiting to hear from agent Blake. There are a few other things they suspect about this jag off."

"Look, we have more than we think. We just have to figure out how it all falls together. This prick will make a mistake sooner or later."

~~~~

Wayne Philips had a spring in his step as the heavy wooden doors of courtroom 808 slowly vacuum closed behind him. He had just reached a 30 million dollar product liability settlement for his client.

John Hook's artificial knee replacement was defective. For seven long years, he walked around on a fractured femur and a right knee that had to be drained dozens of times because it filled up with synovial fluid like an empty gas tank in need of super premium octane.

The firm of Albanese, Copland, Byers and Brittan would receive 14 million from that lawsuit. It was a perfect time to celebrate with the new woman in his life.

Juanita Alverez was a Whitney Houston lookalike. Stunningly beautiful. She was a fashion designer who worked out of her studio on Chicago's Magnificent Mile. Their 7:30 reservation for the 95th Floor in the Hancock Building would make their first romantic date unforgettable.

Wayne Philips felt like the high school president of his class getting ready for the senior prom. He was picturing his outfit for the night as he floated across the federal plaza towards his car. His new hand tailored light blue Italian sport coat with an opened collared white linen shirt and tan slacks with his Berluti Scritto brown leather slip on loafers and no socks would all be accentuated with his brilliant smile and his perfectly straight white teeth.

He was excited as he reached out and unsuspectingly pulled open the driver's door of his navy blue Maserati. He never felt the microscopic incisions the talc glass made on his fingertips as the poison entered his system. He glided into his seat and started the powerful engine. It was quite the day. He was beaming. He hadn't been this happy in a very long time then his fingertips began to itch.

CHAPTER 21

D r. Cyril Dobonovich disappeared from the face of the earth on July 7, 2015, the day after he was released from the Madison Mental Health Center where he spent seven years, four months and 13 days. He knew he would never be missed and he could care less. He had only one friend in the world, and he was scheduled to be released six months later if all went according to plan.

~~~~

Fittingly, on Halloween Day, 2006, Dr. Dobonovich was working on an antidote for Oxymodorin Protivea, a virus he reengineered to attack the central nervous system within a specific amount of time. Once infected with the Oxymodorin virus, the body's entire nervous system would completely shutdown except for the brain, it would last for at least another hour while the rest of the body's organs lost all function and then mercifully; death. While alive, any form of communication would be completely eliminated. No speech. No movement. Just eye contact. One would rather be dead than live a life that consisted of breathing only.

Dr. Helen Lesenski was a pathologist. Her medical studies at Rush University Medical Center were completed in 2004. She was a brilliant student with an incredible future in research. Her stellar academic achievements would never be surpassed. At age 29, she had yet to be asked out on a date. Her five foot-three inch frame was plump. Her brown eyes hid behind little hills of flesh on her tumid cheeks. Her ankles appeared to be swollen in her shoes. He hair was jet black and always looked greasy even though she washed it daily with the fashionable shampoos advertised in popular women magazines by Hollywood starlets.

She never thought of Dr. Dobonovich as anomalous because for some strange reason she identified with him. So, when he offered her a job at his private laboratory at twice the salary and better benefits than she would receive from the University of Chicago Hospital, she didn't think twice. She had accumulated over a $120,000 in student loan debts. The prospect of knowing she could easily handle her payments gave her a great feeling of satisfaction as well as accomplishment that's why she accepted the job.

After a long tedious day with nothing to eat and nine cups of strong black coffee gnawing away at her nerves, Dr. Lesenski suggested that Dr. Dobonovich had used the wrong anti-agent for his Oxymodorin antidote. He had just taken four extra strength ibuprofen Advils to curtail his migraine headache but they had no effect, and his schizophrenic temper flared, "You stupid bitch! How dare you challenge my formula." The swift, backhanded swing of his left fist knocked her off the stool she was sitting on. He started kicking her before she hit the floor. His nostrils were flaring and saliva was dripping from his mouth in his blind rage.

Dr. Lesenski frantically squirmed, trying to get purchase to escape her mad attacker. Her glasses were knocked off her face with the initial blow. Her eyes bulged in surprise and fear. She tried to evade his blows by pushing herself away from his feet and crossing her arms in front of her face to protect it from this murderous tirade. "Conrad. Conrad. Call the police." She hollered.

Conrad Corbett was a student intern, who worked 20 hours a week at the lab for Biology credits at Columbia College. He heard the screams, ran into the room and saw Dr. Dobonovich lashing out with his feet. He could not see his friend on the ground as he grabbed his cell phone. His hands were trembling, fear shadowed his face and horror filled his eyes when he dialed 911 and told the operator, "Dr. Dobonovich is attacking Dr. Lesenski." He gave the address then rushed to her aid.

Dobonovich sensed the young man's approach. He grabbed a microscope that was sitting on the stainless steel counter and with a circular motion timed perfectly, he swung around and met Corbett's left lower jaw, cheek and temple with a crushing blow. The young man was unconscious before he hit the edge of the counter and then the floor. His white lab coat absorbed the blood streaming down his face.

Dobonovich was now in a dark rage. Foam formed on both sides of his mouth. His eyes were wide and filled with wild terror with every step he took. Every fiber in his being was afire. He imagined Professor James McKenzie and all his classmates that laughed at him and mocked him all of his life. He lost sight of his prey and she heaved herself around the tables and into a corner, trying to push herself up along the wall. With the microscope still in his right hand, breathing hard and stomping towards her. He raised both his arms and screamed, "You fucking bitch."

Fear struck, she squealed, "Don't! Please don't!" The last thing she remembered was putting her hands in front of her face in a feeble attempted to stop the microscope from crashing down on her skull.

The police arrived as he was about to deliver the fatal blow to Dr. Lesenski's left temple. The shot from officer Diane Lanning was meant for Dobonovich's back but missed completely, however the loud echo that reverberated through the room startled him, and he dropped the microscope and raised his hands. His protuberant eyes registered surrender but his malodorous grin reflected defiance. His mind was already devising his "mental health" defense.

Dr. Helen Lesenski wished the police would have been five seconds later. She had been in a coma ever since and had not utter a single word for eight years but her mind produced constant nightmares of the raging mad man.

~~~~

Dobonovich leaned close into the bright but softly lite mirror examining his new face, gently touching himself, delicately and slowly moving his fingers about his perfect features.

The last of his seven plastic surgeries was in Paris six months earlier where his cheekbones were raised almost an inch. His nose was altered dramatically, slimmed and shorten in Mexico City. The clef in his chin was removed in Argentina. His thick lips were thinned in Montreal. His Neanderthal forehead was shaved significantly in Palm Springs. His ears were trimmed and rounded in Dallas. His upper and lower blepharoplasty to make his eyes look more open took place in Chicago.

Every one of the surgeries was performed on a man with a different name. From a different country. With a different passport. All performed in elite, private, expensive clinics. All paid for in crisp, new, one hundred dollar bills to assure that no medical records of any kind ever existed. All of his recovery time was spent in luxurious resorts in presidential suites with confidentiality guaranteed by the untraceable cash payments.

A portion of all 25-hair removal treatments took place in all of these cities as he slowly changed his appearance over a two-year period. He was thinking how sly he was; like a "Fox." Not a single person in his life would recognize him with his new appearance not even his lover from Madison Mental Health Center. *I am the "Fox."* He fantasized with an approving smile of admiration.

His glee suddenly morphed into a look of trepidation as his mind flashed back to Eddie Jenkins's office and the hand movement that he couldn't control no matter how much surgery he had endured. He had a "tell" that may have given him away. Cyril Dobonovich, AKA Brandon Martin, AKA Charles Darrow, AKA Ruth Hayward, AKA Sister Mary Thomas, AKA Clarence Tomas, AKA anyone he would create to be a new alias had a couple of flaws that he couldn't change, and he had to constantly work at to control.

The way he raised his right hand was distinctive because of a compound fracture from the severally broken arm he suffered after he fell out of a tree trying to kill a squirrel when he was eight-years-old. He also developed an unintended gait of walking like a shackled prisoner after he fell down a flight of stairs at the Madison Mental Health Center guaranteeing that imperfection forever. Physical therapy and severe concentration helped him correct the flaws superficially but he knew if he slipped out of that awareness when he rushed or lost focus it would haunt him.

He was keenly aware that the police had an imagine of a blonde woman in a gray p-coat at the KTC but he was confident he controlled his tell.

CHAPTER 22

"Do you see it?" asked the frustrated FBI consultant Donna Blake.

"See what?" responded detective Jack Warren. His face was just inches away from the monitor in the JTTF video room as he strained to watch the grainy picture.

Blake rewound the videotape a little further back and punched the forward key ... and waited. "There." Blake said with her eyes widening with anticipation.

"I don't see shit. Do it again." Warren said, despondently.

"It doesn't happen with every step. Like she or he is concentrating on it. He knows he does it."

"Does what?"

"See the lift with the left foot. Up on his toes ever so slightly. Every so often." Blake, now pointing at the picture, said.

Warren noticed it on the eighth playback. "What does it mean?"

"He probably broke his ankle or foot at some time. There is definitely a hitch in his step." Blake said, smiling, relieved Warren finally saw what she was describing.

"So, every ten or twelve steps he lifts up on his left toe. So what?"

"It's like a fingerprint. If we ever get this guy on tape again, he will do it. It's a positive identification marker."

"What was the other tell?"

Blake rewound the tape back to the food line. "Watch the way she or he lifts the ladle."

Warren noticed it on the third try. "Yeah, I see there is some kind of jerky motion. What causes that?"

"I don't know … but … it's a tell."

~~~~

Peter Michaels convinced the show producer that a pre-taped report was all they needed from him for the Six O'clock News. He fired up his "Street Bob," covered his head with his Harley "Love to Ride" skull cap and drove back to the homeless encampment under Michigan Avenue. Several eyes shifted towards him in recognition as he shut down his Screaming Eagles and gracefully eased off his bike in one fluid motion. Michaels walked up to a tall African American man dressed in a long woolen coat draped over his shoulders sitting next to his makeshift bed. It was stifling hot.

"Hey Henry, what's up?" He asked as he offered a fist bump and a slap of the hand, palm first then knuckles back. A greeting he developed with the underground community during his expose.

"Same day. Different shit, Man. What's chew doin' here, man?" Henry asked, knowing the answer.

"I'm looking for Alice. Have you seen her?" Michaels asked, scanning the area.

Alice was Chris Chalmers's friend. They shared the food and water and cigarettes they gathered during their daily runs. She was on the street before him. Their cardboard houses were next to each other.

"Ain't seen her since he gone." Henry said, rubbing his chin.

"Where's his stuff?"

"Over dar. Peoples been pickin' at it. You know what I'm sayin'?"

"Yeah." Michaels said as he walked over to Chalmers's shopping cart. He put on his leather riding gloves and picked at the contents. An empty Styrofoam container stained with ketchup, a piece of gray clothe with a pocket, a single yellow rubber kitchen glove, a worn old gym shoe and a collection of nonsensical junk.

He stopped and picked up the gray clothe again. A hint of recognition crossed his mind. He turned it around in his hand and tossed it back into the shopping cart. *What was it?* His mind asked.

"If you see her tell her I'm looking for her. I need to talk to her." Michaels said, looking more intently over the encampment, searching.

"Yeah. Hey man … you know." The tall man said with a slight nod towards his outstretched hand with a filthy brown gardening glove on it.

Michaels reached in his pocket, pull out a twenty and placed in his hand. "Don't forget."

Henry took the money. His face broke out in a wide grin as he saluted Michaels. "Got it."

~~~~

The hot shower relaxed all his muscles after a very grueling day in federal court. His headache seemed to disappear as well. Wayne Philips was wrapped in a thick fluffy white bath towel. He was pedantic about his appearance so when he noticed that his chest was dappled with what appeared to be a rash, he was perturbed. He leaned forward to take a closer look when a sudden flash of light-headedness flushed through him. He grabbed the black granite bath-room countertop for balance and as suddenly as the light-headedness appeared, it disappeared. He smiled and looked at his straight white teeth in the wall-to-wall mirror.

He was actually getting a little aroused as he went into his double walk-in closet to get dressed. His clothes were perfectly matched and laid out. He tried to imagine what Juanita would be wearing as he slipped into his Berluti Scritto loafers when another flash of lightheadedness hit him. *What the fuck,* He thought as he regained his composure. *What is this woman doing to me?*

~~~~

Juanita Alverez was sitting at the end of bar on the 95th floor of the John Hancock building. Her dirty martini tasted good and settled her nerves. She wondered if she was overdressed in her black, backless dress that clung to her magnificent body revealing a perfectly straight spine with flawless light brown skin. A single diamond hung on a thin white gold chain around her neck. Her voluptuous full lips matched the red in her perfectly manicured fingernails. She looked elegant and she knew it. Every male that walked into the room stole a glance with desire. Every female feigned recognition with envious jealousy.

Chicago's Magnificent Mile was always a beautiful sight to behold on a clear night. She noticed a number of police cars and three or four fire department ambulances responding to some sort of emergency on Michigan Avenue. Traffic was backed up for what seemed like miles. Sipping her second drink, she glanced at her Cartier, 18K diamond watch. *I can't believe he would stand me up, that bastard!*

"Are you alright ma'am?" The bartender in a starched white shirt with a black bowtie and red vest asked.

"Check please," she said defiantly, standing up, "But if a gentleman comes and asks about me, tell him I went home," She collected her cocktail purse, smoothed her dress, wiggled her hips, threw her shoulders back and said, "And tell him to go fuck himself."

~~~~

Squad 1818 was the first CPD car on the scene. The rookie patrolman keyed his mic and asked for assistance; multiple injuries, probably three or four dead. An expensive navy blue Gran Turismo Maserati was wrapped around the traffic light pole at Erie and Michigan Avenue. The driver was unresponsive. His arms hung down with his palms towards the seat, his forehead was laying on the black leather covered steering wheel as if he fell asleep face first. His eyes were wide open and there appeared to be foam coming from his mouth. His skin had a distinct blue tone.

Officer Taylor Evans was on his knees frantically searching for signs of life that he knew weren't there under the car's chasse. His flashlight's beam stopped when he discovered a woman with white hair, cut in bob that reminded him of his mother. Her arm and leg looked as if they were gift wrapped in a silver ribbon. He immediately knew it was her walker. He said a silent prayer and then he noticed the soles of a pair of brown shoes. A man. The husband. Evans got up and went to the other side of the car for a different perspective and gagged. It was the first time in his life he saw bodies this mangled. No one could survive such a tremendous blow.

"I got two people … crushed under this vehicle. Request immediate assistance." Evans nervously said into his radio mic as he stood up.

The night was hot. The air was muggy. The sky was clear. An elderly couple was pinned and crushed under the car. They never saw it coming. There was no horn. No screeching of tires. No warning. The woman with a walker was crossing the street. Her husband close by her side. The light was green so they had the right of way. Minutes before, they were smiling and joking. They just thanked the pharmacist at the Walgreens where they picked up their new prescription of sotalol for their weakened and pacemaker assisted hearts.

Sirens were screaming. Red and blue lights were flashing. The first responders seemed to be there by the time Officer Evans straightened up. The dispatcher's emergency alert was instinctive. Police officers on their ten-speed bicycles immediately took control of the snarled traffic. The fire department's first responders went to work trying to evacuate the elderly couple. The CPD's Major Accident Unit was in route.

Paramedic Kay French came up to the supervising Police Sergeant, who was talking to Officer Evans, "You better come over and look at this."

"What?" said Sgt. Bob King.

"Something ain't right." French said as she led the policemen over to the body of the driver.

"Whatta got?"

"At first, it sounded like a heart attack but ... look at this," she said as she projected her flashlight's beam on the driver's mouth.

"What is that?" Sgt. King asked.

"You might want to get your homicide guys over here. I think this guy was murdered ... poisoned." French said, as she continued to concentrate the beam of light and her flummoxed eyes on the mouth of the well-dressed man behind the steering wheel.

Sgt. Bob King was a soft-spoken man but when he gave orders, they were loud and clear. "Officer Evans don't let anyone touch anything around this car. Let the fire department do their thing and then you preserve this area as a crime scene."

CHAPTER 23

His chili was cooling in its bowl on the bar, the bottle neck on his Miller Lite was sweating and Peter Michaels was lost in deep thought as detective Jack Warren walked into Lindy's Chili Bar on Archer Avenue.

The gray laminate bar top was nicked and blemished, the old pseudo black leather stools were worn and torn. The two by two drop ceiling tiles were tarnished with cigarette smoke and grease. The floor was scuffed and scarred with an obsidian appearance from the feet of thousands of patrons that flooded this neighborhood watering hole for more than a half of century.

Lindy's was a typical Southside Chicago bar that drew drinkers, bettors and braggers for the Bears, the White Sox, the Blackhawks and the Bulls. Not a lot of Cubs fans hung out in this tavern. Lots of money changed hands under the bar from strip cards, ten dollars a square football pools and private bets.

"What's new Jack?" Michaels asked as Warren settled in on the stool next to him.

Warren looked over at Jenny, the bartender and pointed at the bottle of Miller Lite and then at himself. Jenny stopped in her tracks, nodded, reached into the ice cooler, uncapped a fresh bottle and slid it down the bar like a perfect pass from Mitch Trubisky to Allen Robinson in the end zone. It stopped directly in front of the detective.

"I think you are right; something doesn't add up with this terrorist shit." Warren said.

"I can't stop thinking about it." Michaels said as he looked over at his young friend with a puzzled expression.

Warren was shaking his head, "It could have been so much worse. Why just poison one of the salad dressings? No one claiming responsibility. No chatter. Nothing. It makes no sense. None."

"Hum."

"We know he dumped the worms ..."

"Worms?" Michaels started recalling his conversation with Carter Hix and the yellowish-green globs of stuff he had cleaned up in the chunky blue cheese dressing container.

"Yeah, rat lungworms. He dumped them at exactly 12:10. Anyone who ate at the KTC before that was lucky if they liked blue cheese dressing on their salad."

"Got any leads?" Michaels asked as he took a sip of his beer. "Do you know who 'he' is?"

Warren finished a long pull and set his bottle on the bar, "You didn't hear this from me but our bad guy was a man dressed as a woman. We got video of it all but no clear pictures."

"How do you know it's a man?"

"Forensic analysis by the FBI. They spot all kinds of shit, man. It's amazing."

Michaels phone rang to the sound of Jimmy Buffet's "Cheeseburger in Paradise" and he knew it was his producer David Beedy. He motioned with his finger, *just a minute,* answered and listened.

"When." Pause. "You fucking kidding me? I'll be right there."

"What?"

"Attorney, Wayne Phillips. He's dead. They think he was poisoned. That's five of my sources in the last three days. All murdered. All poisoned." Michaels said, as he stood up and dropped a twenty on the bar.

~~~~

Crime Scene Investigator Gary Landis was literally examining Wayne Philips's Maserati with a magnifying glass in the police auto pound. Landis was tall and lanky. He always looked tired. After 33 years on the job, he wanted to retire but cases like this just reenergized him. He walked with a slow, uneasy gait. It seemed he was contemplating something with every step. He went from the steering wheel to the driver's door and back to the steering wheel, four times. A slight discoloration on the steering wheel's hand stitched black leather covering apparently from the middle finger, caught his attention. He was delicately and diligently placing clear tape on the smudge when detective Tony Quag walked in.

"Whatta got, Gary?"

He looked up at his good friend. Landis was 13 years older. Quag had great admiration for the CSI officer because Landis took him under his wing and taught him how to skeet shoot. Landis was a national champion with 12, 16 and 20 gauge shotguns. While he was an expert marksmen, Landis never drew his service revolver in the line of duty in his entire career. He hated the thought of killing some-one although he loved pulling the trigger on his Glock 22.

Looking over his glasses, Landis said. "I'm pretty sure Philips was poisoned when he opened his car door."

"How do you know that?" Quag asked, a quizzical look cur-tained his face.

"First of all, he had foam spewing out of his mouth. It landed on the edge of the horn plate on the steering wheel and there was a lump of it on the carpet between his feet. I know one thing for sure." Landis said pursing his lips.

"What's that?"

"It wasn't arsenic."

"How do you know?"

"He was driving. Arsenic kills almost instantly."

Tony Quag had bewildered look as he waited for Landis to continue.

"He had to be poisoned earlier in the day. No doubt about it."

Tony Quag turned his focus on Landis's hands. "What's that?"

"My guess, this is proof positive." Landis put the tape of the evidence he just gathered on a clear piece of plastic and inserted it into an evidence bag, dated it, and signed it. It took him a while to kneel down again. He was pointing his razor knife at the detective and then he explained, "I took a sample of some surface trace on the door handle here. There wasn't much. It's indecipherable to the human eye but it's there."

"Hum" Quag whimpered as he looked intently at the evidence bag. "What else?"

"I assume Philips was meticulous about his car but looked at this," Landis said and diverted Quag's attention to a tiny blemish under the driver's door handle.

Tony Quag bent over to examine the door and noticed a spidery abrasion with Landis' magnifying glass. "What is that?"

"My guess is, when the bad guy put the poison on the door handle, some of it dripped and hit the door ... so he wiped it off," Landis said as took his razor knife and scrapped a four-inch patch of the navy blue paint off the $185,000 car's door and placed it into another evidence bag. "We'll see."

Landis struggle to get up so Tony Quag offered a hand to pull him to his feet. "What do you got for me from Eddie Jenkins?"

Landis smiled, "Coffee can kill you. No doubt his killer put the poison in his coffee cup. I am waiting for the lab results but I am pretty sure that's how the killer did it." Landis said confidently as pushed his glasses back on his nose with his middle finger. "Soon as I hear, I'll call you."

CHAPTER 24

Detective Tony Quag parked his dirty, green Crown Vic illegally in front of the Cook County Medical Examiner's Office located at 2121 Harrison Street. The ME's Office was created in 1976 after the Office of the Coroner was abolished. The Office is the only Medical Examiner system in Illinois and it covers half the state's population. With Chicago's high crime rate, it is a very busy place.

Dr. Robert Crine was waiting in his office as his assistant prepared the corpse of Wayne Phillips for an autopsy. "What's going on here?" Dr. Crine asked.

"I don't know. First Eddie Jenkins and now Wayne Philips. Its freaky." Quag said.

Dr. Crine was stroking his goatee softly in deep thought. As he stood up, he said, "Don't forget the 28 people in the terrorist attack. They were all poisoned as well."

It was a verbal punch to Tony Quag's gut. He had not been thinking along those lines. "Hey doc, I know you are really backed up here but ... I got a strange request."

"What now?" Crine asked irritatingly looking over his red dime store reading glasses that were perched on the end of his nose.

"There is this homeless guy. Named ... Chalmers. Chris Chalmers. He was a decorated war hero. Peter Michaels brought him to my attention the other day. He may have stumbled onto some poison in his daily travels. Do you think you can at least look at him and see if there is any connection to any of this?" Tony Quag implored.

"Shit, Tony! I'm not sure I can get to it. We had three more shooting deaths today. You know we are averaging 17 shootings a day in July." said Dr. Crine with a forlorn expression. He threw up his hands in defeat. "I'll send a requisition for the body. No promises."

"Thanks. Let me know what you find with Philips."

~~~~

Michaels was slouched deep down in his favorite chair in front of Ron Magers' desk. "Do you believe in coincidence, Mage?"

"Not really, why?" Magers answered as he turned from his computer to look at his familiar uninvited daily guest.

Michaels had a reflective look, fingers spired, lips pursed, "I'm not making this about me, but five of my sources in the last three days are dead. All murdered. I'm pretty sure they were all poisoned. Can that be coincidence?"

"Come on, Michaels. Two of those people were killed in a terrorist attack." Magers always referred to him by his last name when he brought up a different point of view than everyone else in the world had. "You can't be saying, the terrorist is the same person who killed Eddie and Philips?"

"I don't know. Three of them worked in the court system. Philips was a prosecutor for a long time in the same courtroom that Toni Barettelli worked in. I don't know."

"Look Michaels that could be just a coincidence. Philips has been in private practice for years now. He was thriving," Magers said looking straight at his colleague intensely.

Michaels pushed himself out of his comfy chair with effort, his knees were killing him. He winced in pain, "I don't know Mage. I'm going to talk to judge Wolfe. Something ain't right, here. It's gnawing at me."

~~~~

Courtroom 1204 was typical of most courtrooms in the Daley Center. The walls were covered with mahogany wood panels, not expensive, not cheap, that reached up too, but did not touch the12 foot high ceiling that was covered with off-white two by two foot fiberglass, fireproof tiles. The fluorescent lighting constantly hummed as a re-minder of its purpose. Recessed LED lights surrounded the perimeter of the fluorescent bulbs ever four feet but they did their work quietly. An American flag stood in the left corner of the room. The Cook County flag adorned the other corner inside the jury box that con-tained twelve black leather, well-worn swivel chairs that are corralled by a two-foot high solid wooden railing. The judge's bench was posi-tioned in the middle, three feet from the back wall and perched four feet higher than the court's well. An attached six by three foot gray laminated table provided attorneys a platform for their legal docu-ments directly in front of the judge. The walls were barren, except for the paper calendars with information about the court's docket that were attached with scotch tape that was turning brown with age and . beginning to lose its adhesive grip. The cheap, brown and grayish carpeting was well worn from the constant traffic to and from the judge's bench. A small three-foot steel partition akin to a fence with a gate in the center separated the gallery from the courtroom's well. The gallery itself provided seating for eighty people on four rows of church pew style benches that were interrupted by a six-foot wide aisle.

The room provided a businesslike atmosphere. Comfort was not a consideration. Decisions that were made in this courtroom deter-mined the number of years one would serve for their crimes, some life without parole, some death penalties, and some guilty by reason of insanity.

~~~~

The attorney who was dressed in a charcoal gray Armani suit set his briefcase down on the platform in front of the judge's bench. His eyes that were covered with black rimmed Harry Potter type glasses were darting back and forth taking mental pictures of the judge's bench area and its access routes. It looked different from the last time he sat in the last row of the gallery dressed very differently.

The judge was left handed making contact with his gavel just slightly harder because the pathway to the elevated platform was on his left. The jury box blocked admission on the right and the attorney in the Armani suit was not tall enough to reach over the top even in his elevator shoes.

"Can I help you?" The tired looking substitute elderly clerk asked as he entered the courtroom from judge Wolfe's chambers. His brown pants with a yellow strip running down the legs lost their press long ago. His black plastic nametag identified him as Baratucci.

Caught off guard, the attorney slammed shut his briefcase that was filled with empty files and a tightly sealed medical jar. "I'm sorry. I am new from Carlin and Miller. I am supposed to appear here soon and I was just anxious to get the feel of the courtroom." He lied.

"Well, I am going to lock up. We finished early today. We have been a little off around here. We lost our regular clerk recently. We'll be back to normal next week." Baratucci said walking slowly towards the door, signaling the guest with his right hand making a circular motion.

"What's it like tomorrow?"

"Nothing until ten o'clock. Minor motions."

"What time do you generally open for business?"

"Maintenance generally opens the doors around 7:30 but we won't get started until later, tomorrow." He said with a bored expression, leaning his cheek on the door's edge.

"Thanks for your time. I'll see you soon. I hope."

"Yeah. Like I said, we'll be back to normal next week."

No, you won't—you dumb fuck. After tomorrow, nothing will ever be the same in this courtroom. The attorney in the charcoal gray suit thought as he passed through the double doors with a slight lift in his left foot every few steps. The Fox's decision of the death penalty for judge Harold Wolfe was made more than a decade ago, and it will be carried out very soon.

CHAPTER 25

The Chicago Bears were at their Bourbonnais, Illinois summer training camp preparing for their first game with the Green Bay Packers at home in mid-September. The 2018 season was supposed to be spectacular, but it wasn't. The Bears defense was considered the best in the NFL. They were ranked fifth in Las Vegas to win the Super Bowl that year until they played the Philadelphia Eagles in the Wild Card playoff game that they lost in the first round 16-15. The Bears kicker missed a 43-yard field goal in the last 10 seconds of the game. They've been licking their wounds ever since, and looking for a new kicker.

The Chicago media was unashamedly touting the 2019 Bears as the next Super Bowl champs. Their maturing quarterback was reaching top form and his offensive line was melding together.

Producer David Beedy, a diehard Bears fan, was grinning from ear to ear reading the sports section of the Herald when Peter Michaels walked into the office. "What are you smiling about?"

"The Chicago media just jerks itself off with this Bears coverage. They're saying we are going to the Super Bowl."

"They won't be eight and eight this year. They suck." Michaels said with a mocking smile.

"So, you think your Lions are better?"

"Lions don't have a running back or an offensive line. They suck too."

The phone interrupted their conversation. "News ... Michaels." There was a pause, "Yeah, I'll accept."

"Mr. Michaels. This is Alice."

The look on Michaels face morphed from happy to solemn immediately. "Alice ... how are you?"

"Not so good. Henry said I should call you." Alice's voice was so low that Michaels had to strain to hear her.

"Yeah. I need to talk with you about Chris. Where are you?"

"I'm at the camp."

"Did Chris say anything to you? Anything at all about what happened?"

"Yeah. He said there was this weird guy, you know. He said he was just walking from one trashcan to another dumping something. He said he found some shit that he thought was cocaine and he tasted the shit and now he's dead. Fuck, Mr. Michaels, I can't believe it." Alice said, her voice quivering.

"How long you gonna be there?"

"I don't know. Why?"

"Cuz, I want to talk to you. I'll be there shortly. I'm on my way. Stay there. Okay."

~~~~

Conrad Corbett did his student teaching at the Jane Byrne Charter School ten years ago and has been working there ever since he graduated from Columbia College. Corbett loved teaching biology and the Byrne Charter provided him with one of the greatest high school biology labs in the country. All the equipment from the student workstations to their microscopes was the best, making his students' laboratory experiences memorable.

Corbett was never denied anything he needed from insects, to plants and small animals that were to be dissected, to the I-pads his students used to download their daily lessons.

The Jane Byrne Charter School was built right in the middle of the old Cabrini Green housing projects on some of the most prime real estate property on the near North side. The Chicago Board of Education spared no expense in construction, most of the money came from the federal government.

Almost 900 students attended the gifted school. All wore uniforms. If a student couldn't afford a uniform, one was provided. The uniform was a prerequisite that administrators believe helped provide a strict form of discipline. Entrance requirements were ridged. Admission was considered an honor. The natural sciences were the school's top priority in its curriculum.

Philanthropic donations allowed the school to provide the very best education to Chicago's most gifted public school students. So, when Mr. Clarence Tomas walked into the principal's office with checkbook in hand, he was greeted with great enthusiasm. Mr. Tomas' stylish haircut and flawlessly trimmed brown beard and horn rimmed eyeglasses made him look scholarly. His brown contact lenses disguised his bright green eyes. His hand tailored blue Giorgio Armani suit fit him perfectly and his black Gucci elevator loafers made him appear five feet eight inches tall.

"I am considering making a million dollar donation to your school, Mr. Zreibewski," he said as he extended his hand to the school's principal.

"Please just call me Mr. Zee." The principal was tall and thin like a runner but his face defied his structure. It was square, giving him an odd appearance at first glance. His blue suit looked expensive but it wasn't. Men's Outfitters sold high-end suits that may be slightly flawed at bargain prices. "That is very generous of you, Mr.?"

"Oh, I'm sorry. My name is Clarence Tomas. I have researched your school extensively. Very impressive." It was the first time a beard was part of his disguise. He liked the idea of facial hair.

"Well, thank you. We do pride ourselves as one of the finest school in the nation." Mr. Zee beamed. "Do you have any particular interest, Mr. Thomas?"

"It's Tomas, not Thomas." He corrected the nervous new principal. "But yes, I have a keen interest in biology and the sciences. Can I see your labs?"

"I'm sorry. Yes, Mr. Corbett just finished his summer school lab class for the day. Please follow me." Mr. Zee said, motioning the new donor to the door.

The man in the perfectly tailored blue suit had already spent three days observing the school. He knew exactly what the school's summer schedule was. His timing was impeccable.

"I would love to meet Mr. Corbett. I understand his students love him."

~~~~

Detective Jack Warren's curly hair was messier than usual. He had been running his fingers through it for the last hour. His tie was loose and the collar on his blue oxford shirt was open. The questioning look on his face caught Special Agent Tom Eiseman's attention as he walked into the SAC's office unannounced.

"What's on your mind, Warren?"

"Boss ... I don't think we're approaching this thing the right way. It is not making any sense to me."

"Look ... we've talked about this before. Nothing has changed." Eiseman retorted. His fingers were interlaced with his chin resting on top of them. He had a contemplative look in his eyes.

"Yeah. That's just it. Nothing has changed. No one has yet to claimed responsibility. No one has claimed credit. Nothing. Notta. It makes no sense. It's been, what nine days now? And nothing."

He lowered his hands and folded them on his desk before he asked. "What are you thinking now?"

"We are pretty sure it ain't a woman. Quantico tells us it's a short man. He has a slight tell with the way he walks. This just doesn't add up."

"What do you propose?"

"Let me work it from another angle."

"What would that be?"

Warren's expression suddenly changed, the puzzle pieces in his mind took on a linear order, as he looked straight into Eiseman's eyes and said, "It's murder. Pure and simple … murder. Toni Barettelli was a target. That's what I think. The other 27 people were just collateral damage."

CHAPTER 26

Doctor Robert Crine was reading the toxicology report that was just emailed to him from the State Police Crime Lab when his cell phone's loud chime interrupted his thoughts. "Yes."

"Hey doc ... it's Quag."

"Quag ... Your timing is eerie." Crine straightened in his chair and lifted his reading glasses off his nose and let them drop. A thin chain caught them at the third button of his blue shirt.

Detective Tony Quagliaroli still smiles when people use his sobriquet because they can't pronounce his real name. "What do you have?"

"Eddie Jenkins was poisoned." Crine responded standing up.

"Yeah ... so what's new?"

"It's not your typical poison."

"What does that mean?"

"It means, the lab people are not quite sure yet what kind of poison it is but they do know it is really rare. Almost undecipherable."

"So." A look of interest and full concentration veiled Quag's face.

"So. We might have to send it out to a more sophisticated lab for further analysis." Crine responded while pacing around his desk.

"Any results from Wayne Phillips?"

"It should be here soon but I think it will also be a little more complicated."

Detective Quag was now fully alert as he reached for his supplemental police report of Eddie Jenkins's death.

"Hey doc … just for the sake of conversation. It's not my case, but what did all those people die from last week? Do you know?"

"Yeah. Anglostrongylus Cantonensis." Dr. Crine said with a huge smile knowing he just knocked Quag off his feet.

"Anglo … strong … pause … what-the-fuck is that?"

"Rat lungworms."

"Doc … that's fucking weird."

"You want to know what's really weird?"

"Yeah … what? What could be weirder than that?"

"They were home grown. Scientists from Fort Doom have never seen rat lungworms that large before … Ever!"

Quag just stared at his cell phone as he hit the red button to end the call, *What the fuck is going on here?*

~~~~

The homeless people in the lower Wacker encampment didn't bother to look up when Peter Michaels' Screaming Eagles announced his arrival. He locked his black Harley Street Bob between two filthy concrete pillars and eased away from his bike. He tried not to cough from the noxious smell of exhaust fumes that filled the air as he made his way to Henry's place.

Alice was sitting on a plastic red, yellow and green beach chair talking to Henry, who was hidden in the shadows of his stained cardboard box house. She turned and watched as Michaels approached with two plastic brown bags, each with a ham and cheese sandwich. She stood and accepted the bag with a slight nod and a thin grin.

Michaels knew they probably hadn't eaten anything today maybe not for days. He had a very soft spot in his heart for these people huddled together as if prisoners of their misfortunes. Their faces expressionless. Their movements slow. Their eyes distant.

Chris Chalmers was the centerpiece of his expose' of the homeless people lost in this dark under-world. A world of despair, hunger, and psychological mistreatment created by cuts in mental health funding on all levels of government. The public walking above them on Michigan Avenue whether shopping or going to their offices were totally oblivious to the misery under their feet.

"Alice ... how are you?" Michaels asked with pleading eyes, feeling her anguish in the pit of his stomach.

She was shaking from the inside out. Her hands were covered in brown gardening gloves with the fingers cut out. Her fingernails were black with dirt and grime. They hadn't felt soap in weeks. Her long gray coat was so filthy it appeared black. It only had one button. She wrapped the coat around her skinny five foot-two-inch frame like a blanket, holding onto the sandwich bag with her right hand.

"I'm scared. I don't know what I'm going to do without Chris," she said with her sad, downcast eyes.

Henry's booming voice echoed out from the darkness of his shelter, "Don't you go saying shit now girl. You gonna be okay. I be watching over you. You knows dat." Henry remained in the shadows, but he was keenly focused on his newly adopted ward.

Michaels had no place to sit so he reached with his hand as if inviting Alice to follow him as they slowly walked over to his Harley. She pulled her woolen cap down over her ears with the hand that held the brown bag even though it was swelteringly hot. The exhaust fumes that could not escape their surroundings were making

Michaels nauseous. He motioned for Alice to sit on his bike's seat and then asked, "What can you tell me about that day? The day Chris died. What did he say to you?" Michaels needed to confirm what she had told him earlier.

"He said, he saw this little weird, bald, sunburned guy dumping shit into trash cans along Lake Street."

"What kind of stuff?"

Alice shrugged her shoulders in that *I don't know sort of look* and responded, "Mainly gray pieces of cloth."

"Cloth? Gray cloth."

"Yeah." She reached into her coat pocket and pulled out three pieces of the material. "Here … this one had a pocket and the shit that he tasted was in the pocket." Michaels got goose bumps when she produced the pieces of cloth.

"Shit. What do you mean 'shit'?"

"He thought it was cocaine. He tasted some and snorted it, that's when he yelled 'fuck, fuck.'" He said, "It was bitter and burned his nose." Alice's eyes filled with tears, she put her filthy hand over her mouth, and she began to shiver.

Michaels' eyes also started to well with tears even though they were widening in anticipation, "Then what happened?"

"I don't know! A couple hours later, he started shaking and gagging and shit. Then he fell to the ground, grabbing at his throat. I started screaming and everyone came running over, but there was nothing any of us could do. He just laid there and shook and then … he died." She said, now sobbing uncontrollably. "Mr. Michaels it was awful."

Michaels instinctively put his arms around Alice. He was absolutely speechless. The smell from her coat was ghastly but he didn't seem to care. He just heard the exact description of how Eddie Jenkins was murdered.

Alice pulled back, uncomfortable with his embrace, "Can you do anything, Mr. Michaels?" Her beseeching eyes were lingering on his.

Michaels held her out, gripping both her arms, looking straight at her and said, "I promise you one thing Alice, I will do everything in my power to get to the bottom of this. I am pushing for an autopsy for Chris. I think, I just got the ammunition that I need to get it done."

Michaels opened his saddlebags looking for something to put the gray cloth pieces into but he couldn't find anything. "I'm sorry. Do you mind, please can I have that bag? I need to take this cloth with me."

Alice looked sadly down into her bag, removed the rest of her sandwich and absent-mindedly put it in her coat pocket. She then handed Michaels the bag with her dirty shaky hand.

"Oh … Alice can you describe the weird bald guys? How was he dressed?"

"Chris hates the Cubs; you know what I mean? He said, 'the guy was wearing a Cubs tee shirt and hat'. And that 'he looked really red from sunburn or something'. Oh yeah … 'he had on khaki shorts, gym shoes and he sorta walked funny at times' or something like that."

Michaels mind began to race with the realization that Chris Chalmers was an unintended victim of Eddie Jenkins's killer.

~~~~

Conrad Corbett's desk was in the middle of the wall across from the entrance door to his classroom/lab. He was disinfecting his black marble top desk when Mr. Zee and his guest walked into the room but he didn't hear them. His ear buds were in place and he was listening to Classical music. His long, full, black hair that was prematurely turning gray at his temples, hadn't been cut in at least two months. Corbett had his sleeves rolled up and his tie was loosened around his neck. Summer school rules were slightly relaxed particularly on hot July days.

A loud cough from Mr. Zee brought the biology teacher back to awareness.

"Oh ... Sorry Mr. Zee, I didn't hear you come in," he said as he pulled out his ear buds with a smile. His eyes were locked on the stranger.

"This is Mr. Tomas. He is thinking of becoming a benefactor and he has a keen interest in biology." Mr. Zee announced with a hand gesture.

"Nice to meet you." Corbett said extending his hand, a benevolent smile on his face.

The stranger replied "The pleasure is all mine. I am sure." He reached forward and gripped Corbett's hand strongly but never took his eyes off the teacher's. At the same time, he hit the record button of a tiny camera he had hidden in his pocket. If there was a glimpse of recognition it was not reflected in his eyes that were surround by red designer glasses.

"Too what do I owe the pleasure?" Corbett asked.

"I was just interested in seeing your lab. My, Oh, my, how things have changed since I have been in high school. You have quite a place here, Mr. Corbett," he said as he reached up to push his glasses further up on his nose, a nervous old habit that he immediately recognized as a mistake. *Shit!* His face remained frozen but his eyes flinched behind his tinted glasses.

A flash of something from Corbett's past caught the teacher off guard as his mind pressed the reverse button of his memory. Was it triggered by *the sound of his richly dressed visitor's voice or was it something else? Or both?* He thought.

The new philanthropist quickly moved to a microscope that was sitting on the desk nearest him. He nonchalantly peeked into the lens and took a deep breath, gathering his composure.

"Mr. Tomas is thinking about making a generous contribution and he just wanted to see what we are doing with the sciences here at Byrne Charter." Mr. Zee intervened.

"I can assure you we have all the latest in technology. Our students unlike many other schools have a deep love of the sciences and math. Would you like me to show you around Mr. Tomas?" Corbett said as his inner self seemed to ease.

The man known as Mr. Tomas looked over the room slowly rotating his body to calm himself, trying to leave the impression that he actually cared. All he really want to know was should he killed Corbett here or at his apartment in the South Loop.

"No ... I think I have made up mind. I have seen enough. Thank you."

He turned and started to walk away next to the principal and waved, mouthing *Thank you* hoping to offset his mental mistake with the gesture.

As his visitors left, Corbett was frozen there in time, but his mind began racing again to his past. There was something about the man ... his voice ... his mannerisms ... his gait. Conrad Corbett was speechless as the door closed behind them. He started to tremble and he felt something he had not felt in a long time ... *FEAR!*

CHAPTER 27

P eter Michaels parked his Harley Davidson Street Bob in the garage and headed toward the elevator and his tenth floor condo. His mind was darting back and forth like a cue ball in a game of bumper pool. The afternoon sun was beating through his living room window and his air conditioning was working perfectly to keep all of the rooms' temperatures at 76 degrees Fahrenheit. He smiled as he walked in. His mind began to slow down as the cool air refreshed his face.

Michaels had a small atrium-like room with a glass high top table and two chairs positioned to offer a beautiful view of Grant Park and Lake Michigan. It was his favorite spot to entertain his female friends when he cooked gourmet meals for them. He wanted to examine the pieces of gray cloth that he retrieved from Alice in real light. He slipped on a pair of blue latex gloves to avoid contaminating the evidence. He was fingering the material when he heard the knock on the front door. His cell phone rang as he stood up to answer the door. He knew who it was because he called his detective neighbor Jack Warren before he left the lower Wacker homeless encampment and asked him to come right over. "It was important"

Michaels was on his cell phone talking to Gertrude Van Hee, Eddie Jenkins's private secretary when he got up and answered the door. He motioned for Warren to come in.

Warren looked a little haggard. His hair never seem to be combed but he always appeared stylish. His summer tan sport coat hung naturally around his shoulders almost like it was perfectly tailored just for him but he bought it at the Goodwill store off Lake Street.

"What's so important?"

Michaels looked at him, pointed in the air with his right forefinger, motioning "Hold on" and said "Thank you" into the phone and hung up.

"Remember our conversation the other night at Lindy's?"

"Yeah. Why?"

"You said your tech people think the killer is man not a woman." Michaels said with an eager look and then he continued, "I am pretty sure Eddie Jenkins's killer was a man dressed up like a nun."

"Are you outta your fucking mind?"

"No! Not at all and I think this material was part of the habit, he or she … was wearing when he killed Eddie." Michaels said, as he pointed to the material sitting on his table.

Now Warren's expression became more serious. "What are you saying?"

"I know that I have lost five sources. All murdered. You told me that the video you have of a person dressed like a woman probably poisoned all those people last week at KTC. Right?"

Warren was staring at his friend in disbelief. "I just suggested to my boss that those deaths were not the work of a terrorist. The agents think I'm nuts."

"You're not nuts. Eddie Jenkins's last client was a nun, dressed in a gray habit according to Gertrude Van Hee. I bet you if you could get the security video from his building you will see a nun come in but I guarantee you will not see that nun leave."

"What makes you so sure?" Warren responded now with eager eyes.

"These scraps of cloth. I'll bet you my condo for yours that this is the material from the habit the nun wore."

"Come on Peter that is way out there."

"Remember the homeless series I did last year?"

"Yeah."

"Well, the guy I featured in the piece saw a short, bald, sun-burned guy dump these scraps in trashcans along Lake Street." Michaels said as he was fingering the pieces of cloth on the table. "And now he's dead, he sniffed some white shit that was in this pocket." Michaels handed Warren the cloth to study and continued, "A few hours later my source died the same way Eddie Jenkins died. A horrible painful death."

Warren snapped on a pair of latex gloves that he had in his pocket and accepted the material. "I can have our guys analyze this stuff. You got a baggie; I can put this in?"

Michaels got up and walked over to his kitchen cabinets to find some baggies. "I talked to Quag and asked him to get an autopsy for Chalmers. I don't think there will be any question that the two deaths are related." Michaels handed Warren the baggies.

Warren put the gray material into three bags and said, "Hey … give me another one for this plastic bag. If any other trace fell off of this stuff, it will be captured inside."

Warren pulled out his cell phone and called the JTTF walking down the hall for some privacy when he returned, he said, "This case is starting to add up a little better to me."

"Me too. I think judge Wolfe may be in danger."

"Why do you say that?"

"Because on the day Eddie Jenkins died, I saw a small nun dressed in a gray habit sitting in the last row of his courtroom. I think they are connected and I think this is a pure and simple, premeditated murder, and I think I looked right into the eyes of the killer."

~~~~

"The judge just left about a half hour ago." The new temporary clerk for Judge Harold Wolfe told Peter Michaels.

"He lives in Schaumberg doesn't he?"

"I don't think I can tell you that."

"You better tell me! This is a matter of life and death, and I think judge Wolfe is in grave danger."

~~~~

"This is Quag." Detective Tony Quagliaroli was about to smile, he knew it was Michaels from his directory screen but the smile never materialized, a look of concern did.

"Quag. I think Judge Harold Wolfe is the next victim. You gotta get some squads to look for him on the Ike. The Ike is the Eisenhower Expressway, the I-90 runs directly west out of the city to the suburbs.

"I saw Eddie Jenkins killer the day he died."

"Come on Peter. That's pretty far out there. Even from you." Quag said, as he perked up in his chair. He knew this was a very strange case and he also knew that Michaels had an intuitive mind about crime.

"No listen to me." He told Quag everything he knew, and then he continued, "You know that homeless guy, I asked you to see if we could get an autopsy on?. His was killed by the same person but the killer doesn't even know it."

"Now I know you're fucking nuts."

"No. No. Jack Warren brought the gray cloth to the FBI for analysis. We have got to find out if Chris Chambers died of the same poison as Eddie. It's critical." Michaels said pleadingly. "Warren's getting a warrant to pull the security video from Eddie's building. I'm telling you they're connected. I wouldn't be surprised if Wayne Phillips' murder isn't part of this either. Think about it Quag, Toni Barettelli, Phillips and Eddie. They were in judge Wolfe's courtroom all the time for years."

"Fuck!" Quag exploded.

"What?"

"Wayne Phillips was the prosecutor in Wolfe's courtroom for more than ten years."

"I'm telling you. They're connected."

~~~~

The man with the oversized aviator glasses hiding his striking green eyes, wore a gray Armani suit the last time he visited courtroom 1204. Today, he was dressed in a blue work uniform with the name "Chuck" stenciled in red on the front of his shirt and ABC Services was stitched in white letters on the back. His red toolbox had only a few tools in the upper tray and a jar of Oxymodrin Protivea sealed very cautiously and secured in the bottom.

He tested his newly created poison on rats, cats and dogs the week before. All the animals died within his predicted timeframe once infected. It was produced to last at least three to five hours in a human before a painful death. Every time he thought about his deadly creations an evil smile inched across his lips and he felt a warmth in his loins.

No one saw him entered the courtroom after it was cleared when the morning call ended and the lunch recess began. The gadget he held in his hand to measure the output from the building's air-conditioning system was non-functional. It was just a prop in case he got questioned. He didn't. He pointed the pretend measuring device in front of him as he made his way around the courtroom and up to the judge's bench. It took less than 30 seconds to apply the poison on the handle of judge's gavel. It would remain lethal for two hours.

The AC man knew judge Wolfe had only one case on his after-noon docket and the new clerk mentioned that the judge always left early on Friday afternoons, something about a "standing weekly appointment."

The man from ABC Services closed his toolbox, stood up and took a couple of deep breaths to calm himself. This had gone a lot smoother than he anticipated. He looked at his watch and he knew his poison had plenty of time before the judge would call his court to order for the last time.

He exited courtroom 1204 with a grin and a slight limp in his stride every few steps, but he was certain no security camera would capture his image on this hot August afternoon.

He would kill again tonight but his next victim would go undetected for at least three days because Conrad Corbett's final biology exam was scheduled for Tuesday. Besides every poison was different making it harder to trace and connect the crimes. The Fox, Cyril Dobonovich's scheme was working totally as planned. His evil smile widened with every step.

CHAPTER 28

P eter Michaels loved to visit the station's chief attorney Sam Pfeiffer at his office on the 79th floor of the Willis Tower formally known as the Sears Tower. He called Pfeiffer as soon as he hung up the phone with Quag. He wanted advice on reporting what he thought was Chicago's newest serial killer and he didn't want the scare the entire city. Sam was on his way to U.S. Cellular Field and the evening White Sox game against the Detroit Tigers but when he heard what was troubling Michaels he changed his plans and invited him over.

Michaels had a lot on his mind as he pressed button number 40 for the first of his two elevator rides that took at least ten minutes to go up or down. Pfeiffer's office had spectacular views through over-sized windows that made up two of the walls. One captured Chicago's changing landscape as new office towers soared skyward revealing Chicago's new skyline. The other gave way to breath taking views of Lake Michigan and on a clear day you could see as far as the Indiana Dunes and the shoreline of Michigan.

Pfeiffer had a large, modern, cherry wood desk with a bowed front that allowed a platform to write on. Four comfortable designer chairs with black leather seats and backs with highly polished stain-less steel armrests and lower supports, encircled his desk. Pfeiffer's executive leather desk chair was like his private toy, it made him feel like he was on an amusement park ride, and every time he swiveled or rolled from his desk to a file drawer, he would instinctively smile like a little kid that was swathed in a big man's body.

The walls were covered with contemporary, timeless, limited edition prints and an original oil work in vague pastels. Bookshelves housed dozens of legal works and massive three ring binders filled with already tried cases were neatly arranged side by side along with red bound leather copies of useful appellate court decisions.

On the wall behind his desk were bar admission certificates to the U.S. Supreme Court, Illinois Supreme Court and U.S. Federal Court displayed in stainless steel frames.

The walls were painted eggshell white and the floors were covered with black wool carpeting that refused to show stains from coffee or tea. Reflective fluorescent ceiling lights brought the room to life when darkness covered the city. Visitors never noticed the lights on bright days even though they were humming 20 hours a day.

Michaels and Sam where die hard baseball fans. Michaels loved the Detroit Tigers and Pfeiffer had a grotto of Nellie Fox and other White Sox Paraphernalia decorating his egalitarian office. Often when the two teams were in town they would share peanuts, Crackerjacks and witticisms at the ballpark if they didn't have to work. Michaels drank beer, Pfeiffer diet coke.

Sam looked like a professor particularly when he wore a bowtie. His six-foot five frame was thin but not lithe. He lumbered when he walked with his size 14 shoes. His suits looked a little too big on him. His brown wavy hair was long over his ears, neatly trimmed but not combed and his brown eyes were framed with a pair of brown horn-rimmed glasses. He was not imperious but witty and smart. Reporters respected him and more importantly, they liked him. Pfeiffer loved to interact with them. He had an insatiable appetite for gossip.

Pfeiffer offered Michaels a firm handshake but not a seat in his expansive office. He motioned for Michaels to follow him as he moseyed down the hallway, "Peter—come on; let's use the Frankfurter Conference Room."

Sam's law firm had numerous conference rooms, all gathered on a single floor—they were named after outstanding U.S. Supreme Court Justices: Marshall, Warren, Stone, Jackson, Holmes. They were very big rooms but the one named after Felix Frankfurter, for whom one of the firm's founders had clerked, was, oddly, the biggest.

"It's not being used; Carol said we can have it for an hour but I hope we won't need it for that long."

Michaels was awe struck when he first entered the room. It was strikingly sizeable and could hold 40 or more people at a massive table, surrounded by hefty comfortable leather executive high back chairs. Its tall windows on one wall offered an expansive northern view of Lake Michigan's Gold Coast shoreline. Portraits of mostly deceased law firm partners were expensively arranged on the opposite wall. They seemed to be listening intently to whatever was about to be said from inside their cherry wood frames. The room was filled with natural daylight.

Michaels was staring out the window watching the traffic on Lake Shore Drive and he was glad he wasn't in it. An accident had things backed up for miles.

~~~~

The Chicago Fire Department's Squad 83 responded to the multicar accident at the intersection of North Lake Shore Drive where it turns into Hollywood Avenue and Sheridan Road. Four CFD ambulances were also on the scene. Fire fighters with the Jaws of Life were working frantically to reach the man with stylish white hair. His lifeless body was draped over the 2016 black Ford Edge's steering wheel and a deflated airbag. His face was frozen with a look of agony and his opened eyes somehow revealed fear.

Four cars were involved. The Ford Edge just plowed through the busy intersection's red light. No horns. No brakes. Just screams. The EMT's were relentlessly trying to administer aid to the eight victims from the other three cars. Passers bye were taking video with their cell phones as police officers tried to cordon off the area.

Three CPD squad cars managed to edge their way to the intersection. News helicopters that report traffic conditions were hovering overhead as life on Chicago's northside streets was standing still. Angry drivers were blaring their horns and exiting their vehicles trying to get a glimpse at what was causing this gridlock.

Patrolman Tom Martilotti, who had been on the job for two years approached the CFD squad leader as he just cut through the front door of the SUV.

"What do you have?"

"Not sure. Maybe a heart attack or a stroke. Something's strange about this though." The squad leader said with a puzzled, concerned expression.

"What do you mean?"

"Look at his face. That ain't a normal look." The squad leader implored as he pointed to the corpse.

Martilotti bent over and looked into the car and his eyes widened when he recognized the victim. He immediately reached for his mic, "Hey Sarge, the victim in this accident is Judge Harold Wolfe. I don't think this is your run of the mill type of accident. It's pretty weird."

"What do you mean weird, Martilotti?" asked the Sergeant.

"You gotta see the look on the judge's face. It looks like he was tortured."

"Lock it down as a crime scene." The sergeant said urgently. "I'm just around the corner. I'll be right there."

"Copy that." Martilotti said, as he hurried to the CFD first responders.

CHAPTER 29

C yril Dobonovich erased the identity of the man named Clarence Tomas and then created a new one. George Rollins' driver's license listed him with blonde hair, weighing 145 pounds, and he needed glasses to drive. His checking account had $55,000 dollars in it with checks already printed. Scores of other identities had been created, stockpiled and hidden in his home office. Dobonovich had years to plot his revenge. The rest of his plan was taking form as the symbiosis of his prototype Anthrax plus a new nerve pathogen was progressing daily for both a dry and wet application.

Besides his studies in the sciences, Dobonovich loved the fine arts. He was totally infatuated with anything that was artistic and creative. He thought Hans Robichard was a true artist. They met in Innsbruck for first time when he needed a new identity to get grants for his studies from the World Health Organization. Robichard could fashion a passport, a birth certificate and a driver's license from any city in the world with CIA spy-like perfection. His equipment was expensive and faultless, half of which was designed and built with Robichard's steady hands. He charged ten thousand Euros for each of his identity creations. They were masterpieces and were never discovered as forgeries during the last half-century of scrutiny.

Dobonovich visited the artist often at his workshop located in the cellar of an antique bookstore that he used as the cover for his real business. The store was inconspicuous in Innsbruck's landscape. The many skiers and tourists that visited these specialty shops in the capitol of the Alps never suspected any wrongdoing.

Robichard became enamored with the young, odd scientists. He was in his late 80's. His once broad shoulders were now hunched over and rounded making him look almost feeble. The blonde hair of his youth was now snow white and thin, and what was left of it was long, unkempt, and hung over his shirt collar. His brown eyes were tired but active, darting from side to side. His knees were worn out from a lifetime of skiing the Alps and his body ached all over. He wanted to retire so he proposed that Dobonovich become his protégé and he would teach him all of his skills in return for a percentage of the profits from everything Dobonovich created from Robichard's never ending list of clients.

The lessons took place over a two-year period whenever Dobonovich came from Vienna. Robichard not only taught him how to use the counterfeiting machinery with great skill, but he also tutored him in photography and how to gain access to all the materials needed to create new people on paper.

Dobonovich paid his last visit to Hans Robichard a week before he was scheduled to return to the United States. His bank accounts in Europe, the United Kingdom, South Africa and America were generating enormous amounts of interest every day on the millions of dollars he had on deposit. He defrauded over 100 million dollars from the unsuspecting pharmaceutical institutions that supported his scientific research of creating antibodies and vaccines for new diseases and pandemics that seemed to flourish every year around flu season.

Dobonovich smiled as he shook the old man's hand and then walked around behind him to slit his throat with a Norwegian fishing knife that Robichard prided as one of his most treasured possessions. He simply packed the knife with all the counterfeiting gear into four separate crates and shipped the cargo to a newly rented storage locker on Ogden Avenue in Chicago. Before he exited the bookstore, Dobonovich rigged a bomb that would explode when the propane gas trigger expanded to its ignition point.

Dobonovich fell asleep happily on the train in his first class seat on his way back to Vienna and the Austrian Institute of Virology. He would be sound asleep by the time the building exploded.

~~~~

Crime scene investigator Gary Landis was examining the corpse that was laying atop a blue tarp on the sidewalk, next to the wreckage that paralyzed Chicago's late afternoon traffic. Ghoulish spectators were stretching their necks and arms as they attempted to take cellphone pictures of the police activity. Landis deployed his lightweight portable tent for privacy and some shade from the hot late afternoon sun as he conducted his investigation.

"Hey whatta got for me, Sherlock?" Detective Tony Quagliaroli asked as he ducked into the makeshift crime lab watching CSI Landis looking into the mouth of victim with his oversized magnifying glass. Detective Quag had on a white short-sleeved shirt with a red tie that hung loosely around his neck. He was sweating profusely as he entered the sauna like suffocating environment, and that only made him more irritable.

"Took you long enough." Landis responded looking up over the rim of his glasses that always seemed to slide down to the end of his nose but miraculously never fell off.

"Do you know what traffic is like out there?" Quag made it sound more like a statement than a question, and he continued his frustration. "I was running hot, north on Clark Street in the south-bound lanes to get here. What a mess."

"Well, the firefighters fucked up the crime scene. They had to cut the judge out of his car." Landis responded shaking his head. He hated any contamination on his crime scenes.

"I'm sorry to tell you this buddy but the car ain't the crime scene."

"What are you talking about?"

"I called the sheriff and asked them to seal off the judge's court-room. I assure you that's where he was poisoned."

"So now you're taking over my job?"

"Nope. Look at those lips. I bet you that Dr. Crine will discover that he was poisoned. My bet is that it is a similar type of poison to those used to kill at least two other people," Quag opined.

"You think these crimes are connected?" Landis asked with a speculative look.

"Yeah ... I do."

~~~~

Peter Michaels just finished outlining his theory about a new serial killer to Attorney Sam Pfeiffer when his phone rang loudly to the theme of the Lone Ranger ... Beethoven's Fifth Symphony.

Pfeiffer's eyes rolled. "Really?"

"It's a cop. Detective Quag." Michaels said answering, "Michaels."

Sam's look turned from a grin to one of intensity as he noticed the look on Michaels face.

"Are you shitting me. I told you, you had to find him."

"Yeah ... He wasn't heading west towards home. He was on his way to Evanston. Turn on your TV. He crashed his car on Sheridan. He was probably dead by the time he hit the first car in that intersection."

"Was he poisoned?" Michaels asked squinting his eyes.

"I'd bet my pension on it. Hey, I got an emergency call into Dr. Crine. I am going to make sure he does an autopsy on your friend, that homeless guy. He may offer more clues."

Michaels looked down at his phone and pressed the end button as he looked Pfeiffer in the eyes. "Judge Wolfe is dead. Poisoned. Sorry to ruin your game tonight but I gotta run with this story."

"You sure?"

"Yeah ... I'm sure. Something very strange is going on in the city. There is no doubt in my mind that all these murders are connected to some really weird son of a bitch."

CHAPTER 30

D etective Jack Warren was sitting in the video room at the Joint Terrorism Task Force. The security people from Eddie Jenkins building were very obliging to provide their security videotape without a warrant. He slipped the worn, overused cassette into the playback machine as FBI consultant Donna Blake entered the room with a determined look and focused eyes.

It didn't take them long to find what they were looking for even though the tape was grainy and out of focus. The nun in the gray habit entered the building at 9:33 am. He/she looked peculiar in her white gym shoes. The spongy soles and a lift in the right shoe helped disguise the every now and then slight limp. He/she exited the elevator on the tenth floor and entered Jenkins's office at 9:39 am.

Jenkins's office did not have a security camera in the lobby or waiting room. The nun disappeared from view once she entered the law firm's reception area.

Blake played the few seconds of tape with the nun on camera at least a dozen times. The nun appeared to be the same height as the woman in the gray p-coat at the Kale Town Cafe but the experts at Quantico would have to verify that. Blake could not say with certainty that the nun had the same slight limp. The awkward camera angles and the flowing habit help conceal the tell adding to Blake's frustration.

Warren was reading detective Quag's supplementary police report. "It says here that the nun's appointment was for ten that morning and Jenkins had a very easy day. So, I assume the appointment started on time, so go to 10:30 and let's see if we can find the nun leaving."

Blake fast forwarded the tape and found the nun exiting the office at 10:53. The picture of the nun from this angle provided no distinctive results. Her nostrils were flaring, her frustration mounting.

"Shit. This tells us nodda." Blake said, running her fingers through her long flowing premature gray hair as she moved closer to the screen looking at the video sequence several more times.

"Okay … Let's assume he gets off on another floor and sheds his clothes. How long do you think that would take?" Warren squinted his eyes as he studied the pictures.

"We don't know what he did. Do we?"

"We are theorizing that he took off the habit and cut it into pieces afterwards, and he exited the building wearing shorts, a Cubs tee shirt and a Cubs hat." Warren was moving the mystery puzzle pieces in his mind. He could feel the gray fabric he collected at Peter Michael's as if he was still holding it. He instinctively rubbed his thumb and forefinger as if he were still holding the cloth.

The time code on the tape read 11:09 when the first person in a Cubs tee shirt came into frame.

"That's not him." Blake exclaimed.

"How do you know?"

"Too tall and he has long hair. Our guy doesn't have any hair you said. Right?"

The time code moved to 11:19 "There." Warren said, as he moved closer to the screen as if the picture would become clearer. The video quality was fuzzy at best and with the sunlight glaring into the lobby through the dirty windows, the more washed out the video looked.

"That's him but this ain't gonna help us." Warren said exasperated.

"I'll get this tape and the cloth samples to Quantico, maybe they can do something with the quality of this shit. Hopefully we can get some DNA from the nun's habit." Blake said.

"Yeah … there should be some poison trace in that one pocket. With any luck we'll get a match." Warren responded rubbing his chin as he continued to move the puzzle pieces in his mind.

~~~~

Producer David Beedy was in the editing suite putting the final touches on the video package that Peter Michaels was about to deliver on the ten o'clock news.

Michaels was meeting with the ten o'clock show producer and Ron Magers in the anchorman's office. The show would lead with the multi-vehicle accident that gridlocked the city's traffic for hours earlier that day. Magers would read that story as a lead-in and then throw it to Michaels, who was given five and half minutes to tell the story that would shock every person watching television news that night, and they would be talking about it for days.

Every person in the newsroom, and in all the editing suites were frozen in time, motionless, watching the monitors. They were totally engrossed as Peter Michaels boldly proclaimed that the deaths of all the office workers more than two weeks ago were not the work of terrorists but that they were all victims of a maniacal killer, he labeled "The Bug Man."

The story tied the deaths of Attorneys Wayne Phillips, Eddie Jenkins and Judge Harold Wolfe along with his law clerk Antoinette Barettelli to "The Bug Man."

Michaels saved best for last when the screen dissolved to a picture of a man, who looked very much alive on television, then he continued, "This man is Chris Chalmers. He was homeless. He lost his mind in the war, fighting terrorists in the mountains of Afghanistan, but tonight he may offer the first real clue to 'The Bug Man's' identity. Police believe that Chalmers died from the same poison that killed attorney Eddie Jenkins, but more importantly our I-Team has learned that Chalmers actually saw the killer."

Michaels swiveled in his chair to face Magers as he continued. "Ron, I have turned over physical evidence to the police and the FBI that may help them break this case wide open."

"What kind of evidence, Peter?"

"Pieces of clothing and perhaps a sample of the poison that 'The Bug Man' used to kill Chris Chalmers and Eddie Jenkins."

"Who would have thought" Magers said.

"Ron, 'The Bug Man' may have killed as many as 32 people so far but I think he just made his first fatal mistake."

~~~~

His headache was treacherous as he stepped out of his hot than cold shower. They have been increasing in frequency and discomfort. Extreme hot water helped him relax and the cold forced him to refocus his pain tolerance, but he knew his health was showing signs of deterioration. It did not deterred his determination to leave his deadly mark on the city of his childhood. The city he grew to hate.

The "Bug Man" heard the familiar voices of Ron Magers and Peter Michaels coming from the television set in his bedroom. He walked into the room rubbing the back of his neck with his pure white towel and sat at the end of the bed. He bristled when he heard Michaels give him the moniker "The Bug Man."

He gritted his teeth, massaged the back of his neck as he stared at the 75 inch screen hanging on the wall at the foot of his bed and a feeling of Deja' vu enveloped his being, *I thought I felt someone watching me that day but I couldn't see him ... I'm going to kill that fucking Peter Michaels.*

CHAPTER 31

T
he basement apartment of the two flat brownstone on
Chestnut Street was not sterile. It looked rather normal com-
pared to the pristine rooms of the upper floors. The living
room and dining area floors were covered with a beige carpet. Two
sump pumps that were constantly and quietly working were strategically placed near the drains in the front and rear of the basement.
They were guaranteed for ten years. The floors in the kitchen and
bathroom were a darker beige tile. The modern furniture was purchased online from Restoration Outfitters. The dishware, silverware,
towels and linens were bought at Target by a short redhead and paid
for with a credit card that would prove to be fraudulent and
untraceable.

The man that lived there didn't care about the furnishings because his current living conditions were superior to those he had for
the last ten years at the Madison Mental Health Center. The air
smelled like pinecones similar to that from a car wash deodorizer. It
was so overpowering that it would make an ordinary person gag. The
temperature was always set at a constant 72 degrees. He and Dr.
Cyril Dobonovich grew accustomed to it when they shared a room
for almost seven years and became intimate friends.

In Chicago he was known as Yang Sung Choi. His six-foot-three
inch frame was bent over the dark brown composite wood dining

room table. The overhead chandelier provided ample light as Choi's brown eyes determinedly focused on the maps of the Museum Campus, including the tunnels and walkways to Soldier Field and the detailed blueprints of Chicago's famed Buckingham Fountain.

He looked at his watch and was relieved because he was so engrossed in the documents in front him that he lost all concept of time. Cyril would be upset with him if he didn't carry out his assignment with precision. He had two hours to change his clothes, retrieve the Oxymodorin Protivea from the lab upstairs and find a seat at the Southside bar.

Dobonovich specifically chose Oxymodorin Protivea to kill the Judge, Corbett and that bitch cop who tried to kill him when he was working on the antidote for the poison the day he beat that ignorant, irritating Dr. Helen Lesenski to death.

~~~~

Dr. Robert Crine hung up the phone after a short conversation with detective Tony Quag and he started to think about the last time he worked on a case involving a serial killer. His mind drifted to the book **The Devil in the White City** and H. H. Holmes, Chicago's first recorded serial killer. Holmes' changed his name from Herman Webster Mudgett.

Authorities believe that H.H. Holmes was responsible for more than two-dozen murders but they could officially only connect him to nine. They believe his first kill occurred on the night of Christmas Eve in 1891 with the disappearance of his mistress and her daughter although they were never found.

Dr. Crine's thoughts were disrupted when a computer chime alerted him to the search that he requested the day before. The body of Chris Chalmers was stored in a refrigeration truck and was scheduled to be buried in a pauper's grave in two days. He felt relief as he read the email and then he sent a requisition form asking that

Chalmers' corpse be delivered to the Medical Examiner's Office first thing in the morning.

The Saturday autopsy would take him away from his family again on a weekend but his curiosity got the better of him. He leaned back in his chair, closed his eyes and started thinking about John Wayne Gacy and the dozens of boys and young men he killed. It sent chills down his spine and he shuttered, wondering, *How many more bodies would end up in his morgue before this was all over.*

~~~~

Detective Jack Warren was not surprised or upset with the bad news he just received over the phone from FBI consultant Donna Blake. They had no clear shot of the nun's or the Cubs' fan's face. The tape could not be enhanced because it had been recorded over too many times and it became brittle. The only good news was that the Unsub was the same height as the suspected terrorist. No limp could be determined however because the camera angles were too high and provided the suspect with a stroppy appearance.

"You got any good news?" Blake asked frustrated.

"Yeah … We think a homeless guy was killed from the very same poison that killed Eddie Jenkins." Warren responded.

"That's great news."

"Yeah … It is. We know that the killer is positively a male and a bald short fuck."

"Why are so positive?"

"Because the poor bastard lived long enough to talk about it to some of his friends."

"How did you find out?"

"Peter Michaels knew him very well."

~~~~

Crime scene investigator Gary Landis was so tired he was swearing under his breath like he did hundreds of times when he was shuffled from one crime scene to another. This particular case however motivated him deeply because he always felt it involved a serial killer but more importantly he knew each of the victims from testifying in court.

Courtroom 1204 was cordoned off. Landis went directly to the judge's bench to examine his gavel. He immediately saw traces of a familiar substance that he knew would be there. He was absolutely convinced that was how the judge was poisoned. He called Tony Quag immediately after he bagged what evidence he found.

"Hey buddy I suggest you get your ass over here and talk to anyone who was in the courtroom today. This is where he was poisoned. I'm positive."

"Is anybody still around?" Quag asked.

"Yeah, the clerk. He's a grumpy bastard and pissed that he can't get out of here."

"You tell him to keep his sorry ass there. I'm on my way."

~~~~

Conrad Corbett was sitting at the end of the bar watching the White Sox game when his attention shifted to a corner television monitor and the ten o'clock news as the station's announcer revealed an exclusive report about a serial killer roaming the streets of Chicago. Elmer's Grill was one of the most popular sports bars in the resurging South Loop. It was very unusual for someone to watch the news here, but a number of sets now switched over to Ron Magers with a bold graphic that read **EXCLUSIVE**.

A hush fell over the entire barroom as Peter Michaels reported that a serial killer was on the loose in Chicago and that police are now theorizing that the recent rash of murders of attorneys and a judge were all related. There was a buzz in Elmer's for a few moments after the story ended but the sets switched back to the Sox and the Cubs games and the Bears training camp.

Corbett returned to his stool and motioned for Howie to bring him another Coors Light. His mind was racing. *What was it about that new contributor I meet at school?* He was fingering his garlic and parmesan cheese chicken wings lost deep in thought.

The bartender with the Marine type of haircut was wearing a purple Grateful Dead tee shirt with a white towel draped over his left shoulder as he approached his friend. In one motion he flipped off the bottle cap and expertly disposed of it in the waste bucket behind the bar without looking, "You okay Corb?"

Corbett sucked the juices off his fingers and wiped his hands in a soiled paper napkin. "Yeah ... That story on those murders is really bugging me."

"You know that Peter Michaels comes up with some crazy shit, man." Howie was looking at his bar buddy quizzically. "He comes in here all the time."

"Do you know him?" Corbett asked eagerly with a surprised look.

"Well ... sorta ... yeah. He's funny and a good tipper. Why?"

"I'd like to talk him about those murders. Something is really gnawing at me."

"Hold on a sec." Howie said as he turned and went over to a stack of business cards bound together by a rubber band next to the cash register.

Corbett ate the last of his wings, wiped his hands and took the business card. He placed it on the bar in front of him and studied it.

"He told me to give anyone a card if they ever asked for his number." Howie said wiping his hands in his damp bar towel. "You really think you know something about those murders?"

"I'm not sure but I think so. I sorta know ... knew, all those people who were poisoned."

"Come on man. You bullshitting me?"

"Maybe." Corbett said as he drained the remainder of his beer and ordered another.

~~~~

The tall Asian looking man with long auburn hair was sitting in the shadows at a small two top table in the dark corner by the door. His face was obscured because his Blackhawks hat blocked any illumination from the small, dim overhead ceiling lights. He recognized his target at first glance from the video that Dobonovich provided him. He couldn't hear the conversation between the biology teacher and the bartender but he could read the perplexed look on Corbett's face. He smiled to himself, *You little prick! You will be dead in a few hours.*

Earlier, the stranger eased away from his table as if he was going to use the rear bathroom. He slithered over to bar and sprinkled the Oxymodorin Protivea over Corbett's chicken wings as his target was engrossed in the news story he was watching. He knew the garlic would conceal any after taste from the poison. His contemptuous smile widen as he pulled off his latex gloves and dropped them into the trash container next to Corbett's stool. *You are going to die from the same poison that caused your friend Helen Lesenski's death.*

CHAPTER 32

I f you had a casual conversation with Bruce Chambers for just 30 seconds you would know he was a psychiatrist, psychologist or sociologist. Dr. Chambers, a forensic psychologist, practiced for more than 15 years. His thick brown hair turned gray at the temples at an early age and now it has filtered down into his stubby beard. His aplomb personality was reassuring. His blue eyes offered comfort. His pudgy physique was non-threatening. His patients immediately opened up to him.

Two high back easy chairs faced each other at a slight angle giving his patients a comfortable feeling when they entered his office. A sofa had no place in his room. His desk was behind the chairs. Sachets in two corners of the room provided a pleasant peaceful aroma that reminded his patients of an outdoor garden. Every type of criminal behavior imaginable was on display in the books that lined his office library. He had been an expert witness hundreds of times across the country. He preferred to work for the prosecution.

Dr. Chambers had been helpful to Peter Michaels for the last eight years. He had the ability to articulate complicated criminal behaviors in terms that most lay people could understand. He hated to go on camera but he also didn't mind the notoriety that resulted from it. Michaels knew that the stories he was currently doing on terrorists, serial killers or a revenge killer would intrigue him.

Michaels sat to the right of Dr. Chambers as he took out his digital tape recorder from his backpack. He gave a questioning look as if to ask if it was okay to audio tape their interview. Dr. Chambers returned the look with his little boyish grin, rolled his smiling eyes and he nodded. *Sure.*

"Hey, long time no see. How ya' doing?" Michaels started, looking at his recorder making sure the red recording light was on.

"That was quite a story you did last night." Chambers said making himself more comfortable in his thick chair.

"I have no doubt these murders are connected."

"Sounds like it. Look I don't have that much time. So, let's get started."

"Thanks for seeing me on such short notice." Michaels called Dr. Chambers immediately after he got off the air last night. "What are the common misperceptions about serial killers?"

"What you see in the movies and TV is a lot of bullshit. The entertainment industry has put forward many inaccurate depictions of psychopathic killers in film, television, theater, and books. Psychopaths are often incorrectly presented as ghoulish predators or monsters that readily stand out in a crowd.

"In reality, a psychopathic killer like Ted Bundy, John Wayne Gacy or Gary Ridgway, the 'Green River Killer,' can be anyone—a neighbor, co-worker, lover, or a homeless person on the street. Any one of these seemingly harmless people may be a stone-cold killer who preys on others. Psychopaths are social chameleons that rarely stand out in a crowd. This characteristic makes them unobtrusive and, therefore, difficult to apprehend."

"So, they stay under the radar?"

"Yep ... Many of the most infamous and prolific serial killers in U.S. history have exhibited key traits of psychopathy, and many have been diagnosed as psychopaths by forensic psychologists following their capture. A cool and unemotional demeanor combined with a keen intellect and a charming personality make the psychopath a very effective predator. A lack of interpersonal empathy and an inability to feel pity or remorse also characterize psychopathic serial killers. They do not value human life, and do not care about the consequences of their crimes. They are callous, indifferent, and extremely brutal in their interactions with their victims."

"What about a person like Ted Bundy, for example?"

"This is particularly evident in so-called power/control serial killers, such as Ted Bundy. They may kidnap, torture, and/or rape and murder their prey without any outward signs of remorse."

"Does law enforcement have adequate profiling capabilities of these serial killers?"

"Increased attention has been given to the connection between psychopathy and serial murder in recent years both by researchers and criminal justice professionals. For example, the FBI concluded that psychopathy is manifested in a specific cluster of interpersonal, affective lifestyle, and antisocial traits and behaviors frequently found among serial killers.

"As reported by FBI forensic psychologists, these traits and behaviors involve deception, manipulation, irresponsibility, impulsivity, stimulation seeking, poor behavioral controls, shallow affect, lack of empathy, guilt, or remorse, a callous disregard for the rights of others, and unethical and antisocial behaviors."

"When do these patterns usually show their ugly heads?"

"These traits define adult psychopathy, but they begin to manifest in early childhood. Children who have chronic assaultive behavior disorders and abuse animals are known to evolve into killers. It is important to recognize that psychopathic serial killers know right from wrong and are able to comprehend criminal law. In particular, they know that murder violates the laws and mores of society. They do understand that they are subject to society's rules, but they disregard them to satisfy their own selfish interests and desires."

"Does a mental health defense have any merit for these killers?"

"In court, psychopathic serial killers are rarely found not guilty by reason of insanity, simply because psychopathy does not qualify as insanity in the criminal justice system. But contrary to popular mythology, psychopathic serial killers are **not** out of touch with reality and, as such, are not mentally ill in either a clinical or a legal sense. They rarely suffer from delusions unless they also have a separate mental illness such as psychosis nor do they tend to abuse drugs such as amphetamines or cocaine.

In the criminal courts, the attorney of a psychopathic serial killer occasionally presents psychotic delusions as a defense. Normally, prosecutors and forensic psychologists easily challenge such claims, because psychotic delusions are not a characteristic of psychopathy."

"Do these killers have any remorse at all?"

"A lack of interpersonal empathy and disregard for the suffering of their victims are key characteristics of psychopathic serial killers. They generally do not feel anger toward their victims. Instead, they are more likely to feel cool indifference toward them. Many serial killers seem to go into a trance when they are stalking and killing a victim, and the violence they commit often has a dissociative effect on them emotionally.

"Psychopathic serial killers are emotionally disconnected from their actions and, therefore, indifferent to the suffering of their victims. Their ability to dissociate themselves emotionally from their actions and their denial of responsibility effectively neutralizes any guilt or remorse that other people would feel in similar circumstances."

"What about revenge killers?"

"A revenge killer more than likely is just like a serial killer. One of the big difference is a revenge killer can and probably does have anger or even hates his or her victims."

Chambers looked at his wristwatch and abruptly said, "Peter, I am sorry but I gotta go. I need to pick up my wife and if I'm late, I am afraid she is going to kill me."

CHAPTER 33

"*S* *hit*" Peter Michaels' brain exclaimed as he left Dr. Chambers' office. He was looking at his cell phone and realized that he forgot to forward all his calls from his office phone. He dialed his retrieve number and had several voicemails from someone he had never heard from before.

"Hey, Mr. Michaels my name is Conrad Corbett. I saw your story on the news tonight, and I think, I may have some information that may help you. You can reach me at 530-626-6316. Thanks."

Michaels immediately dialed the number but the call after seven rings went to voicemail.

Corbett's cell phone was in his back pocket. After his sixth or was it his seventh beer, he started feeling queasy and left Elmer's shortly before midnight. He looked like any other patron who was over served as he started to make his way to his apartment building on South Indiana. His hands were trembling as he fumbled with his key to open his front door. The elevator ride to the fourth floor seemed to take forever. He felt like he wanted to vomit and a high fever added to his discomfort. The closest bathroom was to left as he entered the apartment. He felt something rise in his esophagus as he hit the highly varnished wooden floor face first. The last few minutes of his life were extremely painful.

"Hey, Mr. Corbett … This is Peter Michaels from the Channel Six Investigative Team. When you get this message please give me a call. I'd love to talk with you about your information. You've got my number."

~~~~

The man with the auburn hair and the Chicago Blackhawks hat was rethinking all of his movements from the night before, making sure in his mind that he left no clues behind as he followed Corbett home. He was careful. He stayed a strategic 15 feet behind Corbett after he exited Elmer's. A night breeze that whispered through the leaves of the red maple trees that lined the street camouflaged his footfalls and cooled his sweaty face. The killer sensed that Corbett was beginning to feel excruciating pain by the way he stumbled and grabbed onto the trees for support to keep from falling. He was confident that the teacher couldn't hear anything. He was like a wounded animal trying to find its way home. The streetlights created eerie shadows on the sidewalks between the parked vehicles and the facades of the neighboring buildings giving him a place to hide if the someone happened outside at that late hour.

He closed his eyes and pictured himself as a nimble cat when he rushed up the three porch steps and grabbed the glass security door just as it was about to close and lock. His mordant eyes searched the street over his shoulder for any onlookers. There were none. He eased into the elevator with Corbett, but he knew the dying man had no idea he had company. He watched as Corbett braced himself up on the wall as the teacher struggled his way to unit 404.

The killer did not need to go into the apartment, he just wanted to make sure Corbett got inside so no one could discover his body in the hallway. The Fox assured him nobody would notice Corbett's absence until late Tuesday morning when the popular teacher didn't show up for his final biology exam of the summer session.

Only his sinful, lifeless eyes matched his wicked grin as he made sure Corbett's door was locked before he exited the building. Gray storm clouds curtained the night's half-moon leaving the street a dark abyss of death.

He breathed a sigh of relief as he hailed a cab on Michigan Avenue that would drop him off three blocks from his Chestnut Street apartment. He was now positive he left no trace. No one noticed him. He laid down on his bed and put his hands in his pants and smiled.

~~~~

Dr. Robert Crine had the autopsy room's high beam surgical light zeroed in on the blue lips of Chris Chalmers. The corpse had been stored in a refrigerated trailer for more than a week. Dr. Crine's magnifying goggles barely brought what was left of the thin line of crusty foam that settled there to life. He used a thin cotton swab to gather the evidence. He flipped up his clear plastic facemask and smelled the tip. He detected no odor but his gut told him it was the same poison that killed Eddie Jenkins because it appeared to be the same color and texture from what he could tell with his magnifying glass.

Crine removed every dried fragment of the trace material from Chalmers' lips and mouth and then he cut off a small portion for his microscopic examination. He bagged the sample, sealed it and signed it. He knew he salvaged enough for a DNA analysis. When the ME examined the swatch under his microscope a feeling of great satisfaction enveloped him. He had no doubt the crime lab would confirm what he had already surmised ... It was a match.

The homeless soldier preformed one more heroic act by providing another piece of evidence that would hopefully lead to the "Bug Man."

~~~~

Dr. James McBride's spectrometer signaled that his specimen revealed the presence of Darmadodimine Extract a very, very rare bio-microorganism that attacks the central nervous system. The Fort Detrick scientist shook his head, closed his eyes and wondered how painful death was for the attorney, named Edmund Jenkins. The mutations in the sample exposed a signature almost identical to that of the rat lungworm he discovered just two weeks before.

Another new sample he was about to test came from a lawyer named Wayne Phillips and the report he just read from the Chicago Joint Terrorism Task Force suspected that the Darmadodimine Extract was also used to kill the former prosecutor. Dr. McBride didn't want to waste time going to square one so he set the same parameters for the rare bio-microorganism for the second test. The spectrometer went through a single cycle before his delicate machine signaled a match not to the same poison that killed Eddie Jenkins but to a different compound with a very similar chemical structure.

McBride was staring at his computer screen with his chin resting in his right hand. He removed the sample and then examined it under the most powerful microscope they had in the lab. "Holy Shit," he exclaimed to himself, then he said out loud, "This stuff was also engineered."

"What did you discover?" His lab assistant Michael Kearney asked.

"There is one, sick son of a bitch out there creating organisms of death, Michael. The bastard can even predict the amount of time it will take for the poison to kill you." Dr. McBride reached for his phone and called the detective who signed the evidence container.

~~~~

"Jack Warren," the young, handsome detective said answering his desk phone almost bored.

"Hey, detective, this Dr. McBride from Fort Detrick. The poison that killed your Mr. Jenkins and the prosecutor Phillips are not the same."

Warren now standing, adrenalin rushing through his entire body. "Are you positive?"

"Yes, it is similar but not the same."

"What is it?"

"Paradomaxia Orthogenics. It also attacks the nervous system and causes a painful death but it's different for sure."

"Was it made by the 'Bug Man' though?" Warren asked hoping for a positive answer. The puzzle pieces once again started moving around in his mind.

"I am 100 percent positive. It was made by the same nut bag that created the rat lungworm that killed all those people up there and what killed Mr. Jenkins."

"How can you be so sure?" Warren asked as he paced around his workstation stretching the cord of his desk phone, eyes wide open and alert.

"Same signature. No doubt! No doubt! You have one sick bastard up there in Chicago."

Jack Warren was biting his lower lip and he retorted, "Does that surprise you? It's fucking Chicago."

~~~~

Detective Tony Quag was talking to CSI Gary Landis. "Can you tell what you got off his gavel."

"I can't give you anything affirmative other than there was trace that looked similar to the trace I got from Phillips car. What did the court clerk say?"

"He was an 'I don't give a shit type of guy'. He just wants to retire."

"Did he see anything unusual yesterday?"

"No. He wasn't around much. He just wanted to get out of there but when I pushed him a little, he said there was a new attorney lurking around the courtroom a few days ago but couldn't remember much about the guy."

"Nothing at all?"

"He said the guy was well dressed. Said he was new at Carlin and Miller. Short. Glasses, like round rimmed. Said he wanted to familiarize himself with the courtroom because he would have a case there soon."

"That sounds a little lame, doesn't it? An attorney casing a courtroom because he has a trial coming up there in a few weeks?" Landis inquired.

"Sounds goofy to me but I'll check with the firm on Monday about any new associates."

~~~~

Dr. Louis Yako didn't see patients on Saturdays. This was his time to review his notes and prepare for any upcoming trial that he was scheduled to provide expert testimony. Yako had an almost perfect record. He lost only one case as far as he was concerned and it bothered him for more than a decade. He would never use his impeccable credentials to help a defense attorney. He worked only for the prosecution. Although he was paid generously for his time and services, he would do it for nothing if he had too, but he chose only those cases that interested him and the one that interested him the most he lost on a technicality. The victim was still alive at the time of trial.

His office was attached to his house on Ridgeland Avenue in Oak Park, Illinois, a western suburb that bordered Chicago. It was a modest yellow brick structure. He could have lived anywhere he wanted. He had amassed tens of millions of dollars in his Merrill Lynch accounts over the years with very shrewd investments. He bought two thousands of shares of Apple when it first went public on December 12, 1980, at $22.00 a share. The stock split seven times, currently leaving him with 112,000 shares or $25,000,000. Money never mattered to him. He was not cheap. He just loved his house and it was the only one he ever wanted lived in. He shared it with his wife of 50 years before she had succumbed to breast cancer two years earlier.

He was thinking of retiring to his summer home in the Travis City, Michigan area overlooking Lake Michigan and to his condo on the white sand beach of Marco Island, Florida in the winter. He promised himself he would make up his mind after the Bears won the Super Bowl this season. He was a diehard Bear fan all of his life. His father and George Halas, affectionately known as "Papa Bear" were lifelong friends. Halas was the team's first player-coach and Louis Yako senior was the team's doctor for 14 years.

~~~~

Very few people had any idea about his wealth or his lifestyle but none of that matter to the man sitting in the rented white Kia parked down the street, never taking his eyes off the modest yellow-brick house. "The Fox" knew Dr. Louis Yako would go to his favorite restaurant La Notte Italiano Ristorante on Marion Street just off Lake Street at 12:30 for lunch.

The good doctor's premier, spotless 1985 white Mercedes-Benz backed into the alley, out of the garage. He had to drive around the block and then north towards downtown Oak Park like he has done for the last four weeks. Dr. Louis Yako was a creature of habit.

CHAPTER 34

T
he employment records of Williamson Waterworks Inc. indicated that Yang Sung-Choi was being transferred from the Detroit, Michigan regional office on Monday, May 20, 2019, to fill the vacancy in the Chicago office that was created by the sudden death of 55-year-old Edward Harris, a senior engineer of what appeared to be natural causes. The family didn't want an autopsy. Harris's family had a history of congenital heart disease.

Even if an autopsy had been performed it probably would not have determined that a concoction of prescription drugs for high blood pressure, Clonidine and Gossypol, were mixed together and dropped into his coffee. The lethal combination caused the fatal heart attack within in minutes. Harris's response was typical and therefore unsuspecting. He reached for his heart and he keeled over face first into his chicken parmesan sandwich. Everyone sitting at the table for a corporate luncheon meeting was shocked. It never crossed their minds that he was murdered.

Williamson Waterworks Inc. was an independent contractor that operated, maintained and serviced all the water pumps in Chicago and Cook County's recreational parks and tourist attractions. The Golf course ponds that had irrigation pumps to keep the water flowing to prevent pond scum and algae build up were in constant need of W.W. Inc's services.

The city's famed Clarence Buckingham Memorial Fountain produces a major water display for twenty minutes every hour, weather permitting. The fountain's center jet shoots water 150 feet into the air when wind conditions are perfect. On blustery days the center jet may shoot the water only 20 feet. The final major water display begins precisely at 10:35 p.m. every night the fountain is operational.

Yang Sung-Choi's resume indicated that he graduated with honors from Purdue University with a civil engineering degree, class of 2005. Sung-Choi never set foot in Detroit nor on the campus of Purdue in West Lafayette, Indiana. His credentials were created on a powerful computer, housed in a two flat brownstone on Chestnut Street.

~~~~

Peter Michaels was having coffee in his atrium room looking out over Lake Michigan when detective Jack Warren knock on his door.

"It's open." Michaels yelled as he got up and walked over to his Keurig coffee machine. "You want a cup of coffee?"

"Sounds good." The young detective said as he ambled down the long hallway. Warren looked horrible, like he hadn't slept in a week. His eyes were bloodshot and his lids were drooping. He was disheveled and his usually stylish frumpy hair appeared oily and gathered.

"You look like shit … Cream?" Michaels said dryly as coffee dripped into his NBC cup. Michaels pulled open the refrigerator and grabbed the half and half from the door.

"Quantico thinks the nun is our guy but we couldn't identify the limp because the tape was so bad."

"I already know that."

"Yeah but we now know that the poison that killed Eddie and we think your Army guy are the same," Warren said as he poured half and half into his coffee. "The analyst are now comparing the powder from the nun's habit to the chemical structure of Darmadodimine Extract and it appears to be the same. The scientists from Fort Detrick should be able to determine if it's the same fingerprint and if was created by the 'Bug Man.' They're fairly certain it came from the same batch."

"What about Phillips?"

"The stuff that killed him is a very different toxin but there is no question it was created by the 'Bug Man.'"

Michaels was a little taken aback. He had surmised correctly that the victims were poisoned and he reported it on Friday night. "I concluded that Eddie and Chris had to be poisoned the same way because there seems to be a direct connection. But?"

Michaels always had trouble with medical terms and stumbled trying to pronounce, "Darma … whatever … Extract. How does it kill?"

"It slowly moves through your body as it suffocates you … then BAAM, all of sudden it's like a bullet to the brain. I'm told it is a very painful way to die."

"Was it Darmadodime Extract that killed the judge?"

"We're not sure yet. They don't have the results of the autopsy yet but we are now operating on the theory that it was made by the same guy."

Michaels raised his eyebrow as he loaded a decaf K-cup into the Keurig machine and pressed BREW. He was totally alert now. "How can you tell?"

"First of all, the signatures are the same. This Extract stuff is very, very rare. You know how a bomb maker leaves a signature on his bombs. Right?" Warren asked quizzically.

Michaels nodded. He was totally focused on Warren's face as he continued.

"This fucker leaves his signature. Quantico says he genetically modified the organisms with a distinct RNA fingerprint. He left a similar signature or RNA fingerprint on the rat lungworm, shit. It's all homemade and it's made by the same crazy person."

Michaels added some half and half to his coffee, stirred it aimlessly and blew on it to cool it down out of habit before he took a sip. "So, we have 30 some people dead and you have found at least three different types of poisons."

"This 'Bug Guy' as you call him, without question left his signature on the rat lungworms. It is some sort of biological ego thing he does. It is very subtle but very distinct."

"What about judge Wolfe? Is that the same stuff?"

"Have no idea. The autopsy won't be completed until tomorrow at the earliest. Dr. Crine did that autopsy on your buddy and he couldn't get to Wolfe. So, we are not sure, but I'd be surprised if it wasn't different though."

"Well, we know for sure that the three of the poisons were home brewed … Right?"

Warren nodded, took a sip of his coffee and blinked, "You know that rat shit that killed those 28 people was homegrown with steroids. This 'Bug Man' guy is one sick son of a bitch. He wants us to know its him."

Michaels blinked as he remembered his late Friday night phone call.

"Some guy named Corbett … Conrad Corbett called me after I got off the air the other night. He said he may know something about the murders, but he hasn't answered his phone in two days. I've called him at least six times."

"Did he sound credible?" Warren asked as a puzzled look crossed his face.

"I don't know but in his voicemail he sounded … he sounded excited."

~~~~

Kathy Broderick left her apartment, 403, and locked her door as she always did when she left for the eleven o'clock Sunday morning mass at St. Mary's, a short walk away. She heard a phone softly ringing in some tropical musical tone in her neighbor's apartment but didn't think much of it. After a few rings, it stopped or faded.

Rigor mortise had already set in and the blood in Conrad Corbett's body had settled. His skin was turning black. The foam that oozed from his nostrils and his parted lips was crusty and dry. It appeared to be colorless. The room's temperature was set at 78 degrees. The corpse's decomposition odor already started to drift towards the exhaust vents as the air conditioning unit struggled to keep the apartment's temperature to its assigned level.

The only neighbor that Conrad Corbett associated with and was fairly friendly with since he moved in a year ago, lived in 406. Rodney Harvey always had a smile on his face and he engaged anyone in conversation easily. He retired from the Chicago Police Department three years earlier as a Deputy Superintendent. He was away most weekends during the summer, fishing with his best friend in Indiana. He was not due home until late Monday afternoon or evening, but that depended on how the fish were biting and the amount of the Balvenie scotch was left in the bottle.

CHAPTER 35

Peter Michaels had a restless night. Sleep was fleeting, he was bothered because this Conrad Corbett, guy, wasn't answering his phone after he left a message that he had some information about the "Bug Man" and more importantly, Corbett sounded so excited to talk. Michaels was also pissed off because he worked all weekend, and he didn't get a chance to take advantage of some southerly winds on Lake Michigan. The other seven members of his racing team took out his boat, Dr. Detroit, to practice for the upcoming Chicago to Mackinaw Race. The Mac is 330 nautical miles, making it the longest freshwater sailboat race in the world. It was a great challenge but for the first time in a decade, Michaels was losing interest because the "Bug Man" was consuming all of his time and interest.

His latte was sufficiently cooled as he sleepily walked into the I-Team office. David Beedy was already at his desk, reading the sports section. Dah Bears were the highlight of the morning, both the White Sox and the Cubs got shutout on Sunday and interest in Chicago baseball was already waning.

"Did you guys sail this weekend?" Beedy asked as he lowered the newspaper he was reading.

"No. I worked all weekend." He walked over and sat on the edge of his producer's desk. The meditative expression on Michaels' face was alarming to Beedy.

"Are you okay?"

"Actually, No … I'm obsessed with this 'Bug Man' stuff. Let's do a Lexis-Nexis search connecting all the cases that involved judge Wolfe, Wayne Phillips and Eddie Jenkins. Let's go back ten years and see what we find."

"No problem," Beedy said enthusiastically as he flexed his fingers and started to punch his keyboard bringing his computer to life.

Michaels ambled over to his desk, pulled out his cell phone, sat aimlessly down and dialed Conrad Corbett's number again.

"This is Conrad. Please a leave a message and I will get back to you as soon as I am able."

This guy uses proper English Michaels thought as Conrad's voicemail would not accept his ninth call in less than 48 hours.

~~~~

The engineer from Purdue walked into the offices in the lower bunker of Buckingham Fountain. One of the maintenance men, wearing a blue work uniform, was laying on his back tightening a nut on one of the water pumps that started to leak over the weekend. The weather had been fabulous and the fountain produced shows that pumped water 120 feet into the air every hour for 20 minutes at a time.

"Who are you?" the man on his back asked, wiping water and sweat from his right eye, looking up at the tall bald stranger.

"I'm Choi. It's my first day over here. I just got transferred from the Forest Preserve Unit." Yang Sung-Choi explained hiding his smile. It had taken him five weeks and $2,500 to obtain the position, the "good old, Chicago way."

The maintenance man's nametag identified him as "Elberto." He was five feet-eight when he stood up. His beer belly made him look heavier than he actually was. His jet-black hair and brown eyes defied his perfect English. "This is a great place to hide out. No trouble here. Just do your job and nobody bothers you," he said as he extended his hand to the new man.

"You here a lot?" Choi asked as a fake smile perched his lips.

"I work on the main pumps all over the county. I'm only around if there is a problem."

"Hey … can you show me how the pumps work for the main fountain and how you gain access to them?"

Elberto's brown eyes expressed puzzlement. *Why would an engineer not know these things?* "Sure, follow me," Elberto said as he led the new guy down the stairs into a room that was sweaty and loud. The giant pumps' gears whirred and the pistons cranked making the area sound like an engine room from a United States Navy battleship.

Choi could hardly contain his excitement. The room looked exactly like the blueprints he had been studying for weeks. He knew precisely where the anthrax combo would go. Now he had to figure out how long it would take him to plant the poison concoction.

~~~~

Kathy Broderick from 403 was meeting some girlfriends for lunch at Molly Sullivan's. It would be a nice walk on the beautiful summer day. She wore a wild, yellow and red flowery sleeveless summer dress that hung loosely over her body. Her long curly thick black hair was damp dry and smelled of lilac shampoo. She locked her door and turned towards the elevators when the smell of what she thought was rotten eggshells caught her attention.

Yuck, she thought as she made her way down the hallway. She had only met Conrad a couple of times but he always seemed like a nice boy. She knew he was a science teacher. *Maybe he's conducting some sort of experiment,* she assumed as the odor eased the further away she got from his door.

~~~~

"That's weird," Peter Michaels said out loud as he hung up the phone.

"What's weird?" Beedy asked looking up from his computer screen.

"I talked with Tony Quag this morning. They dusted judge Wolfe's courtroom and got some trace. They think he was poisoned when he picked up his gavel. Quag said, he talked with the new court clerk, you know that lazy son of a bitch Baratucci and he told him the only odd thing he remembered last week was some little, greasy attorney poking around the courtroom."

"What's so weird about that?" Beedy responded.

"The guy said he was new at Carlin and Miller and wanted to get a feel for the courtroom that he would be in for the first time in a couple of weeks from now."

"That is weird. The associates at Carlin and Miller are pretty experienced. I don't think, they would do that. A courtroom is a courtroom."

"Yeah. That's what Bob Franey said. But he also said that they haven't hired any new associates in the last two years." Michaels pondered, combing his hair with his fingers. "The clerk also said the attorney was a short, a little creepy looking weasel type, dressed in a very rich suit, wearing tinted glasses."

"You don't think?"

Michaels interrupted Beedy in midsentence, "I have no doubt the 'Bug Man' cased the courtroom long before he put the poison on the judge's gavel."

CHAPTER 36

D r. Robert Crine was turning an evidence bag, containing the sample of poison he took from Wayne Phillips's lips, around in his hands, his mind drifted back to the time his mother hit him across his shoulders with a broom handle. He was a teenager and he dropped a pint container of coffee cream as he was putting it back into the refrigerator.

He was snapped out of his nightmarish thoughts when the phone rang, bringing him back to the present. "This is Dr. Crine."

"Hey Doc. It's Quag. I wanna tell you, I'm glad we did that autopsy on Chris Chalmers, just heard from the docs at Fort Detrick. We were right. The poison that killed Eddie is the same that killed Chris," the detective said as he was driving from police headquarters to the FBI's JTTF office.

"I felt that about those two, for sure, but I am not so sure what will happen with Phillips and Wolfe. I am positive its poison but I don't think they're the same." Crine said, still holding the sample up to the high beam light, gazing at it curiously, slightly squinting.

"Detective Warren just filled me in. How's it going over there?"

"I just finished with Wayne Phillips. I'll start Judge Wolfe in a bit. I'm sending samples to both the state lab and to Fort Detrick. But … I don't know."

"Whadda yah mean?" asked Quag dubiously.

"Like I ... its poison, but it doesn't appear to be exactly the same from what I can see with my eyes." Crine responded putting the evidence bag on his desk. "I'll get these samples out before the end of the day."

"Warren says the poisons in the salad dressing and from Eddie were manufactured by the same guy."

Dr. Crine's expression morphed from studious to concern, "Are you sure?"

"Oh Yeah! The scientist at Detrick is now positive."

"Tony, I believe this is going to get a lot worse before this all ends. I'll let you know when I'm finished here. Keep me in the loop."

"Soon as I know, you'll know, and Doc thanks for doing the autopsy on the homeless vet. It may be the break we need because I gotta tell yah ... We don't have a lot to go on."

~~~~

Jacob Cohen worked as a security guard for 40 years. He looked a lot older than his 62 years. His white hair once combed straight back was now thin and stood at a 45-degree angle. Cat hair speckled his blue sport coat that was now his uniform along with gray pants that lost their crease after years of getting up and down from his lobby chair to greet the residents of 880 South Michigan when they entered the lobby through a revolving thick glass door that keeps the cold outside in the winter and the cool air inside during the summer.

"Can I help you sir?" Cohen asked as the workman in the blue uniform that had ABC Services stitched on his back walked in the front door. His nametag identified him as "Chuck."

"Yes, thank you. I am here to see a Mr. Larry Schmidt. He had a problem with his refrigerator." The workman lied with a fake smile disguising his distain.

Cohen looked down at his spiral notebook binder searching for the work order, licking his fingertip, flipping a couple of pages before looking up. "I don't see anything here telling us you were coming. Let me call up there."

"Thank you. Let me check my log maybe I have the wrong day." The Fox pulled out a little notebook from his shirt pocket and replied, "I think I have the wrong day. I'll check with the boss and come back another time." He turned from the desk and walked to the revolving doors keeping his head down avoiding the security cameras.

Jacob Cohen had worked at 880 since it opened its doors in 2001. He knew everyone who lived in the building and thought it was strange that Mr. Schmidt wouldn't leave a note that someone was coming to his apartment to fix something. He closed the spiral notebook and dismissed the encounter, making a mental note to check with Mr. Schmidt.

~~~~

Peter Michaels wanted to slam his desk phone down into its cradle after his tenth call to Conrad Corbett in the last two and half days. Every call went straight to his full mailbox. Michaels was frustrated: everyone he called in the last two hours did not answer. He left seven voicemails. "Any luck with the docket search?" he asked David Beedy as he eased himself down into his chair. He put his feet up on the desk, interlaced his fingers, placed his hands behind his head and looked up at the ceiling and began to think.

"I've gone back ten years. There is nothing that jumps out. Every case in judge Wolfe's courtroom seemed fairly routine and the trials didn't last very long." An exasperated Beedy said, bouncing a yellow number 2 pencil off his lower lip.

Michaels was thinking "routine" when a picture of Antoinette Barettelli suddenly flashed back through his memory. He bolted to his feet and yelled, "2005 or 2006."

Beedy was so startled, he almost bit down his pencil. Instinctively, he started typing. "What the fuck, Peter. You scared the shit out of me. What's 2005 … 2006?"

A wide eye, enthusiastic look emerged on Michaels' face. "Before you came to the investigative unit when you were a show producer, do you remember when I did that series on Pookey Meeks, the Southside drug kingpin? He was buried in the handmade casket that resembled a gold Cadillac. Remember? It was shocking."

"Yeah … slightly, that was a long time ago." Beedy responded, taking his eyes off his computer screen as he stopped typing and looked at Michaels, instantly thinking about his twin sons who were five-years old at the time.

"Henry 'The Hammer' Hopkins was arrested for killing him and his trial was held in judge Wolfe's courtroom." Michaels was now pacing the room with a gleeful mien on his face. "When he was found guilty, several gangbangers forced their way into the courtroom and took Toni and some others hostage."

Beedy's memory was now clicking in as he recollected how everyone scrambled to get the story "Live" on the air. "There was a standoff … right?"

"Yeah, for three or four hours. That's when I first met Toni. I did the story that night on the six and ten." Michaels' gleeful expression was now exchanged with one of thoughtfulness and concern. "She told me that was the most scared she ever was while working in Wolfe's courtroom with one other exception. The mad scientist."

"Mad scientist." Beedy countered with a grimace.

"Yes. That trial was about six months later. The guy had a weird name. Russian. Polish or Eastern European or something." Michaels said, walking now in deep thought. "She said he was crazy … beat his assistant with a microscope or something." Michaels mind was racing in a good way. "She was in a coma for years before she died. It was horrible as I remember Toni telling me."

~~~~

The Fox was now sitting at his sterile stainless steel workspace, naked, looking into his powerful microscope, grimacing. He was debating on which poison he would use to kill Peter Michaels. Ricin or Botulinum?

Ricin was the poison of choice used by Russian spies for years. It was dependable, but so easy to detect. He decided that if used the Ricin, he may not get credit for the kill because he couldn't put his signature on the compound. *Fuck that!*

Most scientists agree Botulinum toxin is the most toxic substance known to mankind, and he could manipulate the anaerobic bacteria leaving no doubt that he created it. He smiled as he made his decision … one nanogram per kilogram can kill a human. *It would take only seconds for that fucker to die.*

CHAPTER 37

D avid Beedy immediately went back to his computer and within minutes found the 2006 case of the State of Illinois vs. Cyril Dobonovich. Tiny beads of sweat formed at his hairline. He licked his dry lips and his eyes couldn't move fast enough to take in everything that flickered across his screen. His shirtsleeves were rolled up to his elbows, and his tie was flipped over his shoulder because it kept interfering with his fingers that looked like they belonged to Jerry Lee Lewis as he pounded the keyboard to one of his greatest hits, "Great Balls of Fire."

Michaels didn't realize that a grin eased across his mouth with a sense of pride, he had never seen his producer that focused. "Whatta you got?" Michaels asked apprehensively, his heart now beating faster as he noticed the look of intense concentration on Beedy's face.

"Holy shit!" Beedy exclaimed, his finger now persistently pecking the down arrow on his keyboard, revealing more and more information that he was trying to absorb.

"What? Holy shit! What?" Michaels said now looking over Beedy's shoulder trying to keep up with the downward scrolling green sentences. "You're right, holy shit. He's killing everyone involved in that case that had anything to do with him going to jail."

"Madison. Madison Mental Health Center; not jail." Beedy corrected. "This guy's fucking crazy. He looks like he was found 'Guilty by Reason of Insanity.'" Beedy said as he leaned back in his chair and took a deep breath letting his shoulders totally relax.

~~~~

In state of Illinois, a defendant found "Guilty but Mentally Ill" is required to serve time in a penitentiary. Although psychiatric expert testimony may be heard at trial, the defendant who is found "Guilty but Mentally Ill" is deemed to be capable of understanding that he/she committed a crime and that he/she knew the difference between right and wrong. Sentences are generally the maximum amount of time allowed by law for that particular defense of a heinous crime. Parole is considered for the defendant like any other prisoner serving time.

On the other hand, a defendant being found "Guilty by Reason of Insanity" by a judge or a jury is committed to the Department of Health and Human Services and eventually placed in a mental institution for inpatient treatment. Normally, the convicted person receives the maximum sentence allowed by law. The decision to institutionalize a defendant is primarily contingent on the strength of the testimony from psychiatrists and mental health experts. A guilty verdict, however, in these types of cases is considered a medical decision and therefore, sentence times may be shortened and early release may be granted after the patient successfully responds to treatment that is proscribed.

Cyril Dobonovich did just that and served only 25 percent of his sentence utilizing every second to plan his revenge.

~~~~

"Print it." Michaels said excitedly as he checked the paper tray to make sure it was full.

Beedy smiled and with a great deal of satisfaction, he hit the print button and immediately pages of the twelve-year-old court proceeding began to fill the receiving tray. Exhaustion instantly enveloped the producer as he peacefully eased into his chair and closed his eyes.

Michaels reached for his phone and dialed Sam Pfeiffer, the station's attorney. He wanted to know the legal ramifications of naming a killer who hasn't been convicted of killing anyone, yet. His second call was to his boss, News Director, Phil Rivers to let him know the significance of what they found and get permission to report it no matter what Sam said.

~~~~

Dr. Robert Crine was tying the final knot in the nylon thread from the last stitch of his V-incision on the chest of Judge Harold Wolfe's corpse. He already prepared two samples of what Crine believed to be very different poisons that were the causes of death for the judge and prosecutor Wayne Phillips and the other victims. The evidence bags were already on their way to the State Police Crime Lab and Fort Detrick. The ME knew that the results from Fort Detrick would be determined much faster than the state's lab because they just weren't properly equipped to detect these sophisticated bio-microorganism.

Crine unbuttoned his stained lab coat and let out a low groan of fatigue as he lowered himself into his chair, thinking about the 31 autopsies his office had performed on what he now believed was the work of a single killer. A mild migraine was creeping in. He pulled open his top right hand desk drawer and reached for an Aleve to discover the only thing left in his makeshift medicine kit was Tylenol, not even extra strength. *Fuck!*

The fluorescent bulb from the ceiling light above his desk began to flicker, reminding him of the latest budget cuts, and the lack of professional help that his office so desperately needed to keep up with the growing demands of Chicago's bloody streets. Weekend shootings were multiplying as the city's homicide rate spiked for the second straight year. In the past two-days alone, he had18 new victims stored on refrigerated slabs adjacent to his operating room.

The doctor's mood was not improving, knowing that he had these "routine" autopsies to preform because of drive-by shootings that had become so commonplace over the last two decades. The only thing left to determine was if the victims were killed with an AK-47 or a Glock-19.

Crine felt the wiry hairs from his goatee as he rubbed his hand across his face, wondering how many more victims there would be from this maniacal killer that Peter Michaels labeled the "Bug Man" before this would be all over. He stood up, buttoned his coat, threw back his shoulders with a grimace, and walked back into his operating room, shaking his head.

~~~~

Detective Jack Warren was sitting in the office of FBI Special Agent Tom Eiseman from the Joint Terrorism Task Force, pleading his case that the murders of the 28 people from the KTC were not connected to terrorist.

"I just got off the phone with detective Quag. It's positive. The poison that killed Eddie Jenkins is the very same that killed Chalmers, the vet. That's a positive conclusion from the scientists at Fort Detrick and Quantico says the stuff from the gray material from the nun's habit is an exact match as well."

Eiseman was leaning back in his chair, listening, his fingers forming a steeple, touching his pursed lips with his head slowly nodding, and eyes in agreement. "Hmmm … It makes sense," he said looking up at the young detective as if waiting for a comment, but then he continued. "It's been over two weeks and no one has claimed responsibility, and my gut is finally telling me you are right, but I don't want to give up control. We have the backing of the entire federal government's resources and I think we can use that to our advantage. Where are we with the other autopsies?"

"Dr. Crine was backed up with the autopsies because of all the shootings over the weekend but we should have something on Phillips very soon. I'm not sure if he even did judge Wolfe's yet." Warren was out of his chair, looking out the window at the late afternoon traffic on Roosevelt Road, "This guy is diabolical."

"Yes, he is, but what's his end game?" Eiseman wondered out loud with puzzlement clouding his eyes.

Warren's phone rang to the Blues Brothers tune "Rock Star" signaling that it was Peter Michaels. He looked at Eiseman and motioned with his left forefinger *let me get this*. "Hey ... What's up?" He listened intently as Michaels told him that Cyril Dobonovich was the killer and explained how he came to that conclusion. Warren ran the fingers of his left hand through his curly locks as a grin widen across his face revealing his perfectly straight white teeth. "Yeah ... I'll get back to you. Thanks."

Eiseman was eying his young agent intensely, "Who was that?" he inquired, although he already knew from the sound of the ringtone.

"That was Peter Michaels and he's identified our killer. I think, he is right on target"

The pieces of the mystery puzzle in Warren's brain started to fall into place. He knew Michaels was using him to give credibility to the story he wanted to report on the ten o'clock news, but he also knew that it all made perfect sense.

~~~~

The Fox's headache was crippling. He knew the Kuru that infected him many years ago in Vienna was having its devastating final effects. He worked for years searching for one of the only antidotes that had avoided his demonic skills. He looked up from his microscope when Choi entered the lab through the hidden back door. A vulpine smile emerged as the tall Asian picked him up and kissed him full on the mouth.

In the past, Choi's tongue would excite him as much as his plan for revenge, but it was different now. The Fox knew he had approximately two or three weeks to live and he wanted his fiendish plan to go flawlessly.

"I am sorry my darling," he said obsequiously looking into his only sexual partner's eyes, "but we haven't got the time. I want to show you the anthrax specimens that I have modified extensively." With that he lead his lover/accomplice to the incubators in the center of the bio-safety lab where he was cultivating the deadly toxins. "It will be ready in plenty of time and you must be very careful how you engage it."

"Yes, we have much to talk about." He said as he looked at the Fox with saddened eyes, dreading the inevitable death of his only friend. "I surveyed the fountain's bunker this morning. I have developed a deployment strategy for the wet specimen and I have a good idea for the outdoor garbage can disbursement, but I still need trial runs and more surveillance."

~~~~

Rodney Harvey had tired eyes and a slight hangover as he put his key into the lock of apartment 406. The long weekend of fishing and Balvenie scotch left him drained and longing for his bed. A familiar odor was wafting in the air. An odor that immediately put him on alert. It was the odor that accompanied many homicide scenes that he encountered in his thirty plus years on the job. It was the unmistakable smell of decaying flesh and death.

His tired eyes awoke with suspicion, and his mind became fully aware that something was wrong. He cautiously walked down the hallway, one hand on the wall, the other instinctively reaching for the assurance of his service revolver on his right hip that was not there. Beads of salty perspiration flowing from his forehead stung his eyes when he stopped in front of apartment 404. He hesitated momentarily, wiped his eye with the swollen knuckle of his right forefinger and then he knocked with a closed fist, "Conrad. Conrad are you home?" He put his ear up to the door to listen for foot falls but there were none. He pulled out his handkerchief and grabbed the doorknob. He didn't want to contaminate any possible evidence. He tried the door but it was locked, so the retired police veteran pulled his cellphone off its holder and dialed 911.

After the customary 911 greeting of, "What's your emergency?"

Harvey explained who he was and said, "I think you better send over some detectives. I believe my next door neighbor is dead."

CHAPTER 38

R on Magers was looking out over the newsroom through the glass wall in his office with his hands in his pockets. The sleeves of his white shirt were rolled halfway up, exposing his black hairy forearms making his gold Rolex sparkle. His red tie with an impeccable half Windsor knot hung loosely around his neck. He was in deep thought waiting for Michaels to arrive.

"Hey Mage. Whatta think?" Michaels asked breaking the solitude of the moment as he entered the room not bothering to knock. He had already filled his friend in on all the developments a half hour earlier.

"That was clever of you to share your findings with your buddy, Warren. I've been thinking about the ethics of it all." Magers said as he walked back to his desk and sat down with a contemplative look adorning his face.

When it comes to ethical confrontations, journalists say, they would never share information with law enforcement but the fact is, it happens all the time whether reporters want to admit it or not. It solidifies trust in sources and ensures the flow of more information. Michaels had some LEO sources (Law Enforcement Officials) with whom, he shared info, but there were others that he wouldn't trust no matter how desperate he became.

"Look, I never bought the idea of a terrorist attack after the second day. Nobody claimed responsibility. No chatter. Nodda." Michaels said with a surprised look. He wasn't thinking about talking ethics, he was more concerned with getting the story on the air. "After reading the court proceedings, I am totally convinced that this Dobonovich character is the 'Bug Man.' We still have some digging to do, but I think we have plenty to run with this."

"Do you have a pic of this guy?" Magers asked sitting down at his desk.

"Not yet. That's another reason I shared my info with Jack. The FBI may be able to get deeper into the records than we ever could."

"How old, you reckon this guy is?" Magers asked leaning forward folding his hands, placing his chin on his fist.

"I suspect around 40. Not sure yet. We are going to the Clerk's office in the morning to pull all the physical records of the case. The summary provided a lot of details like the judge, prosecutor and defense attorney, but not all the witnesses. The doctor that Dobonovich attacked didn't die until after he was institutionalized. That prick only served about 20 percent of his sentence before he got out" Michaels said shaking his head in disbelief. "And he's not been seen since. At least until now."

~~~~

FBI consultant Donna Blake was in high gear after she hung up with detective Jack Warren. She started with a simple Google search and then commandeered an FBI supercomputer. Her search engines were grinding away as she hit command button after command button ... until.

"Holy fuck." She exclaimed to herself as a 1993 St. Ignatius high school graduation picture materialized on her computer's screen. With her mouth wide open and her jaw dropping to her gray metal desktop, she hit her speed dial for Jack Warren.

A broad grin instantly flushed across his face as one of Kenny Chesney's favorite songs, "Get Along" alerted him that fellow FBI agent Donna Blake was calling with what he hoped would be good news. "This is Jack Warren. What's up buddy?"

"You are not going to believe this." The excitement in her voice was infectious and considerably loud.

"Believe what?" Warren answered jumping to his feet like an electrical shock just jolted him to a deeper awareness. "What?"

"I can't believe what this motherfucker, Cyril Dobonovich looked like when he graduated from high school. It's just amazing. I'm in shock." She started punching some keys and said, "I just emailed it to you."

A few seconds later his computer announced the pic had arrived. Even though he had been forewarned, he proclaimed, "Son of a bitch," when he opened it. He stared at the 12-year-old graduate with a royal blue diamond shaped cap that was askew because his wild, frizzy, course black, unmanageable hair would not allow it to settle on his head. His eyes looked distorted because of the thick, black-framed eyeglasses along with bushy eyebrows that seemed to shrink his forehead.

Warren's mind was now racing. He was utterly disturbed. "Oh my God! That looks nothing like our nun or the woman in the gray p-coat. Son of a bitch," he mumbled into the phone as he hit the end button, leaving agent Blake with a dumbfounded look on her face.

~~~~

Detective Tony Quag's star hung around his neck over his red tie. His charcoal grey suit was crisp and stylish and unbuttoned. Most of the police officers in the first district knew him by reputation and stopped doing what they were doing when Sergeant Frank DeBono led him up to the fourth floor. They had known each other for years.

"How are the kids?" Quag asked as they exited the elevator.

"Not kids anymore." DeBono responded.

"Tell me about it, Frank. They grow so fast and then they're gone." Quag was involved in little league with DeBono for years before he got divorced. "What do we have here?"

"Teacher from Byrne Charter was found dead by responding officers. Former Deputy Rodney Harvey called it in. He said it was that old familiar smell of death." DeBono responded as he lifted the yellow crime scene tape and nodded to the officer standing guard at the door.

"Where is he now?" Detective Quag asked as the smell of decaying flesh now premeditated the air. Quag reached into his pocket and retrieved his small jar of Vicks and dabbed it under his nostrils.

"At home, next door. He said to come over anytime you want."

Detective Quag walked up to the body that had an odd color, levity suggested that it had been there for some time. The room seemed warmer than it really was maybe because the odor was so overwhelming.

Crime Tech Gary Landis was kneeling over the body, gently probing the teacher's lips with the eraser of a yellow #2 pencil. He looked up when he heard a familiar voice and offered an ever so slight grin.

"Whatta got, Landis?" Quag inquired.

"My guess ... poison." The CSI man responded making it sound more like a question, but with the conviction that he knew he was right.

"Another one? What the fuck." Quad responded looking down at the corpse dumbfounded folding his arms across his chest then resting his chin in his right hand.

"Yep." The dragged out reply was more of a statement.

"Who is he?"

"Neighbors say he's a schoolteacher. His name is Conrad Corbett."

"How long has he been here."

"Days ... maybe three ... four. Won't know until the ME gets here."

"Is that a wallet in his back pocket?"

"No. It's a cellphone ... battery is probably dead. I'll bag it and you can look at it once, one of Crine's guys releases the body." Landis leaned into the wall for support as he struggled to get to his feet.

Quag bent over as he examined the body and slowly walked around it, not to disturb any trace evidence. There was no blood on the floor. He had booties covering his shoes but he knew the crime scene was from the tip of his head to the front door. Conrad Corbett made it all of ten feet before he collapsed and died once he opened his apartment door.

~~~~

Yang Sung-Choi was sitting next to his mastermind lover on the bed looking up at the TV and the ten o'clock news. They were holding hands and Choi's erection went limp when he saw the graduation picture of his lover when he was 12-years old.

The Fox didn't know if he was angry or dismissive after Peter Michaels identified him as Cyril Dobonovich ... the "Bug Man." He knew no one would come close to recognizing him now. The graduation picture only added to his mystique. His appearance began to change dramatically shortly after he was discharged from the Madison Medical Health Center three years ago. None of the plastic surgeons knew his real name.

"What are you going to do?" Choi asked.

"Kill that cocksucker Peter Michaels," responded Dobonovich. His headache was overwhelming and Choi had him lay down and got him situated. "Please set up the recorder for all the news on Channel Six. I want to know what they know."

"I will do some more surveillance work tomorrow. You rest."

"Yes. I want to show you how to pack the anthrax pathogen. It can be very tricky."

CHAPTER 39

P eter Michaels was walking off the set and back to his office
when his phone rang to a familiar tune automatically bringing a smile to his face. "Jack, I can't thank you enough for
that picture of Dobonovich. Man, what a creepy son of a bitch."

Michaels got the email from Warren 30 seconds before he appeared on the ten o'clock news. The producers miraculously got the
picture into graphics and notified Michaels and Magers through their
earpieces that the pic was up and ready to go. When he saw it for the
first time he was almost left speechless.

"Yeah. D-2 got it. She's good." Warren responded.

Michaels knew D-2 was special agent Donna Blake. She got the
moniker D-2 from his adopted sister that he called "Donna One." The
two Donnas went to high school together. That's one of the things
Michaels loved about Chicago. You always knew somebody, who
knew somebody, who went to school with somebody and somehow
that somebody knew somebody that you knew. Michaels' source
book was filled with hundreds of someones, who knew someone.

"That picture may never help us though because I gotta tell ya
that prick doesn't look like that today." Warren said as his mind pictured the bad guy on videotape as a nun and the woman in the p-
coat.

"Yeah, I know but it's a start."

"Yeah. D-2 will be relentless. Maybe she'll find someone who re-members him when he started changing his appearance. You never know. Maybe we'll get lucky."

"Listen, I'm heading home. I just got a new IPA. Stop by for a beer if you want. I gotta go. I have another call coming in." Michaels hit the green button that accepted the next call and ended the last one. "Yeah. It's Michaels."

"Yeah. Hey Peter. It's Quag."

Michaels grinned. It was not that often that detective Quagliaroli called him this late at night. The happy grin suddenly turned to a look of suspicion, "Yeah, What's up Quagliaroli?"

"Do you know someone by the name of Conrad Corbett?"

Michaels closed his eyes and rubbed his forehead, thinking, *Oh … No.*

"I don't know him but … he called me last Friday after I got off the air and said he may have some information for me relating to the deaths of the judge and Phillips. Why?" Michaels responded taking a deep breath, anticipating a negative answer.

"He's dead."

Michaels felt like someone hit him with a sledgehammer right in the middle of his chest. He stopped … shocked, in disbelief and al-most dropped his phone. "What the fuck."

"Yeah. We just charged his cellphone and it looks like you tried to call eight or nine times." Quag asked rhetorically.

"Yeah. I had no idea what he had but …" Michaels voice dropped off. His eyes filled with wonderment. "How did he die?"

"He was poisoned, we think." Quag didn't realize he was whispering.

This time Michaels did drop his phone. *Son of a bitch … this is getting close to home.*

~~~~

Jacob Cohen the doorman/security guard for 880 South Michigan Avenue perked up when he saw Peter Michaels motorcycle enter the garage on Ninth Street. He grimaced as he tried to straighten up his arthritic crippled body when he stood up from his chair and shuffled over to the elevator. He just noticed that he had an unusual amount of cat hair on his blue blazer uniform jacket. He tried to flick them away but knew it wouldn't change a thing. The residents of 880 didn't care what Cohen looked like, it was what he could do for them that mattered. If someone had a friend visiting for a long weekend, he somehow seemed to find a hidden parking spot in the garage that was always full. He never hinted for money but cash always made its way into his pocket. He knew everything that was going on in the building at all times, like he was clairvoyant.

Michaels grinned when he saw the first floor button illuminated as he entered the elevator. He was greeted by the familiar deep, raspy voice of Jake Cohen as the doors opened.

"How are you tonight, Mr. Michaels?"

"I thought you were off at ten. What are you still doing here?"

"Harold got held up at his other job. Marcia doesn't mind." Marcia was Jake's wife of 51 years. She was the cat lover. All the residents knew of her but never met her. They just heard all the stories of the strays that she either adopted or fostered.

"Jake, I need you to do me a favor. Keep your eyes open for anything strange. I am working on a very weird story. If you notice anything out of the ordinary, I mean anything, let me know, and asked the other security people to do the same."

"Yeah. No problem. I'll pass the word. You okay?"

"Yeah. I'm fine. I just have a gut feeling that something very strange could happen. I don't know why."

Michaels reached in his pocket and pulled out a folded ten-dollar bill and slipped it into Jake's hand, like a magician hiding a card. He pressed the elevator button and heard the door chime announce the doors were about to open.

Jake Cohen suddenly stopped as he put his fob on the keycard to open the front lobby door when he turned, "Something strange happened yesterday as a matter of fact." He said as his voice trailed off and a quizzical look flashed across his face.

Michaels' nerves were now on full alert, "What do you mean strange? How?"

"Some guy comes in and says he had some work to do in one of da units. I said 'we had no information about dat.' This guy gets a little squirrely, you know what I mean … den he says, it's his 'mistake' and den he turns around and leaves." Cohen responded in his typical Chicago dialect.

"What did he look like? Do you remember?" Michaels asked as he started to walk back to Cohen, who was frozen in thought.

"Yeah, sure. He wasn't dat big. Blue work uniform. Real white arms. Almost looked unnatural. You know what I mean?"

"Yeah. Anything else?"

Cohen shut his eyes as he pressed his memory. A painful expression crossed his face and then his eyes suddenly popped open, and he exclaimed, "ABC was on da back of his shirt and den he was gone. He never came back and Mr. Schmidt never knew nuttin about any work on his unit cause I checked wit him today. He said, 'I don't need any work done in my place.'"

"What color was his hair?"

"Don't know. He had a baseball cap on his head."

"Cubs … hat?"

"Nope. Nuttin on it."

"Do you turn on the security cameras during the day?"

"Sometimes. It's up to the morning person. You know nuttin ever happens around here for da most part. Let me check."

"Okay, if you find anything let me know."

~~~~

The soft, relaxing, therapeutic sounds of a sailboat's hull slashing through ocean waves greeted him on his surround sound as he unlocked the door and entered his condo. To Michaels listening to the sea was more than music to his ears and it was more soothing than anything that Chopin or Beethoven could offer for his peace of mind. The sea presented a certain tranquility that allowed him to fall into a deep sleep as it gently filtered the competitive hassles of reporting the news in a city like Chicago. He smiled as he drop his keys into his pocket. He knew he had company.

"This IPA has a stringent bite to it." Jack Warren proclaimed from the grand room.

"It's really good when it is ice cold. Hey … I can't thank you enough for the pic of the ugly bastard."

"I gotta be careful. The boss doesn't like the fact that we know each other so well." Warren said with a smile, tilting his beer bottle towards his friend.

"He'll get over it when I give you some more pictures of that fucker."

"What do you mean. Where did you get pictures of him?"

"I am not sure yet but that fucker was here. I think he was scouting out my building."

"How do you know that?"

"You know Jake, the doorman? He talked to him just yesterday. He was trying to get in here, disguised as a plumber or something."

"You think, he's coming after you?"

"I know he is!"

CHAPTER 40

P roducer David Beedy was at the Cook County Clerk of the
Courts office on the fifth floor of the Criminal Courts building
at 26th and California long before most of the clerks signed in
for the workday. The clerk's office stores all the court's records from
every case that is heard in the courthouse. Tens of thousands of file
folders are colored coded and systematically arranged by dates and
stored on gray metal shelves that reach twelve-feet to the ceilings on
the fourth and fifth floors of the building, occupying 25,000 square
feet of floor space not including the vertical shelves that are only four
feet apart.

One would never guess that the walls of conference room 501
were painted just two months ago because it was like putting lipstick
on a pig in terms of aesthetics. The floors were scarred, scratched and
scuffed from years of foot traffic. Maintenance crews had a hard time
keeping up with the fluorescent ceiling lights. A third of them were
always burned out or flickering within the last seconds of life. Most of
the room's illumination came through a filmy, weather blotched, water stained twenty by ten foot double paned glass window on the east
wall.

The furniture offered no redemption. A five by ten foot conference table that sat in the middle of room was sun bleached and bat-
tered and marred from years of abuse by attorneys, reporters and

interested parties seeking information from the court case files just outside the door.

Beedy was sitting in one of nine nonmatching wooden chairs, fidgeting with his cellphone and drinking his now lukewarm black coffee waiting for the case transcripts of "The State of Illinois vs. Cyril Dobonovich."

When his phone vibrated, he got up and walked over to the window and peaked out through the broken venetian blinds that were meant to help filter out any harsh light but they were so bent, twisted and totally unworkable, they couldn't preform the duty for which they were designed. "Hey, what you got?"

"I'm at my condo building, meeting with the secretary to see if we have any video of Dobonovich's visit. Like I told you last night, he was here. I think he's coming after me." Peter Michaels said as if it were no big deal that someone was trying to kill him.

"Doesn't that bother you?" Beedy asked incredulously with a "dah" look on his face.

"Hey … it's happened before. Remember the drug dealers and those other assholes."

"Yeah … but this is different. This fucking guy is absolutely crazy."

"I know. I'll be very vigilant … believe me." Michaels said casually.

Beedy shaking his head said, "Hey I gotta go. I just got the file. I'll call you later." He clicked off and picked up the voluminous file and got to work immediately.

~~~~

The security monitors were set up in an anteroom north of the lobby. Latisha Reynolds, the morning person, was checking the security camera that covered the main entrance. It was live and recording.

"Was it working on Monday at around four o'clock?" Michaels asked.

Latisha was a robust woman with shiny black hair that looked like it could withstand a 30-mile an hour wind. Her long eyelashes were glued onto her eyelids that were colored with different shades of purple eye shadow. Her fingernails were naturally an inch and half long and were beginning to curl at their tips. They were fortified with an acrylic polish for strength and painted fire engine red with bright sprinkles of make believe diamonds.

"Mr. Peter. I believe we do have it right here." Latisha proudly proclaimed. "Let me see here, if I can isolate that exact time period for y'all."

The hair on Michaels' arms stood up. A chill shivered down his spine as he sidestepped behind Latisha leaving her room to work the keyboard. It was amazing to watch her fingertips gently touch the control buttons with the right amount of pressure that produced a light clicking sound but did not allowed any damage to her nail polish.

"There!" Michaels said. "That's got to be him."

The video was a black and white wide shot that was grainy but plain enough to put Cyril Dobonovich in the lobby of 880 South Michigan Avenue. Michaels concentrated first on his face. The focus was very soft revealing no distinguishing features, and when he turned around to walk away the ABC letters embroidered on his back were discernible but blurry, however, it offered little doubt that Dobonovich was there, and the picture clearly offered investigators another mistake made by the "Bug Man."

"Gotcha you little prick." Michaels smiled. "How long is it?"

"Hum ... let me see here." Latisha said and clicked the rewind button with her long forefinger nail. When the tape got to first frame of Dobonovich entering the lobby through the revolving door, Latisha hit the timer button. Jacob Cohen stood in front of him at the front lobby door blocking his entrance to the elevators. The verbal exchange lasted less than 30 seconds. Dobonovich looked at his cell-phone presumably his calendar and without argument ended the conversation and turned to exit the building.

"We got one minute and thirteen seconds." Latisha said with great satisfaction.

"Latisha you are a blessing." Michaels said then he turned to the condo office secretary, "Ms. Langley, I need this tape. It could be evidence in a number of murders."

Stunned that anything that important could have happened in her workplace Denise Langley said, "Mr. Michaels, you can have anything you need, but I have to ask; Are we in danger here? My God this is awful."

"I don't think so but I will tell you. Everybody in this building needs to know what's going on and no strangers should be allowed in this building at any time unless they are verified until this thing is over." Michaels said emphatically.

Latisha handed Michaels the tape and said. "I needs some coffee and a muffin."

Michaels handed her a ten and said, "I'll buy." With that he took out his cellphone and hit speed dial for Special Agent Jack Warren.

"You got it?"

"Yep. Listen, I am going to take this to the station and makes some copies. I suspect you need the original."

"Yeah. That'd be great. I'll get the tape in the hands of D-2. Hopefully she can work some magic with it."

"Come by the station and I'll get you what you need."

CHAPTER 41

C hicago's Museum Campus is brilliantly spaced along Lake Michigan's shoreline, occupying some of the most expensive lakefront property in the world. This cultural campus offers millions of visitors each year, three of the city's most outstanding institutions of knowledge, unique pleasures and pure enjoyment. The Shedd Aquarium houses 32,000 aquatic animals. Some of which you can interact with and actually touch. Maximo, the Titanosaur, the largest dinosaur to ever walk the face of the earth, greets visitors to Field Museum of Natural History. The Adler Planetarium has a state-of-the-art theatre that gives future astronauts and astrologers an exciting place to visit swirling galaxies, mysterious planets and the most brilliant stars that shine in space.

Tens of thousands of people walk daily on the cement pathways that weave and twist through the Museum Campus. These sidewalks essentially start further north at Buckingham Fountain and parallel the lakefront offering breath-taking views of sailboats and power yachts moored in picturesque Monroe Harbor. Some of these pathways widen to 20 feet as they lead to another one of city's most recognized institutions ... Soldier Field, where the Chicago Bears play all their home football games.

Yang Sung Choi looked like any other tourist walking through the hustle and bustle of the museum campus on this very hot summer morning. His nondescript blue baseball cap revealed very little of the sweat that was running down his back. His white opened collared linen shirt fell loosely over his tight sinewy body; however, steam was forming on the lenses of his Maui Jim wraparound sunglasses. He was systematically counting the number of trashcans that lined the pathways that will be used by the rabid Chicago Bears and Green Bay Packer fans who wear obnoxious giant size pieces of cheese headgear and paint their bodies in their team's uniform colors to prove how loyal they are.

Sick Fucks, he thought as he counted each specific location along the route to determine how many bombs he would need to build for the maximum amount of exposure and offered the least of amount of detection. It is seven tenths of a mile from the back of the Field Museum to the first entrance gates of Soldier Field: approximately 50 trashcans, 25 on each pathway. *No problem.*

Heavy autumn air generally meant cooler nights; it was the winds that were completely unpredictable. September winds offered sailors the most challenging and thrilling conditions on Lake Michigan before they put their boats into winter storage. No one, not even Tim Skelly, Chicago's most famous weatherman can predict the atmospheric conditions weeks out from the opening day of this year's football season. *Fifty toxic bombs should be enough to offset any winds nature presented that fall night.* Choi thought smiling devilishly.

~~~~

Dr. James McBride's long curly gray hair looked like it hadn't been cut in months. It crept four inches below the collar of his white lab coat when he peered through his powerful microscope. His shoulders were hunched forward as he focused on the slide containing the poison that killed the victim, the JTTF identified as Wayne Phillips. The glow in his brown eyes matched the smile that crossed his lips as another signature poison from Cyril Dobonovich appeared on his spectroscope.

"Paradomaxia Orthogenics ... something," He declared loudly causing his young lab partner to jump up from his workstation.

"What do you mean ... something?" The young lab assistant asked in a sardonic tone, rushing over to his mentor's side.

Dr. McBride pushed his glasses closer to the microscope's eye-piece as if the extra effort would increase the size of the specimen and the diffracted image on the focal plane. "It's Paradomaxia Orthogenics and its been enhanced and that's his signature." He announced in a cadence tone and then he stated affirmatively. "There is absolutely, no doubt about it."

Michael Kearney, the lab assistant, became academically involved immediately and combed his long blonde hair with the fingers of his left hand across his forehead to his right ear, an old habit he acquired in graduate school. "Why would anyone have to enhance that pathogen? It is one of the deadliest poisons known to mankind." Kearney asked curiously.

"That's just it. He didn't want it to kill immediately. He mutated it so it took more time to take its full deadly affect. The bastard doesn't want his victims to die right away. He wants them all to suffer. He wants them all to know," he suddenly stopped talking, his voice grew softer almost to a whisper. "He wants them to know they are about to die."

Dr. McBride stood up. Almost paralyzed in deep thought as his right hand went to his chin and his left grasped his right rib cage. His thirty seconds of silence was broken as he ordered Kearney to look into high-powered microscope. "Can you identify his evil signature?"

Kearney pressed his eyes into the lens and turned the focusing knobs to his satisfaction and looked up at the spectrometer monitor. "Is that what you are talking about?"

The mutation on the screen looked like a Rorschach Test that was undeniably similar to all the other poisons' mutations that were already related to Cyril Dobonovich.

~~~~

The Fox was steaming as he squirmed in the seat of his new rental car focusing on the house of Dr. Louis Yako. He never returned home from his favorite restaurant, LaNotte Italiano on Marion Street last Saturday afternoon. After he followed the old man into Oak Park, and then returned to the yellow house on Ridgeland, and prepared two kill zones. The first was the garage door handle just in case the automatic door opener didn't work. He then picked the side door lock and smothered the inner doorknob that led into the house with Balamuthia Mandrillaris. He wanted to kill Dr. Yako with the same poison, Oxymodorin Protivea, that led to his argument and the bludgeoning of Dr. Helen Lesenski on Halloween day on 2006 but he changed his mind to Balamuthia Mandrillaris because he wanted him to really suffer. *That fucking Dr. Yako did everything he could to get me life in prison instead of Madison. Fuck him.*

Cyril Dobonovich never stopped to realize that if Dr. Lesenski died instead of remaining in a coma at the time he was committed to the Madison Mental Health Center, he might still be institutionalized or in prison for the rest of his life.

He obsessed constantly about Dr. Yako's brilliant testimony that led to his demise. He hated to recognize another man's intellect. His narcissism would not allow him to acknowledge an intellect that matched his or that was superior to his.

The migraine headache was derisively relentless as he pounded on the steering wheel as if that action would relieve his pain and frustration. He feed two more 10mg Hydrocodone/Acetaminophen pills into his mouth and chewed them. The eighth of the day and it was just noon. He threw his empty water bottle at the passenger side window. The pressure in his head was not relenting to the effects of the opiate drugs.

Dobonovich made up his mind that if he had any time left he would research Yako's family tree and kill someone related to him. His hatred was erupting with an internal volcanic force when he realized the good doctor had escaped his grip by one week. He should have made him his first kill instead of the orange haired lady whom everyone seem to like and then he thought. *I will kill that fucking Peter Michaels with Balamuthia Mandrillaris.*

CHAPTER 42

D r. Louis Yako not only loved LaNotte's because the food was superb, but because he was always treated like family whenever he went there. He ate his favorite meals, sitting in his favorite spot at a small private linen covered table in the kitchen, next to the hot ovens and boiling pots of pasta water, talking with his friend, the owner Jimmy Naccarodo.

The pasta fagioli was to die for because of the unorthodox way it was prepared. It started with a base of sautéed onions and hot Italian sausage. All of the ingredients were added separately and cooked slowly over low heat for various periods of time. It was never rushed. It took at least five and half-hours to bring this mouthwatering recipe to the table. The main course was orgasmic. The good doctor would often dream about the garlic butter, the creamy asparagus and mushroom sauce with the pappardelle noodles for days on end after he consumed it.

Besides what he ate that beautiful sunny Saturday afternoon, along with his leftovers; he ordered four other meals to go, all with lots of garlic. He decided late that morning to spend the rest of the summer at his home on Grand Traverse Bay in Michigan. It was very unlike him to make any impromptu decisions ... three years ago on this day, his beloved wife Beatrice died a horrible death of cancer. He wanted seclusion and isolation.

He was tired and he had no pending trials because currently there were no cases that excited him enough to put out the exhausting effort to convince a jury of twelve that someone was criminally insane.

He was ready for some solitude and some peace, but most of all quiet, except for the lovely, soft, passive sounds of nature, and he knew that in just six hours he would have it. For forty years, he and Beatrice drove to the mission peninsula, at the 45th parallel, where the Grand Travers Bay was divided into east and west. The spectacular views from his home offered the most glorious sunsets imaginable and served as a reminder of how fortunate he was to be enjoying heaven on earth.

Dr. Louis Yako had absolutely no idea that Cyril Dobonovich, the insane microbiologist, he hadn't thought about in more than a decade, was currently at his house in Oak Park, smothering his door knob with Balamuthia Mandrillaris, a very rare poison that would painfully eat away at his brain for more than two hours before death would gratefully end his misery.

~~~~

Peter Michaels was perusing the case files his producer David Beedy Xeroxed from the trial transcripts of Cyril Dobonovich. His theory was that the mad scientist was killing everyone who had anything to do with his trial and his commitment to the Madison Mental Health Center, but now he was shaking his head.

"You know, if the O.J. Simpson trial were held in the Cook County Criminal Courts, it would have been over in two weeks not the months it took in California."

"Yeah, but there certainly would have still been a lot of courtroom theatrics and drama with the cast of characters involved don't you think?" Beedy responded. "And what about those comedic parodies of the 'Dancing Itos' on the Tonight Show?"

"That bullshit would have never happened in Chicago because murder trials here are adjudicated quickly. The 'Bug Man's' lasted only seventeen hours over a three day period."

"Yeah, but that asshole waived his right to a jury making Judge Harold Wolfe the sole arbitrator of his fate."

"He was charged with aggravated assault and the attempted murder of Dr. Helen Lesenski. The prosecutor only presented five witnesses; the first responding police officer, who by the way I dated."

"You dated Diane Lanning?"

"Yeah for over a year. She was hot." Michaels said looking up at the ceiling, smiling as memories flashed back, and then he abruptly stood up and refocused. "We should try to find this Decker, the EMT who treated Dr. Lesenski at the scene. And the ER doc, the neurosurgeon and this psychiatrist Dr. Louis Yako."

"Man, I bet this Conrad Corbett, the only witness to the crime would have been great to talk with … don't cha think?" Beedy interrupted.

"Poor bastard. I'm waiting to hear what kind of poison that sick son of a bitch used on him." Michaels said as he paced around his desk and continued, "You know, no one knows where this Dr. Louis Yako is."

"I hope he's still alive." Beedy interpolated.

"Me too. I've asked Warren if he can find him. But anyway … my original theory was that Dobonovich was going to kill everyone that had anything to do with his trial, but so far nothing has happened to the first responding officer, the EMT and all the doctors." Michaels said perplexed.

"That doesn't change our theory. Look, these doctors … they never interacted with Dobonovich. They just presented their medical findings. Now, on the other hand, I would worry about Diane. She shot at the son of a bitch. That's what made him drop the microscope according to the court record. She also tasered him."

"Her police report and testimony were very damaging. She said when she cuffed him he was mumbling gibberish and he made no sense at all."

"Yeah. Well to bad she didn't hit him. We wouldn't be investigating the deaths of what ... 32 ... 33 people?"

"I talked to Quag about Diane. He said they took her off active street duty at the time but now she's retired." Michaels said as he reached for his phone. "I still have her number after all these years."

~~~~

"Your buddy Michaels is lucky to be alive." Special Agent Donna Blake said looking away from the video monitor.

"What are you talking about?" Agent Jack Warren said.

"This is the same fucking guy. This is Cyril Dobonovich." Blake said pressing the right button on her computer mouse trying to magnify the image on the grainy videotape that Peter Michaels gave to the FBI. "This guy who came to Peter's condo. There is no doubt in my mind that he was there to kill Michaels." She stated empathically.

"Are you positive? You can hardly see his face."

"He's got the walk. I can spot it now. I don't care how fuzzy the picture is. That's him. I guarantee you that he is carrying some lethal agent in that toolbox."

"Thank God for Jake, the doorman."

CHAPTER 43

T he drive to Traverse City took a little over seven hours with road construction projects causing minor traffic jams, but Dr. Louis Yako loved every second of every mile. It was a ride he'd taken for 40 years usually with joyful expectations, but this particular ride was filled with mixed emotions, melancholic tears interrupted by burst of joyful laughter, familiar sights and exits along the road triggered memories of the love of his life. Louis Yako loved his solitude, but for the last two years he didn't like the loneliness of the spectacular sunsets without his Beatrice by his side sharing a glass of their favorite Latour Puligay-Montrachet Chardonnay.

Harold Hunter, Junior, a local handyman, had Yako's wooden welcoming sign in place at the foot of the steps leading up to his magnificent summer home. The hand carved sign displayed trees and a sailboat floating on ripples of blue water; it served as an announcement to neighbors that Dr. Yako was back in town.

Decades ago, when he first bought the getaway on East Grand Traverse Bay, it was a simple one-bedroom ranch style home on a dead end private road, surrounded by gorgeous white birch trees that had been there forever. It had a perfectly groomed and manageable Kentucky blue grass lawn that was accentuated by flowerbeds bestowing every color in the rainbow. Over the years, four more bedrooms with wall-sized windows allowing in natural light were added along with three very modern bathrooms. Every room, particularly the kitchen with its surrounding weatherized picture windows, presented breath-taking views of Lake Michigan, Grand Traverse Bay and of course the grand natural forests of the Old Mission Peninsula.

Dr. Yako stopped in Elk Rapids, the nearest town, 6.7 miles from his refuge, for fresh groceries and other supplies he would need for his stay, and naturally, he ordered his daily Chicago newspapers that he would collect every three days. Reading the paper while drinking two or three cups of black robust coffee on his cedar deck that wrapped around the main floor was the one morning pleasure that he allowed himself. He needed to know what was happening with his Chicago Bears even if the news was old news by the time he read it.

Not many people from the city knew about his sanctuary away from his busy schedule in Chicago because he ordered his very expensive lawyers to tie up his holdings in so many blind trust that even the FBI would have trouble finding him.

Darkness began to envelope his view as the sun disappeared into the leaves of the birch trees that frame the horizon behind the Leelanau Peninsula. The outside LED lights however still produced enough illumination for him to see his 23-foot Hurricane Fun Deck that was tied to the last of the seven sections of dock extending into the water offering him yet another avenue of peace and quiet. He smiled as he buttoned up his pajama top and lumbered into his bedroom and slid between his clean, fresh sheets. He drifted into a deep sleep with a slight tinge of Macallan 15 Scotch tickling his tongue and the back of his throat.

Dr. Louis Yako had no idea the Chicago Police, the FBI and Peter Michaels that vexatious investigative reporter were frantically searching for him in order to warn him that his life was in extreme danger from a mad man he tried to get sentenced to prison and not committed to a mental institution more than ten years ago.

~~~~

Peter Michaels was staring at the ceiling, mesmerized by the dust particles that were illuminated by the sun's rays as if they were floating in air seemingly defying gravity. He was lost in thought, slowing his breathing, wondering if those specks could infect his lungs, when his phone chimed to the obnoxious soundtrack of "The Lone Ranger" startling him back to reality.

"News … Michaels." He said as he touched his heart thinking it was about to jump out of his chest.

"Mr. Michaels. This professor James McKenzie. I saw your report on Cyril Dobonovich the other night and debated whether or not I should call you. I taught that crazy son of a bitch at Loyola University years ago. I thought he was nuts then, and now I am convinced he is."

Michaels took a deep breath, grabbed his notebook, "Tell me everything you can remember about him." His hands were literally shaking realizing that he was talking to someone who actually knew the "Bug Man."

"He was a student, who thought he knew more than every professor at the university. I gave him a B+ on a paper and he went crazy. He may have been the smartest student I have ever taught. He had an amazing mind, but as a teenager he thought he was infallible." Professor McKenzie, closed his eyes, thinking as he continued to outline Dobonovich's behavior, "He was very antisocial, perhaps because of his weird appearance. I don't know. Other students just gawked at him. He was very withdrawn."

Michaels inhaled deeply, "What was the reason he was so pissed off?" Michaels asked and then felt a little embarrassed by the way he phrased his question.

"It was about Kuru."

"Kuru?"

"Yes that's the short name for Creurtzfelt-Jakob disease. It's a brain-eating microorganism that can take years and years to work its way through your system and kill you, and there is no known cure for it. He was obsessed with it for some strange reason."

"So, he was angry? Did he threaten you at any time?"

"He was very angry with his grade. He had an outrageous ego, but I didn't think he was capable of hurting anyone until he came to visit me after he finished his studies abroad."

"He came back to Loyola and threatened you? When was that?"

"I think it was before he killed that woman."

Michaels was almost speechless, his mind racing, "That happened in 2005 or 2006?"

"Yes ... but when I saw your report that was really the first time, I heard he killed someone."

"Technically when he went to trial, the victim, a doctor Lesenski hadn't died yet. She was in a coma for almost ten years, I think. Anyway, how did he threaten you?"

"He barged into my office like a raving mad man, screaming at the top of his lungs, spittle was spewing from his mouth as he yelled at me. He said, I was 'going to suffer' and I told him to get the hell out before I called security."

"What did he mean you were going to suffer?"

"I really don't know but he stormed out of my office and slammed the door. I was very upset, to say the least. I thought I was going to have a heart attack. I reached for my coffee cup and went to take a drink but my hand was trembling so badly I put it down. Then I took an alprazolam to calm my nerves."

"Is it Doctor McKenzie?"

"Yes. I have PhDs in Biology and Natural Sciences but I am retired now. I live up in Lake Geneva in the summer."

"Will you do an interview and tell your story?"

"When do you want to do it?"

"Right now. I can leave right now." Michaels said but in the back of his mind he was wondering if there were any videographers available.

"I tell you what. I need to pick up some things. Let's meet at my house in Wilmette."

Michaels got the address and said, "See you in a few." He looked over at his producer and said. "Shit, I hope I can get a shooter. This is going to make a great piece for the Ten."

~~~~

Crime scene investigator Gary Landis was scrapping the knob of the yellow house's entrance door inside of the garage at the home of Dr. Louis Yako in Oak Park. His glasses were fogging up and sliding down his nose as sweat drizzled down his forehead, his knees ached from kneeling so long on the cool cement stoop, and the scowl on his face was one of determination, not irritation. His years of experience told him, if there was any trace evidence left on this area, there was only one way to get it, apply his skills and work through the pain.

The particles he gathered were visible on the edge of his sharp knife but as he brushed them into his clear plastic evidence bag they appeared to be invisible to the human eye as he sealed and labeled his findings. He then reached for an alcohol swab but changed his mind and took a dry sterile black cloth to wipe the doorknob. As an afterthought, he then swabbed the knob with an alcohol patch completely obliterating any trace evidence left on the door, but hopefully it would be engrained into the gauze pad.

He was not concerned about poisoning himself, he knew the viral microorganism was no longer potent as an infectious agent, he just hoped there was enough DNA and/or RNA intact so the scientists at Fort Detrick could determine what type of poison it was and how lethal it could have been.

RNA is the chromosomal cousin of DNA. Ribonucleic acid is present in every living cell. It primarily acts as a messenger to carry instructions from DNA for controlling the synthesis of proteins, although in some viruses it's the RNA rather than DNA that carries the genetic information. If there was a microscopic dot of the poison undamaged in any one of the three evidence bags, the scientists would be able to identify it.

Landis had no idea if there was any poison present. He was ordered to gather the samples by the Chief of Detectives because detective Tony Quag thought that the owner, some hotshot psychiatrist, was on the kill list of this "Bug Man."

CHAPTER 44

D r. Robert Crine was leaning back in his chair with his head cradle in his interlaced fingers, looking up at the ceiling, lost in deep thought. The guacamole that came with his Mexican lunch reminded him of the times he was slapped across the side of his head as a kid because he never finished his peas at dinner. The smirk on his face eased when his phone rang and brought him back into the moment. "Yeah ... this is Crine."

"Hey Doc, this is Dr. McBride at Detrick, you were right, the poison that killed judge Wolfe was made by the same person but it was different than the poison that killed Mr. Phillips."

"Thought so, don't know why. It just seem to have a different hue. What was it?"

"Pardomaxia Orthogenics ... it's a very rare microorganism that invades the nervous system and eventually shuts down all your organs. It is a very painful way to die. Judge Wolfe on the other hand was killed with Oxymodrin Protivea. His death was also very painful."

"And you're sure they were made by the 'Bug Man?' You know the same guy?" Dr. Crine said looking for reassurance.

"Yep. Positive. No doubt. He uses an agent that mutates some cells. It is the same fingerprint. 'Bug Man', how did he get that name?"

"I don't know if you've heard of this investigative reporter we got here in Chicago, Peter Michaels? He has been all over this story and he identified him as Cyril Dobonovich and gave him the name, 'Bug Man.'"

"You better warn that Michaels guy to be careful. This guy is crazy. He might be going after him." Dr. McBride cautioned.

"Oh … He has. From what the cops tell me, they already got pictures of the him in the lobby of Michaels building."

"No shit! This gets crazier and crazier every day." McBride said shaking his head.

"Did you get the stuff from the Corbett case?"

"Yes. I just got it within the hour. I should have some answers soon. Hopefully by the end of the day and I guess I have another batch coming in from some psychiatrist."

"Yeah … Dr. Yako. We can't find him. We have been looking for him. We don't know if he's dead somewhere or not." Dr. Crine related with a grim expression.

~~~~

Michaels was grinning from ear to ear as he dialed the number he still had for Diane Lanning. He was thinking about the time he took her to the opera on opening night years ago. She was dressed in a low cut, tight fitting silver glittery dress that accentuated every curve of her five foot four inch sculpted body. When she walked it sparkled, every person in the opera house noticed her movements. Her light brown hair with blonde highlights was in a tight braid, giving her an aristocratic look. Her high cheekbones and deep blue eyes added to her mystic that night.

"Hi honey." Lanning said answering the phone with her ever exciting, fun loving voice. Lanning called everyone "honey".

"Hey Diane. I was just thinking about you. I'm sure you have this macho attitude because you were the police and all that, but this prick Dobonovich may still have some revenge in mind for you and … I am concerned about you. This guy is nuts."

"Yeah … Tony Quag already talked to me. I've been retired for a couple of years. Do you really think this guy can find me?"

"From what I am learning he's got a boatload of money. He definitely has the resources to do anything he wants, so just be careful."

"What should I do, grab every door handle with a dishrag or something?"

"You know, that's not a bad idea. Be vigilant and be careful. Please. This guy is scary."

Lanning hung up the phone, went to her kitchen and starting wiping down all the handles and cabinet knobs with a Lysol wipe and then took out a dishtowel and put it next to her purse and keys.

~~~~

Peter Michaels heard the "Swoosh" sound on his cellphone while talking to Diane Lanning alerting him to an incoming text. "Call me ASAP"

Michaels dialed Jack Warren.

"Hey, I've been trying to reach you. We got the lab results back from Phillips and Wolfe."

"And?"

"Two different poisons … same signature. It was Dobonovich without a doubt."

"What are they?"

"I'll email them to you. You know how much trouble you have pronouncing these compounds."

"He enhanced them didn't he?"

"Oh, yeah. They both died very painful deaths. That sick bastard."

"This guy has disappeared from the face of the earth."

"We have our guys from Quantico trying to use that high school picture to come up with a bunch of different identities from the three videotapes we have of him."

"Is Donna-2 working that?"

"She is absolutely obsessed with this case. I don't know if she is even sleeping. I'm getting text from her day and night. It was her idea about the facial recognition stuff to see if they could project some identities."

"Can they really get a positive type of picture from that old high school photo? It's not very clear." Michaels inquired.

"It is an amazing what these apps can do. They can manipulate all sorts of features. Big nose. Small nose. Cheek bones. Foreheads. Just amazing."

"I can't wait to see that projection."

"D-2 will work on it, day and night."

"I'd hate to get on her bad side."

"Hey … you be careful. Don't let our guard down."

"Tony Quag gave me some cloth stuff to wipe my door handle when I go home. If I notice anything he wants me call him right away."

"You know that fucker is crazy, so be vigilant."

"Don't worry. I am not going to let him get me," he warned again.

~~~~

Videographer Paul Nagaro had his camera set up in the house office of Dr. James McKenzie. Nagaro was fanatical about lighting his subjects if he had the time to do it right. Generally, news pieces were always shot on the fly and a single light mounted on top of the camera was the only source of usually washed out light, so this was an opportunity to create a very dramatic affect.

Peter Michaels was ten minutes behind schedule and traffic on the Lake Shore Drive was typical for late afternoon particularly with threatening skies. A light drizzle made everyone touch their brakes too many times on the drive out to Wilmette in Chicago's northern suburbs.

Dr. James McKenzie looked exactly as Michaels pictured him. He smiled broadly as they shook hands for the first time. McKenzie wore a navy blue blazer with a blue oxford shirt and a yellow bow tie. He had a rack on his desk filled with crusty old pipes with evidence of years of use, their bowls only half their original size, caked with thousands of loads of tobacco, making every drag memorable.

His long, white, wavy hair was combed back and over his ears, neatly trimmed. His gold wire rimmed glasses sat perfectly on his nose, not distracting from his hazel eyes. His forehead was tanned and lined and the crows-feet around his eyes announced a lot of time in the sun. His callous fingers presented evidence that he tied a lot of flies for his fishing rods.

"I have not done a TV interview in a long time. I hope I don't mess up too badly."

"Don't worry. If you screw up or feel uncomfortable we can stop and start over. This is not like a hardcore investigative target interview." Michaels assured him and thought *I just hope you are half as good on camera as you were on the phone.*

Nagaro announced they were rolling and the interview went flawlessly. Dr. McKenzie's facial expressions were made more dramatic by the lighting as he recalled his student Cyril Dobonovich threatening his life so many years ago. An actor could not have done a better job but the reality of his fear was captured on every frame, and every viewer would recognize his genuine terror.

When the interview was over, Michaels called his partner, "Dave, go asked the show producer for five minutes on the ten. This interview was unbelievable and it's going to rock Chicago."

~~~~

The Fox was watching the early Channel Six news, debating if he should make another attempt to get into Peter Michaels condo building and place Balamuthia Mandrillaris on his doorknob. The overcast gray storm clouds cloaked the late afternoon's daylight and increased the killer's opportunity to hide in plain sight.

He intensified his production of the anthrax and ricin compound over the last two weeks. He had killed everyone he wanted too so far except for that Dr. Louis Yako, who had somehow disappeared and Michaels. He decided months ago not to kill that bitch cop. He did not want to gamble on the death of a Chicago police officer to interfere with his other goals.

Choi was out shopping for materials that he would use for the bombs, and his headache was not yet throbbing, so he decided why not give it another try. He dressed in dark gray cargo pants and long sleeve black tee shirt. He decided to carry the poison and talc in his fanny pack.

He walked three blocks to the west and called an UBER that dropped him off at the Hilton Hotel three blocks north of Michaels' building. The charge was on a fake credit card that would be eliminated after he used it the one time. If an opportunity arose to enter the building, he would take advantage of it, but he would not linger in the area for more than 30 minutes.

As soon as he turned onto ninth street, he heard the garage door of 880 South Michigan Avenue going up. He smiled and slithered into the shadow of the ramp against the wall like a snake sneaking under a door without any weather protection. As he melted into the darkness, he looked around for a security camera. There wasn't one, so he slinked further up the ramp looking for the stairwell. He moved like a fox, silently and quickly hoping that no one would enter or exit the garage.

By the time he got to the tenth floor, he was perspiring and his head began to throb. He pulled his black baseball cap down camouflaging his face and walked down the hallway as if he was a tenant. He felt the excitement of the mission as he approached Michaels' unit. His hands were already covered with latex gloves. His fingers slowing opened the zipper of his pouch. He premixed the poison with the talc that formed the adhesive for the poison to grip the metal. He opened the sealed container, dipped his small brush into the lethal combination and generously applied it to Michaels' doorknob. It just took a matter of seconds. When he was finished he heard someone taking in the hallway and said, "Thank you, Mr. Michaels, just call if you want me to come back for another treatment."

He quickly turned in the opposite direction to exit the building. The couple walking behind him would only to see his back if they saw him at all.

The poison would remain fatally active for three hours. It was 6:30. A vindictive grin expressed itself; he was confident of success this time. He watched Channel Six all-day and there were no announcements that Peter Michaels had a story on the late news.

He will be dead if he comes home during the next three hours.

CHAPTER 45

T rue Value Hardware boxes and bags were strewn all over the dining room floor of Yang Sung Choi's basement apartment from all the materials he ordered to build his remote controlled bombs. He was experimenting with a number of systems to disperse the deadly anthrax-ricin mixture that was still maturing in Dobonovich's bio-safe containment lab. Choi was intrigued with the butane gas cylinders used for cigar lighters. Their tubular cartridge fit perfectly into the PVC piping that would hold the deadly concoction and the butane gas created enough energy to propel lethal doses of the poison into the atmosphere without producing any excessive noise that would draw attention to the device itself.

Choi went into the house to use the soundproof portion of the BSL to experiment with the exact amount of the explosive materials he needed for the detonators to ignite his pipe bombs. He was investigating a putty like substance with the perfect amount of a C-4 type of mixture capable of blasting off the cap but small enough to kindle the butane gas without exploding the bomb into a small cloud that would defeat the spread of the poison into the night air.

He purchased the military grade explosives from another patient who was released from the Madison Mental Health Center two weeks after he was. His friend just happened to be an explosive expert in the

United States Army before he was dishonorably discharged for psychological reasons.

Choi thought a disposal cellphone, set on the same FM frequency, would work best to trigger the 50 pipe bombs for a simultaneous release. His biggest problem though was developing a light weight, waterproof material that could not only seal 16 ounces of the fatal pathogen into each pipe but would also disintegrate instantly once ignition occurred allowing the light powdery poison to diffuse freely in the kill zone.

~~~~

Peter Michaels could hardly contain the grin on his face as he tried to explain to Ron Magers, the believability of Professor James McKenzie on camera. "He was extremely afraid of this Dobonovich. He was literally shaking when he describe the encounter from years ago. He still doesn't know what Dobonovich meant about killing him or hurting him though."

Michaels infectious grin made Magers smile as well. He loved to see reporters enthusiastic about their stories. "It seems to me, he dodged a fatal bullet of some kind," Magers said. "You sure this can sustain five minutes on the ten?"

"Mage, this guy knew that crazy bastard. It's the first person that has actually meet the 'Bug Man' and is still alive to talk about it. I know sound bites should be short but when you listen to this guy describe him, I guarantee you … You will be mesmerized."

"I hope you're right. Let's go do this thing." Magers said leading the way into the studio.

~~~~

"Fuck. Fuck. Fuck. How did that bastard escape my poison?" Screamed The Fox after he watched Peter Michaels on the ten o'clock news, interviewing Professor James McKenzie. He grabbed his head in both hands knowing that his headache would become very painful shortly. "He should be a shriveled up old man confined to a wheelchair or be dead."

"What are you talking about?" Choi asked touching his partner's forearm trying to console him.

"I put chancroid bacteria in his coffee cup over ten years ago, his balls should have rotted away." Dobonovich seethed as he reached for the oxycodone, 20 mg pills.

"You never told me about that. Who is he?"

"He's that bastard that gave me my only bad grade in college. I told you about him, but maybe I didn't tell you what I did."

"Maybe you scared him too much."

"Probably." Moments passed as he rubbed his temples with his fingers. "I fucked up with that Michaels too. The Balamuthia Mandrillaris will be useless, now. It's been on too long. It will now have no effect on him whatsoever." Dobonovich got off the bed and picked up the glass of water he just drank from for his oxy and threw it directly at his TV creating a giant spider web of cracked glass across the screen. "I will kill that fucking Michaels; I swear to God!"

~~~~

The phones were ringing off the hook when Michaels walked off the set. "Hey Peter, line one … some woman named … Van Hee." Victor Press yelled from the assignment desk.

"Hey Mrs. Van Hee. How are you?"

"Peter, I am fine. Please call me Gertrude."

"I couldn't do that Mrs. Van Hee. My mother would turn over in her grave. Is everything alright?"

"Oh yes. I still can't believe Mr. Jenkins is gone. I have been meaning to call you but I thought what I had to say might be too much speculation but after I saw your interview with that professor, I am going to throw caution to the wind."

"What do you mean?" Michaels asked, a bewildered look shadowing his face.

"I don't know if you knew it or not, but when Mr. Jenkins was on the floor dying, he was trying to say something to me."

"I vaguely remember something like that, but wasn't it gibberish?"

"At the time, I thought so but after seeing all of your reports, I no longer think so."

"What do you think now?" Michaels asked as he walked over to a quieter part of the room, putting his left forefinger in his ear to block out the noise of the busy newsroom.

"I don't think. I am now positive that Mr. Jenkins was telling me who killed him."

Beads of sweat began to form on Michaels' forehead along with a concerned look. "Are you absolutely sure?"

"He figured it out. I am sure of it. It was the nun. She did something, I don't know what, but something happened and it changed him. When I was holding him in my arms, he said at first what I thought was 'It was the mad sea.' I was so confused and distressed at that time. I had no idea what he was saying, but I think he was trying to tell me, 'It was the mad scientist.' He just didn't get it out before he died. Mr. Michaels, It was that Dr. Cyril Dobonovich."

"How can you be so sure?"

"I knew that man better than I know my own husband. I was his secretary for over 25 years and for more than half that time I was with him 14 to16 hours a day. He figured it out. Somehow. I don't know how, but he did."

"You should think about it some more. Would you consider doing an interview with me for television? I think this will add more to the story, but for sure you need to talk to the police. Is it okay if I give your number to Jack Warren?"

"Let me think about all this. Here is my home number ... call me, sometime tomorrow. I will talk to the police. I am not so sure about doing a television interview. I have never done one before. Mr. Jenkins loved to do them. I don't know. I'll think about it."

~~~~

Michaels was exhausted by the time he parked his Harley in the garage. He had his leather backpack slung over his shoulder when he exited the elevator. When he approached his front door, he reached out to put his key into the lock and was just about to grab the knob when he froze. He let out a sigh of recognition and put the key and his backpack on the floor. He took out the cloth that detective Quag gave him earlier in the day and the put on a pair of blue latex gloves. The black 12 by 12 inch cloth felt like the material used to clean eyeglasses. He placed the cloth on the doorknob and with a circular clockwise motion turned it as if he was cleaning the knob. To his surprise, a white dust like substance clung to the cloth. "Son of a bitch, that bastard was here and he tried to kill me again," he said to himself as he opened the door and suddenly felt exhausted.

CHAPTER 46

A s the sounds of the city started to wake Peter Michaels up from a restless night of sleep, his eyes began to burn, his mouth was bone dry and his head was aching from the beeping of a garbage truck backing up to a dumpster in a parking lot off ninth street. The blare from the siren of a police cruiser just added an exclamation point to his weariness. After a quick shower and a hot cup of coffee, he dialed Jack Warren. "He tried to kill me."

"What in the world are you talking about? He tried to kill you? When?"

Michaels rubbed the sleep out of his tired eyes, "I'm looking at the poison shit he put on my door. You should come get this and get it to your lab as quickly as possible."

"What the fuck, Peter. What poison."

Michaels was looking at the plastic quart size freezer bag and rolling it around in his hand looking out at Grant Park. The sky was bright blue and the sun was peeking out over Lake Michigan's horizon announcing it would be another hot day in Chicago. "Come on up and have a cup of coffee and I'll tell you all about it."

Michaels than pressed speed dial for detective Tony Quag. "I didn't want to call you at midnight last night but I think the 'Bug Man' tried to kill me yesterday. Thanks for the advice and the protection."

"What did you find?"

"He put some poison shit on my door handle. I collected the evidence like you told me too. Should I give it to you or to Warren for the FBI lab?" He didn't tell Quag that he already told Warren to come get it.

"The FBI could probably get it analyzed faster than our lab." Quag admitted.

Michaels smiled at the detective's response. "There was all kinds of a white powdery substance that that tacky cloth collected."

"So, you used the latex gloves and hand sanitizer, right? Put that stuff in a separate bag as well," Quag instructed. "It may provide some additional trace."

~~~~

Dr. Robert Crine used a non-penetrating scalpel type of instrument to pry open the mouth of Conrad Corbett. *What a waste of a life,* he thought as he leaned in closer to examine the crusty tan colored foam that ebbed in the corner of his cyanotic lips. Crine had no doubt the young man was the 33rd victim of the "Bug Man."

The look on his contorted face presented a picture of absolute pain and suffering as if he was suffocated from the inside out. His eyes bulged and appeared to weep blood; the sclera was crimson. Crine closed his lids as if in silent prayer and then continued to scrape the brittle froth into an evidence bag.

The ME slowly walked around the corpse and began talking to his patient but more to himself. "How long did you suffer young man? I hope your organs tell me more about how your body was ravaged by this poison."

Satisfied that he collected every piece of trace evidence off of the exterior of the body, Dr. Crine washed the remains and began his Y incision to investigate how the poison devastated Conrad Corbett internally.

As he placed each organ into the weighing tray, he noticed very similar lacerations that he had discovered during judge Wolfe's autopsy with the exception that these abrasions appeared to be more severe. Deeper, more ulcerated and seemingly extremely painful.

He made a mental note to tell the scientists that would be examining the evidence to compare it with judge Wolfe's to save time. He had no doubt that they were the same poison but somehow it had a much more dramatic effect on this 30-year-old man.

~~~~

The only thing different about Latisha Reynolds's appearance today was the royal blue color added to her bangs. Her long fingernails seemed to glitter as they made that distinctive clicking sound when they hit the video keyboard controlling the security cameras. Peter Michaels wondered how in the world she didn't suffer from corporal tunnel syndrome because of the angle of her hands when she typed to protect her sparkling, curling nails.

Both detectives Tony Quag and Jack Warren along with Michaels were each staring at different monitors reviewing all the videotape from the day before.

"Dr. McBride from Fort Detrick said the amount of time the poison stays lethal once its exposed to air can only be about three hours. So, let's not waste a lot of time here. Let's narrow the time frame to between four and seven." Michaels said.

There were nine security cameras set up around the building. Each person took three cameras to examine. After an hour at double speed Tony Quad exclaimed, "There."

Everyone froze and turned their attention to the seventh monitor in the lower left corner of the screens. The movement lasted about a second. "Back it up. That's far enough. Now watch."

Latisha hit the forward button with her finger poised to stop the frame when commanded. "There."

"What?" Michaels bellowed.

Latisha didn't wait to be told what to do. She gently tapped the reverse key. One frame at a time until you saw just a grainy shadow of what looked like a blimp go from daylight into the shadows as the garage door went up allowing a white SUV to exit. "Gotcha," she said as the shadow of the "Bug Man" was frozen in time.

"That's him." Michaels proclaimed. "It's gotta be."

"That be a little after six," Latisha said, pointing to the time code on the monitor with a big smile from ear to ear.

"He probably thought I'd be home after the six."

"You are one lucky son of a bitch." Warren stated.

"You think your guys at Quantico can do anything with that?" Michaels asked, nodding in agreement.

"Doubtful but I'll send it to D-2. If anybody can make something out of it, she can."

"I'll give you the original but I'm making a copy of it. I can use that in my story tonight."

CHAPTER 47

D r. Louis Yako was feeling very relaxed, sitting on his porch overlooking Lake Michigan, the temperature was 69 degrees causing steam to rise from his hot coffee. He was shaking his head reading the front page of the Chicago Herald as the headline proclaimed more about President Trump's Impeachment hearings. All the newspapers are generally a day old because Grand Traverse Bay is seven hours away from Chicago. For the last 40 years he ordered the Herald when he visited his Michigan summer home.

He turned the page and saw the high school picture of Dr. Cyril Dobonovich before he started reading the story that brought back memories from ten years earlier. "I'll be damned," he said as read his name in the copy. He smiled at the moniker "Bug Man," as he continued.

"What in the world," he muttered. "Why are they looking for me?"

~~~~

Agent Jack Warren nervously paced around the video room at JTTF headquarters as he talked to agent Donna Black at Quantico. "I'm sending some more videotape. We know it's Dobonovich sneaking into Peter's building but I don't think you will be able get anything from it. It's really blurry."

"He tried to kill Michaels again?" Blake asked incredulously.

"Yep. We have samples of the poison he used. You should get it shortly and we sent some to Fort Detrick."

"I am surprised we haven't gotten anything back from that Dr. Yako's house. They have been working on that for a couple of days. Have you guys found him yet?"

"No. There has been a lot in the news. I sure hope the 'Bug Man' didn't get to him already."

"What's the total number of deaths now?"

"We know of at least 33 killed, but who knows that son of a bitch would kill anyone who got in his way."

~~~~

Yang Sung Choi turned off his computer as soon as an unknown city engineer entered the office. He stood up, stretched out his hand and introduced himself with a confident grin, "Hi. I'm Choi. I'm new."

"So, you're the new guy. Funny what happened to Eddie? Just 55."

It was not the welcome Choi expected and the counterfeit smile eroded from his face. He knew Eddie Harris was well liked by his fellow workers and the thought of killing the man who never gave his name instantly crossed Choi's mind. "Yes. It was a terrible thing." He responded, changing to a sympathetic look.

"Well good luck," the engineer who didn't introduce himself said as he continued on his way.

Choi wanted to say, "fuck you" and strangle the life out of him but he said nothing and sat back down turning on his computer. He was studying the blueprints of all the pumps for Buckingham Fountain. He needed the exact measurements of the pipes that shot the fountain's water into the air.

He was mad at himself because it never occurred to him to use the water-soluble plastic material that detergent manufactures used for washing machines and dish washer packets until he saw a "Tide" commercial while watching the news last night.

The fountain has three major jet pumps connected to six pipelines and Choi was contemplating if he should just make three different size containers for the anthrax/ricin compound or 18 for the connecting pipes. The lethal agent was almost mature. He would start testing the dissolvability of the plastic material soon. He had just so much time to plant the 50 trashcan pipe bombs and fill the pumps at the precise moment needed for maximum dispersion of his killer cocktail.

He loaded a CAD program into the computer so he could capture and print the drawings on a paper size that he could easily smuggle out of the office. Once he loaded the material he needed for the diagram of death for his poisonous delivery system, he punched the print key and a sour smile crept across his face as he watched the legal size paper filling the copy tray.

~~~~

The alarm on Dr. James McBride's spectrometer began to ding alerting the Fort Detrick scientist that his results were finally in. He tried to streamline the process by running familiar chemical toxicological assets to eliminate known poisons but the Balamuthia Mandrillaris surfaced as the fifth different poison the "Bug Man" had used on his victims. He then quickly determined the killer's fingerprint on the newest agent.

What a sadistic bastard, he thought as he reached for the phone.

Detective/agent Jack Warren answered on the third ring, immediately recognizing Dr. McBride's voice. "Whatta you got?"

"Your 'Bug Man' is one sick son of a bitch. This latest poison, Balamuthia Mandrillaris is one ugly killer." McBride said shaking his head with a disgusted look.

"As far as we know this stuff hasn't killed anyone yet. At least we don't think so. We still haven't located Dr. Yako where this Balamuthia stuff was discovered."

"There is no doubt that this 'Bug Man' is manipulating these agents, making them more powerful and I might add more painful."

"Did you determine the agent that killed Conrad Corbett?"

"Yes. It's easier to compare the chemical structures to the poisons he has already used. It's the same stuff that killed Judge Wolfe. Oxymodrin Protivea."

"But was that much different than the one used on the judge because I talked to Dr. Crine, and he told me it tore apart this Corbett guy."

"My guess is the alcohol he had in his system probably had a profound effect on how the Oxymodrin Protivea unleashed itself through his system. That's just a theory but I think I'm right on with that."

"Thanks. Oh, by the way any luck on the sample we sent you that we found a Peter Michaels' condo?"

"I'll get on that first thing in the morning. I'll compare it to the latest batches and work backwards. I'm betting it'll be Oxymodrin Protivea or Balamuthia Mandrillaris."

~~~~

Peter Michaels and Ron Magers were standing in studio after the Ten O'clock News. Michaels just reported on the latest developments in the "Bug Man" case including the attempt on his life that had been thwarted earlier that day when his cellphone began to vibrate. He pulled it out of his pocket and looked at the caller ID identifying an "Unknown Caller." He started to hit the decline button when the big red sign that hung in his newsroom decades ago in Detroit saying ANSWER THE PHONE appeared in his subconscious. He motioned to Magers with one finger indicting that *I should take this.*

Magers nodded affirmatively.

"News, Michaels."

"Mr. Michaels, this is Cyril Dobonovich or the 'Bug Man' as you have christened me."

Michaels jaw dropped and his hands began to tremble as the screechy, monotone voice of the serial killer registered in his mind.

Magers reached out to grab Michaels, thinking he was about faint, "Are you alright?" He whispered.

Michaels fighting within himself to gain his composer looked Magers in eyes and nodded affirmatively and said loud enough for Magers to hear, "Mr. Dobonovich. I never thought I would hear from you."

After all the years that Magers had spent in the news business, he thought nothing would surprise him, but a shocking look of danger and disbelief materialized on his face. He looked intently at Michaels, and he too was visibly unnerved.

"Would you like to meet?" Michaels asked.

After a short pause, an incredulous look of shock erupted on Michaels' face.

"I think I would like that. You're not afraid of me, are you?"

"No. I am not afraid of you, even though you tried to kill me twice."

"What makes you think I won't try again?"

"I don't think you are a stupid man. Mr. Dobonovich. When and Where?"

"It's doctor and I am not sure yet. You will be hearing from me soon. Oh! Don't bother to trace this phone. It's a burner. This is the only call that I will ever make on it before I destroy it."

"I'll be waiting then."

"Oh, and if I were you, I'd be looking over my shoulder. You may never know when our paths will cross. I know what you look like but you have no idea what I look like." The Fox concluded; a vile sneer seeped across his lips.

CHAPTER 48

T he elevator doors on the tenth floor of Peter Michaels' condo building seemed to open in slow motion. His steps were guarded and unsteady; if a neighbor saw him as he made his way down the corridor he or she surely would have thought he was over served. His bed and sleep were welcomed. The phone call he had received just an hour before kept replaying in his mind. The sound of the "Bug Man's" high screechy voice irritated him like the sound of nails being dragged across a chalkboard. He felt drained from the adrenaline rush that assaulted his emotions after the mad man he has been investigating openly admitted that he tried to kill him yesterday. Michaels felt like he was bouncing off the walls, dizzy, groggy, and tired as he put his key into his door lock. He turned the doorknob and immediately realized he used his bare hand to open it. He grinned and thought *HOW FOOLISH; the Bug Man could never get back in his building ever again*. He steadied himself as he flipped on the hall lights. He turned into his bedroom and suddenly he gasped, taking one deep breath after another, reaching for his throat, fighting for air. Suffocating. The pain in his head became excruciating. Piercing. Unbearable. The room started to spin faster and faster as consciousness raced for the darkness of death.

Michaels shot upright with an audible scream as he awoke from his deep sleep. His favorite, light gray Petosky, Michigan t-shirt was wet and weighty with sweat. His face was painted in perspiration. His body was trembling. His breathing was deep and fast. The beeping sound of garbage truck backing up immediately brought him back to reality. His relief was instant and he immediately comprehended the nightmare that may scorn him forever was just that … a nightmare. He was alive and thankful and now worried.

~~~~

Gang Crimes specialist Chris Franco was on patrol in the Garfield Park neighborhood, one of 77 community areas making up Chicago's ethnic and very distinctive neighborhoods. It was a hot and muggy night … a typical night for violence in this high crime ridden area. Young police officers liked to work in Garfield Park because it offered them the opportunity to chase bad guys with sirens screaming, kicking down doors in drug raids, executing search warrants, and feeling the adrenalin rush from life threatening danger.

Every year, Garfield Park was one of the top three districts to record the most homicides in the city. Franco didn't know why he turned into the dark alley separating two competing drug operations along Superior. A street that began on downtown's multimillion-dollar magnificent mile, running directly west to one of the city's multimillion-dollar drug trading businesses that included crack cocaine, heroin and marijuana. The streetlights had not been replaced for years helping to camouflage the illegal sales of these narcotics. Every time Streets and Sanitation replaced the lights the drug dealers would shoot them out.

With more than seven years on the job, instinctively Franco's protective radar kicked in. He switched on the high beam spotlight as his beat up green Crown Vic slowly crept east down the alley and within seconds, he eased on his brakes and called for backup.

A pair of red Nike gym shoes, heels pointing upward appeared between a rotting wooden fence and an 80-gallon blue Streets and

Sanitation garbage can. Franco exited his car slowly and cautiously as he scanned the scene protectively. He unconsciously placed his right hand on his Glock-19 holstered slightly behind on his right hip and turned on his high-powered mag-flashlight; methodically traversing its beam to the right and to the left as he approached the victim. The shoes belonged to a young black teenager, who was laying almost facedown, head slightly ajar resting on tall weeds, a brown plastic grocery bag, and crushed green glass from a broken beer bottle. He was dressed in blue jeans and a white t-shirt ... the emblematic uniform of a Chicago gangbanger. Chicago Police gang specialists are very familiar with gang members in the areas they work, but Franco had no idea who this victim was.

The young man's dead eyes pictured fear or pain or both. His mouth was slightly opened and the corners of his lips were covered with some thin crusty foam. His t-shirt was dirty from exposure to the elements but there was no sign of blood. He wasn't shot, Franco concluded. He continued his recce of the crime scene, looking for shell casings that he knew were non-existent. There was no apparent evidence that the body was dragged and dumped. His two-way radio interrupted his thoughts and investigation.

"Hey, Sarge. You better get the homicide dicks over here. I'll put yellow tape around the area that I searched. This looks very strange. He's young, dead, and unknown. I don't think he was shot but from the looks of it, he died a painful death."

~~~~

Crime scene investigator Gary Landis arrived at the homicide scene as the sun was rising along with the temperature. He collected his equipment from the trunk of his squad car and slowly ambled over to the body that had already started to decompose. He slowly knelt down, the arthritis in his knees made him cringe. He pushed his glasses back up his nose, squinted, pursed his lips and said, "I think you should get detective Quag over here right away; this may be related to his cases."

Landis then leaned closer to the body and started to scrap the crusty foam off the victim's lips into an evidence bag. Landis had been on the job for 37 years; he had no idea why he suggested contacting his friend Tony Quag but his gut instinct told him too. *How could this dead gangbanger be related to the "Bug Man?"* he asked himself.

~~~~

Cyril Dobonovich had a cold compress on his forehead. The four oxycodone, he took throughout the night to ease his migraine had little effect on the excoriating pain. The soothing words and light touch of his lover's fingers rubbing his neck softly also did nothing to mitigate his agony. The "Bug Man" knew the end was near.

"I have failed. I didn't kill them all, most of all that fucking Yako. I wanted that bastard to die more than any of them. I should have taken him first," he said as he propped himself higher in the bed.

"Your plan was brilliant. You had no idea that bastard was going to leave town. We had a perfect plan and it is still not over." Lin An tried to reassure.

Currently, the world knew Bing Lin An as Yang Sung Choi, a recently hired engineer by the city of Chicago through Williamson Waterworks Inc., the engineering firm that controlled Buckingham Fountain. The Madden Mental Health Center registered him as Lin Bing An, a paranoid psychopathic killer, who murdered his entire family when he was eighteen. He was born in the United States to South Korean parents. By the age of five his brilliance began to blossom in both the arts and sciences. His dream life began with pampering from his teachers and philanthropists that recognized his musical talents and abilities early on. They thought the prodigy would become the next Yo-Yo Ma, one of the greatest cellists in the world.

When Lin Bing An was 16 years old, he traveled to South Korea with his family. The government sponsored a recital too show off their talented countryman. While staying at the five star Hilton Crest Hotel, he contracted the elusive Hantavirus that took eight weeks to diagnose. The Hantavirus is transmitted through infected rodents. Something as simple as their urine could spread the virus. It left Lin An with a hemorrhagic fever with renal syndrome. HFRS is physically debilitating and if it makes its way to the brain, it can leave a victim psychotic. Less than two years after Lin An was diagnosed, he brutally slaughtered his mother, father, brother and two sisters. When the police arrested him, he was sitting in the middle of his living room covered in blood with the murder weapon, a hatchet, in his hands and a Machiavellian smile on his face.

The first time Bing Lin An met Cyril Dobonovich they became instant friends and soon after lovers. Within six months they began plotting the "Bug Man's" revenge.

CHAPTER 49

D avid Beedy was cursing under his breath and Peter Michaels knew exactly what caused his distress and the mumbled tones when he entered the office … The Bears lost their first exhibition game. Beedy was reading the Herald's sports section, "These fucking writers never cease to amaze me. The Carolina Panthers kicked our ass last night and these guys make it sound like the Bears are the second coming. They suck."

Michaels just grinned … he has known and worked with Beedy for more that 20 years and the story was always the same every year, "The Bears suck." Since "Da 1985 Bears" dissolved, the city has been disappointed every season with high hopes and mediocre performances.

"You look like shit." Beedy said as his grin morphed into a look of apprehension. He lowered his newspaper slowly on his desk, never taking his eyes off Michaels, and then straightened up in his chair. "Are you okay?"

"I had a nightmare last night that the 'Bug Man' put poison on my door handle again. It was so real." He paused; his forehead furled with concern. "Scary actually."

"Jack Warren called this morning. He said, he tried to get a hold of you but your phone went straight to voicemail."

"Yeah. I was so tired last night; I forgot to put my phone on charge. Should I call him?"

"No, He said he'd get back to you. Said, he sent that burner phone number you gave him last night over to Quantico."

"Good. That Dobonovich is not as smart as he thinks he is."

"You okay man? You looked troubled." Beedy asked anxiously.

"That bastard shook me up, Dave. Saying he was going to try to kill me again." Michaels had been threatened before from unscrupulous landlords, gangbangers and politicians that he did stories on in the past but he always considered those threats braggadocios banter.

The phone rang and Beedy answered it, leaving Michaels with his thoughts. Beedy's forehead furled and then his eyes lit up with excitement.

"It Dr. Louis Yako, for you."

Michaels sat down quickly the gloom in his eyes transformed into a joyful gleam. "Hello, Doctor. We've been looking for you and so has the FBI and the Chicago Police Department."

"What on earth for?" Dr. Yako responded. "Did I do something wrong?"

"No. No. Nothing like that. Can I be perfectly honest with you?"

"Please, I would have it no other way."

"Well, we all thought you might be dead. We have reason to believe that Cyril Dobonovich tried to kill you. He tried to kill me too by the way." Michaels instinctively put his hand to his forehead and softly caressed it. "Hey, Doc. Do you mind if I record our call? It could be very important and I don't want to miss anything." Michaels pressed the record button without waiting for permission, and then he put Dr. Yako on speaker so his producer could listen and take his notes for future productions.

"Yes, please. No problem. How are you so sure he tried to kill me?"

"The police found traces Balamuthia Mandrillaris poison on the door handle going into your house from your garage. He used the same stuff on my door handle. He is one sick son of a bitch."

"In my opinion, he's a narcissist, sociopath, psychopath and killer. I believe he has killed at least three people."

Michaels was surprised that Dr. Yako mentioned just three victims. "Who are you talking about?"

"Well, as you obviously know I was the psychiatrist at his trial when he killed Dr. Helen Lesenski. He should have gotten the death penalty. Not a mental institution."

Michaels eased back in his chair, looked over at Beedy and said, "We think he's killed more than 30 people so far. What others are you thinking about?"

Dr. Yako was sitting out on his deck looking out over Lake Michigan. He could hear the sounds of the waves crashing against the shore, but he could not see the deep blue waters of the great lake because a London like fog consumed the artistic horizon. He reached for his coffee cup and noticed that his hands were trembling. He got up from the table and walked inside for a fresh cup, and he mumbled as if thinking out loud, "More than 30 people. I don't understand."

Peter Michaels spent the next 20 minutes explaining why he, the police and the FBI believed Dobonovich killed that many people. When he finished, he asked, "Dr. Yako are you okay? Are you still there?"

Dr. Yako was sitting down at his kitchen table, holding onto his warm coffee cup, more startled than he was before, "I knew that bastard was crazy but I never thought in a million years he was that insane." Yako went quiet and his breathing became heavier as if he was deep in thought.

Michaels could hear him, so like any good interviewer, he didn't want to interrupt the moment. Then Yako continued, "You know he was born on March 15th. Does that ring a bell for you?"

A new awareness suddenly gripped Michaels as he began to think but Dr. Yako answered his own question. "It's the 'Ides of March.' The day Brutus stabbed Caesar. I am a man of science and am not superstitious, but for some reason that always bothered me about him."

Michaels let the doctor ponder for a few seconds then asked, "Doctor. Who else do you think he killed?"

"I have interviewed a lot of crazy people during my career. I had a gut feeling when I diagnosed him the first time that he killed before."

"What made you feel that way?"

"It was the way he talked about his parents. I honestly think he killed both of them, and the more I think about it, now, I have no doubt."

Michaels and Beedy locked eyes and Beedy mouthed, "Which one first?"

Michaels immediately asked, "Who do you think, he killed first?"

Without hesitation, Dr. Yako responded, "His father. I believe he hated him. He hated him with a vengeance."

"Do you have any idea, how he killed them?"

"It would not be in a usual way because he was never charged, or anything like that. I believe the authorities thought they died of natural causes and they died years apart." Dr. Yako was transfixed, deep in thought. His mind racing hard, like a thoroughbred trying to reach the finish line. "If I had to guess, I'd say he poisoned them."

CHAPTER 50

A joyful smile curled from ear to ear on FBI agent Donna Blake's face when she heard the voice of fellow agent and friend, Jack Warren. "Hey buddy what's up?"

"Hey, you. You got anything for us?" Warren asked hesitantly. He didn't want to put pressure on her.

"How did you know? You must have ESP. I just figured it out."

"That might be record time. I gave you the phone number less than 48 hours ago."

Blake was multi-tasking, staring intently at her computer screen and carrying on her conversation. She started processing the "Bug Man's" burner phone number within minutes of receiving it after he admitted he tried to kill Peter Michaels. "How is Michaels doing anyway? That phone call had to scare the shit out of him."

Warren ran his long fingers through his shaggy hair. He was leaning back in his chair, but Blake's question brought him to his feet and he started to nervously pace around his workspace, "He's finally settling down. He was pretty shaken by that. So, what do you have?"

"The phone is an *Excel-Tell*. They're made in Mexico. They are the most popular burner type phones in Europe, Australia, Mexico and Russia believe it or not." Blake informed.

"Well, this is America." Warren responded sarcastically with a smile.

"No shit, dude, but Collardy's BEST DEALS has started selling a shitload of them."

"There's a BEST DEALS on North Avenue and Elston. Man, protestors and rioters hit that place every time the shit hits the fan here. I am surprised they keep re-opening."

"That must tell you they make a lot of money. But listen give me a little more time. I just retrieved the serial number, and I should be able to trace where that phone was sold in a couple of hours."

"I'll get started on a warrant to look at security footage of the store if you can identify it?"

"What do you mean, IF?"

~~~~

Detective Tony Quag was in Cook County State's Attorney Michael Pangborn's office trying to get a court order to exhume the body of Theodore Dobonovich, the father of Cyril Dobonovich. Pangborn was in charge of Special Prosecutions for the last 13 years. It was his last week on the job because he was just appointed to the Cook County Circuit Court Bench. After a two-week vacation, his training as a judge was scheduled to start Monday, September ninth.

"What the fuck, Quag. I'm out of here in a few days. I'm not sure we have enough to get a court order on the information you have." Pangborn said, throwing his Cubs souvenir baseball from hand-to-hand.

"Look we believe Cyril Dobonovich killed more than 30 people, including judge Wolfe. I listened to the taped interview that Peter Michaels had with Dr. Louis Yako. We also have evidence that he tried to kill the good doctor." The detective said with a pleading look smothering his face.

Pangborn, a wiry marathon runner, was slowing walking around his spacious office. The collar of his traditional heavily starched white shirt was uncharacteristically unbuttoned, and his red tie hung loosely on his chest. He listened intently to the beseeching detective.

"The doctor interviewed the 'Bug Man' extensively before his murder trial over a decade ago, and he is convinced that the son of a bitch killed his father in 1993 and his mother, a few years later."

"Okay, you get a sworn statement from the doctor. We'll put two affidavits together: one for the father and one for the mother. What's her name?" Pangborn said, looking keenly at the detective.

"Hildegard, I think. I'll check." Quag responded, as his supplicatory look converted into a smile of satisfaction.

"Anything else?" Pangborn asked not expecting another situation.

"Yeah, there is. You know Landis from CSI?"

"What now?" He asked with an inquisitive look, shaking his head, sorry he asked the question.

"I know this sounds crazy, but he thinks the body of a young teenage gangbanger found in an alley in Garfield Park is connected to the 'Bug Man' investigation." Detective Quag said.

"What. Are you serious?" asked a troubled Pangborn.

"We sent the body over to the ME's office. There were traces of what we think is a similar 'Bug Man' poison on the victim's lips."

"Are you shitting me?" an exasperated Pangborn asked.

"No. He also sent a couple of brand new hundred dollar bills to the lab for analysis. The money was found in the victim's pocket and it was, well, just out of place. It just didn't sit well with him. He's been around a long time."

"Who is paying for all this?"

"The Joint Terrorist Task Force. The feds can move on this stuff a lot faster than we can. I'm told they have already identified the burner phone that Dobonovich used when he called Peter Michaels." Detective Quag said with the palms of his hands facing outwards, signaling *what can I say*.

"This thing gets curiouser and curiouser every day," Pangborn opined.

~~~~

The Chicago Police Gold Start Families Memorial and Park is located on five acres of lakefront property adjacent to Burnham Harbor just east of Soldier Field. The memorial pays tribute to the more 592 police officers that were killed in the line of duty. The area known as the "Sacrifice Space" is the spiritual heart of the memorial. The names of those officers killed while serving the city are etched into the black granite walls. It is a very solemn place to visit. Former Superintendent of Police Phil Cline is the executive director. He asked Peter Michaels to meet him there. "I'd like you to be the guest of honor for this year's Candlelight Vigil."

"Phil, I am honored. When will it be held?"

"This year, it will be Thursday night, September 12th, a week before opening night of the Bears' season."

Michaels and Cline were slowly walking around the area talking about the event. Neither of them noticed the "Mutt and Jeff" looking men who were on a recce mission, double checking the number of trash cans lining the walkways that lead to Soldier Field.

The Asian was tall and thin. A plain blue baseball cap fit squarely on his head. Long white sleeves covered his arms with the temperature in the high 90s. The other one was much shorter. He too wore long sleeves. He was prone to sunburn. Every so often when he walked there was a slight limp in his step.

CHAPTER 51

C yril Dobonovich and Choi/Lin An were walking slowly, pre-
tending to throw garbage into the trashcans on the walkways leading to Soldier Field. They were actually re-measur-
ing the height of the cans and the exact angle needed to place their
PVC disbursement devices.

"Are you sure the butane canisters are the way to get the formula
airborne?" Dobonovich inquired, suspiciously looking over his shoulder, to make sure no one was close by to hear any of their
conversation.

"Yes, I am positive, however, I have to be somewhere in the middle in order to detonate them."

"Do you have an escape strategy?" asked Dobonovich looking
up at his tall accomplice and lover.

"Yes. Don't worry about me. As you know the detonator is not
tethered to anything but me, and the wireless signal is limited. My
only concern is the devices at the far ends. I have been experimenting
with a longer antenna to stretch the bandwidth. I am certain the
crowd won't affect the signal." Choi/Lin An responded as he stopped
and looked over the pathway that would turn into a death march in
two weeks.

"I am not that worried about the end units closer to the Field
Museum. There will not be that many people in the area anyway by

the time you detonate the devices. The biggest crowd will be approaching the gates and they'll all be backed up because of the security checks, but by that time you would have pulled the trigger." Dobonovich said with sinful smile bleeding across his face.

As they slowly made their way to the Field Museum, Choi/Lin An asked, "How are your headaches?"

"The Oxy doesn't help much anymore. I am weak most of the time." The "Bug Man" said, and then added, "The steroid compounds I've developed do give me great energy."

"When will you meet with Michaels?"

"I will call him later after I rest. I will kill him tomorrow or the next day." Dobonovich said, closing his dead eyes as a wicked smile crossed his face.

~~~~

Dr. Robert Crine's shoulders were protesting the long hours of work on his autopsy table and his red and exhausted eyes confirmed his decision to retire after this case was solved. He wiped his forehead with the back of his right hand that contained a scalpel. He took a deep breath and continued to scraped a thin layer of suspected poisonous foam that appeared on the teenager's lips like a rash. He could not help to include a fine layer of skin as he prepared the specimen. Dr. Crine held the evidence bag up to the light and smiled. He knew he had enough of a sample for an analysis when his phone rang.

"Hey doc, it's Quag," said the detective with a slight grin. He knew everyone working the "Bug Man" case was burning the candle at both ends.

"Don't tell me, you've got more work for me?" Crine asked but knew his mild remonstration would fall on deaf ears.

"I wish I could say no but I can't, and believe me, it should be challenging."

"What is it, this time?" Crine asked as he sagged his shoulders to release the tension that he felt all day.

"I'm getting a court order to exhume the body of Dobonovich's father, we believe he killed him back in the early ninety's."

Dr. Crine's tired eyes came to life. It had been a long time since he did an autopsy on old skeletal remains. "When will I get the body?" He asked now with a new spirit of a new challenge.

"The prosecutor is appearing before the judge as we speak. I need to make the arrangements with the cemetery to dig it up, but if all goes well, two maybe three days at most."

"Have any idea what we are looking for?"

"Yeah, poison of some kind. I'd bet."

~~~~

"Who was that?" David Beedy asked as he walked into the investigative unit's office.

"That was the administrator of the Madison Mental Health Center." Michaels responded itching his new gray goatee that he started growing after the "Bug Man" threatened to kill him for the second time.

"What's up with that?" Beedy asked as he put a cup of green tea on his desk.

"Dr. Yako called again and he remembered that two orderlies at Madison died mysterious deaths during the time of Dobonovich's commitment. He said, he was so upset with the case that he followed it for years afterwards."

"You know my brother-in-law is a psychologist and works in the mental health field. Maybe I can ask him to look into this for us." Beedy said as he reached for the phone that started to ring. "Yeah, he's here. It's for you. It's Jack." Beedy said as he cradled his phone.

"Hey, JW what's up?" Michaels said with a smile.

"That burner phone the 'Bug Man' called you on was sold at Collardy's BEST DEALS on North and Elston. We're getting a warrant to get the security videos. We know it was sold eight days ago around two o'clock and it was paid for with cash." Warren said with an approving grin.

"You guys can get that exact? That's amazing." Michaels said stroking the stubble on his chin.

"Everything, serial number, model number, is contained in the barcode. It's an inventory thing. It can be very precise. It's an EXCEL-TELL phone made in Mexico. BEST DEALS is the largest distributor of them in the United States." Warren advised.

The moment Michaels click off another call came in, "News, Michaels."

"Hey, Peter. It's Billy."

"Billy Bob what's up?" Billy Bob Winkler was one of Michaels' dear friends. They met years ago at a golf outing and tried to play a round or two during the summer when they could each find the time to get together. His nickname was BBT which stood for Billy Bob Tim and a moniker that was bestowed upon him when he and a couple of his buddies were joking around with some young girls on an airplane heading to a golf outing in Florida. He didn't want to use his real name. So, BBT was born and it's been a standing joke ever since.

"Something has been gnawing at me. I was thinking about call-ing you a while ago but I thought no he'll think I'm nuts." BBT said haltingly.

"No man, you know me better than that. What's going on?" Michaels said now switching modes from friend to reporter.

"As you know I follow you religiously on television. I heard you had a death threat and I just gotta tell you. I did a job for this creepy little bald fuck more than 2 years ago over on Chestnut. He made my skin crawl. He was a clean freak. Scary. He paid in cash. So, I didn't let his personality or his freakiness get in the way of business." BBT said thoughtfully.

"Let's get together. When is it convenient for you?" Michaels asked but he wanted to meet immediately.

"I am way north on a jobsite. I'm closing it down tomorrow. I can meet you in a day or two if that's okay with you." BBT said questionably.

"No problem. Let's have coffee at Pete's on Maxwell Street. Let me know the time when you are available." Michaels said as they clicked off.

He instantly stood as if in a trance and reached for his leather vest to check his pocket for his motorcycle key. He was going to take a late afternoon ride. Chestnut was not a very long street and there were not that many houses on it. Michaels wanted to meet his killer.

CHAPTER 52

T here are only a handful of two and three flats left on Chestnut
Street between LaSalle and State Streets. They all had
wrought iron fences but only one had a paved walkway from
the sidewalk to the porch that glistened in the afternoon sun, just like
Billy Bob Tim explained. Michaels shifted his cycle into second gear
and let off the throttle to muffle the sound of his Screaming Eagle exhaust pipes. He didn't want to draw attention to his presence. On his
third pass, he stop slightly before the gate and pulled his Street Bob to
the curb to study the house. An eerie feeling smothered him instantly,
he shuttered and he knew he was in the presence of evil. Ten minutes
seemed more like an hour. There were no signs of life, but he could
sense that he was being watched.

A man with green, hateful eyes split the pure white drawn cur-
tains ever so slightly to peer out and a supercilious sneer unfolded on
his face knowing he wanted to kill the man he was looking at.

Michaels started his Harley but this time he drove down the alley
and discovered a seven-foot tall white fence with a secure gate that
blocked any view of the rear entrance. He slowly pulled away as his
gut told him the "Bug Man" lived there. He was sure of it.

~~~~

Choi/Lin An moved all his blueprints and materials out of the base-ment apartment to a storage locker on South State street. He also rented an apartment for a year on Indiana, a short walk from his new workspace. A small tabletop saw with a diamond edge cutting blade easily sliced through the fifty, one and half inch PVC pipes that would hold an electronic detonator and at least ten ounces of the anthrax/ricin poisonous powdery compound.

"Fuck, fuck, fuck," Choi/Lin An started hollering, not all his triggering devices were responding to the wireless signal. A frisson feeling electrified his spine once he realized he might have drawn unwanted attention to his locker by his outburst. He slowly opened the door to look if anyone was around; an malicious smile creased his lips. He was alone.

The anthrax and ricin compound was still in its incubator locker back at the house on Chestnut where they would put it into secure, sealed containers that would be place in the pipes for the big night of celebration.

~~~~

It didn't take Assistant State's Attorney Michael Pangborn very long to convince the judge to issue two court orders to exhume the bodies of Theodore and Hildegard Dobonovich using the death of a fellow judge as leverage and the main argument for the order.

Detective Tony Quag was standing at the gravesites of the Dobonovichs at St. Boniface Cemetery on North Clark Street. The grass in section 1332 looked like a manicured emerald green carpet. Flowers planted by family members of the deceased sprinkled the landscape with every color imaginable. Beautiful upright monuments and stone or marble memorial crosses interrupted the peaceful terrain in a tender way, depicting a loved one's final resting place, except for Theodore and Hildegard Dobonovich. Their gravestones were flat, small and unattended. Only their names and dates of birth and death were etched into the cheapest granite available. Both lived 38 years.

When detective Quagliaroli signed in at the office and presented the court orders for the exhumation, he noticed that Theodore and Hildegard Dobonovich never had a visitor.

A well-aged, rusted green and yellow, John Deere backhoe was already in place at the gravesite. Black diesel smoke choked out of the exhaust manifold as the machine came to life to dig out the caskets. Investigators were anxious to find the cause of death of two innocent people. It took less than 20 minutes for the small but powerful shovel to reach the cement vault containing the remains of Theodore. The inexpensive wooden casket was covered in gray velour cloth and set on the ground. Hildegard's casket was a plain wooden box.

Detective Tony Quagliaroli slowly shook his downtrodden head in disbelief as he witnessed pure hatred unfold in front of him, and he made the sign of the cross although he hadn't been to church in years. He then signaled the funeral director to put the caskets into the hearse. In order to maintain the chain of evidence, he followed it to the Medical Examiner's office.

~~~~

JTTC agent Jack Warren was watching the security footage from Collardy's BIG DEALS in his office, listening to agent Donna Blake on his com-set.

"How are things in Washington?" Warren asked his friend smiling.

"I wish I was there with you, but I can control things better here at Quantico." She responded. "The phone was purchased six days ago at 3:37 in the afternoon. Cash register number five."

"It's amazing you can be so accurate."

"Not really. This is inventory control. It all boils down to money." Blake opined. "Bar codes contain an amazing amount of information."

"There!" Warren exclaimed. "That old Landis might be right. Is that a black kid buying … what six phones?" Warren stopped and studied the videotape that was remarkably clear. The look on his face intensified. "Can you freeze it when he turns his head and we get a better look at him?"

Blake stopped the footage and slowly rewound it almost frame by frame, and when the shopper turned his head, she stopped and a clear image of 60 percent of his face froze on the screen. "That should do it. I'll send you the pic."

"Son of a bitch! Why would a gangbanger buy a burner phone for the 'Bug Man?'" asked Warren, bewildered.

"Yeah, and now he's dead." Blake almost whispered.

"Yeah, he's cleaning up loose ends."

"Are thinking, what I'm thinking?"

"I don't know. What are you thinking?"

"I'm thinking something big is about to happen," Blake pronounced.

"Yeah, I think you're right. But what?"

CHAPTER 53

D avid Beedy was typing furiously on his keyboard, his headset was blocking any external sounds, and his eyes were focused on the screen in front of him when Peter Michaels walked into the office. He noticed the intense look on his partner's face as he put a Grande Latte on Beedy's desk. He didn't look up and say "thank you" like he normally would.

Michaels worked with his partner for 20 years and knew this was a do not disturb moment because something very important was happening. He sat down, turned on his computer and called up the Chicago Herald on his screen to read and wait.

A long five minutes later, Beedy let out a long sigh, leaned back in his chair, took a drink of his now cooled off latte and said, "You are not going to believe this."

Michaels stopped reading with Beedy's sigh and looked over at him inquisitively. "I don't think there is anything I wouldn't believe anymore. Whatta you got?"

Beedy's forehead was furled. His eyes worried. "There may be two of them."

"What?" Responded Michaels expressively. "Who were you talking to?"

"My brother-in-law. He confirmed there were two untimely deaths during the time period that Dobonovich was committed to

Madison Mental Health Center. Two orderlies. They both died under very suspicious circumstances within a year and a half. Guess how?" Beedy asked.

"Let me guess. Ah ... poison." Michaels responded sarcastically. "What about the two of them."

"Dobonovich had a boyfriend, lover, acquaintance. They didn't know what the relationship was exactly, but he was very close to some Korean dude." Beedy said as he stood up and walked over to the printer to get copies of his notes.

Michaels scanned the paper before saying, "This ain't good."

"The guy's name is Bing Lin An. A really strange person." Beedy said handing Michaels a copy of his notes. "He apparently was some sort of musical prodigy, who brutally murdered his entire family." Beedy continued, now pacing the floor.

"Just like Dobonovich," whispered Michaels. "Two peas in a pod."

"This Bing guy was tattooed from head to toe. Like a Japanese Yakuza gangster."

"Yeah, but you said he was Korean not Japanese?"

"Yeah, right and yeah, remember, he's also nuts."

A worried look flushed across Michaels' face, "Dave, this could be very, very bad. Two-of-them. Two, 'Bug Men.' Are you kidding me?"

~~~~

Agent Jack Warren answered his cellphone on the third ring. He knew it was Michaels by the *Lone Ranger* ring tone. "I was just going to call you. This thing just got crazier."

"Oh, so you heard?" Michaels said surprised.

"Heard what?" Warren replied curiously.

"There could be two of them."

"What the fuck are you talking about, two of them?" Warren asked pryingly.

Michaels told him the new information they had just developed, and asked, "What the fuck are you talking about?"

"Tony Quag just confirmed that a young gangbanger bought the phone Dobonovich used to call you. And guess what?"

"He's dead. Poisoned." Michaels said in a low voice barely audible, walking over to his desk and sitting down softly, absorbing the new development intensely.

"How did you know, that?" Warren asked.

"That's the way he kills. It doesn't take a genius to figure it out, does it?"

"We are not sure it was poison yet. We are waiting for lab results. Dr. Crine suspects it is and so does Tony Quag."

"I got one more piece of info for you." Michaels said regaining his composure.

"Yeah, what's that?" Warren asked, wondering how a reporter was moving faster than the FBI and the Chicago Police.

"I am pretty sure; I know where the 'Bug Man' lives."

~~~~

Michaels didn't recognize the number that appeared on his cellphone's caller identification screen but he didn't hesitate to answer. "What do you want? You sick son of a bitch!" he asked.

"How did you know it was me?" Dobonovich asked surprised.

"Why did you have to kill that poor kid? He did nothing to you. He knew nothing." Michaels asked angrily but testing the waters to see if Dobonovich would take the bait.

"He saw my face. I couldn't take any chances. He was just, how do you say it, collateral damage. He was a little fucking gangster. Isn't that what you call those kids? Nobody will miss him." Dobonovich said dismissively.

Michaels was astonished and fully alert. *The bastard just admitted to another murder as if it meant nothing.* Michaels thought and then asked, "What kind of man are you? He had a mother, a brother and two little sisters. You bastard." Michaels didn't care if he pissed him off. "What do you want? Do you want to meet?"

"As a matter of fact, I do, and don't talk to me like that or I'll cancel our meeting." Dobonovich said with a sneer.

"I really don't give a fuck if we meet or not." Michaels lied. He really did care. His fingers were crossed; he hoped he didn't push back to hard, then he couldn't help himself and blurted out, "We're gonna get you, very soon. I know where you live."

"Yes, I saw you the other day. Nice Harley," he said defiantly.

An eerie feeling engulfed Michaels because the "Bug Man" just admitted that he lived on Chestnut and he killed the young gangbanger. The police could get a warrant and arrest him.

"When and where?" Michaels asked anxiously, wanting the set up the meeting, but he also wanted to get off the phone so he could call Jack Warren.

"Let's do it on Jeweler's Row at 4:30 tonight. I'll text you the address later."

"See you there." Michaels said and clicked off.

CHAPTER 54

I t looked as if David Beedy was talking to himself when Peter Michaels walked back into the office then he began to type furiously and Michaels smiled. Beedy looked over and motioned with a finger *give me a second.*

Michaels nodded and continued his conversation with Dr. Louis Yako. "Thanks for the heads up on those two orderlies at Madison. They did die under very suspicious circumstances while Cyril Dobonovich was there but the investigations into the deaths were very limited."

"That doesn't surprise me. No one ever suspected anything at that time. No one knew how sick Dobonovich was." The doctor responded shaking his head.

"We should know today or tomorrow if he poisoned his parents. The bodies have been exhumed and the autopsies were performed yesterday. The results were sent to the FBI."

"I have no doubt he killed them. I just don't know how." Yako said.

"I'll let you know what we find. Hey, listen, where are you? Can we do an interview?" Michaels asked eagerly.

"I'm in Michigan. I am not sure when I will be coming back," he declared.

"Please think about it. We can really move this story forward with your participation. I may be meeting with Dobonovich later today. Anything you can tell me. What to look for? Anything?" Michaels eagerly asked.

"I will tell you one thing, don't get too close to him. Watch his hands. He's not going to shoot you with a gun, but he is devious, and he may try to harm you."

"Yeah, well, he's tried it before. Thanks. I'll be in touch." Michaels said clicking off, and then he turned to see that Beedy just ended his conversation. "What do you have?"

"I just got off the phone with Mrs. Agatha Hutchison."

"Who is that?"

"The wife of Phillip Hutchison, one of the orderlies, who died mysteriously at Madison back in the days of Dobonovich. She still doesn't have all the answers she been looking for after all these years."

"Not surprising. No one ever suspected they were murdered." Michaels responded with a questioning look.

"The other orderly was Matthew Stevonski. His wife is going to call me back. Neither of them have any real answers, but Mrs. Hutchinson said, her husband was a fanatic about working out and he was as healthy as horse, and then one day, he just dropped dead." Beedy said shaking his head.

"I guarantee they were poisoned." Michaels said, as his cellphone began to vibrate in his pocket.

~~~~

Dr. James McBride smiled as he recognized the chemical compound that appeared on his spectrometer's screen. "Cyril Dobonovich strikes again," he whispered to himself as he pressed a button to magnify the compound he was studying. "Balamuthia Mandrillaris, the same poison that he used for Dr. Yako and Peter Michaels."

The Fort Detrick scientist then took the third sample he was examining and did an overlay comparison of Dobonovich's signature chemical fingerprint on that drug. "Gotcha," he declared and reached for his phone.

Dr. Robert Crine grimaced as his phone began to ring. He was preforming his third autopsy of the day on another gangbanger who was shot in a drive-by. He wiped his forehead with his forearm, leaving what appeared to be a gray stain on his lab coat's sleeve. His frown turned into smile when he heard Dr. McBride's voice. "What do you have Jim?"

"Well, the poison that killed that young man, the gangbanger, it was Balamuthia Mandrillaris, for sure, and your psycho killer made it."

"So, he used that on Yako, Michaels and the kid?"

"No doubt!"

"Yeah, I am surprised about the kid but not about Yako and the reporter. I've got more for you."

"No problem."

"I am going to send you some samples from the bodies of his parents. We believed they were poisoned years ago but I don't think this is going to be very sophisticated." Crine said.

"Why not?" Dr. McBride said, surprised.

"Because we believe he killed his father when he was 12-years old and his mother a few years later."

"You're kidding right?"

"No, I am not. There may not be much to test. We exhumed their bodies two days ago. I will do their autopsy before the end of the day and overnight any samples to you."

"I'll get right on it as soon as I get it. You guys better find this guy pretty soon. He's killed more than 30 people, right?"

"He's killed at least 34 that we know of, and there may be more."

~~~~

The smoke was so thick it seemed to engulf the enter workspace and everything in the room; chairs, benches, shelves, tools, boxes, PVC pipes disappeared in the man-made fog. Choi/Lin An turned his fan on low and lifted the heavy door to let the fumes slowly seep away unnoticed. His gas mask hid the mischievous smile that curled on his lips. He perfected his wireless detonator to cover the length of the walkway from the Field Museum to Soldier Field.

He moved from his workbench and felt his way to the side door. He slithered through the slight crack he created, dropped his mask on the floor and stepped outside. The afternoon sun pierced his retinas and made his eyes burn and water. He was sure his killing devices would be operational on D-Day just days away.

He wiped his eyes and slipped on his wire-rimmed Maui Jims securely around his ears. The white gaseous fumes seemed to evaporate into the afternoon heat, leaving no trace of its existence. The tattooed killer looked around to see if anyone else was near. Satisfied he was alone, he walked over to his 10-speed bicycle and a short ride to his final meeting with his mentor, friend, lover and killer.

As he buttoned the chinstrap on his protective helmet, he thought how ironic it was that he rented the apartment of the man he killed just weeks before on Indiana Street. He knew Conrad Corbett died a painful death and he was hoping Peter Michaels would suffer the same fate later that day.

CHAPTER 55

T he skeletal form of Theodore Dobonovich laying on the autopsy table was deteriorated, shrunken, and brittle. The high-
resolution surgical light made the fragile remains look
brownish-gray. The condition of the skeleton defied the length of time
the body was in its grave. As soon as Dr. Crine put the slightest pressure on an inelastic bone part with his delicate instrument it seemed
to disintegrate turning the particles into a dusty like material.

This poor bastard suffered a horribly painful death, Dr. Crine
thought, as he pried into the inner bones, searching any possible marrow or useful fragments that could be analyzed. He managed to extract some detritus from the humerus, tibia, femur, sternum and a
couple of ribs.

He put six samples into evidence bags, tagged them and set them
aside.

The remains of Hildegard Dobonovich were not as deteriorated
as the father's. *Maybe he didn't want his mother to suffer as much as
the father,* Crine reckoned.

Using the exact same procedures, the ME extracted six more
samples from the mother's skeleton, and bagged the evidence for
analysis.

~~~~

Special agent Jack Warren and detective Tony Quagliaroli were discussing who should take the lead on having the remains of Phillip Hutchison and Matthew Stevonski exhumed.

Peter Michaels filled them both in on the two orderlies mysterious deaths at the Madison Mental Health Center during Dobonovich's stay, after he confirmed the deaths occurred.

"You really think this bastard has killed more people than John Wayne Gacy?" Warren asked.

"Gacy killed 33 boys and young men, and we know Dobonovich has already killed 34. At first we thought he was a terrorist killing people at random, but with Michaels's persistence we proved that wrong."

"Yeah, I know. How does he find this shit out before we do? My gut tells me he's right about this too." Warren said.

"I don't know. It is a weak link to connected the deaths of these guys to Dobonovich." Detective Quag said.

"Listen some careers could be made with this case. Everybody in Chicago now knows about this guy. The interest is amazing." Warren opined.

"I'll talk to the chief, if he agrees than I'll go to the new guy in charge of special prosecutions at the State's Attorney's office. Getting an exhumation order is not as complicated as getting a search warrant."

"Do you think Crine will go along with it? He is working on overload."

"My guess is, this will certainly interest him more than an autopsy on another drive by shooting victim. Do you know that so far this year, an average of ten or twelve people a day are shot on the streets of Chicago … Every day?"

"And on top of that we've got this 'Bug Man.' Asshole."

~~~~

Dobonovich and Choi/Lin An carefully transferred the enhanced anthrax/ricin mixture into secure plastic bags and packed them into two red toolboxes. It took months to perfect the deadly compound that would be light enough to be dispersed into the air and water soluble enough to withstand the pressure and dampness when packed into the fountain's water pumps.

"Are you sure the temperature in your new workspace will hold at 72 degrees?" Dobonovich probed.

"I've been there over a week already. I am positive. I have all the tools I need to make the preparations."

"They have no idea that thousands of those idiot Bear fans will die." Dobonovich said with an insalubrious grin.

"I can't wait." Choi/Lin An responded, his evil eyes squinting.

"Do you have your escape route figured out?"

"Yes. I'll trigger the devices from the crossover walkway. I'll be on my bike, and be gone by the time the compounds are released."

"Good. Now it's time to kill that fucking pest, Peter Michaels."

"How are you going to do it?"

"TC-24. It will be instant!"

CHAPTER 56

"Y ou have got to get a search warrant and hit his house," Peter Michaels pled, almost screaming at his buddy, detective Jack Warren.

"It is not that easy to get a warrant," Warren responded.

"You do it all the time with confidential informants. I'm your C.I..

"He fucking admitted to me that he killed those people, and he threatened to kill me ... again. That's not hearsay."

"I know. I know. I'll talk to Quag about the warrant. He's very close to the new supervisor of special prosecutions." Warren said as he exhaled deeply.

"Good." Michaels said smiling.

"Are you really going to meet him?" Warren asked with alarm in his voice.

"You bet your ass, I am. I'm supposed to hear from him soon," Michaels said, rubbing his forehead with the back of his left hand.

"I'm going with you. We can arrest him on site. You might not be able to protect yourself." Warren implored.

"I don't know." Michaels responded, walking around his desk, concern creasing his brow.

"You're putting yourself in harm's way, Peter. This guy is very devious. He's not going to shoot you. That's not his thing, but he will try to poison you, somehow, and you ... we have to be ready to react." Warren said beseechingly.

"I know. I know. I'll think about it. Get that warrant. My gut tells me there is something much more sinister going on here. I can feel it in my gut. I've got to talk to my boss." Michaels said, hanging up the phone.

His shoulders were slumped, and his head was down as he walked to his news director's office. *Am I the dumbest ass in the world? Meeting this monster! Am I nuts?* He thought.

~~~~

It was Gary Allmaier's third day as the new supervisor of the special prosecution's unit of the Cook County State's Attorney's office. All the Chicago Cubs baseball paraphernalia from his predecessor was removed from the office and replaced with pictures of the sporting events that he cherished: golf and marathons.

Allmaier's six-foot one frame was lithe. He was a cross-country runner from middle school to the present day. After he ran his first Chicago Marathon, he fell in love with the windy city and moved here, starting a new career as a prosecutor. Now 22 years later, he was throwing the most precious thing he owned from one hand to the other, a golf ball with TW inscribed on it. Allmaier was in the gallery at the 18th hole when Tiger Woods won his first major championship at the Masters in 1997. For whatever reason, Woods's caddy threw him a ball as they walked by.

The only thing Allmaier loves more than hitting a green in regulation, is putting a murderer behind bars. He did that 21 times as a career prosecutor, only losing three cases that were heavily loaded with circumstantial evidence.

Detective Tony Quag walked in with a big smile and an extended hand.

"Hey congratulations," he said.

"Thanks. Now, how are you going to fuck up my day?" Allmaier asked, a wide grin spreading across his face revealing perfect white straight teeth.

"We know where the 'Bug Man' lives and we need a search warrant for his place," the detective stated.

"Are you positive about your information?"

"He confessed to Peter Michaels that he killed all those people. It's unbelievable." Quag responded.

"He admitted to murder?" Allmaier responded incredulously.

"Yes ... and he wants to meet with Michaels."

"Is Peter going to do it?"

"Yes."

"Is he nuts?"

"Probably but he has had the lead on this thing almost from the beginning."

"I don't know about that. Anything else?"

"Yep. We need to exhume the bodies of Phillip Hutchinson and Matthew Stevonski," Quad proclaimed.

"Who are they now?" Allmaier asked, a questioning look spreading across his face.

Quag explained the connection to the Dobonovich case and looked intensely at the prosecutor and said, "Well."

"Give me three hours. I should be able to get it done, but I'm worried this 'Bug Man' guy is trying to commit suicide by cop. Tell Michaels to be careful."

~~~~

Cyril Dobonovich and Choi/Lin An were cleaning out the laboratory in the house on Chestnut Street and preparing for their exit along with the "Bug Man's" meeting with Peter Michaels. Choi/Lin An was steaming the wrinkles out of a green uniform that Dobonovich would wear later that afternoon.

As if one killer was confessing to another, Dobonovich feeling melancholic, started telling his student for the first time that he killed both his parents when he graduated from high school and before he moved to Vienna.

"Why did you kill them?" Choi/Lin An asked surprisingly.

"Why did you kill yours?" Dobonovich countered.

"Because I grew to hate them. They always put pressure on me to be the best. I felt like I was their money ticket," he said thoughtfully, his mind drifting back to the day he butchered them with the hatchet he found in a utility closet. A sinful smile appeared on his lips, but no shame or guilt.

"What are you smiling about?" Dobonovich asked but he instinctively knew that his protégé was reminiscing on how he slaughtered his entire family. He paused momentarily and continued their conversation without any remorse. "I just hated my father. My mother was an experiment."

"How did you do it?" Choi/Lin An asked staring into the lifeless eyes of his mentor.

"In biology class we were studying plants and I ran across Conium Maculatum which of course is hemlock. One of the deadliest plants in the world. I got some hemlock spring rosette, dried it out and put it in my father's tea bag. He fell over at the dining room table sipping his tea. Everyone thought it was an aneurysm. No questions asked. No autopsy. Nothing."

"That was ingenious."

"Yes, it was. Wasn't it?" Dobonovich responded with a malignant smile, forgetting his headache as he reflected to that time years ago when he put his first diabolic plan into action. He had absolutely no repentance.

"And your mother?" Choi/Lin An asked inquisitively.

"That was the best. I used Flourecein-5-Isotiocyanate," the "Bug Man" said with the same ugly smile. "No one suspected anything because she had a nuclear stress test the day before I killed her. I used the same isotopes the doctors use for the test, but I increased the cyanide and she died peacefully in her sleep. No one thought another thing about it because she did have a weak heart."

"So, there was no investigation. Unbelievable." Choi/Lin An said respectfully.

"Yes. Those idiots had no Idea. I always counted on their stupidity, but I must lay down now and rest a little. This afternoon is going take all my energy," he said in debilitated voice.

Choi/Lin An jumped up, grabbed his arm to steady him, led him to the bed and helped him lie down. "Let me fluff up your pillow." Once he got him situated, he looked down, and got a lump in his throat and tears welled in his hateful eyes. *I know you will be dead in a few hours, but so will that pain in the ass reporter.*

Dobonovich took a deep breath and closed his eyes. A wicked smile creased his face as he thought about killing Peter Michaels.

CHAPTER 57

C hicagoans thinking about buying diamond engagement rings, tennis bracelets, gold chains or other fine jewelry consider shopping at Jewelers Row. Chicago's diamond district consist of more than 200 stores that are located on Wabash Avenue between East Washington Street and Monroe Street, right near the center of the Loop. The iconic, early 20th century buildings that house these jewelry stores are city landmarks, and that makes Jewelers Row a tourist attraction. Five different train lines travel on the elevated L-tracks that run north and south on Wabash, utilizing two different stations, located at Adams and Washington. It's easy to get to and it's easy to disappear into the late afternoon crowds of shoppers and office workers.

~~~~

Peter Michaels stopped biting his fingernails when he was in the seminary in the ninth grade, but at the moment, he was nibbling on his right thumbnail waiting for a call from the "Bug Man."

David Beedy was fidgety. His eyes were darting back and forth as he looked for something to do to stay busy. He nervously asked, "Are you sure you want to meet this son of a bitch?"

Michaels' face was painted with anxiety. He stood up stretching his painful lower back from too many years of competitive tennis. Diving for tennis balls had taken its toll on his body. "I'll tell you one thing. I have never met up with anyone who wanted to kill me before."

"What does Phil think?" Beedy asked standing up; beginning to pace.

"He is checking with Sam to see what the legal issues will be, if any at all." Michaels answered. He was so on edge when his cell-phone vibrated in his pocket it felt like an electronic jolt and made him jump.

"Michaels."

"Hey, it's Sam."

Sam Phieffer the station's legal counsel for decades, asked rhetorically, "You know, you are nuts?"

"Yeah. Yeah. I know but …"

"I am going to tell you not to do this, but I know it will be futile. So, if you meet this crazy man, do it in a public place during daylight hours only."

"Got it. Don't worry." Michaels said trying to sound positive.

"You wear a Kevlar vest and a long sleeve shirt. You have some-one keep eyes on you at all times and you have your phone set for a quick dial 911 emergency." Phieffer said authoritatively, laying out the guidelines.

"What if the police are there?"

"That complicates things. They need probable cause to arrest him," Sam said, running his long fingers through his graying hair.

"Oh, I'm pretty sure they have probable cause. He confessed to me that he killed those people. He called that 13-year-old gang-banger, who bought his burner phones, collateral damage."

"Peter … you'd better just be careful. This guy is deranged. He won't care if he dies trying to kill you."

~~~~

Cyril Dobonovich's was winching in pain. His head was pounding. The migraine was the worst he had ever experienced since they started several years ago. His little rest did nothing to relax him. He knew death was imminent and that motivate him even more. He pushed a steroid concoction into his veins knowing that it would give him at least a full hour of energy.

He rigorously shook a vial of yellowish liquid and inserted a 19-gauge needle into the flexible rubber cap to fill a 20cc syringe carefully. He held his instrument of death cautiously over the sink careful not to let the slightest amount leak. The contents meant instant death.

He smiled when Choi/Lin An walked into the room.

"What are you smiling about?" The killer's assistant asked knowing the answer.

"You know why. Peter Michaels will be dead before the end of this day," Dobonovich said as he put a protective cap over the 19-gauge needle, holding it up the light turning the syringe with his fingers.

"What is that stuff?" Choi/Lin An asked curiously putting on a pair of latex gloves.

"It's TC-24. It's extremely lethal," the "Bug Man" responded, carefully putting the syringe into his toolbox. "It's an horse tranquilizer and Peter Michaels will be dead within seconds once I get this into him."

Dobonovich suddenly felt dizzy and had to steady himself, holding onto the stainless steel counter.

Choi/Lin An immediately reacted, grasping his mentor to keep him upright. "Are you alright?"

"I'll be fine. I will do this one last thing, and you must follow the plan to the end." Dobonovich whispered, his eyes desperate.

"I have everything ready to go," Choi/Lin An said with a half-smile.

"Now help me get ready."

~~~~

"News. Michaels."

"Are you ready to meet?" Dobonovich said, forcing his voice to be stronger than it really was.

"Where and when?" Michaels reacted, surprised that the "Bug Man" called on the office phone instead of his cell.

"We will meet at 37 North Wabash, seventh floor at 4:30 and be a time," Dobonovich ordered. "I will not wait for you."

Michaels' mind was racing. "That's Jewelers Row," Michaels rejoined, knowing that it violated all the rules that Sam steadfastly set up. "I'll be there."

Michaels hung up the phone and called his cameraman, Paul Nagaro and asked, "How did the undercover body-cam work?"

"It worked great. Where we going?"

"Jewelers Row."

"That ain't outside," Nagaro said worriedly.

"We'll be fine. Don't worry." Michaels said but his hands were shaking. "I'll meet you at the truck in a few."

Michaels hung up and made one more call.

CHAPTER 58

T he Chicago Fire Department's Engine Company 99, two fire trucks, one ladder truck, an ambulance and a Haz-Mat Incident Team (H.I.T.) greeted detective Tony Quagliaroli and a small SWAT team when they arrived at the "Bug Man's" house on Chestnut Street with a search warrant. The ladder truck was pumping tons of water on the roof.

Quag recognized the Battalion Chief immediately as an old friend and walked over to him. "What the fuck's going on, Red?"

Quag and Red played high school football together at De LaSalle, more than 20 years ago. Quag came from a cop family. Red, Brian Cronin, came from a family of firefighters. They tried to stay close but as their careers moved forward their connection moved apart. They occasionally had a beer.

The Chicago Fire Department responds to 500,000 emergency calls a year. When something unusual happens, they don't hesitate to bring a H.I.T. team. This was one of those incidents.

"A neighbor noticed thick, black billowing smoke coming from the roof and called in the alarm. The ladder truck guys noticed a sophisticated exhaust system up there when they started dosing it." Red responded, and then asked in his typical Southside dialect, "What are you's guys doin here?"

"Gotta search warrant. We think the guy who lives here is a terrorist or serial killer. They call him the 'Bug Man.' You know what I'm talking about?"

The Battalion Chief's eyes widen, he reach for his radio mike and immediately sent an order to get the Haz-Mat team in full protective gear and ready to move on the unknown situation. He knew the "Bug Man" dealt with deadly poisons and this presented an immediate danger to his men. He turned back to his old friend, "Shit man. This ain't good."

"No, it's not. How soon can I get in there? This is important."

"You ain't going nowheres til we clear this scene and make sure there ain't no hazardous materials located in this structure. It could be hours." Red retorted. "I've got to get the Arson squad over here too."

"Yeah. This is a crime scene alright, and that bastard did everything he could to destroy any kind of evidence that may have been left behind."

~~~~

Special agent Jack Warren was rushing out the door wearing a worried expression, knowing he was going to hook up with Peter Michaels for support during his meeting with Cyril Dobonovich when his phone rang to a Kenny Chesney tune. He knew it was agent Donna Blake, so he hesitantly answered it. "Hey, what's up buddy?"

"You are not going to believe this." Blake said excitedly.

"I'd believe anything at this point. Whatta you got?" He asked rolling his right hand in a circular motion silently conveying *hurry up* to himself.

"I just got back from the crime lab. Dobonovich killed his mother with Flourecein-5-Isothiocyanate. In medical terms it is called FITC and generally it is used for diagnostic purposes."

"Yeah ... that's the nuclear dye stuff they shoot into your veins like when they do stress tests and shit like that. How can that kill you?" Warren asked skeptically, stopping in his tracks.

"The bastard did some fooling around with it somehow. He increased the cyanide proportion and over time it killed her."

"What a sick fuck. How did you guys discover it so quickly? That body was in the ground for more than ten years."

"It was by accident."

"Talk to me. I am running out the door."

"After Dr. Crine performed the autopsy, his assistant was cleaning up the operating rooms. When the lights were turned off, she used a blue light as a flashlight to find her way back to the office area, and that's when she noticed it."

"Noticed what?"

"The skeleton had a green aura. She immediately called Dr. Crine. He was on his way out the door and when he returned he was stunned."

"That's incredible. It seems to be one of the only breaks we've had on this investigation."

"So, he called us about this incredible finding and when the crime lab guys got all the samples they did the same thing, and whalla ... FITC. It's probably Dobonovich's first signature poison."

"On his own mother. What a sick fuck." Warren exclaimed shaking his head in disbelief. "How come they didn't find it back then?"

"There was no cytological screening panel for this kind of biomolecule investigation, and his mother apparently had some sort of test that used the stuff, so it probably never occurred to them. Is my guess."

"This case is so weird! I gotta go. I don't want to be late," he implored.

"Where are you going?" Blake asked.

"Michaels is meeting the 'Bug Man,' and I am going to be there to arrest his ass."

~~~~

Cameraman Paul Nagaro was holding hands with show producer Kim Burke acting like they were in love, shopping for a diamond engagement ring on the seventh floor of the 37 Wabash building. She had a small monitor in her purse connected to Nagaro's wireless high definition body cam as he was making final adjustments for camera angles to capture the meeting between Michaels and the "Bug Man." The bulletproof vests they wore were camouflaged with long sleeve baggy shirts but it distorted Nagaro's shot, so, he had to make some modifications.

The happy couple started their shopping spree at Bergenstein's, the largest and one of the most popular stores in Jeweler's Row. The store's name was stenciled in 12-inch gold letters across the store's huge glass window. More importantly, it offered a perfect view of the entire floor and everyone entering or exiting the elevator.

Nagaro knew the owner Marvin Bergenstein for years. Every piece of jewelry he ever bought for his wife, went through Marvin.

"Now Marv when you hear me say 'GO KIM' you take every one into the back room and get down. I am sure there will be no gunfire but we don't want to take any chances."

Bergenstein's smile turned upside down as fear entered his eyes that his thick glasses couldn't conceal. "You're kidding right, Paul?"

"Trust me the only person who is going to get hurt if anyone does, will be this crazy killer. You see that couple over there? They're cops and they plan to arrest him immediately."

Agent/detective Jack Warren never looked like he was the police. Ray-Ban sunglasses shrouded his piercing blue eyes. His two-button khaki colored summer sport coat that fit like it was tailor made accentuated his purple Nirvana tee shirt. His Harley Davidson black jeans hung perfectly on his hips and his alligator skin cowboy boots made him looked like a country western singer. His 9mm Glock was tucked into the small of his back in a quick release holster.

His partner, Sergeant Katie Carruthers' blonde hair tickled the back of her neck at the collar of her bulky white linen shirt that concealed her bulletproof vest. Her Versace sunglasses rested on the top of her head, allowing her alert, green eyes to focus on the surroundings. Her long, slender, muscular legs looked like they were poured into her tight fitting Levi jeans. She too holstered a 9mm Glock in the small of her back.

"Peter we're set," Warren said into his ear com, connecting everyone on the team.

CHAPTER 59

B
eads of sweat from the hot August summer day and nerves began to roll down Peter Michaels' forehead and into his eyes causing them to burn, as he walked down Wabash Avenue to confront his death threat. The dark blue, baggy, long sleeve linen shirt covering his bulletproof vest added to his anxiety and body heat. He constantly and apprehensively looked over his shoulder to make sure no one could rush him from behind and inject him with some lethal poison as he entered the building's revolving door.

Six federal agents from the JTTF were window-shopping along the street to make sure that didn't happen as well. Per instructions, the FBI agents would rotate in the store on the seventh floor to provide maximum cover and protection for Peter Michaels when he met with the "Bug Man." The agents were given strict instructions on safety procedures if they had to fire their weapons in a crowded store at a strategy briefing hours before.

Michaels walked with extreme caution, more aware of his surroundings than he had ever been before in his life. He never met any of the agents assigned to safeguard him, but he knew what they all looked like. Jack Warren emailed him pictures of everyone on the protective detail, hoping it would help calm his nerves, but it had the

opposite effect. It caused Michaels more anxiety: serving as a constant reminder that he could be dead at any moment.

The elevators were in the middle of the ground floor on the right
hand side of the hallway. The gray marble floors lost most of their
luster after millions of people tracked in tar, sand, gravel, mud, rain
and salty winter snow over the years looking for bargain diamonds.
Michaels hugged the left side of the hallway. No agents followed him
in. They would be awaiting instructions from Jack Warren, who was
already in position on the seventh floor.

The elevator door opened and Michaels made sure the car was
empty before he entered. As he reached to press the seventh floor
button, his heart almost burst from the sudden appearance of a gorgeous red head, who moved like a cat with amazing agility and the
grace of a ballerina, slipped in between the doors just as they were
about to close. Michaels recognized her as a FBI agent detailed to
him and breathed a sigh of relief. *Thank you God,* he said to himself.

The tall, muscular agent gave him a slight hint of a smile in
acknowledgement but said nothing when their eyes met. She knew
she had just scared the shit out of him, but her job was to protect him
and prevent Dobonovich from killing him so, she suppressed any
thought of his soiled underwear. No words were exchanged but
Michaels offered a nod and a look of relief. The red head got out first
and turned right. Michaels exited and turned left towards
Bergenstein's. Thankfully the floor didn't appear to be crowded with
shoppers.

~~~~

Jack Warren noticed the small man first out of the corner of his
searching eyes. The electrician was dressed in a green uniform and
baseball cap. He entered through the fire escape door and went directly to the electrical panel on the rear wall. He was short and hairless. Lee's Electrical Company was embroidered on the back of his

uniform. He carried a red toolbox and moved slowly and deliber-ately. Warren did not pick up on it immediately but the slight limp in his gait put Warren's instincts on alert.

The "Bug Man" knew he was being watched but he acted as if he belong there doing his job. He opened his lightweight three-step fold-ing ladder and steadied himself as he climbed one rung. He place a small mirror on the edge of the electrical box door so he could have a clear view of the hallway and shoppers moving in and out the stores. His timetable was firmly established, he would wait no longer than 90 seconds for Michaels to show up before he would make his escape.

He got slightly dizzy after a minute waiting on the ladder but when he saw Michaels coming down the hallway an sinful smile materialized and a new rush of adrenalin energized his body and seemed to relieve his headache. He flicked a switch on his remote interceptor device and the electronic interference immediately cut off all communications between the agents wearing ear coms.

The silence was deafening and Michaels immediately put his right hand to his ear when all the chatter ceased and that's when Dobonovich grabbed his syringe filled with TC-24 to put his plan in motion. Michaels was just ten feet away when Dobonovich turned off the overhead lights in the hallway. Everything went dark except for a few emergency lights that lined the floor and the exit sign above the fire escape door. He turned a little too quickly on the ladder and lost his footing as he lunged forward at the unsuspecting Peter Michaels. He stumbled forward and screamed wildly and loudly as he reached out to stab his target with the syringe he had poised over his head. "You motherfucker. I have been waiting a long time for ..."

Peter Michaels was blinded by the darkness but instinctively threw himself flat against the wall, taking a deep breath as Warren had instructed him to do the night before. The defensive move cut his target size to a third: exposing his left arm instead of his full frontal

body mass. Michaels also slid backwards to increase the distance between himself and his attacker.

~~~~

"Shit!" Jack Warren screamed as he ran out of Bergenstein's and
down the hall towards Michaels. He switched on his mag light as he
raced to his friend's aid thinking the worst, and also feeling guilty that
he screwed up the whole operation by not thinking about the lighting
issue.

"You alright?" He asked Michaels with relief in his voice, seeing
his friend alive clutching the wall with all of his strength as if he were
standing on the ledge of building, afraid to look down for fear of falling off.

"Yeah, I'm fine but that bastard isn't." Michaels said breathing
hard, looking down in disbelief at his would be killer groveling on the
dirty floor.

Warren shifted his light beam to the ground and Cyril
Dobonovich, who was violently convulsing as if suffering from an
epileptic seizure, quivering in pain.

The other agents that just caught up to the action, did the same
with their flashlights. "That doesn't look too good," Warren's partner,
Katie Carruthers said in a low voice.

"What goes around, comes around." Warren said softly, shaking
his head watching the mass murderer die. He reached for his cellphone to call the crime scene investigators and the medical examiner, and a slight grin of satisfaction creased his lips.

The agent with the red hair went over to the electrical box and
turned the lights back on and then she looked for the interceptor device that was magnetically attached to the switch box door and
turned it off.

The "Bug Man" looked like he touched an electrical current. His
body was contorted, as if frozen in time. His eyes were filled with

agonizing fear and appeared to be bulging out of their sockets. His left arm looked like it was grasping for relief and his fingers were bent and curled as if crippled with horrific arthritis. His right hand was clutching a syringe that was pushed deeply into the left side of his stomach. It took less that 30 seconds for him to die a horrific death. No one attempted to render aid. There was no sympathy in the air, only gratification.

Michaels was overcome with nausea as he looked down at the "Bug Man's" corpse. "I think, I'm going to throw up. That could have been me." Michaels whispered and placed his hands on his knees bending over taking deep breaths.

~~~~

Nagaro and producer Kim Burke arrived a few seconds later. Both had astonishing looks attached to their faces. Nagaro had videotaped many dead people over the years as a photojournalist, but the sight of the man who tried to kill his friend unnerved him. It was the first time Burke had ever seen a dead person other than at a funeral parlor. She turned her head away from everyone and vomited.

Nagaro patted her on the back trying sooth her agony and looked over at Michaels and said, "I got everything on tape until he shut off the lights."

"And you missed the money shot!" Michaels proclaimed trying not to grin, but then he realized, he had just escape death, and he started to gag.

CHAPTER 60

Peter Michaels sat at his high-top table in his atrium alone with his thoughts, his peace of mind disturbed with all the questions that pricked and pierced at his sub consciousness. The "Bug Man" was gone but Michaels gut told him, his deadly mission was not over. He reached for his coffee that was tipped off with Rum Chita. It warmed his throat and calmed his nerves. Michaels could not believe how drained he was after his ordeal with death. He had no adrenalin left and his hands were trembling.

The debriefing took almost three hours at the Joint Terrorism Task Force office. Michaels was upset that he couldn't appear on the ten o'clock news, but he dictated everything to Ron Magers and Nagaro had the forethought to have a currier on standby to get his videotape back to the station. The tape was very theatrical particularly when the lights went out at the very moment the attack on Michaels occurred. Magers' dramatic voice inflection had all viewers sitting on the edge of their seats including everyone in the newsroom and they had already viewed the tape multiple times.

The Neilson ratings for that night reflected the highest local television viewership in history with 89 percent of every TV turned on in the Chicago viewing area. Everyone was talking about the attempt on Peter Michaels' life.

~~~~

Choi/Lin An was clenching his fists, and anger flushed his face as he watched the ten o'clock news knowing his mentor, lover and only friend was dead. He began reflecting on their last conversation and his promise to kill as many people as he could before game time in less than a week. He went to the kitchen cupboard to make sure the anthrax/ricin compound was safely tucked away. Every time he past the cupboard he checked it. His hands were beginning to shake.

He needed to stay busy to keep his mind off of Dobonovich so, he started to construct the 50 pipe bombs after his last conversation with his master earlier that day. The butane gas cartages and the wireless detonators fit perfectly into the PVC pipe. He had to drill a small hole to attach a thin wire that would serve as an antenna to receive the ignition signal. His delivery device was nearly complete. The deadly chemical cocktail would be inserted the morning of the game.

He was in a state of depression and he knew it would be hard for him after he dropped off Dobonovich on State Street and Adams at 4:10 pm because he would never see him again until they met in hell. He didn't realize how much he depended on Dobonovich. He had no friends in his life, just faceless enemies and if things went as planned, he would kill thousands of them before the kickoff of the Thursday night game that would launch the 2019 NFL season.

~~~~

Dr. James McBride pressed his eyes hard into the lens of his high-power microscope examining the sample of Theodore Dobonovich's bone marrow and residue. He was taking a shortcut; something he never liked to do, but he felt he had to look for a compound or poison that would not be that sophisticated to administer. He ruled out rat poison immediately because that would be too easy.

After talking to his wife, who loves to garden, over the weekend, he had an epiphany. She was upset because she discovered a tree that she planted by their front steps was poisonous. The first thing he thought of was hemlock. A smile widened on his face, "I'll be a son of a bitch." He literally wanted stand up and dance.

He had read in the case file that the victim drank an inordinate amount of tea, daily. He reached for the phone and called Dr. Robert Crine. "This sick bastard killed his father with hemlock."

"That's odd, but totally believable. How did you figure it out?" Dr. Crine asked rubbing his gray goatee with his right hand.

"I took a wild guess because I had so little to work with. I knew I would only get one, possibly two shots at the most to find anything because the sample was so miniscule and old. I figure he dried the hemlock and somehow mixed it into his father's teabags. The man drank tea constantly throughout the day." Dr. McBride said leaning back in his chair. "Well at least, he won't be killing anymore people. I saw on the news that he tried to kill that reporter and ended up killing himself. Sick bastard."

"I'm not so sure about that. We might have two more deaths that he is responsible for. We think he may have offed two orderlies at the mental health institution where he was committed." Dr. Crine said.

"What is that 30 or so people, he killed?"

"Could be as many as 40 if these two were poisoned."

~~~~

Detective Tony Quag was at the gravesite of Phillip Hutchison at Resurrection Cemetery. The backhoe's shovel had just started to pierce the dried grass when his cellphone rang. "Quagliaroli."

"Hey Tony, it's Jack Warren," he announced wearily.

"Hey, What's up? You sound down."

"No. No. Just tired. A lot of paperwork with that Peter Michaels incident."

"Have you talked to him?"

"Yeah. He's gonna be alright. I don't think he realized until the debrief how close he came to death. If that prick didn't stumble. It might be our friend that's gonna be autopsied today."

"Yeah. I can't believe he allowed himself to be put in that position but I know nothing was going to stop him." Quag responded with a grimace.

"How's it going out there?"

"We exhumed Stevonski this morning and sent his remains to the ME and in another hour we'll do the same with Hutchison."

"Okay. I am going to go over to the 'Bug Man's' house later. I am not sure this is over yet."

"You're starting to sound like Michaels."

"Yeah. That's scary; isn't it?"

CHAPTER 61

T he face of Cyril Dobonovich was twisted with an angry fury and yet his bulging eyes made him look scared as if they were asking the question; "How could this have happened to me … me of all people." His skin had a silver tone, blending in with the stainless steel table on which his hideous corpse was displayed. Dr. Robert Crine was intrigue by this portrait of a complete madman that lay in front of him.

"Now let's see what you can tell me," he whispered as began to make the first incision into the chest cavity. Crine was stunned by the shape and color of every organ that he removed. They looked tormented. Deformed. Discolored. Diluted. "How could you even walk?" he mentally inquired, shaking his head in disbelief. Beads of perspiration began to bubble on his scalp and butterflies erupted in his stomach like the nervous anxiety he felt when he played his first soccer game years ago in high school. Every organ weighed half of its normal weight.

He was actually anxious to dissect the brain. His hands had not shaken like this since the first time he used a saw to open a skull back in medical school; a feeling he had not felt in decades. He was actually exhilarated, but when he extracted the brain, he became nauseous, and almost dropped the matter onto the table and floor.

The brain of a healthy person normally weighs 49 ounces and it is gray with black, white and red fissures running throughout the organ. They are not very pretty to look at; brains are comprised of nerves, veins, blood vessels, cells, nerve fibers and all sorts of neurons and neuron-connectors. Dobonovich's brain weighed 39 ounces and it was black and green almost like it suffered from frostbite.

The ME's face behind his surgical mask took on a look of delight, almost smiling when he thought of how painful it must have been for this serial killer to live his life as his body betrayed him, but that feeling was cut short as he started to gather evidence. His scientific subconscious wondering *what could have caused such a catastrophic invasion of this sort and how long was it going on?*

Dr. Crine carefully sliced samples of every organ, placed them in sealed containers and labeled them to establish a chain of evidence. He could not wait to send them off to Fort Detrick and his friend, Dr. James McCormick to find the answers to the questions that kept pecking at his brain.

He had never seen anything this repugnant in his 30-year career.

~~~~

Detective Jack Warren heard the roar of Peter Michaels' Harley and its screaming eagle pipes before he saw him come around the corner on Chestnut Street. The search warrant was a precaution and it was tucked in his sport coat pocket. Yellow police tape adorned the entrance to serve as a warning to civilians to stay away from the crime scene. Warren had the key to the police padlock that secured the premises. He waited for Michaels on the porch.

Michaels eased off of his bike in one graceful motion, placed his skidlid on his seat, put the key in his pocket and walked up the stairs. "Hey. Has anyone else been in here yet?"

"No. CFD just cleared the area this morning. They said there was some smoke and water damage but their quick response time allowed them to put the fire out fairly quickly but I doubt there will be much trace left behind."

The once clean windows that seemed glassless were now covered with soot and grime, and thousands of gray water spots. Warren slipped on a pair of black latex gloves and handed Michaels a pair. "The crime lab guys will be here shortly so, don't touch anything." Warren said and then he coughed from the heavy odor of smoke.

They walked slowly and carefully through the living room; their bright mag lights cast eerie shadows over the once white head mannequins serving as resting places for the hundreds of wigs that were line up row after row; giving a feeling that they were being watched from another dimension.

"This is apparently were he dressed before he left the house," Michaels uttered … his red eyes burning and seeping with tears.

Warren went to the racks of women clothing and Michaels went to male side, running his hand over the jackets, shirts and pants that were perfectly laid out as he walked through. "This fucker had OCD." Michaels said.

"Yeah. He was a little shit too." Warren said, taking in all the disguises on display. "We might be able to match up some of these outfits to the tape we have."

"I'd say he never wore the same outfit twice and he destroyed everything he ever left the house in. Look what he did to the nun habit." Michaels opined.

"Anybody home in here?" came the familiar voice of Crime Scene Investigator Gary Landis.

"Yeah. We're in the back dressing room." Warren announced as he opened drawers to the dressing table at the end of the room. Each drawer contained different forms of makeup, eyelashes, glues, latex noses and ears, endless containers of contact lenses of every color; anything that aided in changing appearances. Twenty-one soft lights, seven on each side, surrounded the dressing mirror. All the glass was covered with an ashy detritus, and the electricity was turned off, adding to the insalubrious environment. A chill ran down Warren's spine like an irritating sciatic nerve making him shiver.

"I'm going upstairs," Michaels announced and didn't wait for permission, but he was expecting and got an instant warning.

"Don't touch anything. I'll be right up there." Warren said pulling out the last drawer in the dressing table, looking down at dozens of clear plastic boxes of eyeglasses, many with tinted lens.

Michaels pulled himself up the last step of the spiral staircase and froze. He rotated his body moving his flashlight beam from left to right taking in the laboratory where he had no doubt the "Bug Man" created his deadly, signature, killing compounds. "Son of a bitch," he said in a voice just over a whisper. "Son of a bitch."

The sunlight fought to enter the room, but it was depressed. The water that dosed the fire, managed to wash some of the thick black residue off of the inner windows allowing some irregular beams of light to penetrate the rooms. Thick particles of dust danced in the air, energized by a breeze that filled the room through broken windows. Michaels wished he had a mask to cover his mouth. His throat felt dusty, dry and irritated. He put his handkerchief to his mouth and continued his exploration. The water in his red, burning eyes cause him to constantly blink rapidly and his vision to blur.

He found incubators, refrigerators, and microscopes of all sizes, petri dishes, and test tubes. All the equipment needed; to create microscopic organisms of death. He reached up to open a cabinet but then thought better of it.

Warren walked up behind and exclaimed, "Holy shit. This guy wanted for nothing when it came to lab equipment."

"You know, I think anybody who opens any of these cabinets could face exposure to some serious poisons or some trip bomb." Michaels said.

"I agree. Landis has a HAZMAT guy coming over, and I think we should have the bomb squad x-ray these cabinets before we go any further." Warren said.

Michaels' cellphone rang to the tune of "Cheeseburgers in Paradise," he answered it, "What's up Dave?"

"Dr. Yako called. He's on his way back to Chicago. He'll do an interview." Producer David Beedy informed.

"That's fantastic." Michaels responded with a smile curling on his lips.

"One more thing," Beedy announced.

"Good news, I hope," Michaels retorted.

"I got a picture of Dobonovich's partner. It's a few years old but it is something. I think you are right; this thing is not over yet." Beedy said with a troubled reassuring voice.

The hair on Michaels' forearms stood straight up and his stomach did a flip causing an acid reflux. He trusted his gut and his gut was telling him something very big was on the horizon ... but What?

CHAPTER 62

D avid Beedy was on the phone, in what looked like an intense conversation when Peter Michaels walked into the office. Michaels set a cup of black coffee on his desk and gave him a half salute. Beedy acknowledged him with a big grin and joyful eyes.

"You're not going to believe it, but we have a picture of Dobonovich's partner," Beedy proclaimed as he hung up the phone smiling.

"How'd you do that?" Michaels asked with a returning grin.

"My brother-in-law just found it in an old file at Madison, and he's emailing it to me as we speak." Beedy replied as his phone pinged. "This must be it."

Michaels came over to his desk and looked over his shoulder at a black and white picture of an Asian man, who appeared to have high cheekbones, dark eyes and jet-black hair, cut in a crew cut.

"How old is that picture?" Michaels asked almost squinting.

"At least ten years old, I'd guess." Beedy replied. "Maybe older."

"Let's get that to graphics and let them play around with it. Let's see if they can age him a little and make him bald to give us several different looks. Great job. I've got this gnawing feeling in my gut. We have got to find this guy and fast."

"How'd it go at the house?"

"A lot of debris and smoke. I think they pretty much covered their tracks, but ..."

"But what?"

"How big is this guy? This ... What's his name again?"

"His name is Bing Lin An. He's six-three and he is covered with tattoos everywhere on his body from his neck down to his ankles."

"Interesting. I thought there was no evidence at the house but there was apparently."

"What do you mean?"

"Where would this accomplice live? There was nothing in the house that suggested that another person, particularly a taller person stayed with Dobonovich. Had to be somewhere close by. Wouldn't you think? There was a basement apartment but we didn't check it because the house had to be cleared by the bomb squad. We have to go back there."

~~~~

Choi/Lin An was carefully loading the poisonous anthrax/ricin compound into a canister that appeared to be a shotgun shell with a funnel type of tip. The specially made canisters had a firing pin that connected to the wireless detonator that would be activated by his cellphone. Once ignited the butane gas would release for at least a minute and a half, dispensing the deadly mixture into the clean, unsuspecting atmosphere, uncontrolled, and into the crowd of people walking towards the stadium.

He was wearing a gas mask, a yellow PPE surgical hospital gown that was taped airtight around his wrist and latex gloves for protection. Despite the constant 68 degree temperature inside his new workplace, he was sweating profusely and his hands were timorous. The perspiration burned his evil eyes and he fumbled the canister he was filling when he tried to wipe his eyes with the sleeve of his gown without thinking about the consequences. He regained his self-control, steadied the canister on the table, stood up, and took several deep breaths to recovered his composure.

He felt instant wet heat in his loin, looked down at his crotch and realized he had pissed himself. He was infuriated. He kicked over his stool, and started tramping around his workspace, screaming, "Fuck. Fuck. Fuck," as loud as he could, only to discover that his muffled cries of despair fell on deaf ears. He ripped off his protective mask, stomped over to a wall cabinet and punch a hole through the door. He never felt the pain of the broken knuckle of the baby finger on his right hand until his anger finally subsided an hour later.

~~~~

Dr. Louise Yako was sitting in a small conference room in the Channel Six newsroom having a cup of coffee with Peter Michaels. His thick gray hair and neatly trimmed beard framed his intellectual face. Though he was a scholar, his deeply tanned skin had the look of a sailor, scarred by the sun and the sea. His brown horn-rimmed glasses could not conceal the walnut like wrinkles around his tired eyes. Michaels immediately felt a connection with this academic man and made him feel comfortable during their hour-long informative interview.

Cameraman Paul Nagaro was breaking down his equipment. "I'll get this tape to Dave. I am sure he is ready to start editing." He said as he exited the room and nodded to the doctor, smiling. "Good luck, Doc."

The door slowly closed and Michaels yelled out, "Thanks, Paul. We'll do a piece for the ten."

Dr. Yako was turning the picture of Bing Lin An around in his fingers and studying it intently, shaking his head. "Of course, I know nothing about this person. They met after my association with Dobonovich, but I have no doubt that Dobonovich had the personality that could attract another sociopath to do his dirty work or join forces with him." Dr. Yako offered.

"It's hard for me to believe that anyone who looked like Dobonovich years ago could attract anyone to him," Michaels said. "He was freaking odd looking."

"Appearances mean nothing to psychopaths. It's not what they look like. It's what they are capable of doing, and obviously Dobonovich had no problem killing people to take out his revenge." The doctor reached for his coffee and his hands started to quiver. "I told you … he killed his parents. I had no doubt about that when I talked with him years ago. It was like he had a dual personality. Narcissistic. He could do nothing wrong. He should have been put to death for killing his assistant." Yako said as his mind raced back in time; a trouble look materializing on his face.

"Well, thanks to you, we discovered that he killed his father with hemlock and his mother basically with cyanide." Michaels said thoughtfully.

"Yes. That was a clever way to kill his mother. No one would have put the pieces together unless they re-examined the remains." Dr. Yako agreed, then he asked, "You believe he killed those two orderlies as well?"

"Hopefully we will find out, but I'd bet the house on it," Michaels said contemplatively, looking intently at Dr. Yako. After a short pause, he continued. "What will you do now? Are you going to continue to practice or are you calling it quits?"

"I have to think about that, but for now I am going to go home and relax. I can't wait for next Thursday night's game. It will be a good one. Too bad we are playing the Packers instead of the Lions for the opening night of the 2019 football season." Dr. Yako said standing up.

Michaels stood up with him in unison and shook his hand gratefully. All of a sudden, he got a weird feeling in the pit of stomach, and he didn't know why.

"Thanks doctor. You take care of yourself. Be careful. I don't know if this thing is over yet and I don't know why."

"Trust your gut," the doctor said looking up at Michaels through the top of his glasses. "It was nice meeting you. Trust your gut," he said again, and walked out the door.

Michaels said, "Thank you Dr. Yako. It was a pleasure meeting you as well." And he wonder if he would ever see the old man again.

CHAPTER 63

C hoi/Lin An was seething. Peter Michaels just finished the story of how he escaped death at the hands of the "Bug Man." The interview with that bastard Dr. Yako, who said that Cyril Dobonovich should have been sentenced to death instead being committed to a mental health facility gnawed at his nerves. The anger building up inside of him made his face crimson. His blood vessel at a point of exploding.

When he saw his picture on the screen, he threw the bottle of water he was drinking from at the television. It missed and hit the wall with a harsh thud. He could hardly grasp the bottle because his hand was so swollen. The first time he clenched his fist the pain from the broken knuckle of his right hand almost brought him to his knees. Despite icing his hand for hours, the swelling had not subsided and the rest of his knuckles seemed to disappear into a flesh colored marshmallow.

He wondered how the picture could be so accurate because it was taken more than a decade before when he was first admitted to Madison Mental Health Center. He realized he had to go on the defensive and change his appearance, but he never thought of bringing any of the wigs, makeup and disguises from the house on Chestnut Street with him.

He felt an uneasiness about going into survival mode. He knew the people he worked with would surely recognize him and he thought about how he could return to Buckingham Fountain and place the poisonous packets into the water pumps.

Beads of sweat bubbled on his baldhead as he paced around the apartment. "I am going to kill that Peter Michaels and the old fucking doctor," he mumbled to himself. His anger mounted and his eyes filled with revenge; he whispered again, "I'm going to kill them if it's the last thing I do."

He made a fist with his swollen right hand and slammed it down on the kitchen table. He screamed out in horrific pain and hatred filled his malevolent eyes.

~~~~

Michaels and anchorman Ron Magers were walking off the news set talking and smiling. Both had a feeling of satisfaction reflected of their faces. "You know, you are crazy."

"Ron, he tried to kill me three times. It was inevitable that I had to confront him, sooner or later."

"What's next?"

"Well, I think this story tonight will force an autopsy on those two orderlies. I have no doubt that they killed them but it might be very difficult to prove it a hundred percent."

"Peter, you know that TC-24, he tried to kill you with, is a very strong horse tranquilizer. It was taken off the market years ago. Even a small amount could kill a human in seconds."

Michaels knew his friend invested in racehorses and was knowledgeable about certain drugs that could affect horses. "I bet that, Dobonovich enhanced it as well to kill faster."

"I don't know about that. I can tell you it is a very powerful drug and.it had severe side effects on many horses, and that's why they took it off the market."

At that moment, the cellphone in Michaels pocket vibrated. He took it out, looked at it, didn't recognize the number and answered, "Michaels."

"I am going to kill you and that old fucking doctor and thousands of others, you motherfucker."

"Bing Lin An. How are you doing?" Michaels said trying to contain the sudden rush of adrenalin that flashed through his body upon hearing the voice with a slight accent.

Magers stopped in his tracks. He felt a surge of excitement, and immediately knew that the "Bug Man's" partner was on the other end of the call. The sparkle in his eyes morphed into apprehension.

Michaels took a silent deep breath. It felt like he was just punched in the gut. His hand began to tremble but he regained his composure, "You know Mr. Lin An, we know what you look like. Tomorrow morning, You will be the most recognizable face in Chicago."

"Fuck you. You piece of shit. I'll get you."

The line went dead.

"Holy shit!" Michaels exclaimed. "I knew there was more to come, but ..." He looked at his phone and hit the speed dial number for his friend.

"Hey, great piece tonight. How'd you get the doctor to talk to you?" Jack Warren quizzed.

"Listen, you have got to get Dr. Yako out of his house. I just gotta call from Bing Lin An and he threatened to kill Dr. Yako and me. You gotta get him into protective custody." Michaels implored; a look concern crossing his face.

"He actually called you and you talked to him?"

"I told you this isn't over yet. I think something big is planned. He slipped and said he was going to kill thousands. We have to figure out what that means."

~~~~

Chicago police cars were immediately dispatched to Dr. Yako's suburban house. He just watched his interview on the news and was drinking a cup of tea to sooth his nerves when the police knocked on his door. He was startled by the loud noise and became apprehensive when he saw all the flashing lights through his front room windows. He cautiously opened the door, "Yes. Is there a problem?"

"Dr. Yako. I am sergeant Ben Farnsworth. We have reason to believe that you are in danger. We would like for you to come with us."

"Well sergeant, I don't want to go anywhere." He protested. "I don't understand what this is all about."

Sgt. Farnsworth had a deep voice and penetrating blue eyes behind his rimless glasses. He had delivered messages like this before in his 30 years on the job. "Do you have Peter Michaels' phone number?" He asked cutting to the chase.

"Yes. I do."

"Call him please."

Dr. Yako went to his office and called Michaels, who immediately answered. "Doc, I don't mean to alarm you but you told me, you always had a to-go-bag ready in case of an emergency. Well, this is an emergency. You have to go with those police officers."

"What happened?" He asked. His eyes shrouded with puzzlement along with a hint of fear.

"We flushed out Dobonovich's partner with tonight's story. He called me and threatened the both of us. Go with the police until we can work this out. Please." Michaels stated affirmatively.

"Should I be scared?"

"Dr. Yako you did a heroic thing tonight. We just sent out Lin An's picture to every news outlet in the city and state. Everyone in the Chicago area will be looking for him by morning."

"I told you earlier; trust your gut." The doctor said with a big smile.

"You did. Now let's catch the bastard."

CHAPTER 64

I t was another restless night for Peter Michaels. The thought of his life being threatened again had unnerved him. He took off the wet tee shirt that he slept in and hung it over the shower door. He put on a new black "Born to Ride" Harley Davidson tee and staggered to his coffee machine.

The knock on his front door startled him back to reality. He wasn't expecting company. He looked through the peephole, opened the door, and Jack Warren walked in with concern painted across his face and a copy of the Chicago Herald in his hand.

"You should have called. You scared the shit outta me." Michaels said.

"Yeah. Sorry. I am worried about you." Warren announced, and then asked, "Did you see the paper? Lin An's picture is plastered across the city. Thanks to you."

"Let me see that." Michaels said and started to scan the story that was headlined; *Police believe killer had an accomplice.* "I hope we find this fucker before he tries to kill me."

"We will. In the meantime, I think we are going to put a protective detail on your sorry ass."

"I don't think so. Well ... unless that redhead is available," Michaels suggested with a grin spreading across his face, lightening his foul mood.

"You're an asshole."

"Just looking out for my safety." Michaels retorted, throwing his hands out with a "What can I say," gesture and then said, "We need to go look at that basement apartment. Lin An probably lived there, no doubt, and he may have left us some clues."

"We have ordered his fingerprints from Madison Mental Health Center. They are being very cooperative ever since we told them our theory that Dobonovich and Lin An may have killed two of their orderlies."

"Have you heard from the crime lab about the 'Bug Man's' autopsy?" Michaels asked reaching for one of his reporter's note pads. He started flipping some pages.

"Yeah. They say they have never seen anything like it before, and that if he didn't die from the fatal TC-24 injection that he would have died within days from how fucked up he was." Warren responded, and then he asked, "What are you looking for?"

"A short cut." Michaels said as he stopped flipping pages and started to read. "Tell your analyst to look for Kuru."

"What's that?" Warren asked puzzled.

"Remember that interview I did weeks ago with one of his professors from Loyola?" Michaels asked but did not wait for an answer. "He said that Dobonovich was obsessed with it and its antidote."

"Okay. What is it?"

"Creutzfeldt-Jakob disease. It's a neurodegenerative agent that starts to deprive the brain of protein. It can be very slow acting, but it is deadly."

"I'll pass that on to Quantico."

"Let's have a cup of coffee and go look at the basement apartment." Michaels said looking out his window at a spectacular view of the waves building on Lake Michigan. The dog days of summer were over and white bulbous clouds were moving across the deep blue sky's landscape, promising more agreeable September temperatures.

~~~~

Streets and Sanitation crews were busy on Columbus Drive unloading dozens of blue traffic horses that will be used to close the street down on Thursday night for the opening night of the new football season.

Another crew was erecting an outdoor stage where the "Singing Palombos" would provide live entertainment for all the fans on the festive night before the game.

No one noticed the city worker in his blue uniform attaching PVC piping to the trashcans that lined the walkway to Soldier Field. His eyes were covered with cheap aviator sunglass. His hat was pulled down on his forehead covering his Asian features and a theatrical mustache disguised his upper lip. He acted as if he belong there, blending into another busy day on Chicago's lakefront, hiding in plain sight.

~~~~

Dr. James McBride changed the toxicological screen panel to identify Kuru and was astounded at how fast the sample registered a positive result. "I'll be damned." He muttered to himself, a smile creasing his lips.

With a little more probing, he discovered a dozen different uncertified manmade compounds that he surmised were antidotes that Dobonovich self-injected to reduce the spread or to purge his system of the deadly agent. They all had a similar chemical finger-print and appeared to discourage rapid growth but in the end, they failed the test of time.

He also discovered an inordinate amount of steroids in the sam-ples. He surmised that was how Dobonovich was able to function for as long as he had. The condition of his organs looked as if they had been condemned to death for years.

He reached for his phone and called Dr. Crine to share his thoughts and conclusions.

~~~~

The decaying corpse of Phillip Hutchinson, the Madison Mental Health Center orderly, was on Dr. Crine's operating table. His remains were in relatively good shape for the amount of time they were buried. The heart and liver were average size but their coloring was disconcerting. It appeared that green and yellow veins had infiltrated the two organs. "What kind of poison are you?" Dr. Crine mused. He felt it wasn't a giant leap to conclude it was poison, considering poison was Cyril Dobonovich's weapon of choice.

Crine looked up over his reading glassed that were poised on the end of his nose as his approaching assistant who held her thumb and little finger to her mouth and ear indicating a phone call. He nodded approvingly, rinsed his hands, and walked over to the wall phone. "Crine here."

"Hey, Bob. It's McBride. That reporter was right again. It was Kuru," and then the analyst told Dr. Crine his theory about how Dobonovich functioned for so long when he should have been dead years ago.

Dr. Crine listened intently then said. "I agree. I thought it was some sort of survival approach. Good work."

"It was great working with you."

"Oh. We are not done. I did two autopsies today on those orderlies I told you about."

McBride let out silent deep breath, rubbed his forehead with his free hand, and said, "Man … this son of bitch was something."

"No kidding. So, I looked at the first body earlier today. Matt Stevonski. He may have died of lung cancer. He was a very heavy smoker and his lungs were literally on their last breath, but I will send you some samples. See if you can discover anything.

"The second guy is Phil Hutchinson. His heart and liver may provide some evidence of poison, I believe. He was a very health specimen. A workout fanatic. Death they say was very sudden."

"Get the samples to me and I should be able to get at it in a few days. Do you think that will wind it up?"

Crine had his back to wall. He was looking up at the ceiling. "The police think there could be a serious threat to the city. This crazy man, Bing Lin An, is still out there. We think he is plotting something huge but we don't have a clue what it is."

CHAPTER 65

D avid Beedy was chuckling to himself reading the sports section enjoying his favorite past time, the Chicago Bears, when Peter Michaels entered the office. "Your Bears are going to get their asses kicked in a few days, my friend" Michaels prophesied.

"You're right, but they'll still have a better record than your Lions at the end of the year." Beedy countered.

"Yeah. I know. Anything new?"

"There was a voicemail message from some polish sounding guy who said he may have come in contact with Lin An." Beedy said handing over a slip of paper with a phone number and the name of a man identified as "Mr. B."

Michaels took it, looked at it, sat down and dialed the number. After three rings, a man with a husky, cigarette scarred voice and a very heavy accent, answered. "Mr. B, dah handyman."

"This is Peter Michaels from Chanel Six News."

"Oh Yah ... yes. I call you. I have information for you." He said and then proceeded to cough a deep smoker's cough.

"Your message said you may have had contact with Lin An." Michaels stated.

"Yes. Yes. The china man. No."

"Korean, actually, not Chinese. What happened?"

"A few days ago. He call. He say, I need you to build me a rack to hold pipe."

Michaels sat up straighter in his chair. No longer smiling. "What kind of rack?"

"He come to my workshop on Milwaukee Avenue. He wait while I make. He pay me two hundred dollars cash. I do it right dare. It take me twenty minutes."

"Can you describe this rack?"

"Sure. I use inch thick board and four-inch wide wood. He want the hole to hold an inch and a half wide pipe."

"How tall was this rack?"

"Three feet high, exactly," he answered and coughed very loudly, clearing his throat.

Michaels winched, thinking that had to hurt. "Did he say what he needed it for?"

"No. No. I asked but he not answer. He give me money and he go."

"Is there anything about him you can remember? Any scars? Tattoos? Anything?"

"Yeah. Yeah. He had on long sleeve shirt but look to me like he gots lots of tattoos on his chest. He had right hand in sling and top button of his shirt opened and I notice this thing."

Michaels stood up now walking nervously around the office. Excited.

"What do you mean sling?"

"I think that's why he need rack. His hand very swollen. Big swollen. He had like black cast or something like that on hand. I asked, hey, you need some help? I good handyman. I can fix any-thing." Mr. B said shrugging his shoulders.

"Anything else, you can remember?" Michaels asked excitedly.

"Yes. Yes. He said I don't need your help, I'm almost done. He give to me, two one hundred dollar bills, and he leave. No thank you. No kiss my ass. No nothing." Mr. B said coughing uncontrollably.

"Do you have cameras in your workshop?" Michaels asked hopefully.

"No. But, there is bank across the street that have cameras maybe that help you."

"Thanks, I'll be in touch. What's your name?"

"I'm Stanislaus Burcovinchoff."

"I see why they call you Mr. B," Michaels said grinning. "Thanks. Someone will be by to talk with you some more. I'm sure."

~~~~

Bing Lin An was stewing. His right hand was throbbing and swelling consumed his hand, and now his back was aching as he leaned over his new pipe rack finishing the last 20 dispensing devices. He was pissed that he didn't kill the Hungarian handyman to clean up any evidence that may lead back to him. He wished he had the rack made earlier because it did help keep the PVC pipe steadier as he delicately inserted the wire detonators, the butane cartridges, and the shotgun shell like devices that would hold the anthrax and ricin compound into the pipe.

He didn't kill Mr. B for three reasons; He was very popular in the neighborhood and people constantly came in and out of his shop to say hello and his right hand was so swollen that he could not grip a syringe or gun or a knife with sufficient strength to make the kill. The old man was also smart and strong. He worked with his back against the rear wall so no one could get behind him and he always had a defensive tool like a hammer or hatchet near his right hand for protection, probably something he learned in the old country before he immigrated to America.

Lin An had the rack made two days before his picture was plastered all over Chicago. He didn't know it at that time that he would be in disguise constantly. Despite his ailments things were going as planned and all the explosive devices should be in place by

Wednesday night. His big problem, he realized would be getting in and out of Buckingham Fountain's water pump area.

~~~~

Peter Michaels and Jack Warren were getting out of an ugly green Crown Vic police car when his phone rang. He knew it was Dave Beedy by the ringtone. "Hey, what's up?"

"You are not going to believe this," Beedy stated emphatically.

"Try me!"

"Lin An works for the city's water department." Beedy stated with a knowing grin creasing his lips.

"Are you shittin me?" Michaels said in disbelief.

"His name is Yang Sung Choi on the city's payroll. Get this, one of the engineers recognized his picture from our story and called his supervisor immediately. Guess what else."

"There's no Yang Sung Choi." Michaels said.

"Right. City investigators checked the info on his application form that said he graduated from Purdue."

Michaels interrupted his partner and said, "The school has no record of any Choi, in any engineering class or any other classes for that matter."

"Yep and one more thing; he got the job after one of top engineers keeled over and died of a massive heart attack at a business meeting luncheon about six months ago."

"Interesting. Add another death to the list."

"That's gonna be impossible," Beedy interjected. "He was cremated shortly after his death and there is nothing to test."

~~~~

Detective Tony Quag was on his way to the First Federal Bank of Cook County on Milwaukee Avenue to look at the surveillance tape from the day before yesterday. He called ahead and talked to the bank manager who agreed to let him look at the tape without a warrant once he found out what case it involved.

Before he went to the bank however, Quag stopped in to talk with Mr. B. He identified himself and then asked rhetorically, "You wouldn't happen to have any of those one-hundred dollar bills that Lin An paid you with? Do you?"

"Yeah sure. I got both." Mr. B stated with a victorious smile.

The detective counted out ten, twenty-dollar bills, laid them on his workbench, and had Mr. B drop his two bills into an evidence bag.

"We're going to check for prints and the serial numbers on the bills. Thanks," he said and then went across the street to meet the bank manager.

CHAPTER 66

T   he Chestnut Street basement apartment was lit up like a
         Hollywood movie set when Michaels and Jack Warren en-
         tered the room. The electricity was turned off after the fire.
Four 500-watt lights sat on tripods in each corner of the apartment
energized by a portable generator supplied by the Department of
Streets and Sanitation. They were lightweight, adjustable, efficient,
and easy to move. The windowless rooms had a mixture of poignant
odors: pinecone, similar to car wash deodorizers, bleach from sanitiz-
ing any evidence, and rotten chicken from bones that were left in the
garbage under the kitchen sink.

Crime scene investigator Gary Landis was pulling fingerprints
from every flat surface in the room. "What took you so long? I
thought you were going to be here an hour ago." He inquired looking
up over his glasses that always slip down to the tip of nose, and a joyful grin on his face.

"What do you got?" Warren asked.

"There are prints everywhere, but they may not tell us much."
Landis said frowning.

"What do you mean?" Warren asked quizzically.

"It looks as if he burned off his real prints. They are only smudges
but that doesn't mean we can't match him to prints that we believe
are his. He didn't get rid of every telltale ridge." Landis informed.

Michaels knew he should keep his mouth shut because this was an active crime scene, and technically he shouldn't even be anywhere near it, but he couldn't help himself, he started walking around searching for anything he could find.

There were traces of shredded paper on the floor but nothing that could be pieced together, then he noticed the edge of a piece of paper trapped under a thick wooden leg of a dining room chair. He reached to picked it up but thought better of it. "Hey Jack, in here."

"Don't touch anything." Warren ordered when he came into the room.

Landis was shuffling behind him, carrying a light that immediately brightened up the dank room. An anxious looked curtained his face. "Don't touch a thing until I look at it." He got down on one knee and winched in pain. "I'm getting tired of this," he said taking a pair of tweezers from his kit. The piece of paper was the shape of a right angle triangle, the longest edge measured four inches and it was torn. Landis held it to the light and turned it around while examining it. "It looks like a copy of a blueprint of some sort."

"What's it from?" Warren asked.

"What's it say?" Michaels asked in unison.

"It says 'ngham' ..." Landis responded inquisitively.

"Buckingham Fountain." Michaels and Warren said simultaneously.

"That's the target." Warren proclaimed.

"That might be *a* target, but I think there is a lot more to it than we know. It appears that he is making some kind of pipe bombs. It just doesn't make sense to me. Pipe bombs and Buckingham Fountain." Michaels said mystified.

~~~~

Bing Lin An felt confident that he left nothing behind at his old apartment that could be traced back to him as he instinctively rubbed the fingertip of his forefinger with thumb. He was dressed in a summer suit and a straw fedora carrying a thick brown briefcase. Sunglasses hid his evil eyes and he added a short black wig and a goatee to his disguise. It would take just minutes to plant the two water-soluble poison packets into the main pumps at Buckingham Fountain. The door to the engineering room was locked, but the key he was issued still worked which was a good sign that no one had yet made the connection that he worked for the city.

He slithered into the pumping station and was greeted by a loud cacophony of sounds from pumps churning, pistons pushing, the hissing of pressure being released, and the distinct smell of moldy dampness from the sweating walls, mixed with the motor oil that lubricated all the moving mechanical parts that produced the spectacular water and light shows above ground that are witnessed by millions of visitors every year. He had to act quickly like he belonged there if anyone came in unannounced. He found the heavy pipe wrench in the locker where it was normally stored. He turned off the power and proceeded to take off the caps of the two main water pumps that would force the deadly chemical compound into the air for the 7:30 pm, colorful water show this evening. Light winds from the south were predicted, bringing seasonal temperature in the low 70's, creating an unpretentious atmosphere and perfect football weather.

"Hey! What are doing there?" A voice protested behind him.

He continued to work, ignoring the interruption, waiting for the intruder to get closer. His insalubrious eyes squinted and he calculated his timing as the approaching voice got louder.

"Hey. I am talking to you." The unwelcomed visitor said slowly moving toward the hunched over figure.

Lin An stood up suddenly and in one smooth motion, swung the heavy wrench at the head of the engineer who never identified himself at their first meeting.

"It's You!" He exclaimed surprised as his mind recognized the killer, that he knew and saw on television two nights before, and then everything went black ... forever. He was dead before he hit the floor, blood coagulating under his head.

The trace of a sinister smile appeared on Lin An's thin lips. *Fuck you,* he thought, and he immediately went back to work as if the interruption and murder was nothing more than a mere nuisance of a mosquito biting his skin.

After he placed the lethal packet into the second pipe, he tightened the cap, and drag the lifeless body into the janitor's closet and shut the door. He wiped up the trail of blood with some rags he found. He didn't bother to wash the blood off of the wrench and hung it up exactly as he found it.

He changed the timer for the first light show of the night, and he made sure that the fountain would not deliver the anthrax and ricin compound until the exact time when he would detonate the poisonous pipe-bombs.

~~~~

The 12-foot long blue traffic barricades where in place redirecting all traffic from south Lake Shore Drive to avoid Columbus and onto Roosevelt Road. Traffic from the north was directed to LSD at Randolph Street. Unbeknownst to the city, they were creating a kill zone.

The 14 by 14-foot platform for the "Singing Palombos" and their band was securely in place and city electrical workers were testing the speakers, amplifiers, audio boards and the power source for the stage area.

The city issued permits to four politically connected restaurants to set up beer tents that would make enormous profits from the sale of draft beers during a three hour and half hour window of financial opportunity. To insure the city got its cut, they issued sequentially numbered tickets; no cash was allowed for the purchase a beer.

No ticket. No beer. Accountability: the Chicago way.

The Thursday night game was a total sell out. The Chicago Bears and the Green Bay Packers were two of the NFL's biggest rivalries and their fans carried that rivalry over to other areas, like to the amount of beer they consumed. For years, Bear fans prided themselves for drinking every ounce of beer sold in New Orleans's French Quarter during the 1985 Super Bowl weekend by Friday night. Bourbon Street had to be totally resupplied on Saturday morning before the hung over fans staggered out of their hotel rooms or wherever they crashed the night before.

The festivities would began at four o'clock in the afternoon and the crowds were already starting to form lines to buy tickets so the drinking could begin exactly on time.

Lin An was sitting astride his bike looking down at them, the tinge of an malicious smile crept across his face as he anticipated the agonizing deaths of all those drunk fuckers that would begin drinking soon.

His thoughts were interrupted as a cop on bicycle patrol peddled past him and nodded with a pleasant look on his face. *Fuck you,* he thought, *I hope I get you tonight too.*

A flash of recognition was ignited in the police officer. He slowed momentarily, and closed his eyes briefly trying to recall what triggered that impression, but then he continued on his way responding to an alarm at Buckingham Fountain.

CHAPTER 67

D r. James McBride had his spectrometer working overtime trying to identify the neurogenetic compound he discovered from the sample that came from the bone marrow of Phillip Hutchinson. It did not have Dobonovich's chemical signature, but Dr. McBride theorized that the mad man had not yet developed it during his stay at the Madison Mental Health Center. He was positive though that it was a topical type of agent.

The sample from Matt Stevonski produced a trace amount of rat poison. It was highly suggestive but not proof positive that a common household poison killed the orderly whose lungs were so destroyed from smoking. McBride surmised that no one even bother to look for anything suspicious in the death or murder of Stevonski.

It was late Thursday morning and McBride was taking his wife to the shore for the weekend so, he wanted to report back to the FBI before he left at lunchtime.

"Hey, Jack. It's Dr. McBride. I believe Matt Stevonski was killed with rat poison. I found a trace amount in his sample and I still haven't identified the neurogenetic compound that I discovered in Hutchinson, but that's what killed him, but one very important thing to keep in mind is; it was a topical agent."

"Why is that so important?"

"Cuz, it wasn't injected. It somehow got on his skin."

"That's good to know. When will you know for certain what this nerve agent is?"

"Next week. If I want to stay married I have to take my bride to the shore this weekend. Sorry; that is the best I can do for now. I'll have my assistant continue the investigation, and if he discovers anything I'll pass it on."

"Thanks doc. Enjoy yourself and thanks for all your help."

"I hope you get the bastard."

"We will. I just hope we aren't too late."

~~~~

"What's up Jack?" Peter Michaels knew it was detective Warren by the ringtone.

"Hey. Just a thought." Warren said.

"What's that?" Michaels asked.

"Your partner has a great source over at Madison, right?"

"Yeah. Why?"

"See if he could find out if that orderly, Hutchinson, had a run in with Dobonovich or that Lin An guy, a day or two before he died."

"Why?"

"If there was any kind of confrontation, it could be how they poisoned him."

"How do you know?"

"Doctor McBride from Fort Doom said it was a topical nerve agent type of poison but he's still not sure what it is."

"I'll ask Dave if he can check."

"What are you doing?"

"Thinking, waiting and getting nervous."

~~~~

A silent alarm with red flashing lights was triggered in the Buckingham Fountain pumping station when pressure that built up in one of the main water pumps could not be released.

The alarm also went off in the Joint Operations Center of the OEMC, the Office of Emergency Maintenance and Communications, and at the Williams Waterworks office.

Both offices scrambled into action. The OEMC issued an emergency called to the police and streets and sanitation. Williams Waterworks called their most trusted maintenance man and troubleshooter, Elberto Diaz.

The bicycle patrol officer that passed Lin An was the first responder on the scene. His nametag identified his as Wilson. His six-foot-two frame was lithe and muscular from five years of peddling his bike on patrol throughout the South Loop area. His skin was tanned and starting to wrinkle from exposure to the elements. Wrap around Aviator sunglasses protected his deep blue, intelligent eyes. He found the door locked. He heard no alarms, but he could see red flashing lights through the thick, bulletproof window in the door.

A crew from Streets and Sanitation arrived next. The supervisor had a set of keys that opened the door attached to his belt under his beer belly. He moved slowly and without concern. "What's goin on?"

"Open the door and let's find out." The officer named Wilson said authoritatively.

The supervisor fumbled for the right key, found it, opened the door and said, "After you."

Officer Wilson led the way and noticed a number of strange odors in the sweaty room and pursed his lips in disgust. The flashing red lights illuminated a trail of blood on the floor. Wilson put his hand out in the motion that said, "Halt."

Beer Belly froze, a look of apprehension immediately spread across his face. "What's da madder?" He mumbled nervously.

"Don't know yet. Just stay here until I take a look. Stay here," he ordered. He looked at Beer Belly and mimed "Stay," and then he followed the blood trail to the janitor's closet. As soon as he opened the door, his hand went to his shoulder mike and he called it in.

"This is Wilson at Buckingham Fountain responding to that silent alarm. I got a dead body hidden in a closet. Looks like his head was smashed in."

"Secure the scene. Sergeant Yaksich is nearby." The dispatcher announced.

"Copy that." Wilson responded and then he ordered Beer Belly and his crew away from the crime scene.

~~~~

Both detectives Jack Warren and Tony Quag requested that an APB, All Points Bulletin, be issued if anything strange happened in or around Buckingham Fountain. Their notifications happened by text as soon as Wilson found the body. Both responded immediately. Warren called Michaels to inform him of the new development.

"We just found a dead guy at the fountain."

"This is ... way, way out there." Michaels said confounded. "It is right in front of us and we can't see."

"Anything from Dave?"

"Not yet. He's working it."

CHAPTER 68

Sergeant Robert Yaksich and troubleshooter Elberto Diaz arrived at Buckingham Fountain at the same time. Yaksich assumed control and began giving orders. Diaz was pushed to the background as police officers cordoned off the area with yellow tape depicting a crime scene.

Diaz recognized Beer Belly and asked, "What happened here?"

Beer Belly responded in his Southside accent, "Day found a body down dare. I tink his head was bashed in or somethan."

Diaz pushed his way to the front of the police line holding up his identification, "Hey officer, I'm Elberto Diaz. I was sent here to fix the problem. I gotta get in there."

The officer keyed his mike, "Hey Sarge, I got a guy up here that was sent over to fix the alarm problem." He listen for a second and said, "Go on down. See Sergeant Yaksich."

Sergeant Bob Yaksich loved being the police. He was six-foot-three. A little on the paunchy side. His round face and heavy eyelids hid his hazel, inquisitive eyes. When he shook your hand, you were greeted with a welcoming smile that put you at ease. "Mr. Diaz, I am not sure what we have here. Maybe you can provide some answers."

"Who's that ... laying there?" Diaz asked not taking his eyes off the feet of the man he saw on the floor in the janitor's closet.

"I don't know maybe you can tell us."

Diaz walked over to the body, bent down, and shook his head slowly from side to side, "That's David Stackpool He's a supervising engineer for the company. Nice guy … was a nice guy."

"Well, he must have come upon something at the wrong time," Sgt. Yaksich suggested.

Detective Tony Quagliaroli came into the dank, smelly room, "Hey Yak. What do you have here?"

"We don't know what set off the alarms but that's David Stackpool. He's a company engineer and he's dead. Why are you here?"

"Warren will be here soon. We think this has something to do with the 'Bug Man'." Tony Quag stated.

Sgt. Yaksich's eyes widen. He was now speechless, looking over at the pipes and then back at the body.

Quag looked over at Diaz and assumed he was here to figure out the mechanical problem.

Suddenly the hissing sound increased dramatically and an alarm started to scream. Everyone turned towards the massive structure of orange and black horizontal and vertical pipes, pumps and valves that gave the impression of a modern art piece displayed on the wall and floor. Diaz began to immediately assess the problem and commanded, "This thing may blow. You better get out of here."

Everyone looked at each other. Concern flooded their eyes. Investigators had not taken any pictures yet and the crime scene had not been processed. Sgt. Yak said, "Anyone who wants to get out, go now. We need to figure this out."

No one left.

Diaz went over to the main pump, turned off the power, grabbed his pipe wrench, loosened the cap, and the pressure released. Everyone took a deep breath of relief as the hissing sound died down and alarm stopped blaring. Diaz took the cap off the number one main pump. "What the fuck is that?" He exclaimed, looking down in disbelief at a white substance encased in what appeared to be a clear cellophane package that was stuffed into the ejection pipe of the main water pump.

Detective Quag took over. "Don't touch that. I'm sure it is very deadly." He pulled out his cellphone and dialed, "Where are you?"

"About two minutes out. What's up?" Jack Warren asked.

"You were right. Buckingham Fountain was the target."

~~~~

Peter Michaels was pacing the floor. David Beedy was reading the sports section. Tension etched on both their faces.

"This opener tonight is standing room only. I don't know how they do it every year. Season tickets are so freaking expensive and they keep selling out and they keep losing. Bear fans." Beedy said.

"Who else is playing here tonight?" Michaels asked.

"The Sox are at the Twins and the Cubbies are home at Wrigley. They're playing the Cardinals. That's it. Why?"

"I don't know. I'm thinking." Michaels was interrupted by his phone. "Hey Jack, What's up?"

"Two massive packages of some shit was stuffed into the main pumps at Buckingham Fountain. CFD HAZMAT guys are taking it out now. We'll get it analyzed."

"It's poison. No doubt about it. Any pipe bombs around?"

"We're searching. Got the bike guys going all over the place looking, but we may have caught a break."

"What's that?" Michaels asked, sitting down at his desk. His forehead crease with anxiety.

"I was showing a picture of Lin An around and this bike guy, Eric Wilson came over and said he thinks he saw him on a bike on one of the walkways near Soldier Field."

"How sure is he?"

"He said the guy had black hair and a goatee."

"How does that help us?"

"He said, he also had both arms totally tattooed. That's why he remembers him."

Michaels stood, apprehension shaded his face, and "Tonight's game is the real target or the main target There will be more than 80,000 people, maybe even a 100,000 in and around Soldier Field tonight. That's got to be it." Michaels opined, as he slowly sank into his chair, thinking.

CHAPTER 69

B ing Lin An was panicked and pissed. Peter Michaels just showed his picture with his black hair and goatee on the six o'clock news. *How did he know?* Then he remember the cop on the bike that peddled past him after he planted the last pipe bomb on the trashcan where the fans turn in towards Soldier Field.

The story was a warning to be on the lookout for this man, who could be armed and dangerous. The graphic artist created the new disguise with little effort. The story was superficial, but it served two purposes; one, it got a picture of Bing Lin An out there and on the minds of anyone walking the streets of Chicago and two, not to panic people by giving exact location of where authorities suspected the killer would be.

The Chicago's pointed skyline seemed to pierce the sinking, brilliant orange colored sun as it slowly dipped into the horizon producing a spectacular sunset. The temperature responded and cooled considerably from the afternoon's mid 80's to the now low 70's with a slight southerly breeze producing perfect weather for a football game and the disbursement of anthrax and ricin.

The darkness would help cover Lin An's new face now masqueraded with a full beard. Long sleeves secreted his arms, correcting a mistake he swore he would never make again, and a black beret obscured his high forehead.

The detonator and his cellphone were on their final charge. Time seemed to standstill for him as he waited for the precise time he would leave and ignite his mentor's creation and fulfill his legacy. A devilish smile spread across his thin, lifeless lips.

~~~~

The pre-game party was in full swing. Bear and Packer fans were mingling noisily together on Columbus Drive, drinking draft beers by the kegs and dancing to the music of the "Singing Palombos." Packer fans with no shirts, green and yellowed painted chests and Styrofoam blocks of cheese sitting on their heads taunted Bear fans, who were sporting blue and orange chests, bears ears, and oversized foam "Number One" fingers on their hands.

Some fans were itching for a fight. Others wanted nothing more than to see their team kick the other team's ass on the field. The rivalry was living up to its history and reputation.

Undercover cops circulated in the crowd to make sure order was maintained while mounted police were stationed in Grant Park at the ready in case major mayhem broke out.

Not a single person on the streets saw the picture of Bing Lin An. They could care less.

~~~~

Jack Warren picked Peter Michaels up at the studio as soon as he was off the air.

Michaels was amped up. The threat on his life was in the back of his mind. The threat to all the people at the museum campus occupied his consciousness. "Did you get the jamming order?" Michaels asked anxiously.

"Agents are at the federal magistrate's right now with our affida-vit. No word yet though. They are not sure we have enough evidence."

"I'm telling you. It's Soldier Field. Lin An was on surveillance when that bike cop saw him."

"I know that. You know that. But that still is not enough to get the order."

"Let's go to the last known location that prick was seen. He has to come back that way. Wouldn't you think?"

~~~~

Agent Donna Blake convinced Joint Terrorist Task Force Special Agent in Charge, Tom Eiseman to have the cellphone jamming equip-ment in place to be launched at a moment's notice. She trusted Jack Warren's instincts, which were predicated on Peter Michaels' instincts.

She positioned herself in Burnham Harbor on the outdoor patio of the small café that was closed for the night. Four drones, each equipped with an hour's worth of flight battery were ready for launch. From past experience, she knew that if a judge granted a jamming order, it would be for a limited amount of time, and that generally was for one hour.

Her ear com was on, but it was silent.

~~~~

Officer Eric Wilson was peddling back to the rendezvous point at Soldier Field when he spotted a homeless man picking through the contents of a overturned trashcan.

"What are you doing there, Sir?" He inquired; slowly approaching the man with his hand on his 9mm Glock.

The man was not Asian so, Wilson instinctively relaxed. It certainly was not the man he observed earlier that day.

"I was looking for something to eat, but all I found was empty beer cans."

Officer Wilson had his mag light on the overturned trashcan when he noticed what appeared to be PVC piping taped to it. The hairs on his arms stood at attention. He ordered the homeless man, "You better get away from that trashcan sir. It could dangerous. Please move away." He handed him twenty bucks and said, "Get something to eat. Now get out of here."

The homeless man reluctantly stopped his search, took the money, smiled, nodded thank you, and walked away quietly. Wilson clicked his mike, "Sergeant Yaksich, I think I found one of the bombs."

Sgt. Yaksich responded, "What's your position? I'll get the bomb squad over there ASAP." Yaksich noted Wilson's position, called the bomb squad, and then called detective Jack Warren.

~~~~

Bing Lin An took the detonator and his cellphone off of the charger and put them into his fanny pack. He set the timer on a firebomb he planted to blow up his workspace and destroy any evidence he would leave behind. His getaway car was parked at the intersection of Michigan Avenue and Indiana in a legal spot. He paid a young college student a hundred dollars to move her car earlier that day.

He closed the rental space door for the last time, and then got on his bicycle to travel to spot that he called ground zero. His hateful eyes were matched only by sinister smile.

It was 7:50 p.m..

~~~~

Warren picked up on the second ring, "Talk to me."

"Officer Wilson found a pipe bomb taped to a trashcan on the walkway where it curves toward the entrance of Soldier Field, about a block north of Roosevelt Road." Sgt. Yaksich reported in a calm voice, though his stomach was churning with acid. He threw a Tums in his mouth, then another.

"Copy that. We are on the way." Warren hit his siren and lights, and then his speed dial. The agent waiting at the magistrate's office picked it up on the first ring.

"Tell me something good," said agent Fran Valentino with angst in her voice and eyes.

"We found a bomb taped to a trashcan. It's the proof we needed. Now get that order." He said enthusiastically. He then turned on his ear com and said, "We found a bomb. It's a go!"

Everyone's adrenalin started to pump.

The magistrate issued a one-hour jamming device order.

Warren called headquarters and launched their hastily put together emergency response-plan.

It was 7:55 p.m..

CHAPTER 70

T he highly spirited and inebriated football fans formed a human wave weaving their way to the stadium. They were stumbling, singing, laughing, some falling, but hardly anyone paid any attention to the fire fighters and police officers on foot and bicycles rushing to various locations along the pathways they were traversing.

The four drones that were now airborne, flying inconspicuously in a small grid from the Field Museum to the parking structures on 18th Street bordering Soldier Field. Many fans were playing frantically with their cellphones trying get a signal, swearing inwardly, and punching at icons out of frustration. Those still tailgating, drinking and cheering could care less about anything other than getting to their seats. Go Bears!

Agent Donna Blake was very familiar and well trained in the use of drones. She was a 107 FAA certified drone pilot herself, and she loved to collect shots of seascapes, cityscapes and countrysides. She had taken up drone flying as a hobby well before the days when the hum of a drone became almost commonplace. She had developed a surgeon's touch at the controls, and could massage the pitch, yaw and throttle together to create epic buttery-smooth panoramas. The trickier the flight pattern, the more proficient she became. Even though she knew the potential danger that she was trying to prevent, she was grinning from ear to ear.

She initiated the signal-jamming device at 7:59:30 p.m..

~~~~

Sergeant Shelly Bert, the leader of the bomb squad decided to play a hunch and move to the first trashcan she encountered. She didn't think it was a waste of time because she had heard on her ear com that the drones were airborne and working. If she was right this would save an enormous amount of time.

Sgt. Shelly Bert was a bomb chaser in Afghanistan. She was a member of the 77th Army's Explosive Ordinance Disposal Company. When she put on body armor, her courage, skill and intellect kicked into another gear. She was fearless.

Her hunch paid off. She made a quick call after studying the crude device. "Listen up, everyone. This is Sgt. Bert. Do not panic. Take the black plastic garbage can liners out of the trashcans, place them over the bomb and the trashcan, and then turn the can upside down with the nipple tip of the bomb into the ground. If you can place the can on the grass, take the time to do that. If you have any tape, string, rope, even your belts, secure the plastic bags around the can as tight as you possible can in case our jamming device fails. Once you do that, step away from the device."

Sgt. Bert was giving the orders while she was taking apart the bomb in her hands. She felt strongly that it was not really an explosive device like an IAD because of its weight. She surmised that the wire taped to the PVC was acting as an aerial that connected it to a detonator, which was controlled by a wireless ignition system, probably a cellphone.

The bomb chaser was right. She pulled out the wire and felt confident that the bomb was disabled. She took off her gas mask,

shook her head letting her hair catch the night breeze, inhaled deeply
through her nostrils to relax and smiled a wide satisfying smile.

She knew how to disarm bombs, but she knew nothing about
poisons so, she had absolutely no interest to investigate further. She
sat down and waited for the HAZMAT guys.

~~~~

Beads of sweat were gathering under his beret, anxiety was building
with every pump of his peddles, he was sensing failure, and he didn't
know why. The luminous dial on his wristwatch displayed 7:59. He
had a minute to get to ground zero to detonate the bombs. It was
timed perfectly to capture the largest portion of the crowd on the
walkway. Tens of thousands would be exposed at 8:00 p.m.. It was
precisely calculated.

When he reached ground zero, he was awestruck. He got off his
bike and let it drop to the ground. Police officers and firefighters were
lined, up and down the walkway. He pulled out a pair of high-
powered compact night vision binoculars and scanned the scene.
"Motherfucker," he screamed at the top of his lungs. He extracted the
detonator and dialed his cellphone, but there was no signal. He had
failed his mentor, his lover, his only friend.

Anger was building inside his inner being like a volcano ready to
erupt. Sweat was overflowing down his face into his evil eyes, saliva
was foaming on the edges of wicked lips that were quivering. His
hands began to tremble as he raised the binoculars back to his burning red eyes, searching the scene again when suddenly he came to an
abrupt stop when Peter Michaels came into his view. "Motherfucker.
You. I am going to kill you if it is that last thing I do."

The swelling in his hand finally responded to all the icing and it
was almost back to normal. The pain was tolerable. His fury was at
an uncontrollable boiling point reminiscent of the time he slaughtered his family. He felt for the 20cc syringe filled with TC-24. He

could grip it. Flushed with anger, he wanted his revenge. He put the syringe back into his fanny pack, picked up his bicycle and raced down the hill as fast as his legs would pump.

~~~~

Peter Michaels and Jack Warren gave each other a high-five. Smiles spread across their faces as they listened to Sgt. Bert tell the team how to simply disable the bombs. They were crude devices, but if triggered and detonated, they could have killed thousands of people.

Detective Tony Quag came over to join the celebration. "Man, that was cutting it close."

"Those fans will never know how close they came to death tonight."

Warren opined.

"I'm wondering how I should report this story tonight without scaring the entire city. Nagaro should be here shortly with his gear." Michaels said thoughtfully.

Warren noticed the movement out of the corner of his eye, first. All three turned in the direction of the screams of a madman racing down the hill on a bicycle aimed right at them. Michaels was on the right, Warren in the middle and Quag on the left.

They all now recognized Lin An. His face was red with fury, his eyes were filled with hatred. His voice was harsh from screaming. "I'll kill you. You motherfucker." He aimed his bike directly at Peter Michaels.

Michaels sensed the pressure Warren was putting on his left bicep, and a split second before impact he felt a heavier push and he leapt to his right just before he got slightly hit by the end of the handlebar. He regained his balance and turned around to face his attacker.

Lin An slammed on his breaks, his tires tortured the sidewalk as he came to a screeching stop. He threw the bike down hard, reached into his fanny pack, grabbed the deadly syringe, bit off the protective tip of the needle, and raced directly at Peter Michaels screaming, "I'll kill you. I swear to god, I will kill you." He increased his speed, raised the weapon above his head, and continued to charge forward.

Jack Warren and Tony Quag pulled out their 9mm Glocks instinctively and simultaneously, they held them straight out with both hands at shoulder height, moved their fingers from the frame of the trigger guard onto their triggers and screamed at the top of their lungs at the same time, "Stop, or I'll shoot."

Bing Lin An filled with dark rage kept running straight at Peter Michaels screaming, "I'll kill you. I'll ..."

The pleasant unblemished cool night air and the whispers of leaves whisping in the wind were shattered by the distinct sound of gunfire. Everyone in the vicinity turned and watched the vengeful attack come to a sudden end.

Jack Warren's 9mm bullet hit Lin An directly in the middle of his forehead. His head snapped back but his inertia kept him on his feet and moving forward. Tony Quag's 9mm bullet hit him center mass, squarely in his hateful heart, and his forward motion came to a sudden stop as he fell forward landing at the feet of Peter Michaels.

CHAPTER 71

t was a bad night for the Chicago Bears. They lost 10–3 to the Green Bay Packers. It was a boring, mistake riddled defensive game.

On the other hand, it was a great night for Bears' fans, who had no clue of the potentially deadly danger they were exposed to on their way to the game. There was not one single casualty.

~~~~

Paul Nagaro videotaped the entire shooting incident, but that part of the tape never made the air on the ten o'clock news, and Peter Michaels once again did not report the story because he was at a FBI debriefing.

Ron Magers read a voice over videotape story, giving a low-key account of how a major disaster was thwarted on the museum campus. The decision was made to tell the story minimally, in a matter of fact tone, not to alarm the public.

It took hours to debrief Peter Michaels, but surprisingly this time he was not exhausted from this fourth attempt on his life in less than a week. He was thankful that his friends were there once again to protect him.

~~~~

Michaels had Nagaro make two video copies of the shooting incident and gave one to each Jack Warren and Tony Quag. They would face a police board inquiry to justify the shooting. The pictures and audio clearly showed the detectives warned the attacker/killer to stop.

They would be required to see a department mental health specialist to make sure they were fit for duty. Neither had a single regret of what they had done. As a matter of fact, they were proud of it.

Jack Warren was transferred back to the CPD homicide division from the Joint Terrorism Task Force. He wanted to work with Tony Quag because the two detectives developed a very strong bound going through the shooting inquiry. They started to think alike and almost finished each other's sentences.

~~~~

A few days later, Dr. James McBride identified the microbiological agent that killed Phillip Hutchinson as neurocyonotic bromicide. He found traces of the nerve-paralyzing drug in the sample taken from the victim's esophagus. He theorized that Hutchinson died a very painful death.

As far as Matthew Stevonski's death, he reported that he found a miniscule trace of what he believed to be rat poison, but he could not state 100 percent that that was the cause of death because of the disastrous condition of the victim's cancer filled lungs.

David Beedy's brother in law confirmed that two days before Phillip Hutchinson died a sudden death, he broke up an altercation between Dobonovich and Bing Lin An. The incident report indicated that it was a minor skirmish, and that the two patients were wrestling on the floor when Hutchinson intervened.

Detective Jack Warren surmised that it was the perfect opportunity to apply the deadly topical agent and wrote a supplementary report that tied the murder of Phillip Hutchinson to the "Bug Man" and his accomplice Bing Lin An.

~~~~

Bing Lin An's smudgy fingerprints from the basement apartment were matched to the wrench that was used to killed the engineer David Stackpool, and to the pipe bombs that were disabled, and to the packets found stuffed into the main water pumps at Buckingham Fountain.

Everyone was stunned by the boldness of the potential devastating microbiological attack when they discovered the poisonous compound was a combination of anthrax and ricin. The "Bug Man" undoubtedly engineered it. Scientists discovered Dobonovich's signature on the deadly combination.

~~~~

The CFD Arson Squad investigated a fire at a storage garage on State Street in the South Loop that destroyed all the contents. They determined that an accelerant was used to start the fire and apparently to spread it as well.

No connection was made to the "Bug Man," or Bing Lin An, even though investigators were told the unit was paid for in cash and rented for a year to a tall Asian man who was covered with tattoos from head to toe.

~~~~

Peter Michaels finally admitted to himself that he was totally drained and exhausted, and that he needed a break. So, he decided to go to Marco Island, Florida to spend some time with two boyhood friends, but before he left, he visited Sam Phieffer, the station's attorney.

They were sitting in his spacious, egalitarian office looking out at a picturesque view of Lake Michigan from the 70th floor, watching the last of the sailboats cutting through challenging three and four foot waves. Winter was around the corner and Chicagoans were already being forewarned of a cold and snowy season.

Phieffer was leaning forward at his desk with his chin resting in his hand. His inquisitive eyes brightened along with the smile than inched into the corners of his mouth, "You know you are crazier than I thought. What were you thinking … meeting those two crazy people? They both hated you and wanted to kill you."

"You know me, Sam. I like a challenge."

"You should write a book about this bizarre experience. It's the only way the whole story will be told." Phieffer opined.

"I truly don't know how many people Dobonovich killed, or Bing Lin An for that matter. I have no doubt when he studied in Europe he killed some other people. He was ruthless and without a conscience." Michaels responded, pursing his lips as if in thought, staring out at the clear, deep blue September sky.

"How many do you reckon he killed in Chicago?" Phieffer asked, his hands now folded as if in prayer, with his fingertips touching his lips.

"If you count the orderlies, Dobonovich killed … 42, and if you combined the two, it would probably be more than fifty. I don't know if we will ever find out how many people Bing Lin An killed.

"The 'Bug Man' is probably the worst serial/revenge killer in Chicago's history, and that says a lot." Michaels said standing up, getting ready to take his leave.

Phieffer also stood and reached out to shake hands, "Well, what could be worse?"

Michaels stopped shaking his hand but did not let go of it, a pondering look shrouded his face, and he replied. "A pandemic. A worldwide pandemic."

ABOUT THE AUTHOR

Peter Karl is a retired award-winning television investigative reporter who has been inducted into the prestigious Silver Circle of the National Television Society of Arts and Sciences for his work that spanned over 40 years. Karl is the recipient of 11 Chicago Regional Emmy Awards, the esteemed George Foster Peabody Award, two DuPont-Columbia Awards, the Robert F. Kennedy Award for journalism excellence and he was once named the national Sigma Delta Chi Investigative Reporter of the year. Karl has also been the recipient of death threats during his career as he reported on police scandals, corrupt politicians, mafia kingpins, drug dealers and some of Chicago's most ruthless street gangs.